FEUDING
WITH THE
FASHION
Princess

SIENA TRAP

Foreword

A COMPREHENSIVE LIST OF trigger warnings for those who need them can be found on my website: www.sienatrapbooks.com

This is for all the girls who are proper in public but let their naughty side come out to play behind closed doors.

Prologue

Lucy

I WAS MINDING MY own business, playing with my dolls, when pain ripped through one side of my head. Crying out, I turned to discover the source.

Preston had pulled on one of my braided pigtails. He still held a fistful of my hair in his hand, a taunting look on his face. "Let go!" I tried to pry his hand off, but it only resulted in his grip tightening and pulling again.

"When will you grow up and stop being a baby with pigtails?" Preston teased.

"I'm not a baby! I'm eight!"

"Babies have pigtails and wear frilly pink dresses, Princess."

I was a princess, but the way he said it made it seem like a bad thing. *How dare he?*

Preston was eleven and thought he knew everything. He was my big brother Liam's friend from school. I hated when he came over to play with Liam. Preston went out of his way to tease me, but today was different. He crossed a line when he pulled my hair.

"Leave her alone, Preston." Liam approached us and eyed where Preston still held my hair in his hand. Narrowing his eyes, he frowned. "Take your hands off my sister. Now."

Releasing his grasp, Preston backed away, completely ignoring the incident. "Come on. Let's go kick the soccer ball around."

Liam gave me a look to make sure I was all right before running off to play with his friend. He was twelve and always looked out for me. The same couldn't be said for our much older brother, Leo, who was fifteen. Thankfully, he was away at boarding school. He'd have laughed and helped Preston torture me. I was the youngest of the family and the only girl. That meant I was always the odd one out.

Liam and Preston disappeared around the far corner of the courtyard as I left my dolls behind in the grass and ran to where my mother sat reading on a stone bench beneath a tree. Slowing down as I approached her, I pulled at the ribbons securing my braids, working to undo them.

"What are you doing, sweetheart?" My mother's voice was warm, and I looked up to find her smiling at me as I furiously used my fingers to loosen my hair.

"Only babies wear pigtails."

"Is that so?"

"Yes." Pausing, I chewed my lip before asking, "Mama, can you make Preston go home?"

Tilting her head, she responded with her own question. "Why would I do that? Are he and Liam not getting along?"

Unable to keep the whine out of my voice, I complained, "He pulled my braids!"

A corner of her lips quirked up. "Oh, I see. Is that why you're done with pigtails?"

"He's a mean boy, and you should make him go away." I stuck my lower lip out in a pout. Usually, that got me whatever I wanted.

Patting the stone bench, Mama invited me to sit beside her. Trudging over with heavy steps, I slumped beside her as she put her arm around my shoulders.

"You know, Lucy, boys usually tease girls because they like them."

That was the silliest thing I'd ever heard. Who would tease someone they liked? Preston's relentless teasing only made me angry. It didn't make me like him back.

"Well, I hate him," I declared.

Mama laughed. "Someday, you might change your mind."

Crossing my arms, I shook my head. "No. Never. I *hate* Preston Scott. Forever."

CHAPTER 1
Lucy

Twenty Years Later

My ADRENALINE SHOT SKY-HIGH as I bustled behind the curtain that led to the runway. I lived for moments like this. Each model paused before their turn on the catwalk so I could make last-minute adjustments to their look, ensuring it matched my vision. After years of paying my dues, I earned my own show during fashion week. This was my dream come true.

From the time I was ten years old, I had a sketchbook in my hands, drawing dresses on paper during every free moment. When I turned twelve, my parents bought me a sewing machine, which took my obsession with creating fashion to a new level. By fourteen, I knew for certain that fashion was my future. It gave me a creative outlet when so much of my world was rigid.

Maybe now would be a good time to mention that I was not your typical fashion designer.

I was born Princess Lucette Arabella Grace, the third child and only daughter of the Crown Prince and Princess of Belleston, but everyone called me Lucy. Our tiny country of five million people was nestled in the southeastern corner of the Alps, with Italy, Austria, and Switzerland being our closest neighbors.

Having a "real" career for a royal was unheard of, but I'd leveraged my position as the baby of the family to branch out on my own. That didn't mean I was free. I was still expected to make a required number of yearly royal appearances. If you asked my grandfather, King Victor, he would tell you that my work in fashion was just a hobby before I became a full-time working royal—a woman's version of sowing my wild oats.

Fashion was my life.

After attending fashion school in Paris, I searched for investors to start my own line. That's where the family name came in handy, as much as I hated to admit it. My royal status could open doors that might take years to unlock otherwise, and while I had my pride, I was driven by a need to have my designs showcased to the world.

Acquiring capital was only the first step. My vision and skill would need to take me the rest of the way. I decided early on to deviate from the norm, setting myself apart from the thousands of other designers looking to make a splash in a competitive and ever-evolving field.

My evening wear label, Addy June—named for my mother—was completely body-positive. I made it my mission to create a brand that celebrated our differences instead of body-shaming those who didn't fit the mold fabricated by society. Unlike most brands claiming to be "body-positive," we went beyond offering a broad range of sizes. Our models, both in print advertisements and on the runway, came in every shape and size.

For too long, the definition of "plus-sized" had shifted to the point where you were considered fat if you wore a size featuring double digits. People needed to put their blinders on and focus on themselves instead of judging others. Who cared what number was inside your clothing label if you were healthy?

The inspiration came from the women in my life. While I was petite, I was strongly influenced by my two sisters-in-law.

Natalie married my oldest brother Leo, and while she fit into society's definition of "thin," I'd watched her struggle with an eating disorder. She'd wasted away to almost nothing because the tabloids criticized her size. It came out later that Leo had helped the press destroy her self-image, and eventually, she found the strength to divorce his sorry ass. Yes, he was my brother, but he wasn't my favorite person.

Amy only recently married my brother, Liam, but I'd had the pleasure of getting to know her over the years as they helped Natalie—she and Amy were best friends—raise her kids, living together as a sitcom-worthy blended family. While she was a full-figured, plus-sized woman, she didn't apologize for it. I enjoyed the confidence she had in her body, not hiding her curves behind baggy clothes. She inspired my vision to showcase all women in my designs. I wanted every woman to have the opportunity to feel as comfortable in their own skin as Amy did.

My progressive approach was criticized by some within the industry, but the public's overwhelming praise drowned that out—finally, someone was acknowledging real women. Success had been swift, but there was always doubt in the back of my mind that my name and status had driven it.

Grandfather was right in one regard—my passion was a hobby. It was unseemly for a royal to earn their own money, so once I took care of investors and employees, all profits were donated to charity. That only fueled the popularity of my brand, but the fire in my belly kept pushing for more.

I knew my designs were amazing and my approach unique, but my internal drive demanded I prove to myself that I could truly stand on my own in the fashion world. My second label was created with an anony-mous LLC to hide my identity. But we'll talk about that later.

Right now, I was riding high as the music pumped through the venue and models disappeared through the curtain one by one. It was mayhem behind the scenes. Each model had at least four outfit changes during the show and was assigned a team to strip and redress them before my final approval. There was no time to think. I was running purely on instinct and adrenaline.

This was what I was meant to do with my life. I wanted people to hear the name Lucy Remington and not immediately think of a spoiled princess with everything she wanted in life handed to her on a silver platter. I wanted to share my vision for women's fashion with the world, to make an impact through my creativity. While I'd gained a foothold earning my own show, I wasn't quite there yet.

The last model passed through the curtain, and then it would be time for me to show my face as the designer. She returned, and all the models followed me onto the runway. Dressed in all black, my jet-black hair knotted at the nape of my neck, I stepped out to face my critics, whether they were good or bad.

Everyone applauded, but I knew the real test would come tomorrow when the fashion bloggers posted their reviews. My first show was a big deal, but I knew my continued success was reliant on the opinions of others.

Being judged by strangers was nothing new for me. It had been occurring since the day I was born.

Clasping my hands and bowing my head in a silent show of gratitude, I retreated backstage, where the rest of my design team awaited. The excite-ment was palpable. We were showing alongside the biggest brands in the world; this was huge. We were playing with the big boys now, and while it was frightening, it was also exhilarating.

My associate fashion designer, Sophie, pushed through the crowd to hug me tight, squealing, "We did it!"

My arms tightened around her body. "Couldn't have done it without you, Soph." I meant it. She kept the ship afloat when I had to take time away to be a "proper" princess. In my absence, having trusted support at the helm was invaluable.

Pulling back, her brown eyes sparkled, her smile wide. "We need to go out to celebrate!"

For my team, the night was over, but I couldn't rest yet. "I've got tickets to the Arabella Reign show, but I'll meet you guys later."

Eyes widening, she shoved at my shoulder playfully. "No, you don't! That's the hottest ticket this week! Who did you have to sleep with to score that?"

Trying my best to avoid her questions, I shrugged. "Just lucky, I guess."

"Ugh. I'm so jealous! Promise you'll tell me all about it when you meet us for drinks?"

"Of course." Stepping to where I had left my purse, I reached inside, pulled out my credit card, and handed it to Sophie. "First round is on me. Take the team and enjoy the night until I get there."

Plucking the black card from my hand, she smirked. "Hmm. I could do some damage with this. I'll call you from the Maldives."

"Drop a pin when you get there so I can join you." Winking, I left the backstage area, leaving the warehouse building where Addy June's show had been, before hopping into the backseat of a sleek black sedan that would drive me to the location of the Arabella Reign show.

Thirty minutes later, we pulled up to the museum, where the show was set to begin at any moment. Running up the stairs, I thrust my ticket into the hands of the door attendant and took a seat in the only remaining chair. The place was packed; a line extended out the door of people begging entry, even though they hadn't secured a ticket.

The lights changed so they were focused on the extended runway splitting the room. Anticipation was evident as everyone in attendance craned their necks to look where the first model was expected to appear. Music began pumping through the speakers, and a gorgeous curvy woman with caramel skin, clad in only a lavender lace bra and panties set walked out.

Remember when I mentioned a second label where I kept my identity secret?

Arabella Reign was my secret baby—a lingerie label. Next to no one knew I was pulling the strings on what had become the world's hottest intimate apparel brand. Not only was this an opportunity to prove that I could make it in the fashion world without my family name paving the way, but I shuddered to think what would happen if my grandfather found out. He'd either have a heart attack from the scandal or lock me away in the palace dungeons. Either way, that would be the end of my fashion career.

So, I sat in the audience, enjoying the show like I wasn't completely invested. Even my design team didn't know I was in charge. All communication with them was sent through a secure server, keeping my identity anonymous.

My vision for embracing real women extended across both my labels. Every woman deserved to feel sexy and confident, both beneath their clothes and in the bedroom. I'd carefully chosen a selection of models to represent a variety of women. There were women of every shape and size—some with C-section scars, tattoos and piercings, stretch marks, and cellulite, among other "imperfections"—but they all glowed up there on that stage.

They were all beautiful. Their confidence was sexy, and it was intoxicating.

Everyone watching was transfixed, and I hoped every woman could picture themselves in my designs. But more than that, I wanted the men to see that my pieces were meant to accentuate the woman beneath, highlighting their natural beauty. I curated a collection of classic bra and panty sets, baby dolls, silk pajama sets, teddies, and corsets. There was something for everybody, and the size range was unmatched.

When the models paraded together one last time, the audience erupted in applause, and I let out a deep breath. Two shows by a single designer was almost unheard of, especially on the same day. For nearly twenty years, I dreamed of being more than just a princess, and through hard work and dedication, I had an opportunity to make my mark on the world beyond my family name.

The week following my debut shows could launch my career to the next level. Boutique reps in attendance would go back to their home offices and make decisions on which brands and pieces to carry. Celebrities would commission custom pieces based on what styles intrigued them. One day, I might even be able to open my own storefront. To this point, my evening styles were mostly unique pieces sold off the rack or commissions earned through word of mouth, but my lingerie line was selling well online.

Expansion was always the long-term plan, but it rested in the hands of others. Fashion design differed from many other professions—a set standard didn't easily measure success. You weren't working with numbers that needed to add up correctly, teaching children to read, or healing the sick and injured. My success was determined solely by the opinions and whims of others. One day, I could be the hottest label. The next, I could be old news. Constant evolution was required to stay relevant.

Walking into the crowded bar that Sophie and the Addy June team chose for their post-show celebration, my adrenaline rush began to subside, and I was suddenly exhausted. The stifling body heat from the crush inside the bar after walking in the late-September New York evening air probably didn't help either. Pushing my way through the sea of bodies, Sophie's flaming-red hair acted like a beacon, allowing me to find the men and women who had become like a second family.

Truth be told, I spent more time with my team than with my family. Even though I split my time evenly between working in my studio in Milan and my family's home base of Stonecrest Palace in Belleston, I was too busy "working" as a royal for much downtime—especially when combined with still running my design team remotely. Days "at home" were often spent in the community, interfacing with the citizens my grandfather currently ruled over.

The Remingtons had ruled over Belleston for centuries. Grandfather was nearing ninety and had pulled back significantly on his public appearances, leaving the rest of us to pick up the slack. My father, Prince Adrian, was my grandfather's only child, so he and my mother, Princess Adelaide, were even busier with official engagements than I was. These days, spending time with them often required calling their personal secretaries and booking an appointment.

My oldest brother, Leo, was my father's heir. He made it a point to become the face of the family over the years—destined to one day become

King—loving the limelight and taking a larger share of the pool of obligated appearances.

Liam was the second-born son and middle child of our family. Until recently, he spent several years in America with our sister-in-law, Natalie—Leo's ex-wife—and her children, working remotely with several charities in Belleston. That changed somewhat this past year, when he married Amy and they began to take on a more prominent role as part of the family, splitting their time between their home in Connecticut and Belleston.

Liam and Amy's more active royal life would have been good news for me, allowing me to pull back even further, if Leo hadn't dropped off the face of the earth a few months ago. No one seemed to know where he'd gone or why he left, even though the "offical" statement from the palace was that he was tending to a personal matter. That development set me back to square one—sharing our generation's portion of events with one brother instead of two.

So no matter how exhausted I was, tonight, I would enjoy my limited freedom before I hopped a plane back home tomorrow. If only this was my life full-time. A girl could dream, but that was all it would ever be—a dream. An accident of birth ensured a set of invisible shackles for the rest of my life.

Sophie saw my approach and waved a little too enthusiastically, her body leaning just a touch too far to the right, almost causing her to lose her perch on the barstool she occupied. Gripping the bar with both hands, she giggled uncontrollably. There was no doubt I was late to the party. I made a mental note to make sure she made it back to her hotel room in one piece.

Shaking my finger, I pretended to lecture her. "I said *one* round, Soph."

She swatted at my hand. "It started as one, but then a few early reviews came in."

I froze. I couldn't tell if she ordered extra drinks because they were good and they were celebrating, or if they were terrible and they were trying to forget. My chest felt tight, and I tried to take a calming breath to no avail. My heart was racing, and sweat gathered over my entire body.

Almost too afraid, I closed my eyes before asking, "And?"

Tensing my body and bracing for impact, I jumped when she screamed, "They loved it!"

My eyes popped open, and I stared at Sophie, whose smile was so wide that I feared it would split her face in two.

Needing double confirmation, I breathed out, "Say that again."

Jumping off her stool, unsteady on her feet, she gripped my shoulders, shaking me lightly. "They *loved* it!"

"Oh my God." I let the truth of her words wash over me before they finally sank in. "Oh my GOD!"

Hugging Sophie, we jumped up and down, screaming like pre-teen girls at a boy band concert.

Breaking apart, she exclaimed, "You did it!"

I may have been the one at the helm, but I knew when to give due credit. This entire line, this show, had been a team effort. "No," I corrected her. "*We* did it!"

Sophie raised her arm, signaling to one of the bartenders. "Get this girl a drink!"

A burly bald man, with tattooed sleeves peeking out from beneath his tight black t-shirt, appeared before us. His blue eyes assessed me from across the bar before he asked, "What'll it be?"

I sat on the barstool opposite the bartender and felt Sophie plop down next to me when she swayed into my personal space. "I'll take a Moscato." Tilting my head toward my drunk friend, I added, "And she's cut off."

Nodding, he turned his back on us to pour my glass of wine before placing it on the bar in front of me on a square white napkin. "You want to open a tab?"

"I'm fairly certain a black card is already running a tab for my friends here." I gestured to my team to the right of Sophie, having a well-deserved good time. "That's mine."

Eyeing me skeptically, he crossed his arms. "ID, please."

This. This is why I loved being out in the wild. More often than not, people didn't recognize me on sight—especially in America. It was liberating, but the feeling of freedom was an illusion.

My personal protection officer, Myles, always lurked nearby. He was good at his job, fading into the background so well you had to really search to find him, but I always knew he was there. How could you forget there was a man shadowing your every move, trained to take a bullet for you? Not that anyone cared enough to attack little old me; I was the third child, after all.

Unzipping the clutch hanging from my wrist, I withdrew my driver's license before handing it across the bar. Peering down at it, he turned toward the register where the cards running tabs were being held. Cross-referencing that the names matched, he returned to double-check I resembled the picture on the identification. Satisfied, he handed it back to me. "Thank you, Ms. Remington."

He walked away to serve drinks to other customers, and I sipped the cool white wine as Sophie nudged me. Turning to look at her, she had her eyes on the muscled, tattooed bartender.

"He was totally checking you out! You should go for it."

Laughing nervously, I shrugged her off. "He's not my type."

Giving me an exaggerated frown in her intoxicated state, she challenged, "And what exactly *is* your type, Lucy? I've never seen you with a guy."

There's a good reason for that.

"Discreet."

Sophie rolled her eyes. "Come on. He asked for your ID. He had no clue who you were."

"Yeah, but it's just that. He *saw* my ID. One little internet search, and a fun night becomes a PR nightmare."

"Don't you ever just say 'screw it' and let loose?"

Oh, dear, sweet Sophie. You have no idea.

Smiling, I moved my hand up and down in front of her body. "Letting loose looks great on you, Soph. It's just not my thing."

"Fine." She pouted for a second but then exclaimed excitedly, "Tell me about Arabella Reign! I still can't believe you got to go!"

"It was amazing." I couldn't help but smile.

"Can you believe no one knows who owns it? I've heard even the design team doesn't. It's so crazy!"

Trying to play it cool, talking about my secret label without letting any clues slip as to my involvement, I shrugged. "Maybe they were worried about the gamble of showcasing real women."

"We do that, and most people praise us for it."

"I don't know. It's a different story when you're dealing with intimate apparel."

Sophie's mouth twisted. "Maybe, but big is beautiful, and I'm prepared to fight anyone who says otherwise." Jumping off the stool, she looked around, fists raised like she was prepared to physically fight someone.

Standing, I gripped her wrists to lower them. "Easy there, killer."

Taking a calming breath, Sophie collapsed back onto her seat.

"Sorry, I get a little fired up about it. Women like me"—she gestured to her own curvy body—"don't often get represented. It's refreshing that someone finally had the guts to metaphorically give the middle finger to the fashion world and show them that you don't have to fit into their size 00 mold to be confident and feel sexy in your own skin. The standard set for women to have thigh gaps and every rib showing has gotten out of control."

"You know I agree with you, Soph."

"I mean, look around. There are more of us than there are of them. In the US alone, almost three-quarters of the population is overweight or obese. We could take those skinny bitches—you excluded, of course. I will . . . I will sit on someone if I have to!"

I desperately tried to hold back my laughter, but she was too much, and I doubled over laughing so hard my sides hurt. When I finally came up for air, I looked at my friend and colleague. "I'm glad you're on my side, Soph."

Clearly, the liquor was turning on her as I watched her first transform from giggly to feisty, and now emotional. Her coffee-colored eyes grew glassy, and tears slipped down her cheeks. "Lucy, thank you for taking a chance on me and allowing me to design for bigger women everywhere, who deserve the same incredible fashion options as everyone else."

Pulling her in for a tight hug, I shushed her. "Aw, Soph. I love what you bring to the team. It won't be long before you're running your own label. You're talented and have an incredible vision."

Breaking free, she wiped at her wet face. "Enough about me. What are you going to do now that Addy June is hitting it big? You could totally leverage your success into a bridal line."

"When would I find the time? I barely have enough to manage Addy June. Adding another line just doesn't seem possible."

Especially when I am already running a second line.

"But you're so good at it. Just imagine the impact you would have if you brought your talents to offering stunning wedding dresses to women of all sizes."

I tried my hand at bridal when Natalie remarried a year ago. I not only designed her gown, but I also made it myself—by hand. It turned out stunningly, and now I was designing one for Amy. She and Liam got married last fall, but they'd eloped and were now in the process of planning a state wedding. Millions around the world would see the dress I created for Amy.

In another life—if I didn't have royal obligations—I could add a bridal line to my repertoire, but I was already stretched too thin. I should be grateful for what I'd been allowed to accomplish already, but I couldn't help but yearn for more.

Closing out the bar tab, I encouraged Sophie to call it a night, and we returned to our hotel together. Ensuring she arrived safely to her room, I went to mine, barely making it inside before I collapsed on the bed. Falling asleep in my clothes after the whirlwind of a day, my last thought was a silent wish that I could be free.

Chapter 2

Lucy

Leaving New York, I made a quick pit stop in Hartford, Connecticut, to spend a few hours with my nieces, Amelia and Charlotte, and nephews, Jameson and Beau—Natalie's children. Charlotte, who we called Charlie, was from her second marriage, but I loved her just the same.

These kids were given the childhood I always dreamed of—a normal one. Far from Belleston, they weren't constantly hounded by the press and were free to simply be children.

But it was all a façade. Someday, Jameson would be called upon to rule as my brother's eldest son. At least his siblings would be free to live their lives as they chose. Natalie made sure of that when she took sole custody in the divorce.

The real reason for my stopover in Connecticut was to pick up Amy and Liam so we could travel back to Belleston together. They were in the throes of wedding planning, so at least I had dressmaking to look forward to while I was forced into servitude for my country. On top of Amy's bridal gown, I was creating bridesmaid dresses for myself, Natalie, and their other best friend, Hannah.

I was thankful they were traveling home with me. These past few years had been lonely. Liam left with Natalie and the kids to escape Leo over four years ago now, and until this past year, none of them had returned.

You'd think that as a third child, four years younger than my closest sibling, I would be used to being in the palace alone. Liam left for his required military service when he was nineteen and I was fourteen, going on fifteen. His departure coincided with Leo meeting Natalie and bringing her into our lives. She was only two years older than me, and we became close as I showed her the ropes of our public life. Leo was always one to get his way, and by the time Natalie was eighteen, they were married before they quickly had back-to-back babies, Amelia and Jameson. We became almost like true sisters, but I couldn't blame her for breaking free of my cruel brother when she got the chance, even if that meant leaving me behind.

When Liam married Amy and they began returning home more frequently, it helped erase my solitary existence. Liam and I had always been the closest of the three Remington siblings, and Amy was already like a sister to me from her many years of visiting Natalie. I couldn't be more thrilled that they were taking on a more active role. I was excited to spend more time with them.

Far above the Atlantic Ocean in our family's private jet headed back to my gilded cage, I sank into the large, cream leather captain's chair. The eight-seater jet was sleek and stylish. Four seats—two on each side—faced across a lacquered wooden table, the other four placed along the edge of the jet, set in a couch configuration. A door in the back led to a bedroom, and there was a kitchenette in the front. It was essentially an apartment in the sky.

Most people would kill for the luxury of their family owning a private jet. Sure, it was comfortable and convenient, but it came at a price—a price I no longer wanted to pay.

Amy drew me from my thoughts. "The reviews keep pouring in for Addy June. You must be thrilled, Lucy. All your hard work is finally paying off."

Amy and Natalie were my biggest cheerleaders; their support meant the world to me. "Thanks, Ames. I didn't quite expect this kind of response."

Not one to let me wallow in self-doubt, Amy's voice was stern. "Don't do that."

"Do what?"

"You know what. Your designs are brilliant, and your vision for the inclusivity of women of all sizes deserves every bit of praise you've received."

Liam looked up from his laptop. "She's right, LuLu. Everything you've designed for Amy or Natalie has been incredible. Enjoy your success."

I scowled at the use of his childhood nickname for me from when he was small and couldn't say my name correctly. He knew I hated it now that I was a grown woman in my late twenties, but every now and again, he let it slip—old habits and all that. I decided not to dwell on it with more pressing matters at hand.

"I wish I could. There's so much work to be done, and I won't be able to get to Milan for at least a month." Leaning my elbows forward on the table separating our seats, I asked, "How did you do it, Liam?"

"What did I do now?" He was close to rolling his blue eyes—the famous Remington Blue—that matched mine, but he refrained.

"Escape for all those years."

Sighing, he shared a look with Amy. "It was a necessity."

Getting Natalie and the kids away from Leo had been no small feat. Liam and my mother conspired to sneak them out in the middle of the night while Leo was on a state visit to Spain. They'd told no one else of their plans so there wouldn't be a leak. One day, Natalie and the kids were there, the next, they weren't. No one knew where they went, at least for a while. The memory of Leo's rage when he returned home to find his family gone forced an involuntary shudder to rack my body.

Needing to lighten the mood, I joked, "So, what you're saying is . . . I should kidnap Amy in the middle of the night so I can work in peace for the next three years under the guise of protecting her?"

Amy's hand went to her mouth to hide her smile, but I could see her body shaking, trying to hold back laughter. Liam was less than amused. Even though Amy had softened his normally stoic demeanor, it didn't take much to bring back his patented perma-scowl.

"That's not funny, Lucy," he reprimanded.

"Well, do you have any better ideas? Any way I can sweet-talk the Big Wigs into letting me work remotely while things are crazy?" Big Wigs was our code name for our elder royals—Grandfather, Mom, and Dad. They were almost literal gatekeepers; everything went through them.

Liam's expression softened. He never made it a secret that he preferred a quiet, private life. Granted a momentary reprieve due to his mission to protect Natalie, the responsibilities we'd been born to still came knocking at his door. I knew permanent escape was impossible. I just wanted a little time to focus on what made me happy. Our family and our duty weren't going anywhere in my potential absence.

"I'll see what I can do, Lucy. But with Leo gone . . ." His words trailed off.

There was no love lost between my two brothers. They'd never particularly gotten along—Leo preferred the spotlight and flaunting his status while Liam chose to serve our country without the pomp and circumstance—but their relationship was fractured entirely when Liam learned of the tactics Leo used to control and emotionally abuse Natalie behind closed doors. Liam was a protector, so it was automatic that he jumped to Natalie's aid. I was sure Liam didn't particularly mind that Leo had disappeared.

"I know, I know. If I step back, it puts more on Mom and Dad." Our parents were the face of the family right now. Grandfather stepping out of the spotlight had thrust them into it, and we all knew the clock was ticking—the day our father became King was barreling toward us at an unknown date. "I just . . . need more time."

"Don't we all?"

Shocked, I looked at my brother.

That was slightly cryptic. Perhaps, with no one knowing where Leo went, he was referencing the possibility that he might need to step in if he never returned. It seemed unlikely, but stranger things had happened.

Sighing, he added, "We can't change who we are, who we were born to be. All we can do is make the best of the hand we've been dealt."

Ugh. If only I could go back to being ten years old, when I thought being a princess was the coolest thing in the entire world. The novelty wore off during my teenage years, and now the weight of the life forced upon me was suffocating.

Closing my eyes, I let the exhaustion of the past week roll over my body and drag me into the abyss of unconsciousness.

Returning home and resuming my royal duties was like riding a bike; I automatically fell back into the routine. The faces of citizens I met blurred together, and it felt like I was living every day on repeat. I was a prisoner in my own life.

Running on autopilot, I came alive only in the late-night hours when I worked on my designs. I was drowning trying to balance two "careers." There were only so many hours in the day.

Orders to carry Addy June designs were pouring in from boutiques worldwide, and we were looking into streamlining our production on a mass scale. It was exciting, but I was limited by being separated from the team in our Milan studio. I trusted Sophie, but it was difficult to hand over complete control when we were at such a critical point for the label.

My heart and mind were in Milan while my body was stuck in Belleston.

A week into my sentence, I received a summons for an audience with my grandfather. That was never a good sign. Grandfather only requested—more like a loose term for "demanded"—a private audience when he was displeased. With the success of Addy June and his previous objections to my aspirations as a fashion designer, I could only imagine that was the reason for this meeting.

My stomach twisted thinking about it. If he demanded I give up my passion, I wouldn't survive. It would suck the soul from my body, and I'd be left a hollow shell.

I loved my family, but for the first time in my life, I considered walking away. Sure, it would put more pressure on my parents, Liam, and Amy, but didn't *I* matter?

I'd run the numbers. Continuing to donate my Addy June profits, I could live comfortably with the money earned from Arabella Reign. Breaking free would also allow me to expand into a bridal line. I may have to give up the life of private planes and penthouse suites in hotels, but that was a small price to pay. I didn't care about those things as much as I cared about my career.

Dressing smartly in a pair of high-waisted black sailor pants and a sleeveless white lace blouse with a bow collar, I approached Grandfather's private office with a vise-grip squeezing my chest. His personal secretary nodded when I arrived, signaling that I was expected to let myself in. Pausing at the gilded wooden door, I took a deep breath before turning the doorknob and entering.

Sitting behind a massive oak desk, likely centuries old, was the patriarch of our family. King Victor's reign had been long, spanning nearly fifty years, and he was the last link to the old ways. He was a traditionalist, which was a direct threat to my hybrid royal lifestyle.

At almost ninety, he wasn't as mobile as he once was, often using a cane when walking. His head was nearly bald on top, a few gray wisps trimmed closely on the sides. Wrinkles lined his face from all he'd weathered as our monarch, but one thing that had never changed in all the time he was King was the distinguished mustache he wore—the only difference was the gray color which had replaced the once black facial hair. His blue eyes still shone brightly, a distinctive feature he passed down to his only son, and in turn, Liam and me.

Seeing me standing in his doorway, Grandfather gestured for me to enter with his hands. "Lucette, please take a seat."

Dropping into a quick curtsey, I followed his command, settling gracefully into the richly upholstered Victorian wingback chair opposite his desk. This room had been off-limits to us when my brothers and I were growing up. Grandfather used it for important state business, and our parents warned us he couldn't be disturbed.

Being the royal children we were—unaccustomed to being told no—the three of us snuck in one day when we knew Grandfather was traveling.

Leo spent the entire time posturing, telling us how this would be his office when he was King, even being so bold as to sit behind the desk. Liam stood guard at the door, having been unable to deter us from our plan to enter the restricted room. I sat in a corner, taking in the space in awe.

The room was gorgeous, with its rich mahogany walls accented with gold filigree, burgundy and cream furniture, and an entire wall of windows overlooking the courtyard. But that wasn't what intrigued me about this sacred space. This room had seen centuries of Remington monarchs working diligently to create policies to better our country, meeting with foreign dignitaries, or even making military decisions to protect our homeland. Our family history—our legacy—was created within these four walls.

What once had seemed inspiring now felt oppressive. The weight of a responsibility I never asked for held me down, keeping me from achieving my dreams.

Crossing my legs at the ankles, I sat with my back straight and hands clasped in my lap, waiting for Grandfather to begin. The monarch always got the first and last word—and his word was law.

"It's wonderful to see you returned home, Lucette." There was a deeper meaning behind his words, implying he was displeased that I wasn't always at home, ready to be the perfect princess. Bowing my head, I acknowledged his opening statement, allowing him to continue. "You're nearing your thirtieth birthday, and it's long past time to discuss your future."

My breathing became shallow as the walls closed in around me. This was it. I tried to hold back the tears in anticipation of my worst fear to be realized, when he demanded I give up my job—my passion, my life. I would be asked to choose between loyalty to my family and what made me truly happy. My heart and head would war; the choice impossible.

Not needing a partner in this conversation, Grandfather continued, "I'm not getting any younger, and I'd like to see you settled before I'm gone."

Settled? I was suddenly lost.

Politely, I asked, "Pardon my confusion, sir, but settled how?"

His striking blue eyes, which mirrored my own, stared right at me as he stated simply, "It's time for you to marry."

Whoa. Back it up. Married?

"I'm not dating anyone," I blurted out.

Waving his hand, Grandfather brushed off that major obstacle with ease. "Precisely. We can proceed without any complications."

It finally clicked. I was being used as bait in some political game. Okay, I was wrong before. Losing my career wasn't my worst fear anymore. Being forced into an arranged marriage was so terrifying that it had never entered my radar.

The idea was beyond absurd. My parents had married for love, Leo had married for control—but at least he chose his bride—and Liam was so over the moon for Amy that they'd eloped.

There was no time in my life for a man, even if I did want one. My life was too busy to be tied down—metaphorically, at least. I couldn't imagine whoever Grandfather had likely already brokered a deal with would be willing to let me continue working. I'd become a prop for some powerful man. That was so not my jam.

I was reeling but found it deep within myself to push back. "Excuse me for saying so, but don't you think I should have a say in who I marry? Father was granted that right, as were my brothers."

Grandfather steepled his hands before him on the massive desk. "Your father chose well, but your brothers' choices were not ones I would have condoned. We must uphold the Remington family name as one with strong Bellestonian roots."

Translation: Purebred Remington royals full of Bellestonian blue blood were superior to the half-royal children my oldest brother had produced, and my older brother would likely bring forth in the coming years.

Both Leo and Liam had married Americans. Natalie and Amy came from wealthy families—Natalie's father was in tech, and Amy's was an oil tycoon—but they were outsiders. I'd always loved that they came from a different world. Their fresh perspective was such an asset to our country moving forward. Grandfather saw them as a threat to our long-standing traditions, and it had been mentioned more than once that they were a bad influence on me. It was easier to place blame for my need to spread my wings outside of this palace than to accept that maybe I didn't belong.

There was still one part of this that didn't make sense. Finding my response, I questioned the man across the desk—who, at this moment, was more my monarch than my grandfather. "Why is it so important that I produce blue-blooded Bellestonian babies? Leo has three children, and Liam is bound to have his own children. The line of succession is set, and I'm so far down that it makes little difference who I marry."

I was used to the patriarchal society where I lived—in one of the few countries still invoking male-preference primogeniture—but I never thought it would come to this. Sure, I learned long ago that my role was to smile, look pretty, and give my life to service, but I wanted more. I deserved more. That's why it was time to stand up and fight for my own life.

Expecting to be patronized, being told that it was my job as a woman to support a man and obey her king unquestionably, I was surprised when Grandfather softened with a sigh. "Lucy, you're a grown woman now, so I'm going to tell you the truth, but what I have to say can not leave this room. I need your word."

Slightly frightened as to what kind of truth would require absolute secrecy, I wasn't sure I wanted to know. The skeletons in this family's—high-profile and influential—closet could be anything. But curiosity won out; needing to understand why I was being placed on the altar of sacrifice.

Nodding, I accepted his terms. "You have my word."

"Leopold is not your father's son. The circumstances are not mine to share, but he will never ascend the throne, and therefore, neither will any of his children."

Grandfather paused just long enough to allow the bomb he dropped to blow me away.

Had they known this all along? Was that why Leo left? Did Liam know?

Those questions faded into the background of my mind as reality sank in, and I breathed out, "I'm your backup plan."

"You're the spare, Lucy. You must marry well should you ever be called upon to rule."

Fuck. This changed everything.

Grasping at straws, I tried for one last lifeline. "Liam and Amy will have children. Lots of them, if the way they look at each other in the hallways when they think no one is looking is any indication. Each of their children—and their children's children, and so forth—will come before me."

Grandfather glanced at a life-sized portrait of my grandmother, Queen Eleanora. She'd passed away several years ago, but it was clear that he missed her. They were the last arranged marriage our family had seen. It worked out well for them, but that didn't mean it would for me.

"Sometimes, no matter how much you love each other, life has other plans."

My father, Prince Adrian, was an only child. Was he implying they wanted more children and hadn't been able? It didn't matter. It wouldn't change the situation I found myself in.

I couldn't do it. I just couldn't.

Standing, the words left my mouth before I could stop them. "I'm sorry, Grandfather. This isn't what I want for my life. I want to create, live, and love on my own terms. Family is important, but an archaic arranged marriage is a step too far. Please don't make me choose between my love for my family and my passion. I have a feeling you won't like the outcome."

Turning, I walked five steps toward the door when he called out behind me, "What if you can have both?"

Halting my steps, I turned. "Excuse me?"

"If you agree to marry a man I deem worthy, I will fully support your fashion career and allow you to step away from royal duties."

I'd always thought it would come down to my family or fashion, and now he was saying I could have both. But it came at a price. It was up to me to determine whether the cost was too steep, essentially trading one set of shackles for another. But how could I not at least hear him out if it meant obtaining what I once thought was impossible?

Returning to my chair, I sat, at least willing to hear him out. "Do you have a man in mind?"

Looking slightly pleased, Grandfather nodded. "There was a list of candidates, but I've narrowed it down to one with the help of your mother. His pedigree is impeccable. The second son of a local duke, he's not in line for his own title and works as an attorney for the Crown."

Great. I was looking for an escape, but this proposal meant being dragged back into a world I'd come to despise. Most of the nobility were my playmates and schoolmates growing up. They viewed the world as their playground because they were born into privilege. Any of them could be found pictured in the dictionary next to the definition of a God complex.

I was not compatible with that group. I worked hard, and when I found a worthy cause, I volunteered my time because it made me happy and fulfilled. Not because someone was watching to earn good publicity. They played to the cameras when I only wanted them to go away.

The men especially thought they were God's gift to women. They were arrogant and self-absorbed, and from the stories I'd overheard in prep school, they exaggerated their sexual prowess. I had no interest in vanilla sex for the rest of my life, with some red-faced two-pump chump collapsing on top of me, with the cherry on top being the expectation that I should be thankful for the privilege. No thanks.

Crossing my arms defensively, I asked, "*If* I were to agree to this, how would it work?"

"There would be a courtship, time for you to get accustomed to each other. If you deem it a good fit, we will move on to a formal engagement."

"Timeline?"

"I would prefer you to be married by your thirtieth birthday."

That gave me some time. I would turn twenty-nine this December.

"And if I don't deem it a good match?"

"You will." Grandfather's meaning shone through those words. If I didn't like his choice of a husband, there wouldn't be another—the deal would be off.

I needed to make sure it was worth it. "I would be able to move full-time to Milan? Or anywhere else I choose to set up a studio?"

"Yes. You would be free to follow your pursuits as soon as your marriage is made legal."

"Security?"

"That's non-negotiable. You may not be a working royal, but you are still my granddaughter. Our enemies could still use you as leverage, and your protection is paramount."

Being kidnapped sounded like a drag, but there was never a single attempt in almost twenty-nine years. I could work around my constant security presence if need be.

Moving to the next item on my mental checklist, I challenged, "What of my chosen husband? It sounds as though his work requires his presence in Belleston."

Grandfather paused, and I gave myself a mental high-five thinking I'd finally found a snag in his master plan for my life. That hope was dashed when he grinned, answering, "His marriage to you will become his job. Where you go, he will be expected to follow."

Stunned, I processed what that meant. This man would essentially be my consort. That was not a twist I saw coming. What kind of man would allow himself to be led around by the nose by little old me? Who in their right mind was so entranced by the idea of marrying into royalty that they would give up their life?

But on the flip side, maybe this wasn't the worst thing. The role-reversal was appealing in its own way. I wouldn't be some man's ornament—he would be mine.

I began to seriously consider this proposition. There were fourteen months before I absolutely had to get married to this mystery man. If Amy and Liam had a child before then, maybe I could break things off. Even if they didn't, I could bide my time, and eventually, once they had a family, I could arrange for a divorce—Leo and Natalie created a precedent. Once the line of succession was secured, my marriage would be irrelevant.

Riding high on the idea that perhaps I'd found a way to cheat the system and still get what I wanted regarding my freedom, I gave Grandfather my practiced perfect royal smile. "You have a deal."

"You've pleased me greatly, Lucette. I will arrange a meeting in the coming days."

With nothing left to say, I stood, curtseyed, and left the room. Reaching the hallway, I leaned against the wall, closing my eyes. Taking deep breaths, I reminded myself that I wasn't giving my life away; I was gaining my freedom—a chance to live on my terms.

"Well, hello, Princess."

My eyes popped open. I knew that voice—despised that voice—and it belonged to the one man I had hated my entire life. Scanning the hallway, I caught motion when he pushed off the wall further down the hallway, stalking toward where I stood frozen, as his hazel eyes sparkled with amusement.

Standing at six-one, with his chestnut hair perfectly styled away from his forehead and neatly trimmed scruff lining his square jaw, he knew he was attractive, but his good looks held no power over me. When I looked at Preston Scott, all I could think of were the endless years of taunting and teasing I'd endured at his hands.

With those three words, the bubble of glee that had formed in my belly at the idea of my freedom suddenly popped.

CHAPTER 3
Preston

I SHOULD HAVE LEFT after my meeting, but I couldn't help myself when I learned hers was the appointment following mine. I was counting on the prissy girl I knew to turn her nose up at a potential arranged marriage so I could go back to living my life. The last thing I wanted to do was spend the rest of my life babysitting Lucy Remington.

My father had been vague about my audience with King Victor, but his message was clear—you didn't refuse your king, no matter the ask. That alone was enough warning to know I wouldn't like what was requested of me.

After completing my required military service in my early twenties, I attended university before choosing a law school specializing in international law. Upon returning home, I spent a year clerking for a judge in the justice department for the Crown before being granted a position as a junior associate in the offices dealing with the Crown's charitable foundations. Four years later, at thirty-two, I was ready to move up to the treaty law team. I wanted to make a difference for my country, and what better way to do that than to have a hand in fostering our many alliances around the world?

As irony would have it, my father was right, and I knew better than to refuse my king. There would always be at least one man whose orders I was duty-bound to follow blindly, and that disturbed me. Especially now that I'd learned of his request.

King Victor wanted me to marry Lucy.

I sat through his spiel about how important it was that she marry a man of impeccable Bellestonian blood, the whole time wanting to scream in frustration. Our proposed union boiled down to bloodlines and birth order. Talk about romance. I felt like a prized stud won at auction.

None of that mattered because I couldn't say no. Precious Princess Lucy's fashion career was taking off, and it sounded like she was throwing a tantrum to spend more time on her pet projects. The King leveraged this to his advantage to force her into a Crown-approved marriage, and I was caught in the crosshairs. I was the unlucky bastard chosen to become her accessory; I was no more than a designer purse, expected to stand by her side instead of it being the other way around. It was emasculating.

All of this would be bad enough, and I could probably make it work with any other woman, but this was Lucy. We'd never gotten along. The way she was staring at me now with those sparkling blue eyes, I knew she hated me with every fiber of her being. The feeling was mutual.

Befriending Liam Remington early in primary school meant playdates at the palace. Lucy was always hanging around, begging to be included, and when we refused, she cried to her mommy, getting us in trouble. Her entitlement was clearly inherent, and it grated on me. She was bratty and disobedient, and something deep inside my subconscious wanted to punish her for it.

So, I did.

I spent years teasing and torturing her, believing she'd earned it with her bad behavior, and Lucy never forgave me for it—not that I asked for forgiveness. Later in life, I found an outlet for those impulses, but being forced to marry Lucy would put an end to that.

There was an escape clause: Lucy had to agree to the marriage. If she said no, I could walk away unscathed, returning to my life. Knowing that, I'd waited for her emergence from the office, hoping I could tip the scales in my favor. I was counting on her hatred for me outweighing her love of fashion. I liked my odds.

Seeing her leaning against the wall, breathing deeply with eyes closed, I knew she was just as rattled as me. Now, I just had to use that to my advantage. She *hated* when I called her Princess, so I leaned on that tried-and-true provocation.

It gave me a small thrill to watch as her eyes opened in shock, her mouth dropping open slightly as she searched for the source of my voice. Dressed impeccably as always—nothing less was expected of a royal, let alone one at the helm of an emerging fashion empire—her good looks stirred nothing inside me. I only saw the princess who expected the world to cater to her every whim.

Her baby blues narrowed when she saw me down the hallway as I stalked to where she stood.

Crossing her arms, condescension dripped from her words. "How did *you* make it past the guards?"

Smug, I couldn't wait to put her in her place. Flashing her a grin, I answered, "I was invited. Had a private audience with our king."

It was extremely gratifying to watch as reality sank in. Those blue eyes widened in shock at the realization that I was the man her grandfather intended for her to marry, and she whispered, "No. No, no, no."

Stepping away from the wall, she began pacing. I watched, mentally celebrating my victory, as she repeatedly pinched her forearm until it turned a deep red. If she wasn't careful, she'd cause bruising.

Rookie mistake.

Curious, I asked, "What are you doing?"

Shooting me an annoyed glance, Lucy never paused her pacing. "Trying to wake up."

Pouring on the charm, knowing it would annoy the hell out of her, I drawled, "Oh, Princess, why would you want to wake up from the dream come true of forever with me? Hearts will be breaking across Belleston when news gets out that I'm off the market."

Her blue glare bordered on glacial. "God, you are so full of yourself."

I went for the kill. "Aw, are you jealous? Would *you* rather be full of me?" It was crass, but I was trying to offend her enough to have her running back into that office to turn down the offer flat.

A flash of pain radiated on the left side of my face, and it took a moment to register that Lucy had slapped me. Instinct had me reaching for her, but she spun on her heel and stomped down the hallway as fast as her black pumps could carry her. My extended hand instead went to cup my jaw, attempting to rub away the sting her palm left behind. No woman had ever been so bold as to lay a hand on me—they knew better.

Lucy was playing with fire, and she didn't even know it.

She was in such a hurry to get away from me that I watched as she rammed into the back of a man further down the hallway. Watching in fascination, I realized that man was Liam, who had his redheaded wife caged against the wall. Liam shielded his wife from the impact of Lucy's careless retreat before calling something after her. Lucy turned, red-faced, screaming at her older brother.

Yep, she was the same old bratty, self-absorbed Lucy I grew up with. Some things never changed, but at least I was confident she would never agree to be my wife.

Before I could escape, Liam called my name from down the hallway as he approached.

Liam was my best friend growing up, but we'd lost touch over the years. When we got together, it was as if no time had passed, but our lives had taken different paths, and quite honestly, it was challenging to maintain adult friendships. I had my career while everyone I knew was getting married or having babies, but that was where the extent of their adulting ended. Most were happy to fall back on their aristocratic roots, leaning into their privilege—only caring about gossip and the next party to attend. Our lives didn't mesh the way they had when our biggest concern was who to sit next to in history class.

Liam had only recently returned from an extended stint living abroad, caring for his sister-in-law. The distance didn't bother me—it was similar to when he'd re-enlisted in the Bellestonian army, and I'd chosen higher education. Our common thread had been that we were eternal bachelors, but his return included a wife—who was charming and exactly what our country needed, don't get me wrong—and it felt like the final nail in the coffin of our dying friendship.

Liam was taller than me by barely an inch, but his broad form, honed from many years of military service, was barely contained in his perfectly tailored suit. His coloring was identical to Lucy's, with their family's classic Remington Blue eyes and raven black hair, but that's where their similarities ended.

Liam was level-headed, whereas Lucy was short-tempered.

Liam felt a sense of duty toward his family while Lucy ran all over the world, playing dress-up.

Liam preferred a quieter, private life, and Lucy needed to be in the spotlight.

I couldn't pinpoint whether it was her status as the baby of the family or the fact that she was the only girl, but something somewhere turned Lucy into this needy, self-centered, attention-seeking hellion. How could the King possibly think we were a good match?

I was the last person on Earth who would cater to her demands. Perhaps they thought I could tame the wild beast they'd created? How was I supposed to do that when I had to give up my career to follow her around like a love-sick puppy while she got to do whatever she wanted? It wasn't going to work, and the sooner everyone involved figured that out, the better.

"Did I forget a meeting we had scheduled?" Liam's voice dragged me from my thoughts as he got close enough to converse without shouting down the long corridor.

I threw on my practiced charm. "No, you're off the hook, old chap. Although, your wife's new projects are keeping me on my toes."

His wife, Amy, had a background in social work and dove head-first into creating no less than a dozen programs to better the lives of Bellestonians in need. Logistics and legalities for charitable pursuits were one of the many things that landed on my desk.

"Then what brings you here on a Tuesday?"

"I was summoned."

Liam winced. "Oof. That's never good. Anything I can help with?"

"It's complicated. Hell, it may turn out to be nothing." I was tiptoeing around telling one of my oldest friends that I might be defiling his little sister in the very near future.

Just the thought of touching the ice princess had my balls shriveling up, but it was either her or no one if this deal went through. You didn't cheat on the King's granddaughter and live to tell the tale. My duty to obey my sovereign was in direct conflict with the bro code. You didn't mess around with your friends' sisters.

Sensing my discomfort at discussing this out in the open where anyone could overhear, Liam offered, "Come on, let's go to my office. It's more private there."

We were in a more functional palace wing, where the monarchy's press office operated and many of the working royals held their own private offices. It was smart. Even though they worked where they lived, they could create a separation between their public and private lives. Liam opened a door down a side hallway, nodding to his secretary before entering his modest office.

Walking straight to the sideboard, where several liquor decanters waited, he poured brown liquor into two crystal glasses before motioning to the black leather couch along the opposite wall. We sank onto the soft leather, which groaned as it yielded to the weight of two grown men.

Liam handed me a glass, and I took a sip. It was bourbon, aged to perfection. While I'd typically savor the burn of the liquor down my throat, it only served to remind me of the sting of Lucy's palm against my cheek.

Almost like he could read my mind, Liam spoke, "Please tell me my sister didn't slap you."

Had it been that obvious? Shrugging, I replied, "I provoked her."

There was humor in Liam's blue eyes. "You still doing that? You two aren't children anymore."

I blew out a breath. "I'm sorry. I know she's your sister, but there is just something about her that I can't stand."

"You must have really pissed her off. She laid into me over something totally innocent after she nearly knocked me over to get away from you."

"I had a little help."

One of his dark eyebrows rose. "Care to explain?"

"It may turn out to be nothing. God, I hope it does."

"You're going to have to give me a little more than that, old friend."

"Your grandfather proposed to me."

Liam was mid-sip, and bourbon sprayed out of his mouth and onto my face. Always prepared, I pulled a white monogrammed handkerchief from my breast pocket and wiped away the evidence of Liam's shock.

Coughing to clear his throat, he finally croaked out, "I didn't realize you were his type." Regaining his composure, he smirked. "He has been lonely. I'm sure you two will be very happy together."

"Very funny. He wants me to marry Lucy."

"Fuck! Have they learned nothing? Our lives aren't a fucking game!" His anger was the last thing I expected. There was more to what he was saying, but it wasn't my place to ask. I might be the son of a duke, but that didn't even come close in comparison to what the royal family dealt with internally. Liam eyed me. "You said no, right? You two will kill each other."

"It's not up to me." I shrugged.

"Who is it up to?"

"Lucy."

He let out a snort. "Then you're off the hook. She'll never agree to marry you."

"If only it were that simple," I muttered. "If she goes through with it, she gets to focus full-time on her fashion career."

Liam couldn't hold back a chuckle. "Oh, you are so fucked. She's desperate to get out. Desperate enough to even marry you."

I groaned. "Don't say that." Any shred of hope I held onto that she might turn her nose up at the match between us vanished. Desperate people did crazy things. It's why you saw them running back inside burning buildings or throwing themselves into oncoming traffic to save a loved one.

Fashion was Lucy's baby, and she was willing to be burned by me to protect it.

"They couldn't find someone better than you?" There was still laughter in his voice.

"Apparently, I'm the best Belleston has to offer in remaining unwed second sons that aren't too young or too old."

Liam raised his glass in a silent toast. "Welcome to the family."

Fuck my life. This couldn't really be happening.

Suddenly, I regretted the way I'd managed my life. I kept my personal life deeply private while projecting the perception of being squeaky clean by all outward appearances. That was coming back to bite me in the ass. Maybe I should have allowed the world to view me with disdain, throwing ignorant labels my way. Because now, it was all gone. My life would never be the same. Lucy would gain her freedom at the cost of mine.

Spiraling and stuck in limbo while Lucy decided my fate, I left Liam's office. Nothing was official yet. Tonight might be my last chance to exhibit the control I craved. That control was at the root of who I was, how I centered myself. It was therapeutic. Without it, I may very well go insane. Especially if tied to Lucy for the rest of my life. That girl wouldn't know how to obey an order if her life depended on it.

CHAPTER 4

Lucy

I COULDN'T GET TO my room fast enough, especially once I heard Amy calling out behind me. How could I explain that I'd blindly agreed to marry the one man I couldn't stand? All for the sake of a job—a life—I loved.

An arranged marriage was bad enough. But with Preston? This was beyond the worst-case scenario. I could have handled one of the obscenely dull, over-confident men I grew up with. I could have laid there while they got their rocks off, and pretended to like it. Most guys would have been happy enough with the title upgrade this marriage would bring, allowing me to live my life without interference.

Not Preston.

Oh, no. He knew how to push every single button I had, even ones I didn't know existed. It was like he got some kind of sick pleasure out of pissing me off.

He didn't know shit about who I was, and I sure as hell didn't want to get to know him. This would never work.

Bursting into the residence wing, my vision blurred as tears filled my eyes. My pride and dignity demanded that I stand my ground and refuse this marriage. But how could I just walk away from a chance at a life that had only been a pipe dream before today? His constant presence would taint my dream life—I'd never work in peace again. Maybe I could negotiate that he be allowed to resume his work for the Crown, citing its importance, to get him out of my hair.

Finally reaching the door to my private apartment, I turned the knob, rushing as fast as my feet would carry me toward my bedroom. My suite of rooms was directly across the hall from Liam and Amy's and mirrored theirs exactly. Practically a house inside a palace, I had two thousand square feet all to myself, yet I was never alone. There was always someone hovering—housekeepers, maids, butlers, and footmen, to name a few—waiting for my next request like I couldn't fend for myself at almost thirty. Even when I deadbolted my entryway door, secret passageways into my apartment allowed the staff to enter without disrupting our lives.

I couldn't be the first royal to feel suffocated by this life, right?

Running up the stairs as fast as I could in heels, I threw myself on my bed, hugging a pillow to my chest as I curled into the fetal position. I tried pinching myself downstairs, and it hadn't worked to wake me up from this nightmare, but how many movies had I seen where they were still in the dream, even when they felt like they woke up? This could be the opposite of that. I was just stuck, that was all. Closing my eyes, I wished it all away like the bad dream it was.

"Lucy?" Amy's concerned voice was accompanied by a soft knock on my open door.

"Go away." I couldn't hide the hiccup from crying in the middle of those two simple words.

The bed dipped behind me, and I knew I was unsuccessful in gaining the solitude I so desperately required.

Her hand rubbed my bare arm soothingly, and she whispered, "You don't have to talk about it if you don't want to. Just know I'm here for you. It's what sisters do."

Turning to face her, I was slightly shocked to find her lying in bed with me, her emerald-green eyes fixated on my watery ones. Was this what it was like to have sisters or even a best friend? Before Amy, Natalie was the closest thing to a sister I'd ever had. And while I loved her with my whole heart, she was constantly dealing with her own issues—she didn't have the capacity to see beyond herself when she lived here, and I couldn't blame her for that. Amy was her best friend and had dropped everything to move in with her when she needed help, and I could see why Natalie treasured their friendship. It was comforting to have someone in your corner with unwavering support. God bless Liam for bringing her fully into my life.

Wiping at what was surely a mess of mascara running down my cheeks, I sighed. "I'm sorry I yelled at Liam."

Amy gave me an understanding smile. "He knows he isn't the one you're upset with."

"He caught me at a bad time." That was an understatement.

"This have anything to do with the man at the other end of the hallway?"

"I hate him." It was the truth. No point in sugarcoating it.

"Hate's a strong word. Who is he?"

God, I hated that I was even going to utter these words out loud. "He's the asshole I'm going to marry."

If I was going for shock value, I'd found it.

Amy's brilliant jewel-toned eyes widened, and she gasped. "You're getting married? Whoa. I think we need to back this up. Start from the beginning." Amy sat up against my gray quilted headboard, and I mirrored her, still clutching my pillow closely for comfort.

"You wouldn't understand."

There were a few cardinal rules in life—one was that you didn't piss off a redhead. I knew I'd made an error the minute the words left my mouth.

Folding her arms across her chest, there was a steel edge to her tone. "Would you like to try that again?"

"I'm sorry, Ames. My life is ending, and I'm not handling it well."

"Two heads are better than one. Lay it out for me, and maybe we can figure out a solution together."

Leaning my face into my pillow, I took a deep breath. "Okay. I was called to Grandfather's office today, where he made me a deal."

Amy's eyes narrowed. "What kind of deal?"

"If I agree to marry a man of his choosing, then I get to step away from royal duties and focus on fashion."

One of the things I loved most about Amy was that she was level-headed, rational to a fault. She took her time thinking, contemplating the best choice of words instead of blurting out whatever came into her head—something I struggled with, especially when provoked by a certain someone. I could see the wheels turning in her head, but she gave nothing away.

Tilting her head, she assessed me before stating, "You said yes blindly."

Normally, I would be offended that I was so transparent, but barely a week ago, I'd begged Liam to go to bat for me and help me obtain more freedom.

Nodding into my pillow, a fresh set of tears fell from my eyes. "It seemed almost too good to be true. Should have seen it coming."

"Can you take it back? Turn down the offer? Ask for another suitor, perhaps?"

I shook my head. "There won't be another option. It's Preston or no deal. If I go back with my tail between my legs, I'd be giving up on my dream."

Amy's lips twisted in thought. "Well, we can't have that. Why don't you tell me why you hate Preston so much."

Rolling my eyes, I scoffed. "How much time do you have?"

A soft laugh escaped her lips. "For you, dear sister, all the time in the world."

"I'm sure my brother would beg to differ."

"It's a good thing I have him wrapped around my little finger." Amy smirked, holding up her pinky.

"Never thought I'd see the day."

Liam was a control freak and as serious as they came. All that changed when he married Amy. She found a way to soften him, and their power dynamic was one of equality, even if Amy joked that she was in control. Liam was the brother I could always count on to protect me growing up, but I loved the man he became with the woman he loved by his side. He'd always been a good man, but now he was a great one.

Amy brought me back to my new reality. "You're deflecting, Lucy. What's the deal with Preston? Liam seems to like him, and you know he doesn't like many people."

"It's Liam's fault I even know Preston. They were best friends growing up, so he was always over here playing with Liam. I was just the pesky little sister, and he made my life a living hell—teasing me, calling me a baby, pulling on my pigtails. Don't even get me started on the way he calls me *Princess*. Talk about annoying."

"Lucy, you are a princess." Amy was simply stating the obvious.

I groaned. "It's the way he says it. Like he's mocking me."

"The childhood teasing seems pretty standard, however. That's what boys do when they like a girl. Did you ever think that maybe he had a crush on you?"

My head shook violently. "No way. He thinks I'm some spoiled, self-ab-sorbed girl who throws tantrums to get what she wants."

"Then he doesn't know you. Maybe you should show him who you really are. Lucy, you're this incredibly kind, caring, smart, thoughtful, passionate woman. And that's not even touching on your creative genius. If he knew the real you, maybe things would be different."

She had a point, but I was stubborn—a trait I shared with her husband. "He made up his mind about me a long time ago. Why is it my responsi-bility to change his perception?"

"I'm just trying to help."

I sighed. "I know you are. Even if he changed his mind about me, he's still an egotistical, crass, judgmental prick. Just another one of the arrogant, power-hungry men I grew up with. I'm trying to escape this fucked up world with all its politics and power trips. Now, I've become another pawn in that game of chess the powerful men play."

"And you won't even entertain the idea of turning down the deal?" Amy asked.

"I would if I thought I could secure my current arrangement. It's not ideal, but I make it work. What scares me is that I could be recalled to home base and told my career is over at any given time. What then? I'd be worse off than I am now."

Amy gave me a look of pity, and I hated it. I didn't want her to feel sorry for me. I wanted her to help me find a way to have my cake and eat it too, but that seemed like a pipe dream. "It sounds like you've made your choice."

That set me off. "There is no choice, don't you get it, Amy? Everyone else got to choose what made them happy, except me. Mom and Dad got a choice. You and Liam got a choice. Hell, even Natalie got the choice to leave when her marriage didn't work out. I'm being forced into a marriage

I don't want for the sake of the family, wrapped up in pretty packaging and disguised as my freedom. I'll never be free so long as I'm tied to Preston."

Just when I thought I'd stunned Amy into silence with my outburst, she grabbed my hand. "We're sisters now, and I think it's time I share something with you. Something only Natalie, Hannah, and Jaxon know. Not even your parents." Jaxon was Natalie's new husband.

I was honored that Amy wanted to share a secret with me. She was one of the handful of people who knew about Arabella Reign being mine, so she knew I trusted her explicitly. Knowing she returned the sentiment made me feel like we genuinely were sisters.

Curious, I took a deep breath. "Okay."

Amy turned to face me fully while sitting beside me on the bed, tucking a strand of her auburn hair behind her ear. "You know that Liam and I eloped, but you don't know that we had an arrangement."

Wait. I remembered how angry my grandfather and dad were when they got word that Liam ran off to Vegas and married Amy. There was no way they'd had an arranged marriage.

"What kind of an arrangement?"

She sighed. "You know how you're considering this because you love your job?" I nodded, so she continued, "Well, it just so happens that I was up for a promotion at work, and the jerks I worked for made it very clear that unless I was married, I wouldn't get the job."

The pieces fell into place. "Liam offered to marry you." My voice was barely above a whisper.

Amy smiled. "God, I thought he was crazy when he brought the idea to me. I tried to tell him he couldn't fix everything for everyone, but you know how well he takes no for an answer. I was so annoyed that he was right—I needed his help. We signed a contract. Our marriage was to be on paper only so that I could get the promotion. No romantic entanglement, just roommates."

As stunned as I was that their marriage wasn't what it initially seemed, I argued, "But you two were friends first. You knew you could at least tolerate each other."

"He wasn't always my favorite person. You grew up with the stubborn man I married. You know what he's like."

"But you didn't hate him."

She conceded that point. "No. I didn't hate him, but I didn't love him either. I do now. I never saw it coming. We'd lived in the same house for years, and I never thought of him as more than Natalie's brother-in-law who helped us raise the kids. Something shifted when we were forced together. I can't explain it. It didn't happen overnight but built over time. Maybe you and Preston can have that. You never know."

"I appreciate you trying to help me make lemonade, Ames, but I just don't see it. You can't turn a lifetime of hatred into love."

Amy shrugged. "You know what they say about the line between love and hate."

Sinking back into a reclined position on the bed, my thoughts escaped my lips before I could stop them. "Can you two have lots of babies so I can be let off the hook?"

"What did you just say?" Amy tensed beside me, green eyes widening in shock.

Oops. I'd almost forgotten about the whole Leo not being blood thing, but it was somewhere in my subconscious. Now, I realized I may have just spilled a family secret. Grandfather had explicitly told me it didn't leave that room. I tried to play it off with a wave of my hand. "Nothing."

Her eyes narrowed, and she searched my eyes. Calmly, she asked, "You know, don't you?"

Playing dumb, I retorted, "Know what?"

Amy sucked in a sharp breath. "Oh my God, you know."

Deflect. Deflect. Deflect.

"Maybe I know something different? Ever think of that? This family has too many secrets to keep track of anymore."

"Fine. On the count of three, we say it at the same time. Worst case, it's not the same thing, and we trade secrets. We know we're good to keep it quiet."

"Deal." I nodded.

Taking a deep breath, Amy began counting, "One. Two. Three."

At the same time, we said one word.

"Leo."

A look of pure relief crossed Amy's face, that she hadn't spilled something I hadn't already known, but then she realized how it impacted my current situation. "I'm sorry, Lucy."

Raising my hand, I acknowledged my new role. "Yep. I'm the backup plan in case you two don't procreate. Gotta love how my future rests in the hands of others."

My life was reduced to one of those interactive storybooks, where you made choices at critical points within the narrative and the unique combination determined your ending. Except that I wasn't the one making the choices that would ultimately determine my fate. I was at the mercy of my family.

I guess, in a way, I always had been.

Curious about one thing, I asked Amy, "How long have you known? I found out today, so I'm still playing catch up."

Amy bit her lip. "I found out a few months ago. Liam, however, knew before he asked me to marry him."

Sucking in a breath, I winced. "Yikes. The gravity of being the heir had barely sunk in, and he signed you up to be the face of the monarchy with him without telling you? I'm surprised he's still standing."

"Yeah, well, the Penelope scandal overshadowed it. Seemed mild by comparison." Penelope was my brother's ex-girlfriend, and the press sensationalized a couple of pictures of them during one of his visits home without Amy, alluding to an affair.

"You're a better woman than me."

"Addy is better than us both," Amy countered with a sigh.

I knew my mom was this incredible, graceful creature, but the way Amy said it didn't sit right with me. "What do you mean?"

Suddenly uncomfortable, Amy went to slide off my bed. "I better be going."

"Oh, no. You're not going to run off like that. What's going on with my mom?"

Amy bit her lip, stalling, but eventually she asked, "Did you happen to get any of the details on why Leo is out as heir?"

Running the conversation with Grandfather through my mind, I landed on one key piece of information. "Leo's not my father's son," I whispered, almost afraid the walls would tell on me for repeating what I was told in confidence.

So caught up in what that news meant for me, I didn't take the time to analyze what that meant. How was it even possible? My parents loved each other. It didn't make sense that my mother would have an affair, especially so soon after they were married.

"I don't quite understand," I uttered.

Amy grimaced, but explained, "From the very limited information I have on the subject from Liam, Addy was attacked, resulting in Leo's conception. They kept it hidden for years to protect her from public scrutiny."

I scoffed. Public scrutiny. More like, they would have taken a heinous act against my mom and twisted it into a sordid story about how she was meeting men in dark alleyways, cheating on my dad. I couldn't imagine having to keep a secret like that all these years, dealing with the pain in private, while there was a living reminder of your trauma.

The pieces clicked into place why Leo was always so different from the rest of us. He wasn't one of us. His coloring was different. His temperament was different.

He'd grown up in the same loving home as me and Liam, yet was calculating and cruel toward others. He didn't know how to love—not like the rest of us.

It was no wonder they decided after all these years that he couldn't be allowed to rule. They gave him every privilege this world had to offer, but he spit in their faces. Our country dodged a bullet with this decision.

If only it didn't mean my life being sacrificed in an attempt to keep our family line intact.

Sighing, I appealed to Amy, "I learned a long time ago to accept that I can't change the family I was born into. But this is an impossible choice. I *hate* Preston almost as much as I love my job."

Amy took my hands in hers. "I can sympathize with your desperation to hold onto a career you love. You built your labels from the ground up. I was just an employee. You are Lucy Remington—badass boss bitch. Don't let anyone stand in the way of getting what you want. You won't regret being selfish if it makes you happy in the end."

Maybe she was right, but too much information had been thrown at me today, and my brain struggled to process it all. "I think I just need time to figure out what I want to do. I appreciate the talk. It helped a little."

Pulling me in for a tight hug, I clung to her like the lifeline that she was.

When I finally let her go, she smiled. "I believe in you and will always have your back."

Giving my hand one last squeeze, she slid off the bed, leaving me alone with my thoughts. My brain was overloaded, and if I just sat here thinking of all the possibilities for my life, it would likely explode. What I needed more than anything was to shut it off, even if only temporarily. There was only one place I knew where I could make that happen, but it would have to wait until later. Rolling over, I closed my eyes, willing myself to sleep until the time was right.

CHAPTER 5

Lucy

JUST PAST MIDNIGHT, I walked along the darkened underground tunnels connecting the palace to the outside world. Initially designed as an escape route in the event of an attack, they now became my method of slipping my security detail in the middle of the night. Stonecrest Palace was built against the side of a mountain, with the Bellestonian capital city of Remhorn situated below. That meant the tunnels were a maze of steep stairs leading toward the city.

Using the flashlight on my phone, I carefully navigated the path I knew would spit me out closest to my destination. Walking barefoot to avoid slipping on the worn stone steps in four-inch heels, the chill from the Earth surrounding me was seeping into my bones. It didn't matter. I could handle a little discomfort.

After twenty minutes spent underground, I unlatched the heavy metal door that opened on a random cobblestone alleyway in Remhorn. It was one of many exits from the tunnels, all unmarked. If you didn't know they were there, you'd never find them, and they only opened from the inside. Each time I ventured through them, I was taking a risk as I was forced to keep it open with a metal pipe to await my return. My family would kill me if they knew—not only where I was going but that I used the tunnels to do so.

Slipping the familiar silver mask onto the upper half of my face, I strapped on my heels and ventured through the alleyway toward my destination. Two turns later, I knocked on the bolted steel door in a practiced cadence until the horizontal slot at eye level slid open, and I was met with another masked face, asking, "Password?"

Ready for the irony? "Freedom," I replied.

The sound of three deadbolts turning echoed through the small alley, and the door opened, allowing me entry. Stepping inside, I was instantly met with warmth, which was quite welcome on a cool October night in the Alps. Especially after spending almost half an hour scantily dressed underground.

The first few steps inside the building showcased a reception area, where you were expected to hand over your cell phone and any other personal belongings you didn't want to carry. A wallet wasn't needed. Everyone was billed according to their member ID. Spelled out in neon against a brick wall was the name of the club: Desire.

My cell phone was the only possession I brought tonight, so I handed it to the hostess behind the desk to store in the bin associated with my ID. We didn't use names here—not real ones, anyway.

A red curtain separated reception from the rest of the club, and once I was cleared, I stepped through them to encounter another set of stairs that led me right back underground. Reaching the bottom, I felt at peace. This was where I belonged.

The club's main room featured a stage, several seating areas—some secluded, others not—and a bar. Everything was done in black, with red and silver accents, whether it be the art on the walls, the booths, or the carpets. Beyond this area, commonly known as the bullpen, were private rooms paid for by members.

If you haven't figured it out yet, Desire was a sex club.

Now, before you judge me, hear me out.

Do you know how hard it is to have a sex life as a royal?

Let me rephrase that: Do you know how hard it is to have a sex life as a *female* royal?

Outside of this club, there were camera warriors everywhere. We now lived in a world where everyone had a camera in their back pocket, and the moment they recognized who I was, they whipped it out to get either a picture or a video. There had been speculation of a dating history with every man I'd been seen standing within two feet of since I was sixteen.

Even if I kept within the tight upper circles of society, word would get around, and the press would pay handsomely for proof of a scandal. As a teenager, I knew I couldn't risk what they would do to me if a picture or video was ever leaked of me in bed with a man.

There were different sets of rules for men and women. If a man had several sexual partners, they were applauded by society for sowing their wild oats before settling down. If a woman even implied that they enjoyed sex, they were labeled a hussy, slut, whore, or worse.

What's worse than a whore, you ask? I'm not sure, but I'll be damned if I volunteered to be the first to find out.

When I was eighteen, I used a search engine to find discreet ways to lose my virginity. That single search led me down the rabbit hole that the internet provided, and I discovered the world of sex clubs. After months of research, I was sure I'd found the solution to my problem.

Notice how I gave up my cell phone at the door? Discretion was an illusion in the outside world, but down here, it was the law. Beyond that, members were required to wear masks to disguise their identities. Total anonymity was why I chose Desire over other clubs in Belleston—yes, clubs as in plural; the lifestyle was more common than you'd think.

I was terrified the first time I came here, certain that I would be out of my league. I couldn't have been more wrong. It was obvious that I was new, but there was no pressure.

Afforded the time to get to know some members, I found the right man to take my virginity. In this environment, it was something to be cherished—a man was honored to take me on my first sexual journey, and he wanted me to enjoy myself.

Safety was at the forefront of every facet of Desire. Members were required to pass a rigorous background check prior to being granted access to the club's private rooms. A stipulation of continued membership was providing monthly STD screening results, and women were asked to show proof of birth control, the only exception being long-term relationships where both parties agreed otherwise.

The bottom line was that all members, either single or attached, could enjoy their time at the club without worrying about real-world consequences following them home.

This club allowed individuals to explore their sexuality in a safe space—the type of safety varied from member to member. My safety lay in the fact that the kind of men who could afford membership had enough money that selling a story about sleeping with me would barely make a splash in their bank account. That was, if they even knew who I was behind the mask.

Masks came in several colors, and each had a separate meaning.

White meant virgin.

Silver meant submissive.

Black meant Dominant.

Beige was reserved for the club employees, so they were easily identifiable.

Beyond the mask signifying a member's status, it was up to them to clearly communicate their limits with their partners.

I'm sure by now you've noticed my mask was silver, and I know what you're thinking—that I was a hypocrite. Just hours ago, I was railing against the idea of men deciding my life, and now, I was in a club where I willingly gave up control to a man.

But this was different than being assigned some man to "take care of me." Down here, I got my choice of partner. I chose how far it went and if I wanted it to stop at any given moment without question.

The outside world viewed places like these as a dens of depravity—picturing whips, chains, and leather—where men took advantage of women, using and abusing them without their consent. That couldn't be further from the truth. It was about vulnerability, trust, and a deeper physical connection.

Do you know what it's like to have someone anticipate your needs? Who knows your limits better than yourself? All because they can read your body's cues beyond your brain's awareness? You just have to give yourself over to it.

Men seemingly held all the power—which was slightly sexist because there were plenty of female Dommes—and women were perceived as their sex slaves. When in reality, women held the ultimate control. Everything stopped instantly if we felt ourselves being pushed beyond the limits of our comfort level and invoked a prearranged safeword—no questions asked.

This place became my escape. When I was down here, I gave my care over to a man, shutting down my brain to the basic function of obeying my partner's commands. It was liberating, hence the club password of freedom.

Yeah, I knew it was fucked up that I grew up conditioned to take orders and obey. My family circumstances groomed me to need that to get off. Think what you would about me. Everyone had their issues.

Desire catered to a wide range of clientele. Some members kept permanent private rooms while others rented them on a nightly basis. There was no shame in single members coming in to play without a long-term attachment required.

I'd dabbled in almost everything the club had to offer, tried everything. If you were going to experiment, you might as well have found what you liked through trial and error. I've had some long-term Doms, always keeping our relationship restricted to within the club walls. Not everyone did that, but it was all about your comfort level. When I began spending more time in Milan, it wasn't fair to my partner to be gone for long stretches at a time, so I started using the club more for casual play—I enjoyed time with a partner, not looking for commitment, with both parties well aware of the terms.

Tonight, I came down here to forget. Just needing to block out the series of unfortunate events that now defined my life. Once the papers were signed, legally promising me to be Preston's wife, this part of my life would be over. Consider it one last hurrah.

Ugh. The thought of a life with Preston as my only option for sex had my lady bits drying up. He probably had the same routine, no imagination, with his happy ending being the main objective. How was I expected to live like that? I guess I'd need to up my toy budget—variety would be the key to keeping me satisfied getting in off on my own for however long we wound up married.

Cozying up to the bar, I ordered a vodka tonic and gave my member ID to the bartender. I needed a moment to survey the landscape of the club tonight and see if there was anyone I was interested in for play. It might have been after midnight, but it was still early. The club wouldn't become crowded for a few more hours. My nap earlier was strategic preparation for an all-nighter. Thankfully, I had no engagements scheduled for tomorrow.

Returning with my drink, the bartender placed it before me on the smooth black marble surface, tilting his head toward the opposite end of the massive bar. "Courtesy of the gentleman."

This wasn't unusual. It was a Dom's way of making first contact without seeming too pushy. Sometimes, they were out the cost of a drink if there was no interest, but they could afford it.

Turning to where the bartender indicated, my breath caught at the sight of the commanding figure raising his glass in my direction. Dressed in black from head to toe in a perfectly tailored suit, his lips and hands were the only visible skin—a short dark beard covered his face where his black mask didn't. The thought of beard burn on my sensitive skin had my thighs clenching as I took in the accompanying look of his dark, messy hair.

He had potential.

His body was turned sideways as he sat on a barstool, showcasing lean, long legs. This man was tall but not overly broad. I didn't need massive muscles so long as he was fit enough to get the job done without nearly having a heart attack. Willing to at least talk to him to see if we were a good fit for an evening of fun, I lifted my glass in return, silently signaling that he should come and join me.

Let my last night of sexual freedom begin.

CHAPTER 6

Preston

I FELT HER PRESENCE before I saw her. For some reason, my body always had a heightened awareness when Lucy was nearby. I thought maybe my mind was playing tricks on my body because it was fried after a long day. There was no way perfect Lucy would be caught dead in a place like Desire. Hell, her sheltered existence would prevent her from learning such a club even existed.

Lucy was the reason I came here tonight. I was reeling after the events at the palace earlier—this was the only place I was guaranteed to be in control. Needing an outlet, I was more than ready to pour all my energy into playing a random woman's body like a finely tuned instrument with my hands. This might be the last chance I'd get.

Like I said earlier, if the deal to marry Lucy was finalized, it would be her or no one. Desire would become part of my past.

Perched on a seat at the bar, I was on high alert, looking for the perfect woman to play with tonight. That's when she walked in.

Even with the silver mask covering half her face, I knew it was Lucy instantly. Having known her most of my life, I'd recognize her body and how it moved anywhere. The tell-tale blue eyes only provided further confirmation.

There wasn't long to process the shock of Lucy being in a sex club—outwardly promoting that she was submissive—because my body was too busy reacting to what she was wearing. Or, more accurately, not wearing.

A sheer black dress clung to her body, barely held up by thread-thin straps, just long enough to cover her ass. From the front, several gems formed triangles to cover her nipples and the apex of her thighs, giving the illusion that she wore nothing beneath. When she walked through the room, I caught a glimpse of her from behind, the back of the dress featuring another gem pattern of a straight line down her ass crack, the bottom curve of her ass visible through the fabric. There was no illusion—she was bare beneath the see-through dress.

Silently telling my dick to calm down, reminding myself this was Lucy, I watched her take a lap around the room before sidling up to the bar at the opposite end of where I sat.

Growing up around bored rich kids, I knew they were always looking to try new things, pushing boundaries. When you had too much money and a lack of parental oversight, there was a tendency to think you were invincible—the standard rules of society didn't apply. They were always chasing a new high. Maybe that's what this was for Lucy. I wouldn't put it past her to be down here because she felt it was some new fad, and she was missing out. She wouldn't survive down here if that were the case.

Just to be safe, I scanned the rest of her body for any indication that she was currently involved with another Dom. The last thing I needed was to piss someone off and get my membership revoked, considering I was in a fighting mood. Lucy entered alone, and there didn't appear to be any kind of identifying jewelry on her body, but that wasn't a sure sign that she was unattached. Knowing the brat she was, she could be toying with her Dom as an act of defiance.

My jaw clenched thinking about her with another man when she was promised to me, even if I didn't want her. I knew I was being irrational, seeing as I was sitting at the bar in the same club, specifically looking to get laid. It was the principle of the thing—I was willing to be faithful once we were bound, but it didn't look like we were on the same page. Maybe I could use that as a dealbreaker and end this waking nightmare.

Intrigued, wondering how committed she was to this world, I told the bartender to let her know her drink was on me. It wasn't uncommon as an icebreaker for casual play. When he placed whatever clear drink she ordered in front of her seat and indicated that it was taken care of, her blue eyes looked right at me. Lifting my glass of whiskey in her direction, I took a sip while she undressed me with her eyes.

Even from this distance, I could see her shifting in her seat. Well, well, well. Little Miss I Hate You was turned on. I could work with turned on—down here, I made a living with turned on.

Lucy lifted her drink in my direction, essentially inviting me to join her. How could I refuse?

Pushing off my stool, I slowly stalked to where she sat, sipping her drink. The closer I got, the more confident I became that she'd recognize me as easily as I had her. My body was tensing, bracing for her to make the connection between the masked stranger and the man she claimed to hate.

Stopping before her, Lucy flashed me a smile. She didn't recognize me. "Thank you for the drink. I'm Ari."

Ari, huh? No one used real names down here—everyone used an alias, but I saw right through hers. One of her middle names was Arabella, so she'd shortened it. Clever.

Taking the black-velvet-lined barstool next to hers, I decided to try a new alias with her, a play on my name as she'd done with hers.

Dropping my voice an octave to avoid her recognizing my voice, I introduced myself. "Tony."

Her fingers toyed with the rim of her glass. "Tony. I like that."

She really had no idea it was me. This was wild. I'd already come this far, so why not take things further? I'd be lying if I said the idea didn't intrigue me. Seeing if I could command Lucy Remington's body seemed almost like a challenge. Beyond that, I wanted to find out if she would obey. She would never grant the real me that level of trust, but I could see what I was working with should things proceed with our arranged marriage.

Boldy, I dropped my hand to rest on her bare thigh, where her short skirt had ridden up while she sat with her legs crossed at the bar. Her skin was soft, smooth, and surprisingly warm, considering she'd just entered the club from the cool night air. Lucy leaned into my touch, positioning her upper body closer to mine. The signals were clear—she wanted this.

Curious, I asked, "Are you a new member? I haven't seen you around before."

Her brilliant blue eyes never left mine as a corner of her lips turned up. "No, I've been a member for a while but travel a lot for work. I don't get down here as much as I'd like these days."

How long was a while? Months, years? Perfect Princess Lucy was not as she seemed. But then again, neither was I.

On to the next question. If I saw any red flags, I would pull the rip cord and end this charade. For all I knew, she was trying to trap me, using my private life to deem me unfit to marry.

"Are you looking for a permanent partner or more interested in play for the evening?"

Reaching out her hand, she caressed my arm from my shoulder through the thick material of my suit jacket down to where my hand rested on her thigh, where she proceeded to move my hand further up and under her dress.

Voice breathy, she responded, "Play."

Jesus, I did not expect her to be so bold. One final test before I took her behind closed doors. "Limits?"

Blue eyes flaring, she smirked. "None."

None?

I felt my jaw drop slightly. Lucy always struck me as the type of girl who had sex with the lights off, the sight of a penis too offensive for her delicate sensibilities. Now, down here in the sexual underworld, she was saying nothing was off limits?

There was some dark shit that went down behind closed doors. I'd never been the kind of man who got off on their partner's pain, but I knew those who did. I got off on the control, nothing more. If I saw a need to punish, I did so in ways that wouldn't leave marks. But for Lucy to say she was open to all this world had to offer was shocking. Had she been struck by a member in the throes of consensual sexual play? Had she liked it?

I'd asked the question but was not prepared for her answer.

While I was still gathering my bearings, she asked a question of her own. "Do you have a room here?"

That was all it took. One simple question, and my mind switched seamlessly into Dom mode. Hardening my voice, I gripped her thigh tighter. "That will be the last question you ask tonight."

A soft gasp escaped past her lips, and I watched her chest rise and fall rapidly. Dropping her gaze to the floor, she whispered, "Yes, Sir."

Fuck. I'd fully expected her to be the contrary Lucy I knew, but down here, she fell into the submissive role as easily as I assumed my Dominant one. Gripping her chin with my free hand, I forced her face to meet my eyes. "Just play. But for tonight, you're mine."

She tried to nod, but I held her immobile. That was enough for me. Standing, I released both hands from her body, allowing her to mirror my actions.

Lucy was petite, and our size difference was evident once we were both on our feet. Her five-two frame was aided by the addition of heels tonight, but even so, she barely reached my chin. Until now, I hadn't understood those with a size kink, but I could see the appeal. I couldn't wait to experience the feeling of towering over her once I removed her heels.

Placing my hand on her lower back, I guided her toward the curtained entrance to the private rooms. I paid the monthly rate required to have a permanent room at the club. For how much membership cost, I knew the owners could afford the best in sanitation for the nightly room rentals, but I liked knowing my room was for my use only, everything exactly how I preferred it.

Stopping outside Room 203, I punched in my four-digit code, and the door unlocked. Gesturing for Lucy to enter before me, I had the pleasure of watching her from behind as I followed her inside. Her long black hair hung loose tonight, stopping just short of the dimples of her lower back visible through the transparent fabric.

Closing the door behind me, I stepped up behind her, brushing those long, silky tresses to the side, exposing the soft skin of her neck. Lucy tilted her head, giving me greater access as I leaned down and kissed where her neck met her shoulder. God, I'd barely touched her, and my dick was standing at attention, wondering if she was this soft everywhere.

Lucy moaned softly, arching into my touch. My hands dropped to her waist, and I slowly moved them down the sides of her body, dropping to my knees until my face was level with her ass, barely hidden by the see-through material covering her body. This close, I could smell her arousal, and I wanted to bury my face between her legs.

Caressing from her thighs to her ankles, I carefully unstrapped the heel from one foot before placing it bare on the ground. Repeating the motions on the other side, I stood before gripping her shoulders and turning her to face me.

It was satisfying watching her crane her neck to look up at me standing so close, now that there was almost a whole foot in terms of the size difference between us. She looked tiny, fragile almost, and I knew that wasn't the case, but the illusion was intoxicating.

"Take off your dress," I commanded.

Licking her lips, Lucy took a half-step backward. Her hands dropped to the hem of her dress, and she pulled it up her hips and over her head, the fabric so light that it made no sound as it hit the carpet when she dropped it.

Goddamn, her body was perfection. The lighting in the room was dimmed just enough to give the sight before me an even sexier vibe. Every inch of her breathtaking form was on display, and I took my time devouring her with my eyes.

Lucy was thin, but not in a sickly way. She had meat on her bones, and her tiny frame was perfectly proportionate. Her creamy alabaster skin was flawless. Small yet perky breasts, tipped with rosy, pink nipples standing at attention, had my hands itching to tease them. My perusal continued down her body to her trim waist before her hips flared out, showcasing a thatch of dark curls at the juncture of her thighs. Having gotten a good view of her ass through her dress earlier, I knew it was perfectly round and each cheek would be a perfect handful.

I'd never been attracted to Lucy—her attitude was the ultimate turnoff—but right now, as we played these roles, I couldn't deny that I wanted to hear her screaming my name as she came around my cock. That wouldn't happen here tonight because we weren't Lucy and Preston—we were Ari and Tony. I would use her body, and we'd both get off, but tomorrow, nothing would change. We'd still hate each other in our real lives.

Forcing myself to forget about tomorrow, focusing more on now, I didn't need to disguise my voice as it came out husky, unrecognizable to my ears. "Get on the bed."

God help me, she obeyed instantly. The black silk sheets of the queen-sized bed taking up a large portion of the room shifted under her slight weight as she sat on the edge and scooched her body back until it reached the middle. Like the good girl she was, she laid down, offering herself up for whatever I had planned.

Hmm. There were so many ways for this to go. I needed to make this count. I'd meant what I said when I told her it was just for one night.

Approaching the bed from the side, still fully dressed, I climbed up next to her, the mattress dipping slightly under my weight. Lucy's short pants were audible, punctuating the air through the silence. Straddling her waist, I gripped her wrists and pinned them above her head.

One of the many reasons I loved my private room was that I had my choice of furniture. This bed featured a vertically slatted headboard, perfect for what I planned to do to her. Silk ties were already attached to the slats above our heads, and I grasped a single strand of the black fabric before securing her hands with a handcuff knot—so aptly named—and testing its strength.

Now that her hands were bound, I flipped the toggle on the side of her silver mask, watching as the eye holes were blocked with matching silver fabric. Not only did Desire offer total anonymity, but their masks were also ingenious, offering an option to provide a blindfold without removing one's mask. I'd never felt the need to test their efficacy before, but had a moment of doubt as I reached behind my head to remove mine. Hovering over her face, I was given the confirmation I needed when she didn't attempt to knee me in the balls for tricking her.

Satisfied she'd never know it was me, I took her mouth without warning. Lucy moaned, opening to me fully, and I took advantage. My tongue swept inside, and she kissed me back, hungry and eager for what was to come. Not wanting to come up for air, I forced myself to break the kiss, enjoying that she craned her neck to try and capture my lips once more. There was still one matter to attend to before we proceeded.

"Pick a safe word, Pr—" Old habits died hard, and halfway through calling her Princess, I caught myself. Lucy's head tilted to the side as she tugged on the ties restraining her arms, but I quickly recovered, uttering, "Precious." Close enough.

Tugging her lower lip between perfectly straight white teeth, she tried shifting her hips pinned beneath me. Breathless, she whispered, "Red."

Sticking with a classic. That would be easy enough to remember.

"I only have one rule, Ari. You don't come until I say so."

Lucy whimpered beneath me. I smirked, knowing that would be the ultimate test of my control over her. With what I had planned, she'd be hanging on for dear life to hold back her orgasm until I gave permission.

I still wasn't sure she could hack it. She struck me as one of those women who'd only known sub-par former lovers that didn't know how to please them, so they greedily took from a real man when an orgasm was dangled before them during sex. Almost more frightening was the prospect that she *could* handle it, indicating that she had as much experience down here as she alluded to.

It was my job to make her forget every man before me. Tonight, she was mine.

Leaving her, I moved to the foot of the bed, where I had a storage bench waiting. Lifting the quilted lid, I sifted through the items until I found the perfect tool. Closing the bench, I placed the adjustable spreader bar below where her feet rested on the bed.

Climbing up from the bottom, I grasped one of Lucy's ankles, affixing it to the leather cuff at one end of the silver bar before repeating the process with her other ankle. I took my time extending it longer and longer until her legs were spread wide, her glistening pussy available and waiting for my use.

I stood, silently taking my time removing my clothing. The longer it took, the more restless Lucy became—pulling on her restraints, raising her hips, her breathing becoming more erratic—as the anticipation of my next move grew. The psychological aspect of sex could be just as impactful as the physical.

With her legs spread wide, I watched as she grew wetter, simply waiting for me, completely restrained and her vision eliminated. I wanted to save this image for my screensaver to look at it daily. It was that stunning.

Gripping my throbbing cock, I gave it a few hard strokes to relieve the ache, knowing it would be waiting a bit longer before it got in on the action. Stepping forward to the foot of the bed, I anchored the spreader bar to the footboard, rendering Lucy completely immobile as I climbed atop the bed, kneeling between her open thighs.

Sensing my nearness, she arched her body, trying to make contact, but quickly realized her movements had been even further restricted. Her moan of frustration brought a smile to my lips.

It was finally playtime.

Placing my palms beside her head, I lowered my mouth next to her ear, blowing on the sensitive skin behind it before tugging an earlobe between my teeth. The sound of the silk ties straining signaled she was desperate to touch. Bad news for her, that wouldn't be happening tonight.

Slowly, I moved down her neck to her collarbone, keeping my lips a breath away from touching her but close enough that the tiny hairs coating her skin could sense me. Roving over one breast, she tried desperately to raise her chest to my lips, but I bypassed them down to her navel, licking just below. The sound of Lucy's ragged breathing filled the room. She was desperate for more but was entirely at my mercy.

Returning to her breast, I hovered there for what seemed like an eternity. Just long enough to make her think I changed course again when I sucked a pebbled pink nipple into my mouth, flicking it with my tongue while I sucked hard. The groan torn from her throat was the sweetest reward for my patience.

Taking one hand, I ran it down the side of her body, over the curve of her hip, before drawing it between her legs. She was drenched, coating my hand with her arousal, causing a moan to slip from my own lips. Her body was responding beautifully, and I'd barely touched her.

"Fuck, Ari. You're soaking wet."

Her hips desperately tried to rise off the bed to gain friction with my hand, but how she was pinned made that impossible, and she let out a tiny whimper. Dipping one finger inside her, the warm depths gripped it tightly. Damn, she was close already. The rest of this night would be exquisite torture if she obeyed orders and only came when I allowed.

"Please," Lucy begged.

Bringing my body flush with hers, I whispered against her lips, "Oh, sweetheart, I love to hear you beg."

Not allowing her a chance to respond, I took her lips roughly. The little minx met my tongue stroke for stroke, biting my lower lip whenever she could. She'd always been fiery. I should have known it would carry over into the bedroom.

Adding a second finger, I swallowed her moans as my thumb grazed her clit. Lucy's body was trembling beneath mine, so I added more pressure, feeling smug when she tore her mouth from mine in a gasp. She'd never be able to hold off at this rate.

Watching her face, it pleased me to see her desperately trying to stave off her orgasm. Her teeth dug so hard into her lower lip I feared she'd draw blood. Hips squirming, I could tell her body was waging a war with her brain. Her body craved release while her mind knew she would be punished, therefore, it needed to do everything in its power to hold off.

I knew that if I really wanted to, I could wring the climax from her body, and she wouldn't be able to stop me. Toying with her was half the fun. There was only one certainty down here—I was in complete control.

Years had been spent honing my skills and the ability to read a woman's body better than they ever could. Every twitch, sigh, and gasp told a story, creating a unique blueprint on how to pleasure them.

Lucy's inner walls began to grip my fingers, and I decided to grant her mercy, withdrawing as her body sagged in relief. It would be short-lived, however.

Climbing off the bed, I gave her a moment's reprieve while I grabbed a condom off the nightstand. The last thing I needed was for Lucy to end up pregnant. Female members of the club were required to provide proof of birth control, but I wasn't about to tempt fate—or the failure rate, in this case.

Rolling it on, I approached her from the foot of the bed once more. Unlatching the spreader bar from the footboard, she was given no warning as I flipped it, causing her body to land face-down on the mattress.

Positioning myself kneeling just below it, I gripped the bar by her ankles and forced it forward, propping her up on her knees. Lucy's head thrashed side to side against the black silk sheets, her soft whimpering music to my ears. This position left her completely exposed to me, and the view of her pussy presented for my unquestioned use had my cock throbbing painfully.

Pushing who I was with to the back of my mind, I lowered my face level with her dripping folds. Blowing lightly against the dampness, causing a shiver to run down the length of her body with the anticipation my nearness caused, I silently counted out a full minute before burying my face in her pussy.

A shrill scream reached my ears as her hips tried to move forward to escape my tongue lapping at her swollen clit. We both knew how close she was to disobeying the one rule I gave her, but there was nowhere to hide from the relentless oral assault on her pussy.

Fuck, she tasted incredible. If she were anyone else, I could live here, just feasting on her for the rest of my life. As tempted as I was to make her come like this, I wanted to watch as she fell apart. When her thighs began to tremble where I held her spread wide for me, I reluctantly pulled away.

Lucy was teetering on the edge. It wasn't going to take much more.

The urge to continue teasing her, pushing the limits on her restraint, was strong, but my baser instincts threatened to take over. Wiping a hand across my mouth, I smiled, knowing that my short beard was soaked with her juices and I could carry the smell of her home with me—a souvenir of the night Lucy Remington submitted. I still couldn't believe it.

Positioned like this, her pussy taunted me, begging to be filled. What could I say? I'd always been a sucker for begging. Kneeling behind her, I gripped my cock at the base and lined up with her waiting entrance before thrusting fully inside without warning.

Lucy wasn't the only one caught off guard by the action of our bodies joining. I was unprepared for how tightly she surrounded me, squeezing my aching cock where I was buried deep inside. Gripping her hips tightly, I held her steady, relishing the breathtaking sensation.

For the first time in my life, I almost lost control. Almost.

My chest rose and fell with the effort to regain my bearings before I pulled back and slammed home. Lucy's upper body was thrashing against the bed, no doubt using the friction of the sheets against her sensitive nipples while her hips pushed back against mine, inviting me to take even more.

How could I refuse?

Holding her hips steady, I began to pound into her, deaf to the cries of passion echoing off the walls. The rush of blood roaring in my ears was too loud. Far too soon, I could feel the familiar tightening in my balls, signaling my impending release, and I needed to slow things down—I didn't want this to end.

Pulling out, I took a few ragged breaths before using the spreader bar to flip Lucy again. Now on her back, I glided my hands to hold her calves held wide by the bar, pushing down until she was bent nearly in half.

Sliding back inside her, I groaned. My temporary reprieve hadn't been long enough, and my body threatened to betray me, taunted by this insanely deep angle. Lucy's gasp at how deep my dick reached inside her was the tipping point.

Thrusting with all my might, I growled in her ear, "Come freely."

That's all it took, and on command, her pussy gripped my dick like a velvet vise, nearly strangling it as her entire body tensed beneath me, and her cries of pleasure echoed throughout the room. Pumping into her as if my life depended on it, I chased my own release, spurred on by her perfect obedience. That, in and of itself, nearly rivaled her intoxicating body.

These were the moments I lived for. Lucy had been edged repeatedly and was now screaming as I pounded into her overstimulated pussy. Gritting my teeth, the orgasm was ripped from my body, and I practically collapsed on top of Lucy, where she was spread open wide for me.

My brain was sluggish, but I had the wherewithal to remember our significant size difference and forced myself to release her legs before dropping onto the space beside her on the bed.

We laid there for a while, regaining our bearings before I forced myself to get up and dispose of the condom. Stepping on something, I looked down, having completely forgotten that I removed my mask—something I'd never done before. Reaching down, I slid it over my sweaty face before returning to the bed and freeing Lucy's ankles and wrists from their restraints.

Sighing, she stretched her arms and legs, which were undoubtedly sore from being held stationary for so long. Throwing on my boxers, I grabbed a bottle of muscle-relaxing lotion from the bedside table before rejoining her. Flipping the toggle on her mask, I returned her sight before turning her relaxed body onto her stomach.

Squirting the lotion into my palm, I rubbed my hands to warm it before working it into her sore muscles. Taking my time, I started with her thighs, and she melted beneath my touch, moaning at the relief it provided. Working my way up her body, I used my thumbs and the heels of my palms to knead her yielding flesh. When I reached her shoulders and upper arms, it was clear she'd fallen asleep—her breathing even and body lax. I'd worn her out.

I couldn't have planned this better if I tried. Leaving her prone form on the bed, I dressed before heading for the door. She could spend the night; I'd let the hostess stand know I had an overnight guest. Pausing with my hand on the doorknob, I glanced back one last time to make sure I hadn't dreamt the events of the past few hours. Sure enough, Lucy was still there.

Opening the door, I walked through, but not before whispering under my breath, "Good night, Princess."

CHAPTER 7

Preston

DESPITE MY LATE-NIGHT ESCAPADES, I had work to do. I'd reconciled myself to nights of little sleep when I visited the club. Last night especially had been worth it, but I found myself dragging as I entered the breakfast room of my family's estate.

Yes, I was a thirty-two-year-old man who still lived at home.

Foxway Manor had been in my family for centuries and was the ancestral home of the Duke of Ashbridge, the most current one being my father. Thankfully, it was large enough that if I wanted to feel like I was living alone, I could go days without seeing another family member. The perks of a full staff and not having to worry about cooking or cleaning for myself outweighed any fleeting desire to secure more separate living arrangements. It wasn't like I was bringing women home—yet another reason for my private room at Desire.

Downing my second cup of coffee, I was catching up on work emails on my phone when my older brother—and future Duke of Ashbridge—Maxwell, entered the room. He and his wife, Madeline, also lived at Foxway Manor. They were expecting their first child this winter, thus securing the family line.

Loading his plate with various hot and cold breakfast items, he sat across from me at the table. I could feel his eyes on me, so I looked up from my phone to see a smirk on his face—a face that looked very much like mine, minus the scruff.

Annoyed and sleep deprived, I was in no mood for games, so I snapped at him. "What?"

Maxwell leaned back in his chair and started clapping slowly. "Well done, little brother."

Glaring at him, not knowing where this was going, I asked, "What have I done now?"

"I have to say, I'm impressed. The King's only granddaughter? That takes balls. Didn't know you had it in you."

There was a sinking feeling in my stomach. I hadn't told a soul other than Liam about what happened during my audience with the King. How did Maxwell know about it?

Shrugging, I kept my tone light. "It's not a done deal yet."

Sitting upright, he began buttering a piece of toast. "That's not what I heard."

"Care to enlighten me?"

"Father received a call last night that the courtship will begin immediately. We are dining at the palace tonight."

It was a done deal? And no one had thought to tell me? When Lucy last saw me—well, at least when she thought she did—she was livid at the idea of marriage to me. It also begged the question of when she agreed to the match.

The timeline didn't add up. I'd left her sleeping at the club, and Max said the call came in last night. Lucy went to Desire looking for sex *after*

FEUDING WITH THE FASHION PRINCESS   83

agreeing to a courtship with me? Even though I was the man she ended up fucking, anger began to churn in my gut. She didn't know it was me. When exactly did she intend to end her membership? If I was willing to give it up in a marriage, I'd expect the same of her.

Lucy was like a wild stallion that needed to be broken. I wasn't sure I had the strength.

Pushing that to the back of my mind, I circled back to the more pressing matter of being tied to Lucy for life. Liam said she was desperate, but I thought I'd pissed her off enough to extract myself from the situation. My career was on the line—everything I'd worked for—and now I was just a show pony, arm candy for the princess.

My agitation shot through the roof as I rubbed a hand across the scruff along my jaw and caught a whiff of her scent lingering there even after showering—another reminder that I couldn't shake her, no matter how hard I tried.

There had to be some way out of this. I just needed time to figure it out, and that would be impossible with Lucy nearby with alarming frequency. She tended to cloud my judgment; my only instinct was to piss her off. Watching the steam pour out from her ears was far too entertaining. We wouldn't make it out of this courtship alive, let alone an engagement and, eventually, marriage.

A lifetime with Lucy felt like a death sentence.

The clock was counting down on my freedom, and there wasn't a moment to waste. Pushing my chair away from the table, I abandoned what was left of my breakfast without another word to my brother. I needed to get to work. I wasn't throwing in the towel just yet, and I couldn't afford to let my job performance suffer over a potential arranged marriage that may or may not ever result in a walk down the aisle.

Arriving at Stonecrest Palace with my parents, brother, and sister-in-law, we were ushered into the royal family's private sitting room. My mother, Abigail, and Madeline were bursting with excitement at the prospect of being in-laws with *the* royal family. Marriage to a duke or future duke was the highest social standing within the nobility, but it didn't compare to royalty. This match was more than my parents could have ever hoped for regarding their second son. I was their spare, but now it seemed as though I was their golden goose. Lucky me.

Unlike the ladies, the men of the family were unphased by a date at the palace. My father, Harold, had grown up as a childhood friend of Prince Adrian, Lucy's father, while Maxwell and I had been playmates with Leo and Liam, her brothers. We knew the men of the royal family well, and I would be the first to tell you they were human, just like the rest of us.

Social events at the palace were the norm for high-ranking nobility, but merging our family with the Remingtons would set us apart. I'd have much rather remained a part of the crowd. I didn't want to be up on that stage with the world scrutinizing my every move—that was no way to live. It had been too much for Leo's wife, causing her to leave the country with their children. Unlike me, she had somewhere to go, being an American. Belleston was my country; I couldn't walk away from my homeland if the pressure of life in the public eye grew too great.

Trussed up in a formal dinner suit, I couldn't breathe. While we waited for the royal family to join us for pre-dinner cocktails, I constantly pulled at my collar, trying to loosen it, but nothing helped. It foreshadowed what life with Lucy would feel like—suffocating.

Just when I thought I would pass out from a perceived lack of oxygen, the door to the sitting room opened, and the royal family entered. Well, most of them, I should say. Lucy was notably absent.

My family members bowed and curtseyed as the King approached, showing respect for our monarch.

King Victor stopped before me, viewing me with an assessing eye, before stating, "I'm pleased we could make this arrangement work. The union between two of Belleston's longest-standing families will provide a strong future for our country."

His implication that Lucy and I would be expected to procreate was anything but subtle. I clenched my fists, desperate to tell him where to shove his "arrangement," when my father subtly elbowed me.

Clearing my throat, I turned on the charm, smiling, before bowing my head slightly. "I am honored to be chosen as Lucy's suitor." I hated how easily the words rolled off my tongue after a lifetime of conditioning in the proper social etiquette.

"Very good," King Victor replied before walking past where I stood and settling into a sizable wing-backed chair, inviting my father and Prince Adrian—who could very well be Liam's twin, albeit thirty years older—to join him.

It was though I were a child again. The "men" were over there deciding my future while I stood here helpless.

Princess Adelaide, Lucy's mother, was the picture of grace with her gray hair pulled back into her signature French twist, wearing a long-sleeved navy-blue evening gown. Clasping hands with my mother, they gushed over how excited they were about planning yet another royal wedding—after Liam and Amy's, of course. Lucy was their only daughter and first royal female born in over two generations, so plans for her nuptials would be like a wedding on steroids. Lucy was sure to be the ultimate bridezilla.

God help me.

Amy and Liam brought up the rear of the line of royals to approach us, and I was grateful to be among friends. Liam, I knew well, and while I only had the pleasure of speaking with Amy once, her charitable works crossed my desk so frequently that it felt as though we were well-acquainted. She'd taken the country by storm when Liam brought her home after eloping—the people loved her. It was easy to see why when she approached Madeline, gushing over her baby bump and launching into a conversation as if they'd been best friends for years, instead of women who met for the first time this evening. Liam was a lucky man.

Insisting that Maddy get off her feet, Amy led her to a richly appointed settee, leaving me standing with Max and Liam. This was how it always was in these types of social settings, with everyone breaking into smaller groups based on rank and gender.

Liam offered us a pre-dinner bourbon, and I gratefully accepted, needing something to take the edge off. Throwing the brown liquor down my throat in a single swig, I grimaced against the burn.

Eyeing me as he took a sip from his own glass, Liam said, "Lucy will be down soon. She had a wardrobe malfunction and needed to change last minute."

Skeptical, I asked, "Really?"

Liam chuckled. "No, not really."

Almost as if mentioning her name was enough to summon her, Lucy stomped into the room, perfectly put together in a floor-length black silk dress that swirled around her legs in her haste. She stared daggers at me as she passed by where we stood before plopping down on the chaise opposite where Amy and Maddy sat. Crossing her arms and scowling, her body language betrayed that she was just as pleased about tonight as me. She wore her ice princess mask so well that I'd have never believed there was another side to her if I hadn't witnessed it firsthand.

Now, if only I could forget how incredible it felt to have her total obedience. Having the knowledge that she was capable of submission but chose to be defiant when it came to the real me was its own form of torture. There was no denying the sexual chemistry last night, but it only worked because she didn't know my identity.

Leaning to my right, I asked Liam under my breath, "What the hell happened yesterday?"

Liam smirked, enjoying watching me squirm. "A lot of things happened yesterday."

Narrowing my eyes at my oldest friend, I said through clenched teeth, "You know what I'm talking about. Yesterday, she couldn't get away from me fast enough, and now our mothers are practically planning our wedding. What. The. Fuck. Happened?"

Peering around me, he addressed my brother. "Max, Preston seems a little on edge, don't you think?"

Maxwell was along for the ride. If there's one thing I'd learned in life, it was that an older brother enjoyed the discomfort of their younger brother. "You know, Liam, now that you mention it, he does seem tense. Can't imagine why. His bride is a stunning woman."

Liam gave him a conspiratorial grin. "You are right about that, my friend. My baby sis is beautiful. Don't you think so, Preston?"

I was seconds away from causing a scene in front of not only my and Lucy's entire families but also my King. "Cut the shit."

"I don't see how this is my fault. If I recall correctly, I warned you where her priorities lie."

He had warned me she was desperate to break free of the royal life and focus on her fashion career, but like an idiot, I thought there was a tiny chance she might turn it down once she learned I was involved.

Conceding his point, I sighed. "Yes, you did, but I want to know why this is happening so fast? Lucy didn't even take time to think about it?"

There was sympathy in Liam's blue eyes. "Apparently, she agreed to the deal *before* she knew it was you, and Grandfather set the wheels in motion."

Nodding toward Lucy's sulking form, I remarked, "She looks as miserable as I feel about this arrangement. Can't she just take it back?"

Liam took another sip of his drink before glancing in his sister's direction. "She could, but she won't. Lucy is stubborn."

I had to hold back a snort—stubborn was an understatement. "Thanks for the support, man."

Sighing, he gave me a pat on the shoulder. "Look, I get it. Your whole life changed in an instant, and you're trying to make sense of it all. Take a moment, step away from the situation, and look at it with fresh eyes. You might be surprised."

Before I could ask how he could possibly "get it," the butler announced that dinner was set to begin. Lucy bolted from the room, clearly looking to avoid being escorted to dinner by yours truly, so I shoved my hands in the pockets of my suit pants.

She couldn't stand the sight or thought of me. A lifetime of this should be fun.

CHAPTER 8

Lucy

LOOK AT HIM. JUST sitting there across the table, all smiles and charming dinner conversation, while my world was crashing down around me. I bet he thought he hit it big, securing a match with the King's only granddaughter. His family sure looked cozy here at the palace. How long had they been planning this climb up the social ladder?

"Lucette!" Grandfather's voice boomed throughout the dining room, drawing me from my thoughts.

Looking to my right, where he sat at the head of the table, I ducked my head demurely. "My apologies, sir."

Preston made a choking sound across the table, and I glared at him from beneath my eyelashes. What was his problem? Did he think I was incapable of contrition? That just went to show he knew nothing about me.

Addressing my grandfather once more, I asked, "My mind wandered for a minute. How may I be of service?"

Grandfather looked displeased, but repeated himself, "We were discussing the timeline of your engagement."

"Fuck my life," I whispered under my breath.

"What was that, dear?" my mother asked, seated two down on my right, with Amy in the seat between us.

"Nothing," I mumbled.

Amy grasped my hand beneath the table, offering her silent support.

Ignoring the disruption, Grandfather continued, "What would you say to announcing between Christmas and New Year's? We could turn our annual New Year's Eve ball into an engagement party. That gives your courtship a little over two months—a perfectly respectable amount of time."

Respectable, my ass. This was the twenty-first century. No one met, fell in love, and got engaged in two months. That was the kind of thing you saw when an unplanned pregnancy was involved, and that was *not* the case here—if I had my way, it never would be. The harsh reality was that an arranged marriage followed its own set of rules, and I was merely a pawn—a piece in their game, moved around the board at the will of the players.

Mom asked, "Lucy, have you thought about when you'd like the ceremony to occur? Summer or fall would be ideal before it gets too cold and snowy."

How about never?

Most surprising in all of this was that my mom, my closest ally, saw no problem in my current predicament. When I arrived home this morning—after unexpectedly waking up at Desire—I appealed to her, begging for help extracting myself from this outdated practice of an arranged marriage.

She told me it was a good match and that Grandfather was overly generous in allowing me to step back as a working royal. Mom knew how much I loved my job. Looking at her now, a part of me wondered if she was a traitor, who told Grandfather exactly how to trap me into this ridiculous charade.

All eyes were on me, so I played off my silent tirade as time spent thinking about my schedule. "Well, let's see. Amy and Liam are getting married the first week in April. Summer is rough for me, leading up to fashion week in September. Two royal weddings in less than a year seems like a lot of work. Are you sure we can't postpone until the following spring at the very least?"

Waving her hand and smiling at our guests, she brushed off my concerns. "Everything is mostly done for Amy and Liam. I don't see why we can't see you two married by the end of next year."

Feeling defeated since everyone had an answer for everything, I sighed. "Fine. Whatever you think is best."

Pleased, my mother smiled at our dinner guests. "Wonderful. I think mid-October will be perfect."

Grandfather commented, "Sets up perfectly for a summer baby."

Baby? Did he say, *BABY?*

The last shred of my sanity snapped, and I stood from where I was seated, drawing the attention of everyone in the room.

Dad let out a shaky laugh and threw on a fake smile. "Lucy, is everything all right?"

"No, everything is not all right. Not once before tonight was there any mention of a baby. Assuming I'm expected to be the mother of said baby, was anyone planning to clue me in? Marriage is one thing, but you can't seriously expect me to sit here like a good girl and open my body up to unlimited breeding for the sake of our country and this family's survival." Everyone just stared at me, including my intended, who I turned on next. "Did *you* know about this?" I didn't give him time to answer, stating, "You know what, it doesn't matter. This whole situation is insane!"

Shoving the heavy chair out of my way, I turned on my heel and was halfway out of the dining room when my mother called out, "Lucy! We have guests!"

Halting my steps, I turned back to our dinner guests. Throwing my arms wide, I couldn't help the near-hysterical laugh that left my lips, nor the sarcastic tone in my response. "I'm sorry your dinner is ruined. You know what? I'm not, actually, because my *life* is ruined."

The smirk on Preston's face caught my eye, and damn if I didn't want to slap it off his face for the second time in two days.

"You'll have to excuse Lucy. She's not quite herself at the moment." Putting a hand next to his mouth in a conspiratorial fashion, he told the group, "You know . . . That time of the month."

My mouth dropped open in shock as I felt heat rushing to my face. How *dare* he? Speechless, I let out a frustrated scream and fled the room.

This would never work. He was determined to make my life a living hell. A life with Preston would be worse than a life without fashion.

When the dust settled, I'd tell Grandfather the deal was off.

Amy found me in my home workspace—ironically, the same room in my apartment expected to eventually house the nursery.

Knocking on the door as I sketched out my frustrations, she asked softly, "Do you have your computer?"

Confused, I turned to where she stood in the doorway. "Why do I need my computer?"

She was dressed casually in leggings and an oversized sweater, an indication that dinner was over. "I might have an idea, but we're gonna need some help."

"My laptop is in my bedroom."

Standing, I stretched my body, which was stiff from hunching over my sketchbook for what apparently had been hours since I'd left dinner. Usually, losing myself in new designs was therapeutic, but my brain was still fuzzy, unable to focus. I was sure that tomorrow when I looked at my drawings, they would either be genius or garbage.

Amy followed me into my bedroom, where I flopped down on the bed. Groaning, I asked her, "Did I imagine what he said down there? Like I didn't make enough of a fool of myself, he had to kick me while I was down?"

Her green eyes were full of pity. "It was a douche move, but I could see it for what it was. If it makes you feel any better, it made the men visibly uncomfortable, and Liam looked like he wanted to kill him."

I groaned. "No, it doesn't make it any better. They think I'm some hormonal woman when they've planned out my whole life without asking me. I'm allowed to be emotional."

Grabbing my computer from the nightstand, she sat beside me on the bed before opening it. I typed in the password, and she went to work setting up a video call. Seeing my face in the screen preview, I looked terrible—my usually bright blue eyes looked tired and dull, my hair a total mess—and I couldn't summon the energy to care.

A digital ringing sound filled the room before two boxes lit up with faces I knew. The sight of Natalie and Hannah had tears springing to my eyes. The events of the past thirty-six hours finally caught up to me, and I couldn't hold it back anymore.

From an ocean away, Natalie went right into mom mode. "Oh, Lucy. What happened?"

Sniffling as tears streamed down my face, I opened my mouth to explain, but only a sob came out.

Amy threw her arm around my shoulder and spoke for me. "We've got a little situation over here."

Through blurry eyes, I could see Hannah waving her fists in the air. "Whose ass do we need to kick?" A shaky laugh rose from my chest. Hannah was a hockey coach's daughter and had no filter. Don't tell my sisters-in-law, but she might be my favorite of their friend trio.

"Fucking Preston," I muttered.

Natalie's brows drew down through the screen. "Preston? Why does that name sound familiar?" There was a pause, then recognition lit up her face. "Wait. Isn't that Liam's friend?"

"Well, if he's still friends with him after tonight, I'm disowning him as my brother."

If Natalie was the mom of the group, Amy was the rational one. Calmly, she explained my predicament. "King Victor offered Lucy a deal yesterday. If she marries Preston, she can step away from her royal duties and focus on her fashion full-time."

Hannah was the first to react, blurting, "That's fucked up! At least tell me he's hot."

"Hannah!" Natalie chastised.

"What? I feel like that should be part of the consideration. Amy, is he hot?"

Amy answered slowly, "He's not bad-looking . . ."

"That means he's hot," Hannah declared.

Natalie looked at me with her kind chocolate brown eyes, showcasing a hint of sadness. "Lucy, honey, if you don't want to marry him, don't marry him. You don't want to wake up in ten years and realize you should have trusted your gut."

I knew she was talking about her marriage to Leo. She had doubts about their marriage—she was barely eighteen when they wed—but had pushed through at her parents' insistence. My brother was so controlling that he broke her spirit, and I could tell she was concerned the same would happen to me if I allowed myself to be pressured into a marriage I didn't want.

Sighing, I laid it all on the table. "How can I give up what I love? This is my one chance to chase my dream. More than anything, I want to get out of this fishbowl and live my life." Scoffing, I added, "But it looks like they're letting me free, letting me think I can fly, only to find out they merely clipped my wings. You should have heard them at dinner, planning when I would pop out my first baby."

"Whoa, back the fuck up!" Hannah called out. "Babies?"

"Yeah, they hit me with that bomb today. In front of an audience," I grumbled.

Amy jumped in, "No matter what they said, they can't force that on you. Invest in good birth control, and there's nothing they can do about it."

"Pro tip: steer clear of whatever Natalie uses," Hannah interjected.

Natalie rolled her eyes. "Ha ha. Very funny." There was a running joke about Natalie and her failed birth control—not one of her four children had been planned. Steering the conversation back on track, she asked, "How does Preston feel about all of this?"

I snorted. "He's too busy pressing every button I never knew I had to care about much else. Do you know what he did to me tonight?"

Sensing how agitated I was becoming, she winced but took the bait. "What did he do?"

"I was mid-meltdown when that arrogant prick excused my behavior by telling everyone at the table that I was getting my period! I'm pretty sure my grandfather and dad will never look at me the same way again."

Hannah was trying and failing to hold back a smile. "Just asking for the record. Are you getting your period?"

"No! He just lives to piss me off. They couldn't come up with anyone better? At this rate, I'll take one of the boring ones I can lead around by the nose. Anyone but him!"

"What happens if you back out?" Natalie questioned.

"Then I lose any semblance of happiness in my life. Nothing compares to the feeling of sketching a design and then bringing it to life. In a way, the clothes are my babies—my creations."

Amy mused, "We know what happens if you break things off, but what happens if Preston does?"

Too blinded by what this entire situation meant for my future, I hadn't taken a moment to ponder the other half of the equation. Taking a moment to think about it, maybe Amy was onto something. I couldn't be blamed if Preston walked away, and I was confident I could make a compelling argument to my grandfather that I'd held up my end of the bargain. Throw in some tears, and boom—I would be the picture of the sad, jilted woman.

There was only one problem. "Preston has just as much to gain in this match as I do."

"What's in it for him?" Amy asked.

"He's getting a bump in social station. Being the second son of a duke, he holds no title. Marrying me would likely see him granted one."

She paused, choosing her next words carefully. "So, what's the worst that could happen if he ends the courtship? They find someone else? That'll take time, essentially creating a stay of execution on your single life."

"What makes you think he will call it off?"

Amy smiled wide, motioning to the ladies joining us on the computer screen. "That's why we brought in the big guns."

Hannah smirked. "I like how you think, Ames."

I was still lost. "I don't get it."

With a wicked gleam in her sparkling green eyes, Amy clarified, "Between the four of us, I'm sure we can find ways to run Preston off."

"Turnabout is fair play," Hannah offered.

Mulling over their words, my mind slowly put the pieces together, and a light laugh left my lips. "Amy, you're a genius! He's tortured me for my entire life. Now, it's my turn."

Pleased with herself, Amy added, "The best part of this plan is that it's rinse and repeat. New suitor, same plan. It's time to take back some of the control."

She was right. I could scare all the men away until word got out that I was impossible to tame, and they began refusing Grandfather's proposed matches. I couldn't care less if I became known throughout the nobility as difficult. My freedom mattered more than my reputation among a bunch of stuffy old men stuck in the ways of the past.

Ready for battle, I asked my ladies, "So, what's the plan?"

Natalie had been quiet but chose now to speak. "We don't want it to be too obvious, so it's best to start slow. How does a shopping spree sound, Lucy?"

Hannah added, "And not on the weekend, either. Call him in the middle of the workday and say you need to see him urgently. He doesn't need to know it's a fashion emergency."

For the first time in two days, I smiled. "If there's one thing I'm good at, it's being a picky shopper. Preston won't know what hit him." I was filled with hope that we could pull this off. "We have a little more than two months to scare him off. The family wants to announce our engagement right after Christmas."

"Two months is plenty of time. Women have been pushing men away since the beginning of time—they tend to spook easily. Between the four of us, there's no way Team Lucy can lose." Amy's confidence was contagious.

"I love you, girls. I was so ready to throw in the towel, but now I'm excited to watch Preston squirm."

"You've got this, Lucy! Let us know when you need more ideas!" Hannah winked. She was the most mischievous of the bunch, so when it came to fresh plans to push Preston into breaking off our courtship, she was the first one I'd call. As the last single girl in their friend group, whoever ended up with her was in for a wild ride.

Amy and I said our goodbyes, making sure to tell Natalie to give the kids lots of hugs and kisses from us before ending the video call. Sighing with relief, I flopped onto the many decorative pillows propped against my headboard.

"Feel better now?" Amy asked as I heard her closing the laptop.

"You have no idea." I blew out a breath.

"Sometimes, you just need to take a breath and remember how many people are in your corner."

For the millionth time tonight, she was right. I'd have never thought of this plan on my own, but it was brilliant. I couldn't wait to see Preston running to Grandfather with his tail between his legs. It would be the sweetest revenge for all the pain and suffering I endured at his hands.

Let the games begin.

CHAPTER 9

Preston

PATTING MYSELF ON THE back for my quick thinking at the family dinner at the palace, I was convinced Lucy had been pushed past her breaking point. She'd set me up perfectly when she lost her mind over the mention of a baby. Granted, that was also news to me, but I had enough self-control to keep my mouth shut. But Little Miss Drama Queen lost her cool, stealing the show with her theatrical meltdown.

A week later, there was nothing but radio silence from the palace. Life returned to normal, and I could focus on my work.

Grabbing my briefcase, I was ready to head to the office when our family butler, Emerson, intercepted me on my way out the door. "Sir, there's a car here for you."

Confused, having not asked for a car to be brought around, I shrugged him off. "Thank you, Emerson, but I had plans to drive myself today."

As I brushed past him, wondering if perhaps he was getting too old for the job, he called out, "No, sir. This car was sent by the palace."

A bubble of hope rose within my chest. This was it. The King was summoning me to share the news that Lucy had called off our courtship, and I would be free to continue my life without disruption.

With a quick apology to Emerson for the misunderstanding, I sent a short text to my boss, letting him know the situation before walking out the front door. Sure enough, a sleek black sedan sporting Bellestonian flags was waiting in the circle driveway outside Foxway Manor.

Seeing my approach, the driver exited the car to open the back door for me. Sliding onto the gray leather seat, I took a deep breath. This nightmare was about to end. As the driver got behind the wheel and we rolled through the front gates of my family's estate, I wondered what took so long. Maybe they were working through the legal ramifications of breaking the arrangement. As a lawyer, I knew a verbal agreement was legally binding, but I was willing to let them off the hook. I wanted nothing more than to move on with my life and pretend the last week never happened.

Lost in my thoughts, I wasn't paying attention to where we were headed. By the time I glanced out the window and noticed we were driving through town and not up the side of the mountain toward Stonecrest Palace, the car was slowing down and stopping outside a boutique shop.

Confused, I asked the driver, "Aren't I expected at the palace?"

Peering at me through the rearview mirror, he shook his head. "No, sir. This is where you're expected."

Looking out the window once more, I stared at the boutique. It was for women's clothing. What on Earth could require my presence there?

More perplexed than ever, I didn't wait for the driver to open the door before exiting the vehicle. Startled, he jumped into action, joining me on the sidewalk.

Having left my briefcase on the back seat, I asked him, "Will you be waiting here for me?"

Dipping his head, he replied, "Yes, sir. I'll be at your disposal all day."

All day? That couldn't be right. Why would I need to spend all day in a women's boutique? Was Liam pranking me? That was the only rational explanation.

Fully prepared to find Liam laughing in my face before heading to work for the day, I opened the glass door of the boutique but stopped dead in my tracks when I saw Lucy standing on a circular podium, dressed in an all-black ensemble. Catching sight of me in the wall of mirrors before her, I had the perfect view of her blue eyes sparkling with mischief as a smirk graced her lips. Before I could blink, she threw on her perfect princess mask, smiling as she turned in my direction, where I stood frozen just inside the door.

"Oh, Preston! I'm so glad you're here."

One of the employees, a short woman with blonde hair pulled back in a low bun, dressed smartly in a blouse and pencil skirt, approached, offering to take my coat. It was only mid-October, but a cold front had swept in, giving us an early preview of winter temperatures. Not intending to stay long, I declined, striding to where Lucy now stood, rummaging through a rack of clothing.

Giving a quick nod of acknowledgment to her security guard leaning against the far wall, I growled in her ear, "What the fuck, Lucy?"

Pulling back so she could look me in the eye, Lucy gave me her best "cat that ate the canary" grin. "Honey, this is an emergency!"

With this woman, I was sure needing a pedicure was an emergency, so I took her declaration with a grain of salt. Running a hand over my jaw, I asked, "What is so dire that you couldn't manage without me?"

I watched as her face morphed into a look so serious that I was concerned something terrible had happened and she was shopping for funeral attire.

"Preston, it got cold so quickly that I didn't have time to piece together my winter wardrobe!"

This fucking girl. Not in the mood for her games today, I ground out, "I fail to see how that is any of my concern. I need to get to work."

Turning on my heel, she waited until I had the door handle in my grasp before her smug voice called across the tiny boutique. "Oh, but darling, I thought, as per the terms of our arrangement, you are at my disposal. And what I need from you today is to help me choose the perfect items to wear this winter. As a fashion designer, people look to me for inspiration on emerging trends."

Looking over my shoulder in shock that not only was our courtship still on but she expected me to sit here and watch her try on clothes all day, I asked, "Are you serious?"

Putting a perfect pout on her face, she clasped her hands under her breasts. "Pretty please?"

She had to know what she was doing, right? Lucy was trying to give me a little preview of what life would be like as her escort.

Fine.

Shrugging off my dress coat and handing it to the waiting sales associate who had offered to take it previously, I sat in one of the plush chairs situated for the best view of the podium. I could do this and be back at work before lunch. I'd tell Lucy she looked great in everything. How many pieces of clothing did she need for winter anyway?

This must be what hell feels like.

After six hours of this torture, Lucy showed no signs of slowing down. The boutique we began the day in was for business casual attire, and then we stopped in a shop for outerwear. Who needed twenty different winter coats? Lucy, that's who, apparently. After that, it all became a blur, my only job being that of the bag bitch—sometimes, I got upgraded to purse bitch, but that was only a momentary reprieve.

Checking my watch for the hundredth time, I grumbled as Lucy scoured a shop dealing in accessories to find the perfect accent pieces to pair with the thousand outfits she purchased today. All right, maybe not a thousand, but seriously, how many clothes did one tiny woman require?

"I'd really like to stop by the office today before everyone goes home."

Smiling sweetly, Lucy handed over her credit card to the salesman on the opposite side of the glass counter before receiving yet another bag for me to carry. "Don't worry, darling. Only one stop left."

Thank God. There was a light at the end of the tunnel. Sighing in relief, I held open the door to the tiny shop for her to exit. "Lead the way, Princess."

Uh oh.

Lucy's head snapped back to glare at me as those brilliant blue jewels masquerading as eyes narrowed. Yeah, I knew I fucked up. And I had been so close.

The driver was waiting with the black sedan—he'd been carting us around all day—but Lucy waved him off, electing to walk further down the sidewalk toward another shop. Following behind her, I had a perfect view of her ass swaying side to side quickly, her mounting anger evident with each step she took. Part of me was elated that I'd pissed her off after the day of hell she put me through, but the rational part of my brain knew I was about to be punished for it.

Stopping at a corner shop, she threw the door open and disappeared inside before I could catch up. Glancing at the storefront sign, I groaned inwardly—it was a shoe store. Mentally bracing, I opened the door for myself, entering to find Lucy gesturing to the lucky saleswoman who would likely make her entire month's commission this afternoon.

Assuming my position as the doting boyfriend—like *that* didn't turn my stomach—I dropped into a plush chair to view the same show I'd watched on repeat all day.

Two hours later, Lucy had tried on every pair of size-seven shoes the shop carried, and they were now littered around her on the floor. Curious, I bent over to pick up a box sitting near me on the floor, inspecting the pair of pumps.

Musing to myself, I said, "What's the point of red soles on these?"

Lucy cleared her throat, and I peered up at her. Smirking, she sauntered to where I sat, placing her hands on the arms of the chair, effectively caging me in.

Voice low, she held my stare, taunting, "Honey, if you don't know why a pair of red-soled shoes is the sexiest thing a woman can wear, then I can't help you."

Damn her. Now, all I could picture was Lucy naked, wearing only the heels I held in my hands. My cock twitched at the mental image.

Get it together, man. We're trying to get away from her. She's prissy, dramatic, and bratty. Sexual chemistry can't erase that.

The grin on her face told me Lucy knew exactly what she was doing before pulling back and sashaying away with an exaggerated sway of her hips.

Annoyed with not only her, but the situation, my voice was laced with frustration as I asked, "And why aren't there price tags on any of these?"

Turning to face me, she threw both hands on her hips. "Tell me, Preston, are there price tags on the custom-made designer suits *you* wear?"

She had a point, but I didn't have to like it. We lived in a world where if you had to ask the price, you couldn't afford it. While that might seem like a luxury to the casual observer, have you not also noticed that we paid the price in other ways? Like this ridiculous arranged marriage to a woman I despised? No amount of money could extricate me from her.

Silent for too long, not allowing her the satisfaction of knowing she'd backed me into a corner, she pushed further, "Oh, I see. Do you need me to buy you shoes, babe?"

Clenching my jaw so tightly I heard a tiny pop, I breathed out through my nose to keep from losing my temper on this infuriating woman pushing my buttons. Practically growling at her, I forced out, "No, I don't need you to buy me shoes."

Those blue eyes sparkled as Lucy tried to hold back a smile. "Well, let me know if you change your mind. The offer stands." Turning to the saleswoman she'd put through her paces for hours, she waved her hand to the mess before her. "I'll take one of each. Thank you, Mary."

There were no less than fifteen pairs of shoes strewn about the show-room, and she was going to buy every single pair. Mary's eyes lit up with the realization of how lucrative the past few hours had been, and she bustled about, cleaning up the mess and packing each pair of heels with care.

Taking the five massive bags to the car—I'd moved past bag bitch, might as well call me a mule at this point—I gave up trying to stuff more in the trunk and threw them onto the passenger seat. Myles, Lucy's security agent, usually sat there, but he could take my seat in the back. I was done for the day.

Not even bothering to say goodbye, I walked down the street, needing to clear my head in the cool evening air before I exploded. Today was only a preview of what life with the fashion princess would entail, and I wasn't sure how much more I could take.

———⊰❈⊱———

"Everything's all set. This program will do a lot of good for the families of Belleston." I sat back in my chair in Liam's office, having gone over the details of Amy's newest project—residential housing for adults looking to regain custody of their children.

Liam's face shone with pride. "You can take the girl out of social work, but you can't take the social worker out of the girl."

Having done a lot of legwork for this latest project, I knew it mirrored a program Amy had implemented in her hometown of Hartford, Connecticut, before leaving her day job and devoting more time to the people of Belleston. We were lucky to have her, and with each passing day, Bellestonians realized the rare jewel Liam brought home to serve by his side.

Lucy could learn a lot from Amy.

Almost as if he could read my mind, Liam asked, "So, how are things going with Lucy?"

I still had PTSD from the shopping events of last week. Not to mention my team at the office joking around after pictures surfaced of me as Lucy's bag bitch on social media. That was my role now—Lucy's bitch—and there was no escaping it.

Dragging a hand across my jaw, I sighed. "Not great."

Liam's blue eyes—an exact match for Lucy's—sparkled in amusement. "Putting you through your paces, is she?"

"That's putting it mildly. Her emergency shopping trip last week cost me a whole day out of the office."

Raising an eyebrow, he asked, "What's an emergency shopping trip?"

"That's an excellent question, my friend. Until last week, I had no idea how urgent it was to have a fresh wardrobe the second the weather turned. God forbid she wears a stitch of clothing from last year."

"She does work in fashion," Liam said without sarcasm, simply stating that fact.

Frustrated, I groaned. "You sound exactly like her. I don't know why she needed me there at all. I didn't do anything other than sit in a chair watching her nitpick about every piece she tried on, which was pointless because, more often than not, she bought it anyway. Then, I was forced to carry it all to the car, lest dear little Lucy break a nail." Liam was practically snickering by this point, which only fueled my anger. "I know she's your sister, but she's driving me insane! If I didn't know any better, I'd think she intentionally dragged out the day to keep me from getting to work."

That last remark was met with silence. The hairs on the back of my neck raised, and I glanced at my oldest friend. Liam's eyes were cast down, not wanting to meet mine. His body language only confirmed my suspicions.

"Liam . . ."

Guilty blue eyes met mine, and he grimaced. "I'm sorry, man. Amy may have let it slip that Lucy's trying to get you to break things off. I can only imagine your little shopping adventure was part of that plan."

She was trying to force my hand, expecting that I'd go back on my word to the King? Oh, that was rich, but I didn't know why I was surprised. Of course, Lucy would want to come out smelling like a rose while getting everything she wanted, and I'd be the disgrace whose word was worthless.

I would happily spend the rest of my life as Lucy's bag bitch before I let the country I loved think I disrespected my King.

The only way I would get out of life with Lucy was if *she* broke it off. I couldn't be held responsible for the whims of a spoiled princess who changed her mind. *She* would be the one who hung her head in shame for disappointing her grandfather. *She* would be the one who lost it all by being unable to follow through. Not me.

The wheels began turning in my brain, which must have been obvious to Liam because he chuckled. "Oh, boy. I know what that face means."

I shrugged. "I don't know what you're talking about."

"I've known you most of my life, Preston, and right now, you're plotting your revenge. Just remember what you said before. She's my little sister. If you hurt her, I'll have to hurt you."

A corner of my lips quirked up as the perfect idea to push her past her breaking point struck me. It was brilliant, but I was going to have to pour on the charm to pull it off. Chuckling to myself, picturing how pissed Lucy would be, I stood from my chair.

Liam looked at me warily like I'd lost my mind before warning, "Preston . . ."

"Don't worry. I won't hurt her; I'm just going to rough her up a little bit." I winked.

"God help us all," Liam muttered.

He knew as well as I did that Lucy's actions were a declaration of war. Growing up together, I'd never been one to back down from a challenge, and I wasn't about to start now.

If Lucy wanted to play games, then it was game on.

One thing I knew for sure, it wouldn't be nearly as pleasurable as the last time we played together.

CHAPTER 10

Lucy

"HONEY, I'M HOME!"

What the hell?

I was upstairs in my workspace, in the beginning stages of cutting fabric for Amy's wedding dress, when I heard someone enter my apartment, loudly announcing their presence. Setting down my shears on the worktable, I closed and locked the door behind me before walking down the stairs to the first floor.

Standing in my entry hallway was Preston, casually dressed in khakis and a cable-knit sweater. Momentarily blinded by my annoyance and the smirk on his face, it took longer than it should have to notice he had a large suitcase in each hand.

Why does he have suitcases?

Crossing my arms, trying to tamp down my panic, I tried to play it cool. "What are you doing here?"

Like a predator, he stalked toward me. With his long legs, it only took three strides before he invaded my personal space, forcing me to crane my neck to look up at him. Even his height annoyed me. Who needed to be that tall anyway? As long as you could see over a steering wheel and hit the height limit for the best rides at amusement parks, anything over that was just bragging. There wasn't a trophy to be won for doing the best job growing up.

Smug, he glanced down from above. "I live here now, Princess."

"The fuck you do!" The words were out like a reflex.

"Language, Princess." Preston was so calm.

Why was he so calm?

"You're not moving in here." Let's try this again.

"We're going to be married. I have to move in at some point."

"Not today! It's not proper!"

Taking a half step forward, Preston was close enough that my breasts were brushing against his upper abs as my chest rose and fell rapidly, trying to figure out what was happening.

Dropping his voice an octave, his voice was husky. "Since when do you care about proper?"

No. His charm and sex appeal weren't going to work on me.

Closing my eyes, I took a calming breath. "You *can't* move in because it would create a media frenzy. They would eat up the scandal of us living in sin."

Confident I'd made my point, considering the pictures of Preston seen carting my bags out of every shop in downtown Belleston were still circulating, I was about to open my eyes when I felt his breath hot on my ear as he whispered, "Are you trying to tell me you're a virgin?"

Eyes popping open, I shoved at his chest to create space. I'd gone from annoyed to panicked to pissed in the span of the five minutes Preston had been inside my home. There was no way I would survive the emotional whiplash he provoked within me for the rest of my life.

Glowering at him from a few feet back, I held my head up high. "That's none of your business."

Shoving his hands into the pockets of his tan slacks, he rocked back on his heels. "It will be. Might as well put it all out on the table now."

"Not if I have my way," I muttered.

"Just think, Princess, I'll be so much more accessible the next time you want to go shopping."

Yeah, he was still pissed about that. Too bad I didn't care. That was the whole point.

Pulling out the big guns, I tried desperately to end this charade. "Grandfather would never allow this."

There was that damn smirk again. "Funny you should say that. I had a lovely conversation with our King and your mother, and they both agreed this was a wonderful idea."

Excuse me? Did he just say my grandfather and my *mother* signed off on this? No, that couldn't be right. Mom would never betray me like this.

Pushing past him, I ran out of my apartment on the verge of hyperventilation. Putting a hand to my rapidly rising chest as blackness crept into the edges of my vision, I tried to calm myself, but it was useless. I wouldn't be able to calm down until I got to the bottom of why Preston thought he was moving in with me.

Bursting into the sitting room my mother favored for her afternoons when she wasn't out at an engagement, I was thankful to find her at home.

Startled by my sudden entry into her private oasis, Mom stood at the sight of me bent over and breathing heavily as a result of both my panic and the sprint to find her. "Lucy! What's happened?"

Closing my eyes, I took a few more ragged breaths to calm myself before facing my mother. Straightening, I collapsed on the nearest chair before forcing out, "Preston. Apartment. Living together."

"Oh, that." Mom said it so casually, as if it were no big deal.

"Oh, that? That's all you have to say about this? Living together, Mom! Think of what people will say!"

"Lucy, we live in a different world than the one in which I got married almost forty years ago. People live together before marriage all the time, and virgin brides are a thing of the past. You might as well take him for a test drive. Better to find out if you're compatible now before it's too late."

Blinking rapidly, I gaped at my mother. Take him for a test drive? Who was this woman? Putting my tongue back inside my mouth, I scoffed. "I don't need a test drive, *Mother*. I already know we aren't compatible."

She waved me off. "Preston had a very compelling point when we met with him yesterday. He said he hadn't seen you in two weeks and that living together, you'd see each other daily. What better way to get to know each other than by spending time together? There's no pressure from the press inside the palace walls, and you can be yourselves."

"I've known him most of my life, and I already know I don't like him."

Mom assessed me with my arms crossed across my chest, practically pouting. "Lucy, no matter what you think, you can't really know a person's heart until you have those deep conversations. Everyone wears a mask in public. You, of all people, should know that. Get to know the person underneath. You might be surprised at what you discover."

There was nothing to discover. I already knew Preston didn't have a heart. He was the same jerk who pulled my pigtails when we were kids, only now he was bigger, with a larger arsenal of weapons trained to piss me off.

Accepting that I wouldn't get the help I needed from her, I excused myself, on a mission to find the one person living here I knew would always have my back. Walking down the hallway of the residence wing, I stopped at the door opposite my apartment. Testing the knob, I sighed in relief that it wasn't locked—a locked door to this apartment meant Amy and Liam were having "private time." It was the middle of the afternoon, but they were still technically newlyweds, so nothing was off the table.

Letting myself into my brother and sister-in-law's apartment, I prayed they were home. Luckily, I found them in their living room, working independently on their respective laptops.

"Amy!" I yelled, startling them both enough to look up at me.

Liam glared at me as I plopped onto the couch opposite them. The emotional ups and downs of the past half hour had exhausted me. "You can't just barge in here anytime you want, LuLu," he chastised.

That was it—the final straw. Shooting to my feet, I lunged at him, finger in his face for full effect as he held his ground. "Call me that one more time, and I swear to God, I'll cut your tongue out of your mouth. You don't want to fuck with me right now."

Liam opened his mouth for a rebuttal when Amy cried out, "Wait a minute, I like his tongue!"

That took all the wind out of Liam's sails, and his face turned red. "Amy!"

Unapologetically, she shrugged. "What? It's true."

Liam gestured to me. "You don't need to tell my sister that!"

Taking advantage of his discomfort, wanting to get back at him, I patted his arm. "Don't worry, big brother. Amy tells me *everything*."

Eyes bulging out of their sockets, he looked between us in disbelief. I may have been embellishing a little, but Amy merely shrugged, confirming I knew enough.

See? I told you she always had my back.

Liam groaned into his hands, realizing that his sex life wasn't as private as he once thought, and I was satisfied that he would think twice before using my childhood nickname again.

Ignoring her uncomfortable husband, Amy walked me back to the couch, sitting beside me. "What's going on, Lucy?"

Flailing my arms, I yelled, "He moved in!"

Amy's brows drew down. "Who moved in?"

"Preston!"

Her green eyes grew large. "He moved in?"

"That's what I've been trying to say!"

"But why?

I scoffed. "Sold some crap to Grandfather and Mom about wanting time to get to know me better. And get this—Mom told me to take him for a test drive. As in, have sex with him and see if I liked it!"

Liam made a choking sound from across the room before croaking out, "I'm still here."

Waving my hand in his direction, I brushed him off. "We know. Just don't care. If you're uncomfortable, leave. Take Preston with you while you're at it."

Amy was sorting through all this in her mind, carefully processing the information. "This doesn't make any sense. He already knows you. We all know you two can't stand each other, so why make a push to live together? Something's missing here. Did he say anything to you that would give us any clues as to his motives?"

Racking my brain, I tried to replay my conversation with Preston—it was short, and my memory was spotty due to how angry he'd made me. The virgin comment was on brand for him, aiming for maximum shock value. Now that I thought about it, there was one thing he said that was a little odd.

Seeing realization dawning on my face, Amy exclaimed, "You figured it out, didn't you?"

Chewing on my bottom lip, I mused, "Well, he did say something about being accessible the next time I wanted to go shopping. You don't think he knows . . ."

"How could he know?" She paused. "Liam, did he say anything to you when he met with you last week about the reunification center?" Turning our heads to look at Liam, we found him hiding behind his newspaper. Instantly suspicious, Amy narrowed her eyes. "Liam . . ."

Lowering the newspaper only enough that his bright blue eyes peered over the top, he replied, "Yes, sweetheart?"

"Does Preston know that Lucy took him shopping all day to get him to break off their courtship?" When he didn't answer, she fixed him with a look. "If you don't spill right now, you can sleep in your own master bedroom tonight."

Oh, did I mention that each apartment featured dual master bedrooms? That would come in handy if I couldn't evict Preston for a few days.

Liam lowered the paper completely, sighing. "He may have an idea that there's a plot afoot."

Standing, I put my hands on my hips, staring down my big brother. "And how exactly did he come across *that* idea?"

Putting his hands up, he tried defending himself. "I didn't tell him. He guessed."

Amy stood next to me in solidarity. "Whose team are you on?"

A pained expression crossed Liam's face. "Why must there always be teams? Why can't I be Switzerland?"

She challenged him, "You picked a team when it came to Natalie and Jaxon."

Liam had been the only man in Natalie's life for years when she became entangled with Jaxon, causing him to become overprotective to the point of endangering their relationship. It had taken time and a lot of work on his part, but they eventually made peace with each other. Liam asked Jaxon to stand by his side during their state wedding, but unfortunately, he would be too busy with his hockey team at that time, hopefully gearing up for the playoffs.

Grumbling, he responded, "Yeah, and look how well that turned out. I'm always on the losing team."

Gloating, she prompted, "And who is always on the winning team?"

"You are, sweetheart."

"I suggest you keep that in mind because I am on Team Lucy right now."

"Noted." Standing, he grabbed his laptop and headed for the door before adding, "I'll leave you two to your war plans. The less I know, the better. I don't want to end up in the middle of this."

Amy walked to where he stood, lifting up on her toes to press a kiss on his lips. Patting the side of his cheek, she smiled. "Smart man."

Once he was gone, she latched the door to the living room, rejoining me on the couch, all business. "Okay, we have clearly underestimated Preston. Moving in is a bold move. Involving the Big Wigs was crossing a major line."

Shaking my head, I was slightly dazed. "I still can't believe what my mom said."

Amy smirked. "I can."

Eyeing her, I asked, "What is that supposed to mean?"

Slightly bashful, some color rose to her pale cheeks. "Addy is slightly more progressive than you give her credit for."

"Apparently," I muttered.

"Let's not focus on that. Right now, we need to deal with Preston. What can we do that trumps him invading your personal space? There has to be something he really cares about that we can exploit."

"Hmm. Well, he did spend the entire day I was shopping complaining about needing to get back to work."

Amy's eyes lit up. "That's it! You're both workaholics. Maybe he needs reminding that a life with you means your career trumps his." A sly smile graced her lips. "When do you head back to Milan?"

Oh, I liked the way her mind worked. "A little over a week."

"And how long will you be gone?"

"Three weeks, maybe four."

"Make it three weeks. He may want to work remotely, which I don't have to tell you is a real pain in the ass. Then, we throw in a monkey wrench and pick you up to spend Thanksgiving with us in Connecticut. The time change will make it impossible for him to work unless he gives up sleeping."

Throwing my arms around her neck, I squealed. "You're a genius!"

Pulling back, she appeared pleased with herself. "Stick with me, kid. We'll get you through this single and free."

Liam may have run for the hills at the first sign of conflict, but his wife was willingly in the trenches with me.

Preston had declared an all-out war with his actions today, but he'd be the one waving the white flag when all was said and done.

CHAPTER 11

Preston

WATCHING LUCY RUN OUT of the apartment in shock was well worth the uncomfortable audience I had with the King, begging him to let me shack up with Lucy. Surprisingly, it hadn't taken much convincing—he seemed desperate to make the match work. Princess Adelaide was eerily enthusiastic about the idea as well. I knew Lucy was a royal pain, but I never expected her family to want to get rid of her so badly.

Moving in without warning made us even for her little shopping stunt. You might be thinking my counterstrike was a bit more aggressive, and you'd be right. Lucy may have been the one to start this war, but I was bound and determined to finish it.

Not anticipating a long residency here at the palace, I packed lightly. The two large suitcases I wheeled in upon arrival were mostly empty, containing a few sets of clothing and basic toiletries. If, by some miracle, she survived the weekend, I'd send for my suits.

While she was gone, I took inventory of her private space. Her apartment seemed to span two floors. The first contained what looked like a breakfast room, living room, dining room, and modest kitchen. I doubted that she had ever touched a kitchen appliance in her life.

Carting my bags up the stairs, I found a locked door on one side of the upstairs hallway.

Interesting.

I wondered what she could be hiding in there. The other door on the opposite side opened to reveal a large private sitting room and two bedrooms. Unashamed, I walked into both, quickly identifying which was hers by the gray, pink, and cream color scheme—classic for a princess in her ivory tower.

Sitting on the oversized couch facing a small flatscreen TV, I relaxed, awaiting Lucy's reappearance. Best case scenario, I'd be back at Foxway Manor by dinnertime.

Passing the time scrolling through emails on my phone, I heard the steps on the stairs signaling Lucy's return. Ready to be thrown out on my ass, I pocketed my phone, spreading my arms wide across the back of the couch to look like I'd made myself at home in her absence. Every move I made from this point forward was carefully crafted to piss her off.

Turning the corner into the sitting room, Lucy stopped dead in her tracks at the sight of me. Narrowing those twin blue flames at me, she challenged, "What do you think you're doing up here?"

Gesturing around, I replied, "I live here now."

"You've mentioned that," she muttered.

"Have a nice chat with your mother?"

Lucy may have been pissed before, but that sent her over the edge to murderous rage. Between gritted teeth, she forced out, "Stay away from my mother."

I made a point of ignoring her demand. "Lovely woman. She was overjoyed at the prospect of us cozying up here together." Conspiratorially, I added, "Between you and me, I think she's hoping we have a little whoopsie and have to move up the wedding, if you know what I mean." I threw in a wink for good measure.

There it was—the reaction I was aiming for. Lucy's face turned bright red, and she screamed in frustration, stomping into her bedroom and slamming the door.

I took pride in my powers of observation—they would have come in handy had I chosen to pursue criminal law—and Lucy's reaction the night of our "family" dinner at the mention of a baby was stored deep in the vault. Knowing Lucy, her aversion to starting a family could stem from one of many reasons. Maybe she wanted to continue focusing on her career and the company she'd built from the ground up. Perhaps she didn't want to bring children into this life of bullshit social rules, where your life wasn't your own. My guess was that it was something vain, like she didn't want to ruin her figure. Whatever the reason, it was a fun new button to press.

Now, to leverage living here into discovering and exploiting more of Lucy's weak spots until she finally snapped and kicked me out, effectively ending our courtship and letting me off the hook.

Feuding with the fashion princess promised to be more fun than I initially thought.

I kept to myself for the first twenty-four hours living in the palace, hoping to lull Lucy into a false sense of security that we could cohabitate without disrupting her life.

Now it was time to flip the switch and show her how annoying I could be as a roommate.

I took dinner in my room and waited until I heard her watching TV in our shared sitting room before taking a hot shower. I couldn't help but chuckle as the water cascaded over my body, picturing the look on Lucy's face when I interrupted what she thought would be a quiet evening.

Turning off the water, I toweled off, leaving extra water in my hair. I wanted to see her reaction to errant beads of water running down my bare chest. When tying the towel around my hips, I made sure it was low enough to make her fearful that if it slipped an inch, I'd be indecently exposed.

Half-naked, I was ready to ruin Lucy's evening.

Turning the knob of my bedroom door slowly, I silently opened it. Luckily, the couch faced away from the bedroom doors, so I could see her but she couldn't see me. Leaning against the doorframe, arms crossed, I began calculating my next move.

The volume was low on the television, but from what I could tell, it was one of those ridiculous reality dating shows with one girl and a dozen guys, where she is looking for love and must choose between them. It didn't seem like something Lucy would watch, however. She was going out of her way to make sure she could remain without a man, and when she wanted her "needs" met, she wasn't looking for romance—I knew that better than anyone.

Intrigued by the enigma of a woman who was my chosen mate—for now, at least—I observed her reactions to the contestants on her show. How could she watch this crap? The girl, Talia, was looking for a connection, but all these guys wanted was to get in her pants. The fact that she couldn't see right through them was slightly unnerving.

The final straw was when one of the men told Talia that her body was beautiful but the smile on her face was his favorite.

Rolling my eyes, I scoffed. "What a line."

Lucy's head whipped around, realizing she wasn't alone. When she saw me, clad only in my towel, she stood abruptly. Clearly, she expected to spend the evening alone, indulging in trashy reality TV, as she was dressed in a set of black silk shorts with a matching camisole, her hair piled atop her head in a messy bun. Old castles tended to be drafty, and she must have been slightly chilled because her nipples stood at attention, visible through the silky fabric clinging to her breasts.

Blue eyes wide, she stood there stunned, mouth dropping open as her pink tongue peeked out to wet her lips.

That's right, Princess, get a good look.

Enjoying a rare moment of silence in the company of Lucy, I unfolded my arms and walked toward her.

That seemed to jolt her out of her shock, but not quite enough, as she practically tripped over her words. "Wh-what are you d-doing?"

Playing it cool, I moved a few steps closer, motioning to the television. "Catching up on my favorite show."

That seemed to snap her out of her stupor, and her baby blues narrowed at me. "You watch *Last Chance at True Love*?"

Christ, even the show's name was cheesy as hell, but I was committed. "Never miss an episode."

More suspicious than ever, she eyed my lack of clothing. "Uh-huh. And you just happened to forget to get dressed?"

I shrugged. "When I heard you watching, I couldn't risk any spoilers. There wasn't time to stop for clothes." Grinning, I remarked, "I'm really rooting for Fernando. What about you?" I played to win, so you could bet your ass I paid enough attention before revealing myself to note the name of the least douchey guy I saw.

Momentarily distracted, Lucy paused, chewing her bottom lip. "I'd have to say Rich— No! I know what you're doing."

Raising a single eyebrow, I challenged, "What am I doing? Other than catching up on my guilty pleasure?"

"Very funny. I see right through you."

Throwing my arms wide, I felt my towel slip a fraction of an inch. "Like what you see?"

Lucy's upper lip curled in disgust. "Get over yourself."

Reverting to our earlier conversation about her stupid reality show, I grinned. "Why, yes, I would love to watch with you." Plopping down in the middle of the couch, I left her no choice but to sit next to me with our thighs a breath apart from touching or to retreat to her room.

I had to give her credit. Lucy wasn't one to back down from a fight, electing to sit down to my left, bending her knees and pulling them to her chest to create extra space between our bodies.

Smirking, I taunted, "What's the problem, Princess? Afraid if you get too close, you won't be able to stop yourself from jumping my bones? Don't let my toned body fool you. My lap is quite comfortable."

Lucy pretended to fake a gag before firing back, "You know what they say about a man with a big ego? That he's got a tiny dick."

She shot me a smug look, thinking that insulting my manhood would provoke a hypermasculine reaction. The joke was on her, and she didn't even know it. Only I knew the truth that I'd already been buried deep inside her molten heat, making her scream, yet she would be unable to pick my dick out of a lineup.

There was only one way to remedy that.

Gripping the edge of my towel, I began to lift where it crossed over my legs. "There's only one way to find out."

Lucy's eyes dropped to my lap, and when the skin of my knee became visible, she jumped up like she'd been burned and ran from the room.

For anyone keeping score at home, the count currently rested at Preston 2 : Lucy 1.

CHAPTER 12

Lucy

AFTER PRESTON'S LITTLE TOWEL stunt, I decided to keep our re-location to Milan for most of the month to myself for longer than I normally would have.

I'd stewed over that interaction for a week, berating myself for being a coward and running. I should have called his bluff. He would never have exposed himself to me completely—Preston was all talk.

He knew exactly what he was doing. Liam spilling the beans about Preston's knowledge of my plans changed nothing. It only meant we were now both aware of the rules of the game. There would either be one winner or two losers.

Unlike me, he didn't have a support team waiting in the wings, constantly devising new plans to get him to throw in the towel.

Ugh, towel. I needed that image to leave my brain!

I mean, could you blame me? I hadn't had sex since the night my world tilted on its axis, and I'd snuck out to Desire. Tony had been everything I needed in that moment, and for some reason, my night with him still hung around in the back of my mind. We said one night, and I'd meant it, but Preston was driving me insane, and I needed a night to forget—again.

In the end, it didn't matter. We were headed for Milan tonight.

Sauntering into the breakfast room, I was delighted to find Preston dressed for work in a gray suit, sipping his coffee and checking his emails, blissfully unaware that I was about to throw him for a loop. Maybe today would be the day, and I'd push him too far. Traveling to Milan free as a bird sounded like heaven.

Stepping over to the sideboard, I poured myself a cup of tea. Biting back a grin, I tossed over my shoulder, "Are you packed yet?"

Completely oblivious, Preston fired back, "I told you, Princess, I'm not going anywhere. You're stuck with me."

Thanks for the reminder, jackass.

Turning, I took a slow sip of my tea. "I meant for Milan."

That got his attention. Tearing his gaze away from his phone, he looked up at me with those hazel eyes, which today appeared more green than brown—spending more time with him, I noticed they shifted depending on the light and sometimes his mood.

"Why would I pack for Milan?"

"Well, we leave tonight, darling."

Folding his arms across his chest, he stared me down. "I'm going to need more information than that. What's in Milan, when are we going, and how long will we be gone?"

Feeling the urge to play with my food before I ate it, I taunted, "I thought you knew everything . . ."

Unamused, he snapped, "Answer the questions if you expect me to accompany you out of the country."

Smirking, I retorted, "Not like you have a choice."

He blew out a breath in surrender, remembering that he was at my beck and call. "Fine. *Please* may I know how long we are going for, so I know how much to pack?" Under his breath, he added, "Maybe if I make it sound like a fashion crisis, she'll be able to understand."

Pleased that I had him visibly agitated, it was time to lower the boom. Smiling sweetly, I replied, "Well, since you asked so nicely . . . My fashion studio is headquartered in Milan." The first piece of news was met with understanding by Preston, but I wasn't done yet. The next part was what would set him off. "We are leaving tonight after dinner, and we will return on the first of December."

Now, it was time to sit back and enjoy the show.

It took Preston a minute to fully process the reality that he would be away from work for an entire month. When it sank in, he jumped to his feet, eyes menacing. "You can't be serious."

Playing coy, I batted my eyelashes at him. "Is there a problem?"

"You know damn well that there's a problem!"

I'd never heard Preston yell before, and I was slightly taken aback but carefully schooled my features to appear unfazed. This was the reaction I was hoping for, and I couldn't flinch now.

Standing my ground, I challenged, "Should I tell the flight crew it will only be me this evening?"

Watching his face carefully for any sign that he was about to break, I was disappointed when he calmed down. "Would have been nice to have more than a few hours' notice, Lucy."

Feigning innocence, I placed my free hand on my chest. "I'm sorry, honey. I thought I told you last week. My bad."

"Your bad. Yeah, right." Preston's words dripped with sarcasm. "If you'll excuse me, *Princess*, I need to get to work and tie up any loose ends before our little getaway."

Not sparing me another glance, he moved to leave the breakfast room, so I called out to his back, "Have a great day!" The second he was gone, I burst into a fit of giggles.

Point for me.

God, how I'd missed Milan. Not only was the city gorgeous, but I could finally take a deep breath—Belleston was slowly suffocating me to death. This was where I belonged.

If I kept pushing Preston, eventually, this would be my life full-time.

I *had* to win. There was no alternative.

Like the infuriating man that he was, he sorted out a remote working situation and was waiting for me inside the private jet when I arrived that night. When he wasn't anywhere to be found in our apartment and missed the car to the airstrip, I thought I'd done it, but nope. It would seem he was just as stubborn as I was.

Two weeks later, I was dragging the stubborn ass to the studio each day, enjoying the view as he struggled to communicate with his team over two hundred miles away. There was humor to be found in Preston's frustration due to his co-workers moving forward without him on projects he'd formerly held the lead, as he quickly realized that he was replaceable. Oops.

It still wasn't enough to force him to pack up and go home, however. I needed something more.

Addy June was alive with activity in the wake of fashion week. Expansion was on the horizon, and I spent my days designing, working out the logistics of mass production, and interviewing candidates for new positions created by our overnight popularity. That left me little free time to devise new ways to torture Preston into calling it quits.

The clock was ticking. If I wanted him gone before it was too late, I would need to carve out some time in my busy schedule to brainstorm my next attack. Natalie and Amy's ideas had been brilliant. Still, it was time for me to develop an idea on my own—this was a team effort, and I needed to carry my weight, considering I was the beneficiary.

Luckily for me, inspiration struck suddenly during our last week in Milan before flying to the States for Thanksgiving—yet another detail I decided to keep from Preston. Sophie brought me a design for a dress suited for a plus-sized model, one larger than any of the mannequins we kept in the studio.

Using my long hair as a curtain, I bent over a sketchbook, trying to hide the evil smile on my face as Sophie oversaw the cutting of fabrics to be pieced together to make the dress she envisioned.

This was going to be *so* good.

Once all the pieces were ready, I put on my professional mask, inspecting the cut fabric laid on the large worktable before approaching the podium in the center of the studio. Preston was huddled in a corner, trying to get work done. Did I mention I wasn't benevolent enough to provide him with a desk? I couldn't stop the small smile that crossed my lips at the sight of him trying to juggle his laptop on his lap while seated in a folding chair.

Erasing the smile, I kept my voice cool. "Oh, Preston?"

Satisfaction coursed through my veins when he closed his eyes and took a deep breath before answering, "Yes, dear?"

"Would you be so kind as to assist me over here?"

Sighing, he closed his laptop before standing and placing it on the chair he'd vacated. Trudging over to where I stood, he looked resigned.

Perfect.

I had him right where I wanted him. Today's stunt had to be the final straw, and I couldn't wait to breathe in the sweet smell of victory.

Instructing him, I gestured to the podium. "If you could please step up there."

Following orders like a soldier being led to their slaughter, he stepped onto the raised circular platform without a word. Walking to the worktable, I grabbed the longest piece of blue silk before turning to Preston standing there like a statue—or a mannequin, in this case—and getting close enough to drape it over one of his shoulders.

The second the fabric touched him, he jumped back, nearly stumbling off the podium. Hands held up before him, eyes wide, he asked, "What do you think you're doing?"

Tilting my head, the long swatch of silk still held in my hands, I replied, "Piecing together a dress. Last time I checked, this was a fashion studio."

Those hazel eyes flashed gold. Honestly, the past few weeks had been anticlimactic. I'd been too busy with work to focus on provoking a reaction from Preston, and I had to admit, seeing him riled up now, I missed it. Nothing made me feel more alive than having the knowledge that I was the thorn in his side after the years of torture he put me through. He'd do well not to forget I could make his life a living hell. Today would serve as a reminder.

Preston was breathing heavily, trying to control his temper. It took every ounce of willpower not to burst out laughing. This was the stuff sitcoms were made of.

Pretending to be annoyed, I tapped my foot. "I don't have all day. The sooner I get this dress pinned, the sooner I can hand it off to the seam-stresses."

His eyes floated between my face and the fabric I held in my hands. "You can't be serious. I'm a man. That's a dress."

Rolling my eyes, I retorted, "I'm not stupid, Preston. I know that. This is a plus-sized dress; none of my mannequins are large enough. Your proportions are perfect."

Panic set in, and he looked around the room, hoping to find something to save him from his fate. His eyes lit up when they landed on Sophie. "Her! She can be your mannequin."

Sophie's eyes went wide when she realized he meant her, but I brushed him off. "Oh, Sophie? No, that won't do. She's far too short for this dress. The model I have in mind is much closer to your height. Now, if you could please step into the center and stop wasting precious time. We only have a few more days here."

Preston was observant. No doubt he remembered that I mentioned a December return to Belleston, but it was only the third week in November. If he wanted to get his hopes up of going home early, who was I to crush his spirit? He didn't need to know that when we boarded the plane, we were crossing the Atlantic. That would be a fun little surprise.

With the hope of getting back to his daily routine and his precious job dangling like a carrot before him, his shoulders slumped, and he stepped forward once more.

Damn, I really thought this was going to be the one that sent him running home with his tail between his legs, but to my chagrin, he stood there for two hours while I pinned the dress together around his body.

This was going to be harder than I thought, and time was running out.

Chapter 13

Lucy

Preston was suspicious when we boarded the private jet to find Amy and Liam waiting for us on board, but seeing a friendly face distracted him enough that he didn't ask questions. It didn't sink in until the third hour of the flight, when he checked his watch and realized that we should have already landed in Belleston.

When he looked to his friend for answers, Liam was visibly uncomfortable. I felt slightly guilty for placing him in the middle of our war when he asked me to leave him out, but it couldn't be helped. This was part of Amy's plan, after all. I was sure she'd make it up to him once we landed and they were back in their natural habitat—if Milan was my escape, then Connecticut was theirs.

After nine hours in the air, we landed in Hartford, Connecticut, and Preston was a bomb, ready to explode. Somewhere over the ocean, he figured out that the time difference would make working impossible.

Another point for me. I hadn't been keeping score, but if forced to guess, I'd say the scales were tipped in my favor.

Two black SUVs were waiting on the tarmac, and I quickly grabbed Amy's arm and jumped into one so the boys would be forced to ride together. After nine hours spent in a metal tube with Preston, I needed some breathing room.

The ride to the gated community where Amy and Liam lived was short. As luck—or fate—would have it, Natalie and Jaxon lived next door to my brother and his wife. Over the years, they played a little game of musical houses. Natalie, Amy, and Liam had once lived in the big house with the kids, with Jaxon as their neighbor. Lines were crossed, leading to Natalie and Jaxon's relationship, as well as Amy and Liam's, so they swapped. It was perfect, really. They found the loves of their lives and kept their best friend close—if you could no longer live together, living next door was the next best thing.

Wasting no time, I barely waited for the tires of the SUV to stop before jumping out. The second car was pulling up behind us in the drive of Amy and Liam's house as I grabbed my bags from the trunk. I heard the doors open behind me as I made a beeline for the path that led to Natalie's house.

"Where are you going?" Preston's weary voice called out.

Why did he even care?

Turning to face him, I threw a thumb over my shoulder. "Natalie's house. I'm staying there. You're staying here."

He simply shrugged in response. I was sure he needed a break from me as much as I needed one from him. Amy left her bags for Liam, and met me at the entrance to the path.

Liam groaned. "Ames, where are you going?"

Amy bit her lip, slightly conflicted, before answering, "Girls' night?"

Running a hand down his face, Liam grumbled, "Of course. Why wouldn't you plan for a girls' night the second we get off a trans-Atlantic flight? Makes perfect sense. I'm going to bed."

Preston watched their exchange, turning to his friend. "What's girls' night?"

Liam shook his head, grabbing the bags before him. "You don't even want to know."

With that, I considered the matter settled and embarked down the path. Before we took off from Milan, I sent an emergency text to Natalie and Hannah, letting them know we needed a brainstorming session. More than happy to oblige, they said they'd be ready when we landed with one of their signature girls' nights. Up to this point, they were almost like an urban legend, these nights where the trio of friends got together, either at home or out in the wild. But now I was being brought into that inner circle. Being considered worthy of a spot at their exclusive table was humbling.

They must have heard our driveway conversation because the front door was wide open when we emerged on the other side of the stone pathway.

Hannah stood there with a serious look on her face, arms crossed over her chest. Eyeing us, she said, "I have one question."

Nervous, I glanced over at Amy. Was this some kind of initiation, where I would be denied entry if I answered incorrectly? A cool sweat broke out along my body as I answered in a shaky voice, "Okay."

Hannah's blue eyes glittered with mischief. "Caffeine or booze?"

"Booze?" I replied, uncertain.

Pushing off the doorframe, she nodded. "Good. I was afraid after a long flight, you'd be jet lagged, and our best ideas for taking down men come when we are good and drunk."

Relieved that the question was innocent and they were ready to craft a plan to win the war, I remembered why Hannah was my favorite. She was feisty and wasn't lovestruck like my sisters-in-law. Sure, they were on my side in this fight, but they'd both had their emotional walls scaled by their respective knights in shining armor. I needed a single girl to help keep our eyes on the prize.

Hannah pulled me into a hug when I reached the open doorway. Close to my ear, she spoke, "Don't worry. He's going down."

That pulled a laugh from deep within my chest. It was only a few words, but I needed that reassurance—I wasn't alone in this fight.

Natalie was making a pitcher of margaritas in the kitchen, but when she saw me, she stopped everything, throwing herself into my arms, squealing, "I'm so glad you're here! When Amy told me she was bringing you home, I thought she was messing with me."

Smiling weakly at my eldest sister-in-law, I squeezed her hands. "Just needed a change in scenery."

Hannah was all business. "Is the enemy next door?"

"And that's my cue to leave." I hadn't realized Jaxon was in the kitchen until he spoke. Nodding to me, he flashed his perfectly straight teeth—a wonder, considering he played professional hockey. "I'll leave you ladies to it. Lucy, make yourself at home."

"Thanks, Jaxon." I watched as he dropped a kiss on Natalie's forehead before leaving the room. Jaxon was a total teddy bear and was so good to Natalie and the kids. As heartwarming as that was, it only made it glaringly obvious that Preston was the exact opposite.

Amy grabbed margarita glasses from a high cabinet, being the tallest of us all at five-foot-nine. "Let's get to work. Lucy may be wide awake, but I'm fading fast. Liam mentioning going to bed didn't help, either."

Hannah waggled her eyebrows. "Damn, girl. Still in the honeymoon phase?"

Rolling her eyes, Amy tried to hold back a yawn. "Not that kind of bed. Get your mind out of the gutter."

"But it's so much more fun in the gutter," Hannah protested.

Natalie took charge, pouring the green mixed drink into the glasses and garnishing them with a wedge of lime before handing them out. The first sip was heaven on my tongue, the perfect mixture of sweet and tart. It was exactly what I needed.

Ushering us into the two-storied open living room, Natalie curled up on the chaise, inviting us to take a seat. I grabbed the ottoman while Hannah and Amy sat on the oversized couch.

Sighing, I vented, "He's not backing down! I'm running out of time. When we set this plan in motion, I had months, and now I have weeks left! What happens if he doesn't walk? This might be the most expensive gamble of my life."

A sympathetic look crossed Natalie's face before she prompted, "Okay, Lucy. Catch us up. Last we heard, he went behind your back and got permission to move in, and then you forced him to accompany you to Milan."

I scoffed. "He really thought he had me with moving in. Then, there was the towel stunt."

Hannah leaned forward, tucking her caramel-brown hair behind her ears. "What towel stunt?"

Groaning, I filled them in. "I was watching my shows, and he walked in wearing nothing but a towel, acting like he owned the place, sitting his ass right in the middle of my couch. I may have insulted his manhood, and in retaliation, he started to lift the towel . . ."

Natalie's brown eyes went wide. "Don't tell me you two . . ."

Offended, I waved my arms. "Of course not!"

Chuckling, Hannah added, "Geez, Nat, don't paint her with your brush. Not everyone mauls a guy they've known forever the first chance they find themselves alone with a bed in the immediate vicinity."

"Hey!" Natalie protested.

Leveling her with a glare, Hannah challenged, "Tell me I'm wrong."

She was referring to Natalie and Jaxon's initial hookup, when Natalie went next door to retrieve a ball Jameson had thrown over the fence. I'd heard variations of the story over the years, but that single encounter was the reason for Charlie's existence, and the rest was history.

Twisting her lips, Natalie grumbled to herself before changing the subject. "We are here to talk about Lucy." Turning to me, she gestured a hand in my direction. "Proceed."

Taking another sip of my margarita, I continued, "I ran before he could expose himself. As a punishment, I didn't warn him about our month away until the morning we left. I wasn't exactly his favorite person after dropping that bomb."

"Were you ever?" Hannah asked.

"Good point."

"How was Milan?" Amy asked.

"Busy." I sighed. "I got caught up in my work." Smirking, I added, "Preston struggled in that arena, at least. It'll be a miracle if he has a job to come home to."

Natalie nodded. "Well played."

"I did have one flash of brilliance, however."

Hannah clapped her hands together. "Do tell."

A giggle escaped my lips just thinking about Preston trussed up in the royal blue silk. "I may or may not have used him as a plus-sized mannequin."

The room went silent as all three women stared at me.

Amy was the first to recover, asking for clarification. "You put him in a dress?"

I shrugged. "Technically, I pinned a dress around him."

"Please, dear God, tell me there is photographic evidence." Hannah threw her hands together as if she were praying.

Pulling my phone out of my pocket, I scrolled until I found it. Passing it over, I stated, "You can thank Sophie for being stealthy enough to capture this without his knowledge."

Huddled together, they looked at the picture on my phone in shock before all three burst out laughing.

Natalie was gripping her sides; she was laughing so hard but forced out, "And he still got on a plane to come here after that?"

I gave her a sly grin. "He thought we were going home."

Hannah looked at me in awe. "That's cold. I fucking love it!"

Draining the rest of my glass, I placed it on the coffee table. "Well, it wasn't enough. He could be on a commercial flight home right now, but he's not. And what's worse is we all know something else is coming—he hasn't tried anything since we left Belleston. I need something more!"

Standing, I went back into the kitchen to get a refill. When I came back, I was only met with silence; all three women appeared deep in thought. I remained quiet, wanting to give them the time to think of a grand idea that would finally drive Preston away for good.

When I couldn't take it anymore, I yelled in frustration, "Someone has to have something!" Looking between them, I honed in on Hannah. "It's your turn. Nat came up with shopping. Amy was the genius behind dragging him kicking and screaming to Milan. You've got to have something up your sleeve. I'm desperate."

Hannah knew the pressure was on and held up a finger, indicating she was almost there. Lowering her hand, she spoke, "You know what scares single men?"

In no mood for a guessing game, I snapped at her, "Just tell me!"

"Babies." It was only one word, but maybe she was onto something. How many times had Preston used that against me?

"You know, that's not half bad, Hannah," I praised as she grinned triumphantly.

"Wouldn't work on Liam," Amy grumbled. "He can't shut up about wanting babies."

Natalie chimed in, "Jaxon, either. He's been begging for one more. Spoiler alert—never gonna happen. Shop's closed."

Hannah glared at them. "Jaxon and Liam are exceptions to the rule. But I'm not talking about the idea of babies. I mean real, live ones."

Intrigued, I prompted, "Okay, I'm listening."

"Even when a man is fully on board with bringing a baby into the world, newborns terrify them—they're fragile. Do you know what would be even scarier? Super tiny newborns. . ."

Hannah waited for me to catch on to what she was implying. It took a minute, but then it hit me, and I sat bolt upright. "Hannah! I think you just won!"

Brushing the imaginary dirt off her shoulder, she smirked. "Oh, I know."

Amy cleared her throat. "Would anyone care to clue the rest of us in?"

Before I could open my mouth, Natalie beat me to it. "You're going to take him to Jameson's NICU."

An uncomfortable silence engulfed us. The last thing I wanted to do was upset Natalie in my quest to send Preston packing. Barely above a whisper, I asked, "Is that okay?"

Nodding slowly, I could tell she was mulling over the idea in her head. "Make sure you give them my regards when you go."

The NICU at Alpine Slope Women's Hospital in Remhorn held a special significance to our family, particularly Natalie. Jameson, her second-born and eldest son, was born nearly two months premature, requiring their life-saving medical care. While my brother blamed his heir's early arrival on his wife and left her to deal with the aftermath, I came and sat with her and teeny tiny baby Jameson every day after school.

Every day, I witnessed the emotional rollercoaster contained within its pale pink walls. Watching how the mood shifted from sorrow to triumph so quickly was overwhelming—it was enough to give anyone watching whiplash. The nurses and doctors were the real heroes, working tirelessly, even when the unimaginable happened.

Jameson was one of the lucky ones who made it out, growing into the perfectly happy and healthy ten-year-old we all knew and loved. But even over a decade later, I could see the haunted look in Natalie's eyes just thinking about it. She'd put her professional focus behind serving those whose babies were in the fight of their lives, and when she left the country, I took over championing that worthy cause.

Hannah's suggestion couldn't have come at a better time. I was due for a holiday visit. It would seem that Preston and I were about to spread some Christmas cheer when we returned home.

CHAPTER 14

Preston

A MONTH AWAY FROM Belleston with Lucy. I wasn't sure how I was still standing, especially after she forced me to stand while her entire team watched as she created a dress around my body.

A dress!

Talk about keeping my balls in a jar on her shelf as a trophy. I'd never been more humiliated in my entire life.

As much as I hated to admit it, she was winning, and she knew it.

Just when I thought we were going home and I could do some damage control at work, getting back on track, she carted me to America without even telling me. At this rate, I'd be lucky to have a job when I returned. Lucy was demolishing my life brick by brick.

Then, there's me.

Clearly, I blew my load by moving in because I hadn't been able to strike back since. Could you blame me? I figured I'd go big or go home, but when it didn't work, I wasn't left with many options. What could I do to top that? I was drawing a blank, and time wasn't on my side.

I had no intention of backing down. The only uncertainty remaining was finding out if holding my ground meant being forced into seeing this arrangement through, meaning I wound up married to Lucy.

When we landed Stateside, Lucy disappeared to Natalie's house while I remained in a guest room at Amy and Liam's. After the last month, I welcomed the breathing room but was very conscious that I was residing with newlyweds—I felt like a third wheel.

Having grown up with wealthy parents, I was well-traveled, and this wasn't my first trip to the United States. However, Central Connecticut wasn't a popular tourist destination, and I hadn't crossed the Atlantic in nearly a decade. Add in a holiday exclusive to America and their northern neighbor—hosted by a couple I mainly knew by reputation—and I was at a disadvantage.

Well played, Lucy.

I wasn't a coward, but I dragged my feet going next door, allowing Amy and Liam to leave before me. When an hour passed and I hadn't made an appearance, Liam walked through the front door to find me sitting on the couch, scrolling my phone.

Chuckling to himself, he stopped at the edge of the couch. "You planning on hiding out here all day?"

Taking a deep breath, I sighed. "No, just needed a moment to mentally prepare myself."

"I can personally assure you that I've inspected the house, and there don't appear to be any booby traps set up for you."

That would be a first.

"I'm trying. I just can't seem to force myself to get up off this couch."

A devilish gleam entered Liam's striking blue eyes as he deadpanned, "Amy and I have had sex on that couch."

That was enough to light a fire under my ass, and I jumped up, brushing off the back of my suit pants. "Not cool, man."

Not the least bit remorseful, his gaze scanned me from head to toe. "You're not seriously wearing a suit to Thanksgiving, are you?"

Looking down at my navy-blue suit, I thought I looked respectable, so I was confused. "Isn't this the Americans' mini-Christmas?"

Liam's chest vibrated as he held in his laughter. "No. This is way more casual. You have to change. I can't vouch for you if you show up like this."

Noting Liam's choice of clothing for the day of jeans and a sweater, I nodded before heading to the guest room to change. You'd think packing for a month away would mean I had various clothing options at my disposal, but that couldn't be further from the truth. When Lucy dropped the bomb that we were leaving, with only a few hours' notice, I panicked, grabbing what I could and throwing it into a single suitcase. Milan was one of the fashion capitals of the world, so I figured I could just buy anything I forgot.

That wasn't helpful now as I surveyed my inventory of clothing. I had a lone pair of dark wash jeans but no sweaters, so I opted for a navy-blue button-down instead. It was still less formal than the suit, so it would have to do.

Trudging back down the stairs, Liam was still waiting in their open-concept living room.

Annoyed, I grumbled, "I'm not a flight risk."

Unconvinced, he shrugged. "Just saving myself the trouble of coming back here to retrieve you a second time."

Resigned, I followed him out the door and across the stone pathway between the two houses. When Liam let himself in a side door, it hit me why I'd been so apprehensive about joining the festivities. I felt like an intruder. I wasn't part of this family.

There wasn't long to ponder that reality as I crossed the threshold and was hit with a wall of sound—adult and child voices alike—creating a cacophony the likes of which I'd never heard before. It was evident that the side door we entered through wasn't the main entry, given the mudroom to our right and the narrow hallway to our left. Liam turned left down the hallway, and I followed him further into the house. The noises got louder with every step we took.

Finally, we were spit out into a kitchen that could rival that of any estate back home. It was massive, easily larger than some of the more modest dwellings in Belleston, and featuring gray threaded marble and stainless-steel appliances. Most shocking of all was that it was filled with people. Some cooking, some chatting, and some of the smaller ones running around—a majority of them were strangers to me.

To say that this kind of scene was foreign to me would be an understatement. Growing up, our kitchen was in the basement, and the staff handled the cooking. Sure, as a child, I occasionally snuck down for a snack, but it was never like this.

Drawn from my thoughts, a petite woman with honey-blonde hair approached where I stood staring, a smile on her face. "You must be Preston! If we have met before, please forgive me for not remembering. The faces started to blur together after a while."

Blinking at the woman, it took a moment to place her. Stunned, it hit me. "Natalie?"

Flashing me with a brilliant smile, she blushed. "That's me. Welcome to our home."

She looked nothing like the girl I remembered. The Natalie I knew was frighteningly thin, fragile, and kept her eyes down. Her submission was not given freely—it had been practically beaten into her. The woman who stood before me looked healthy, vibrant, and happy. It was incredible to see her transformation.

Astonished, I breathed out, "I almost didn't recognize you."

Reaching a hand up, she touched her head, almost laughing. "It's the way I do my hair now, isn't it?"

Damn, and she was funny too. Smiling, I nodded. "That must be it."

Taking my hand like we were old friends, she pulled me further into the kitchen past an older couple I couldn't place, stopping once we stood before a dark-haired man about my height, holding a raven-haired toddler on his hip. Dressed even more casually than Liam in jeans and a black t-shirt, his prominent arm muscles bunched as he juggled the squirming little girl. I could have sworn I heard mention of Natalie ending up with a professional athlete, but I couldn't recall which sport he played.

Natalie's chocolate brown eyes sparkled as she looked at this man before introducing him. "This is my husband, Jaxon."

Shifting the toddler to his opposite hip, he reached his right hand out to shake mine. "Nice to meet you. Make yourself at home."

Returning his firm grip, I shook his hand. "Thank you for making room for me. I know I wasn't on the original guest list."

Glazing over that comment, Natalie tickled the belly of the toddler in Jaxon's arms, causing her to giggle. "And this is Charlie."

Liam reached over, plucking Charlie from Jaxon's arms. "Stop hogging the baby."

Natalie laughed, her eyes full of adoration for her brother-in-law. "Charlie has her Uncle Liam wrapped around her little finger."

Amy called out from the stove, where she stirred something hot. "Someone better tell that girl I won't be cooking forever, and I'll want my husband back."

Liam walked up next to his wife, kissing her temple while she worked. "Now, now, sweetheart. There's more than enough of me to go around."

Everyone chuckled, a testament to the relaxed nature of the gathering. Lucy's family and mine were so formal, stuffy almost. It was refreshing to see that there was a softer side to some families. I could see why Liam had been so reluctant to return home after his time spent away.

Natalie dragged me around to every person in the room, introducing me to her new in-laws, a few of Jaxon's teammates—I learned quickly that they played ice hockey—and the rest of her children.

The kids, at least the three older ones, were the future of my country. It brought a smile to my face to see that they were living a happy, carefree childhood. The oldest, Amelia, was eleven and helped her aunts in the kitchen. Jameson, my future King, was ten, and his blond mop of curls bounced as he tore through the kitchen, snagging the occasional snack from the kitchen island. Beau was the youngest of the royal children and was only five. What struck me most about him was that he seemed to be Jaxon's shadow—where Jaxon went, so did Beau.

Lucy ignored me as she worked alongside Amy in the kitchen, preparing what promised to be quite the feast for dinner. Truth be told, I didn't mind it. Sitting at the huge kitchen island, I watched her work for a while. Seeing her outside of her natural habitat was slightly jarring.

Not only was I shocked she knew how to cook, but she also looked different. Her jet-black hair was held back and off her neck by some kind of clip, with pieces falling out every time she moved her head. The cream cashmere sweater hanging off one shoulder was one I recognized from our little shopping adventure, but as my perusal moved lower, I was surprised to see her wearing a pair of skinny jeans, her feet bare on the kitchen hardwood.

Those feet transfixed me as she went up on her tiptoes to reach certain shelves. When she was stationary, I smiled to myself as she absentmindedly moved them into ballet positions—no doubt the result of muscle memory after many years of classes. Most unsettling of all was that I could recall with vivid clarity how delicate those ankles felt in my hands as I wrapped the cuffs of the spreader bar around them.

Okay, time to focus your attention elsewhere before you embarrass yourself.

Looking around the room, a different set of blue eyes caught my attention. These were attached to a brunette at the kitchen table, chopping various vegetables. Shifting in my seat, her gaze was so blistering it felt like I was being skinned alive.

Feeling slightly threatened, I kept my eyes on her as I leaned to my right, nudging Jaxon's teammate. The big one—Cal, I think his name was. "Who is the one at the table that looks like she wants the floor to open up and swallow me whole?"

Glancing over, Cal scoffed. "Oh, that's Hannah. It's probably meant for me. Don't worry about it."

Turning away from Hannah, I said low enough that she couldn't overhear, "What'd you do?"

Rolling his eyes, he shrugged. "Today? Could be anything, really. My very existence pisses her off."

Interesting. Apparently, I wasn't the only one with a female adversary in this group. Cal was vague enough that I wasn't sure if the pair were involved or not—for all I knew, they were in the middle of a lover's spat. For his sake, I hoped his situation was better than mine.

I was stuffed.

I didn't think I'd ever eaten this much in my life. No wonder the Americans only did this once a year. Not only was it a ton of work to make the feast that this holiday demanded, but it was more food than any single person should consume in one sitting. The giant roasted bird was one thing, but who needed eight different side dishes and four desserts? It made our long, drawn-out, multi-course meals back at home seem like child's play.

Making myself useful, I was clearing plates and bringing them into the kitchen when I heard Liam say quietly to Jaxon, "Grab the scotch and meet us next door."

What was that about?

Jaxon and Natalie were finishing their hosting duties, saying goodbye to their guests, when Liam found me still in the kitchen after he had helped put the kids to bed. Nodding toward the hallway we used when entering the house, he said, "The girls are staying. Us guys are heading next door."

I wondered if this was something they did often. From Liam's reaction to a girls' night when we landed a few days ago, I'd say so. After thanking Natalie and Jaxon for having me, I ventured out into the cold November night, returning to Liam's house.

Liam was getting a fire started in a pit on their back patio when Jaxon arrived with a bottle of scotch and three glasses. Placing them on the patio table, he dropped onto a cushioned outdoor chair, remarking, "This stuff is usually saved for special occasions."

Curious, I turned the bottle to get a look at the label. The brand wasn't anything high-end that I would recognize, so I couldn't help but ask, "What makes it special?"

Liam chuckled. "For some reason, this scotch makes an appearance at important moments in our lives—most notably, when our now-wives throw us for a loop. You're about to marry my sister, so I figured you could use some."

Protesting, I shook my head, "No. I'm not like you guys—you're in love. I'm fucking miserable."

"Been there." Jaxon raised his hand.

"Me, too," Liam offered. "Usually, we are drinking this scotch when we don't know which way is up. Sounds like you could use all the help you can get."

I honed in on a single word—help. That's what I was missing, so I jumped on the opportunity. Taking Jaxon's offered glass of scotch, I took a sip before laying out my proposal. "I need you guys to help me."

Jaxon took the bait. "Help with what?"

I sighed. "I'm not sure how much you've heard from Liam, but I'm kind of in a tight spot right now. Lucy and I are expected to get married, but we *hate* each other. It'll never work; we'll end up killing each other before the wedding. Right now, I find myself in an epic battle of wills with her—she's trying to get me to call it off while I'm doing the same. I need new ideas if I'm going to get myself out of this jam. That's where you two come in."

Liam nearly choked on his sip of scotch. "You want us to go against the girls?"

Jaxon's eyes went wide. "No, man. I get you're struggling, but that's a suicide mission."

Eyeing the two of them, I asked, "Are you scared of a bunch of women?"

Shaking his head, Liam answered, "Not scared, just playing it smart. They always win."

"What are you talking about?"

Tilting his head toward Jaxon, Liam explained, "When they wanted this one to end up with Natalie, there was nothing I could do to stop them. Trust me, I tried."

Jaxon continued, "And with Liam . . . Well, let's just say he was holding out on his wife, and they fixed *that* problem."

That was a lot to unpack. These guys looked spooked. Almost unable to believe what they were saying, I tried one more time. "Are you serious?"

"And if Hannah's in any way involved, you better watch out." Liam shuddered at the thought. "That girl is crazier than the rest, especially when she's been drinking."

"Can confirm," Jaxon added.

Thinking back to the girl in the kitchen that Cal identified as Hannah, I shook my head slowly. "So, she was glaring at me. Cal thought it was him."

Jaxon chuckled. "Oh, she's got it in for Cal too. But if she's on Team Lucy, you're toast. Accept it."

"Team Lucy . . ." I scoffed. Maybe these two were the crazy ones.

Liam was dead serious, declaring, "These girls don't mess around. Once team names are announced, they won't stop until they complete their mission. So, you have two options—either call it off yourself, or resign yourself to life with Lucy. That's it. Game over."

Silence descended upon our small gathering, with only the occasional crackling of the fire between us. That's when I heard it—the distant laughter of women. When it became apparent the other men heard it too, it only confirmed what I suspected. That laughter belonged to the women in question.

Mulling over my options and the resigned men before me, I took another sip of the scotch. "Humor me, gentlemen. I can't simply give up my life. That's what will happen if I'm backed into a corner with only those two choices—the result will be the same. I just need an idea or two. Liam, you know her better than anyone. Help out an old friend, even if it doesn't work. I'm desperate."

Liam was placed in an impossible position—either to help me or his sister. I knew it was unfair to ask him to choose, but that was where I found myself.

Sighing, he offered, "I don't know. Amy really doesn't like it when I interrupt her while she's working. Maybe try that. Lucy's a workaholic."

Frustrated, I groaned. "That's it? That's all you've got? You two are whipped." I accused Liam, "Being happy has made you soft. It wasn't that long ago you swore off women."

Leaning back in his seat, he propped one ankle on the opposite knee. "I've learned the error of my ways."

Jaxon threw a thumb in Liam's direction. "The girls did that to him."

"Says the guy who was in love with Natalie for ten years before she gave him the time of day."

Unfazed, Jaxon replied, "And I also have the girls to thank for that." Turning to me, he said, "Who knows, maybe a year from now, you'll be thanking them as well."

"Doubtful," I muttered. Steering the conversation back to the task at hand, I asked, "Fine. Say I want to interrupt her at work. How would I go about doing that? We just spent a month at her studio in Milan while she worked, and—knock on wood—we are headed back home after the weekend. Seems too little, too late for your suggestion."

Liam didn't see the problem. "Interrupt her when she's working from home."

Confused, I asked, "What are you talking about?"

"Lucy doesn't just turn that part of herself off when she's at the palace. She burns the midnight oil most nights in her workspace."

Now, I was really lost. "What workspace?"

"The room across the hall from the master suite in her apartment."

Understanding dawned. "Oh, the locked door."

Liam frowned. "Locked? That's odd."

Odd, indeed. It would seem Lucy was keeping more secrets than the ones I'd already uncovered. When we returned home, my objective would be to discover exactly what she was hiding, and if somehow that led to the destruction of our courtship, then that would just be a happy accident.

CHAPTER 15

Preston

WE WERE HOME AT last, but the damage caused by a month away was already done. Most of my projects were handed off to other attorneys in my department, and I was left with fluff projects that required very little oversight.

The writing was on the wall—they were preparing for my inevitable departure. It was no secret that I was involved with Lucy, and as much as I hated it, I couldn't blame them for setting up a contingency plan.

I wasn't ready to wave the white flag just yet.

Lucy was back to ignoring me, which was fine by me. I was busy observing the pattern of her routine, trying to find a way to catch her going into that locked room, and dealing with another one of her antics trying to drive me away would have only stolen my focus. Time was running out; I couldn't afford unnecessary distractions.

We'd been home for a few days, and each night, I sat beside my bedroom door, listening to her movements. After dinner, she would watch TV for an hour or so, then go into her bedroom, where she'd stay for an additional hour before venturing back out. Each night, I watched the shadow her body created beneath the crack in my bedroom door—she was check-ing to see if I was still awake.

Once satisfied that she was the only one awake, I heard her pad almost silently to the door of the suite before latching it behind her. If Liam's intel was correct, she was venturing across the hall into her locked workspace.

A flicker of doubt crossed my mind. What if she was sneaking out to Desire every night? The thought made my blood boil. Talking myself off the ledge, I clung to the fact that we had only crossed paths once in all the years I'd been a member. If she were a nightly visitor, I would have noticed her long before now.

After four days of observing Lucy's unchanging nightly routine, I decided to make my move. Listening intently by my door once again, I waited just long enough to hear her unlatching the entrance to the suite before I snuck out. Moving swiftly through the sitting room, I caught up to her just as she was about to shut the door across the hallway.

Reaching out, I gripped the edge of the door, halting its progress, startling Lucy enough that she screamed. Forcing the door open, un-sure what I was about to uncover, I braced myself for Lucy's wrath at the intrusion on her privacy.

What I didn't expect to find was four mannequins in the middle of the room, each showcasing dresses in various stages of completion. Three of them were the same color blue as Lucy's eyes, but one stood out from the rest. Stark white, still in the process of being pieced together, there was no denying what I was looking at—a wedding dress.

Dumbfounded, I asked quietly, "What's going on here?"

With fire in her eyes, Lucy seethed, "What does it look like?"

My chest tightened as panic set in, but I managed to force out, "Who—whose wedding dress is that?"

Crossing her arms over her chest, Lucy looked at me like I was stupid. "Amy's."

Relief washed over me like a tidal wave. If she had said it was her dress, that would mean she was resigned to our mutual fate, rendering any last-minute Hail Mary attempt to stop this madness futile. Lucy giving up hope with weeks to spare would be catastrophic; her acceptance of our union would be impossible to overcome.

Walking further into the room, I recognized many of the same items she kept in her main studio in Milan. There was a large table with cut pieces of fabric, a raised circular podium—this one on wheels as opposed to affixed permanently to the floor—and a sketch desk cluttered with dozens of papers featuring dresses obviously of Lucy's creation.

Liam wasn't kidding when he said Lucy was a workaholic. I knew for a fact that she spent most of today at the capital city's largest library, and I could only imagine how exhausted she was from pretending to be the gracious princess she portrayed to the public. Now, here she was, past midnight, working on Amy's wedding dress. It didn't take much to figure out the blue dresses were for the bridesmaids.

"You're working on this all by yourself?" I questioned.

Lucy was instantly defensive. "Why? Don't think I'm good enough?"

That took me aback. Given our history, it made sense she would think I didn't value her work, but she couldn't be more wrong. Spending those weeks in Milan, I'd be a fool not to admit she was talented. I could see why she was willing to fight for her career—her company—to the death.

That should have been my first warning sign that I was fighting a losing battle, but I was too stubborn to accept defeat. Just like her.

Reminding myself that we were at war, I quipped, "Don't you have people you can hire to do this?"

Mouth dropping open in shock, Lucy stared at me. Finally, she found her voice, stating angrily, "No."

I mocked her. "What? Run out of money?" I knew that was the furthest from the truth, but my goal was to push her over the edge, and I could sense I was close.

"Because it's important to me!" Lucy screamed before pushing past me and crossing the hallway. The slam of her bedroom door signaled that she'd given up on working tonight.

Stunned, I could only stare in the direction she fled. With only a handful of words, Lucy put a crack in my perception of her.

The Lucy I knew was selfish. She didn't stay up late to create a handmade wedding dress for her sister-in-law. At the very least, she brought in a team to help, not tackling such a monumental task solo.

That begged the question—what else was I wrong about?

Before I could spend too much time pondering this contradiction to the woman I thought I had pegged, my phone buzzed in my back pocket.

Who would be texting at this hour?

Desire Concierge: *The submissive from October 7th would like an encore.*

Well, *that* was a twist.

October 7th was the night I dominated Lucy at the club. There was an irony to be found in the knowledge that in running from me, she was unknowingly seeking comfort in my arms.

For a fleeting moment, I thought perhaps this was my chance to end this farce once and for all. If I revealed myself to her, scaring her into thinking I would expose her darkest secret, she'd have no option but to bow out.

Unfortunately for me, blackmail wasn't my style. I couldn't sink that low and be able to live with myself. Not to mention, she'd have the same dirt on me, and if either of us spoke of our knowledge, we would be in breach of the contract we signed as members.

Simply put, it wasn't a viable option. Back to the drawing board.

However, that didn't mean I couldn't work off some of the pent-up frustration I constantly carried as a result of the woman looking for an encore of our one night together. Who better than her to offer me release?

Tapping my fingers against the smooth screen of my phone, I typed out my reply.

Room 203 Dom: *Tomorrow night at midnight.*

Desire Concierge: *Very well, sir. Your message will be relayed.*

That gave me just shy of twenty-four hours to dream up how I planned to make Lucy submit to me—again. Heading back to my bedroom, a smile crept onto my lips. This time, I was going to have some fun.

Turned out, it was a good thing my workload had been reduced to the most menial tasks at the office because I couldn't focus on anything beyond the thoughts of my meeting with Lucy that evening at the club. Clockwatching became my new hobby, willing time to pass faster so I could confirm our first encounter hadn't been a fluke.

I convinced myself over the past two months that perhaps I had imagined how willingly Lucy submitted. It was as if she were two separate people—the self-absorbed princess and the obedient submissive—and my brain was working overtime trying to reconcile the two. As hard as I tried, my dominant nature slipped into facets of my everyday life, so how could Lucy compartmentalize so well? Nothing about the woman I'd spent the past six weeks living with gave any hints of her secret submissive nature.

When evening finally approached, I returned home, ate dinner alone—no different than most nights—and resumed my nightly stake out behind my bedroom door. Lucy's routine remained the same, regardless of her after-dark plans. The TV could be heard softly through the wood of my door, and I dressed in pajama pants and a t-shirt, venturing from my room, passing by where she sat in a show of getting a glass of water before bed. Tonight would be spoiled if Lucy suspected I was the man behind the mask in Room 203.

Returning to my room with a cool glass in my hand, I mumbled, "Good night," before closing the door. Wasting no time, I dressed in my club suit. The all-black ensemble was my favorite for portraying an air of danger. Submissives were drawn to the illusion of danger but knowing they were completely safe in my care—it had worked with Lucy.

As I slipped on my tie, I heard Lucy turning off the television and retreating to her bedroom. All that was left to do was wait until she made her move.

Like clockwork, after an hour, I heard the telltale click of Lucy's door opening. Giving her a fifteen-minute head start—more for myself to avoid bumping into her if she forgot something and doubled back—I cracked my door and carefully peered out to ensure the sitting room was empty. Checking her bedroom and her studio, both were quiet and dark, confirming what I already knew.

Lucy was headed to Desire.

It was no small feat leaving the palace this late at night. I explained to five security agents that I had an emergency at work and needed to gather files from my office before morning. They gave me a hard time, but I would expect nothing less from the men appointed to protect the royal family at all costs. Finally, sweet-talking my way into exiting the grounds, I was permitted to drive myself off the property.

If it was this difficult for me to leave, how did Lucy manage it? Her status came with a personal bodyguard, and I couldn't see Myles allowing her to enter an underground sex club, where there were dark corners everywhere and everyone wore masks. Simply put, it was a security nightmare. However, it wasn't at all surprising that Lucy would do whatever she wanted, damn the consequences to her personal safety—that girl thought she was bulletproof.

Pushing away thoughts of how vulnerable Lucy would be if anyone else discovered her identity beneath the silver mask, I drove down the side of the mountain to the city of Remhorn below.

Parking down the street from Desire, I slipped my black mask over my face and exited my car. I'd done this so many times that it became automatic—password at the door, handing over personal effects, then passing through the red curtain and down the stairs to the bullpen.

Tonight, there was a demonstration occurring on stage, showcasing a woman affixed to a St. Andrews Cross as her Dom presented different ways to use it in bringing a submissive pleasure.

Demonstrations had always intrigued me. It was captivating to watch as those participating were able to proceed as if they were the only people in the room. I wasn't a voyeur but had been involved with several subs who were, so I watched them occasionally. I wasn't one to kink shame, so if it got my sub all hot and bothered, I was more than willing to watch others. As for participation, I wasn't a man who liked to share.

The St. Andrews Cross demonstration held my attention longer than most I'd seen over the years. The X-shaped apparatus that hinged in the middle had me picturing Lucy's body helpless, spread open, affixed to the restraints at each of the four arms of the cross. There were playrooms for rent with larger pieces of equipment—such as the one showcased on stage—and I itched to take Lucy to one someday but knew that this would likely be our last encounter. Either we would go our separate ways in two weeks or be stuck together forever. Both scenarios would put an end to whatever we were doing down here. I wasn't willing to risk discovery, and she would likely never trust me enough to reveal her deepest sexual desires, so we would put on different masks for each other and have a boring sexual relationship, if we had one at all.

That was why I had to make tonight count.

Grabbing a seat at the bar, I ordered a whisky neat while I continued to watch the show. The Dom had just turned the crank on the side of the cross, slowly bending his submissive over and presenting her intimately to the room before teasing her soft skin with feather-light touches.

Keeping one eye on the door, I awaited the moment when Lucy would emerge, finding myself curious as to how she traveled to Desire. She wasn't allowed to drive herself, and it would not go unnoticed if she took a car—the security at the gate would recognize her and alert Myles immediately. Hell, he would probably lose his job if it was ever discovered she was down here with or without him.

As the minutes ticked by, I became nervous that she bailed on our rendezvous. Maybe it was for the best. We shouldn't be doing this, especially when I held the knowledge of her identity while she was blind to mine.

I was crossing a line, and I knew it.

Just when I was about to give up hope and head home, the bartender handed me a note. Unfolding the paper, my heart began to race as I read the message.

Your submissive is waiting in your room.

I'd been so distracted by the thought of Lucy and how I could put the demonstration to use that the idea of her beating me to the club never crossed my mind—regardless of the fact that I gave her a head start.

Pushing off the barstool, I took several deep breaths to calm my racing heart. She came, and was waiting for me. I needed to be calm and in control—two things that proved challenging when Lucy was near.

Nerves threatened to unravel the careful control I'd honed over the years. What if she finally put the pieces together and figured out my identity? Would she feel used? That was the last thing I wanted, but I knew I was playing with fire each time we met like this.

Reaching the door to Room 203, I reminded myself that she requested this encore, so who was I to ruin that? Punching in the key code, I heard the digital sound of it unlocking before I slipped fully into Dom mode as I opened the door.

I nearly stumbled when I looked up from the doorknob to find the sight that awaited inside the room.

Fuck. Me.

Lucy was facing away from the open door, kneeling on the floor at the foot of the bed, with her hands clasped behind her back and her head bowed—a perfect "submissive ready" posture. There was nothing more arousing than a ready and willing sub. Not moving a muscle, she gave no visible reaction to my entry into the room. She was waiting for me to command her.

Clad in a silver sequined dress, no doubt an exact color match to her mask, it was a contrast to the see-through outfit she wore the first time we met down here. Every subtle detail gave me another piece of the puzzle of Lucy's involvement in this world. She knew enough that asking for an encore meant her body wasn't for others to see. She knew exactly how to wait for her Dominant.

I wondered if she had any long-term Doms in her past.

There had to be at least one. A sub didn't learn their role this well without proper instruction, and that didn't come from casual play partners.

That thought was quickly forgotten when I saw the flash of red at the bottom of the heels she wore, with the soles presented to me, seated as she was in this position. I had to hand it to Lucy; she was right about those being sexy as hell.

Getting a grip on myself after finding her like this, I lowered my voice not to give myself away. "Hello, Ari."

Demurely, she answered, "Hello, Sir."

Fuck. That one word went straight to my dick. It was a submissive's show of respect—this was the one place on Earth where Lucy gave that to me. If I weren't already hard at the sight of her, that would have done it.

Approaching her from the right, I reached down to take her chin in my hand, turning and tilting her masked face to look at mine. Tsking, I chided, "I remember telling you this arrangement was for one night only."

Lucy tried to dip her head to avoid meeting my gaze, but I held her chin firmly in my grasp, not allowing her to look away. When she remained silent, I commanded, "Tell me why you asked for more."

Taking in a shaky breath, she responded, "I needed to escape, Sir."

I knew what she meant, but the words were still a knife to the gut. I drove her to this, even if I was also the one she trusted to make her troubles forgotten for a time.

Feeling like a fraud, knowing what we were doing was an abuse of the unconditional trust Lucy handed over so freely, I had a moment of doubt. The right thing would be to end this now, telling Lucy the truth and letting her do with it what she would. But I couldn't ignore that she *needed* this tonight, and it was my job as her temporary Dom to see to her needs.

"On your feet." I kept my tone as detached as possible in my demand. That was the only way I would survive this night. We couldn't keep doing this.

No doubt her muscles were sore from the time spent in the ready position, but Lucy gracefully maneuvered her body to stand before me. My eyes trailed down her body, and I noted that while her dress wasn't transparent, it was short—short enough that the act of walking was enough to shift the hem and expose her.

Opening my mouth to reprimand her for risking the gaze of a Dom she didn't belong to, the words died on my lips when her blue eyes flashed to mine. It was a bold move for a submissive to make eye contact without permission, and that was the first time I saw a spark of Lucy down here. A part of me wanted her to push me too far, just so I could punish her for the hell she put me through these past couple of months. I couldn't use outside actions as a reason, especially since she didn't know I was acting as her Dom. I needed blatant defiance while we held these roles.

Silently, I watched as her pink tongue peeked out to wet her lower lip, biting it lightly before speaking, "Sir, I have a confession."

Maybe I'd have a chance to administer that punishment after all. "Go on."

"Since our last meeting, my orgasms have belonged exclusively to you."

Groaning, I closed my eyes. Not only did it dispel any concern I had about her sneaking down here without me, it was also an admission that she hadn't pleasured herself in all that time. Lucy's confession was aimed at pleasing me, and I'd never been more pleased with a submissive than I was at that very moment.

Cupping her cheek, I nearly whispered, "That's a good girl."

Lucy's eyes fluttered shut at my words, and a moan slipped from her lips. Most subs enjoyed praise, but her reaction was so erotic that I found myself needing release, or I wouldn't be able to play her body properly—I couldn't think past the cloud of lust to adequately worship her in the way she deserved.

With that thought in mind, I growled, "Down on your knees. I want to watch my good girl suck my cock."

Satisfaction coursed through my veins as I watched her breathing hitch and the pulse point at the base of her throat flutter due to her increased heart rate; she was excited to please me in this way.

Almost as if in slow motion, Lucy dropped to her knees on the plush carpet. Her tiny hands landed on my belt buckle, but I stopped her by placing mine over hers. Blinking up at me in confusion, there was still one last box to check before we proceeded this evening. "Do you remember your safeword?"

Relief flashed in her blue eyes, and she breathed out, "Red, Sir."

Removing my hands that halted her progress, I used one to tangle in her hair's long silky black tresses. "You may proceed."

It was an exquisite torture to watch as she undid my belt before unbuttoning my suit pants and slowly lowering my zipper. God, I swore she did it so slowly that I could hear each individual tooth of the zipper as it came undone. It was a miracle I could hear anything over the roaring rush of blood in my ears.

With my pants undone, my erection pushed through the fly, still contained within my boxer briefs. I hissed when Lucy's soft hand grazed the waistband, dipping inside to grip the throbbing flesh. Closing my eyes, I threw my head back, reveling in the sensation.

A rush of cool air met with my heated skin, and I forced my eyes open to look down at Lucy as she came face-to-face with my aching cock. Seeing her on her knees before me was so overwhelming that I swallowed uncontrollably before forcing out, "Eyes on me."

God help me, those blue eyes flared, and I knew she was just as turned on by what she was about to do as I was. Without a moment's hesitation, eyes locked on mine, Lucy parted her perfectly plush lips and wrapped them around my cock. The heat was almost too much to bear, and when she hollowed out her cheeks, creating a vacuum with her mouth, it nearly brought me to my knees.

Usually, I wasn't one to take my pleasure before my submissives, but I'd make it up to her before the night was done.

Lucy was gorgeous as she moved over my length, never breaking eye contact. It took every ounce of my willpower not to close my eyes and give myself over to the pleasure her mouth provided.

Unlike her, I hadn't been a saint. More often than I cared to admit, I gave myself a helping hand in the shower, but nothing compared to this.

Watching her added to the mounting pressure I felt building in my balls, seeing her hips shifting to relieve the ache between her own thighs. Then she moaned around my shaft, and I couldn't stop the explosion. I didn't know it was possible to have the breath stolen from your lungs while simultaneously having a roar ripped from your chest, but somehow that's what happened as Lucy's mouth coaxed the climax from my body while our eyes remained locked.

Goddamn, she was something else.

I was transfixed as her throat worked to swallow every drop, never faltering for a moment. When I had nothing left to give, Lucy's mouth continued to move along my hypersensitive flesh. The sensations were too much, forcing me to step back, breaking the contact between our two bodies. My chest was heaving, trying to come back down from the high Lucy provided so effortlessly.

There was a give and take within these walls that we couldn't replicate in our daily lives. It was a damn shame because I was reasonably certain I'd met my match in the bedroom.

CHAPTER 16

Lucy

BREATHLESS, I STARED UP at Tony. It was evident he was pleased with me, even as he struggled to breathe. The idea of bringing him to the edge of ecstasy and throwing him over was just as intoxicating as being led to that edge myself. Hearing his sounds of approval from above as his eyes never left mine had slickness coating the insides of my thighs.

He'd kept me waiting for so long, I feared he wouldn't show—even though he set the time—but I should have known that making me wait was intentional. Anticipation was an essential tool used by Dominants to heighten arousal. As frustrating as it was when you were in the throes of it, there was no denying the efficacy—it worked every time.

My muscles ached from holding my posture perfectly still until the moment he arrived. It felt like hours, but I had no way of telling how long it had actually been. That was all forgotten the moment he commanded that I drop to my knees before him, and I parted my lips to take his cock within my mouth.

Now, my body felt like a live wire; the right touch had the power to send me skyrocketing toward the stars. I hadn't lied when I told him he still owned my orgasms. There was something that hadn't felt right about pleasuring myself, even if I had no intention of seeking him out again until Preston invaded my privacy.

No. I wouldn't think about him here. *He* didn't belong here—not in my thoughts or reality. This was *my* sanctuary, and I wouldn't allow him to ruin what I had right here and now.

I waited for my next command as I held my position, kneeling on the floor. The silence stretched between us until Tony's gruff voice finally said, "Stand."

A shiver racked my body, and I couldn't get to my feet fast enough. There was something to be said for entrusting your care to a Dominant—simply shutting off your brain, focused only on obeying, knowing they had your needs at the forefront of their mind.

Tony's intense green-gold eyes held mine as my heart hammered in my chest. Mere inches separated us, the closeness setting my body on fire. If he deemed our evening over right now, I would leave satisfied with the knowledge that I gave him pleasure, accepting there was a reason he denied mine—perhaps as a punishment for reaching out when he'd been firm in his declaration that our last encounter was a one-time deal.

Thankfully, that idea was dispelled when the pads of his fingertips dragged up my thigh. Giving myself over to the sensations his touch provided, I held his stare, even as his hand slipped under the short hem of my dress. Reaching the curve of my hip, he groaned at the discovery that I wore nothing underneath.

"Fuck, Ari," he breathed, closing his captivating eyes for a second before training them on me yet again. "When you get home, destroy any panties you have. I want to know you're always like this—ready and accessible for me."

Never breaking eye contact, my voice was clear in my response. "Yes, Sir."

It didn't matter if this was the last time and our unspoken arrangement was temporary—I was compelled to obey. The same compulsion kept me from seeking personal pleasure these past two months as his dominance extended past our time shared in this dim room. I couldn't quite explain it, but there was something different about Tony, and his commands became law even when he wasn't around.

Pleased, his hand traveled across my hip bone before cupping between my thighs. It took every ounce of strength I had not to thrust my hips into his touch when he dipped a single digit into the wetness he found there. A barely-there circle over my sensitive and throbbing clit had my breath catching in my throat before he ventured further, coating his finger with my arousal.

All too soon, he withdrew his hand from between my legs, holding it up between us. A smirk crossed his lips as he teased in a playful tone, "Fair's fair. You got a taste, so now it's my turn." He drew that same finger between his lips and sucking it, savoring the flavor unique to me.

I locked my knees, desperate to stay upright. The sight of him enjoying the taste of me was breathtakingly erotic. I licked my lips, willing him to kiss me before the remnants left his tongue.

Either not reading the subtle cue or simply not caring about my wants, focused more on my needs, he withdrew the finger from his mouth before reaching down with both hands and pulling the dress over my head, leaving me only in my heels. Cool air rushed over my heated skin, raising goosebumps across my flesh.

Crowding my space, he took a step forward, forcing me to take a step backward—not an easy task in heels—causing me to stumble slightly. A strong arm like an iron band looped around my lower back, keeping me upright, as he continued to force my backward journey until the back of my knees bumped against the side of the bed in the center of the room.

A gentle hand on my shoulder, and my knees finally gave as I dropped onto the silk sheets. Two strong hands cupped my face, and Tony leaned down until our foreheads touched, his lips a breath away from mine. If I tilted my head up just a fraction of an inch, I could capture those lips, but I wouldn't—not without permission first.

His hot breath fanned my face as he whispered, "I'm going to let you have your hands tonight, but you're going to put them to good use."

My response was automatic. "Yes, Sir."

Pulling back, he rose to his full height. God, he was so tall that it made me feel delicate when he stood before me, and I had to crane my neck to look up at him. His gaze raked over my body, so intense that it felt like a physical caress. He knew what he wanted to do to me but wanted to make me squirm.

Spoiler alert—it was working.

I wanted nothing more than to shift my hips to ease the ache between my thighs, but I kept my body still, awaiting my next instruction.

Tony dropped into the armchair facing the side of the bed, and that's when I noticed his cock was still out. A small smile graced his lips when he saw my gaze shift, and he gripped his length that had begun hardening again, stroking it lazily. Last time, he'd activated the blindfold built into my mask, so this was my first time seeing him.

When I'd been on my knees earlier, it was like staring down the barrel of a gun, and my eyes nearly crossed trying to focus on what lay before me. Now, I had a perfect view, and while he wasn't the biggest I'd ever encountered, I knew he knew how to use it, and that was all that mattered.

Just remembering the pleasure he'd wrung from my body during our last time in this room caused a moan to slip past my lips. That was enough to jar Tony from the trance his self-caress had created.

Eyes flashing, his tone brooked no argument as he ordered, "Lay back."

His authoritative tone shot straight to my core, adding to the throbbing there I could no longer ignore. Ready and eager to obey, I scooched my butt back, one of my heels dropping to the floor as my feet left the ground.

Growling, Tony barked out, "Heels stay on."

Fuck, that was hot.

Slipping the errant heel back on, I pulled my body onto the bed more carefully. I laid flat, awaiting further instruction as my chest heaved in anticipation.

"Ass to the edge of the bed, facing me. Knees bent so your heels touch your bottom, legs spread."

God help me. His words alone had me struggling to hold my climax at bay. Tonight was proving to be the ultimate test of my submission, and we'd barely begun. Getting into the position he described, I was laid bare and open for his perusal.

"Touch yourself."

I barely heard the words he said so low over the sounds of my heart hammering in my chest.

Taking a shaky breath, I slid a hand over my torso, past my belly button, and between my thighs. He wanted a show, and I wanted to please him, so I dove right in, slipping two fingers into my slippery heat, penetrating myself as he watched.

"Fucking perfection," he groaned low, his voice rough, gravelly, the words sounding distant, as if they were said at the far end of a tunnel.

Spurred on by his praise, I pumped those fingers inside myself a few times, imagining it was his throbbing cock. My free hand found my nipple, rolling it between my fingers, the touch sending a jolt of pleasure straight to my clit. Moaning, I bit my lip as my hips arched in response, the tingles I knew all too well gathering as I tried to stave them off. I would not fail to obey—it wasn't an option.

With my fingers now well-coated in my arousal, I moved them to my clit, which was so sensitive, the lightest touch sent my back arching. Tony hummed his approval, and I shut my eyes tight, all my effort going into holding back my impending climax.

My legs shook, my breathing became shallow, and just when I felt like I was about to lose myself, Tony gripped my ankles, forcing my legs open impossibly wide, growling, "Now."

There wasn't time to process the single word—the permission I was desperate for—when his teeth clasped around my clit, and he sucked it into his mouth. My soul left my body, and I was deaf to my cries of ecstasy as stars burst behind my eyes. Every muscle seized as release racked my body, but Tony wouldn't let me come down from that high, flicking my overstimulated nub held firmly between his teeth until I crested that wave of pleasure for a second time, my voice hoarse from the screams ripped from my throat.

I was a trembling, shaky mess when he finally stepped away. Gasping for air, my brain was mush. Much more of this, and I was afraid I'd lose consciousness—the pleasure was that intense.

My eyes were still closed, trying to come down from the highest high I'd ever experienced, when I heard rustling in the bedside table and the tell-tale sound of ripping foil.

He wasn't done with me yet.

Soft hands caressed my calf, and my body involuntarily jumped.

Calm words soothed me from above. "Easy. I've got you."

Relaxation rolled over me, easing the tremors of aftershocks from not one but two rapid-fire orgasms. My eyelids felt weighed down, and it took all my effort, but I managed to get them halfway open. Sighing, I took in the sight of Tony's naked body, standing at the edge of the bed. His lean but toned upper body was lightly peppered in dark brown hair, and I itched to run my fingers across his chest.

Unable to move, I watched as his hands moved down my calf, to my ankle, before removing the heel from my foot. Repeating the motion, he did the same to my other leg before pressing his thumbs into the arch of my feet, activating a pressure point that had my body vibrating once more.

The touches were so gentle—reverent almost—that I was caught completely off-guard by the flash of pain as his fingers gripped my hips, and he impaled me without warning. It was so jarring that I couldn't stop the shrill scream that clawed up my throat.

Tony tried to ease my legs around his hips, but my body was so boneless from the pleasure already wrung from it that they dropped, hanging over the edge of the bed. Setting a slow and steady pace, he held my hips firmly in his grasp, and all I could do was remind myself to breathe—in and out, in and out. It was harder than you'd think, the way my body was being driven toward that steep cliff once more.

I was vaguely aware of Tony above me as he pounded into my pussy, and in my lust-induced haze, I recall watching the tendons of his neck straining as he raced toward his own release.

Locking eyes with me, I felt him press on my lower abdomen, right above my pubic bone, and I gasped, shocked by the blinding pleasure that simple act caused. Picking up his pace, pushing down further with his hand, he growled, "Come for me, sweet girl."

Even though I was lost in the fog of bliss, my mind and body instinctively obeyed, and I was careening off that cliff, freefalling into the chasm below.

Breathing was forgotten, and my mouth opened in a wordless scream as tears streamed down my face. This was beyond anything I'd felt before, and I was sure I would be chasing this high for the rest of my days.

Above me, Tony's thrusts became jerky and erratic right before he grunted, stilling as his climax claimed him. I barely felt when he slipped from my body; it was numb and alive simultaneously, the nerve endings misfiring, not knowing how to respond to what felt like a near-death experience.

Sated, I laid there, unmoving, barely aware of my own name. That's what he'd done to me tonight—turned my entire world upside down with just his body and mine.

The mattress dipped beside me, and I felt a cool cloth dragged over my sweaty, heated skin. Swallowing thickly, still trying to gain my bearings, I turned my head to the side to watch Tony as he cared for me gently, with a serene smile on his face.

Catching me watching, he stroked my cheek. "You did so well."

My eyes closed as I soaked in his praise. He knew exactly what I needed tonight and gave it to me as freely as I gave up my power to him. It was a perfect balance. *He* was my perfect balance.

Mourning what could never be, I sighed as he pulled me into his strong arms, holding me in his lap, content to simply stroke my hair as the adrenaline coursing through my veins slowly dissipated. His chest vibrated against my face as the deep timber of his voice sounded above me. "You should stay tonight. You're in no shape to leave."

Hopeful, I asked, "Stay with me?"

Daring to look up at his face, his eyes were laced with regret as he shook his head slightly. "I can't."

I knew better than to push, but a piece of my heart broke. He took care of me so well, but our arrangement was temporary. I was pushing the limits even asking for a second meeting.

He would be the Dom—the man—I used as a measuring stick for all who came after him. The two evenings spent with him were a gift I would cherish for the rest of my life.

CHAPTER 17

Lucy

THIS WAS IT. MY last-ditch effort to drive Preston away.

Christmas was only one week away, and I was officially out of time. It was a great idea, but I wasn't sure it would be enough. Maybe it was time to accept that Preston was as stubborn as me, and we were doomed to a life of driving each other insane. Hey, at least women tended to live longer than men.

Listen to me. I'm already longing for the day my currently young and healthy intended leaves this plane of existence.

That kind of thinking wouldn't help today. I needed to think positive thoughts.

Getting up early enough to catch Preston before he headed to work, I dressed in a pair of black pleated skinny trousers and a cream cashmere sweater—I wanted my clothing to be as soft as possible for holding our tiniest Bellestonians. Tying my long hair back, I made sure not to wear any jewelry, not wanting anything to scratch the sensitive, thin skin of the babies we were going to see.

Taking a deep breath, I checked my appearance in my standing floor-length mirror one last time before venturing from my room and heading for the breakfast room, where Preston was likely enjoying his morning cup of coffee.

Most days, we staggered our morning routine to avoid running into each other over breakfast. Preston was slightly surprised when I entered the room earlier than usual, his raised eyebrows giving him away. Without a word, I stepped to the sideboard laden with cold meats and cheeses, along with assorted pastries and fruit. Placing a few items on a plate, I perched myself on the edge of the settee, enjoying a moment of peace before the festivities began.

Hearing Preston folding his newspaper—a clear sign he was about to leave—I cleared my throat.

Pausing, probably hoping he was hearing things, he asked, "Did you need something, Lucy?"

"Actually, I do," I responded as I placed my plate on the coffee table.

Sighing, Preston was resigned. "What now?"

Throwing on my fake princess smile, the one he believed was the only one I owned, my voice was sickeningly sweet. "Today, you will accompany me to my engagement."

Absorbing the news, he ran a hand down his face in defeat. "Where are we going?"

"No need to worry about that." I purposely brushed him off. The shock factor was necessary today. "Just know that you will be escorting me as my intended. After all, by next week, the news of our betrothal will be spread across the world."

Pleased, I watched his throat bob as he swallowed that hard truth.

There's still time to get out of this, buddy, but the ball is in your court. Man up and do us both a favor by calling this ridiculous arrangement off.

Much to my chagrin, he stood, brushing imaginary wrinkles from his dress slacks with his hands. "When do we leave?"

Plucking a scone from my plate, I replied, "Be ready in an hour."

"Fine," he muttered as he left the breakfast room. The tension was evident in the straining tendons of his neck.

Good. I wanted him slightly aggravated at all times—it increased the odds that the pot would boil over at some point, and he'd say "uncle."

I was putting all my eggs in this final basket. It had to work.

———❈———

As we pulled up to the back entrance of our destination, a mixture of confusion and fear crossed Preston's face. Alpine Slope Women's Hospital was a specialty hospital, providing medical care unique to the female sex. While most of Remhorn's residents were born here, there were also departments devoted to female-specific cancers and preventative care.

Allowing Myles to open the sedan's back door, I stepped out, waiting for Preston to join me before we entered the building. My heels clacked on the polished vinyl flooring just inside the doorway, and I was instantly flooded with memories—this was the same entrance I used all those years ago when Jameson required the highly specialized care of the NICU.

"Princess Lucy!" Hearing my name called from further down the hallway, I plastered the perfect public smile on my face, snapping into the role forced upon me by an accident of birth.

"Ms. Dixon. It's so lovely to see you again," I greeted the public relations representative for the hospital. She was a younger woman herself, dressed in a conservative skirt suit. We'd interacted on many of my previous pre-arranged visits to the hospital over the years.

"The pleasure is all ours, Your Highness." Noticing Preston beside me instead of hanging back like Myles, she dared to ask, "And who have you brought with you today?"

Yeah, I saw the way her eyes devoured him, and I had to tamp down a sudden surge of possessiveness.

Looping my arm through his, I clung to Preston's elbow, peering up at him with an over-the-top fake smile, acting like he was the light of my life. "This is Preston Scott, my intended."

My smile turned genuine when I heard the muffled choking sound he tried to stifle. Ms. Dixon probably hadn't heard it, but I sure did. He knew that explaining our relationship to someone outside our inner circle at the palace would have the news circulating before the end of the day. It wasn't an over-sensationalized media rumor when it came straight from my mouth.

Clapping her hands in glee, Ms. Dixon was quick to hide the jealousy in her eyes as she gushed, "How wonderful! Congratulations to you both."

"Thank you, we are very excited. Aren't we, darling?" I batted my eyelashes at the stiff man beside me.

Preston's arm was rock-hard beneath my touch—every muscle tensed—but he managed to keep up appearances, responding curtly, "Thrilled."

Ignorant of Preston's thinly veiled irritation, Ms. Dixon smiled politely. "Let's not waste any more time down here. They're beyond excited about your visit upstairs."

"The feeling is mutual. Please, lead the way," I encouraged, falling in step behind her as she navigated the maze of hallways.

Releasing Preston's arm, anger radiated off him in waves as we walked side by side, stopping only to travel by elevator to the fourth floor. The sliding doors opened, revealing our destination written out in baby-block letters above a window extending the length of the entire wall before us: Neonatal Intensive Care Unit.

"Here we are!" Ms. Dixon announced with pride. Preston stood silently beside me as we walked up to the giant window, peering inside at the babies, most residing within clear incubators. "As you can see," she explained, "with the funds generously raised by your family, we have been able to extend the size of our unit, with the capacity to care for up to thirty babies at any given time. Beyond that, we have been able to invest in additional training and equipment for our staff, becoming not only the premiere NICU in Belleston but one of the best in all of Central Europe."

Jameson's stint in this very NICU had shone a spotlight on how lucky we were, and my family poured their resources into raising awareness and funds to support advancement in care for the tiniest residents of our great country. Since our involvement, the mortality rate of the unit had sharply declined, and more Bellestonian families were able to leave this hospital whole.

Swiping her security badge on the door to the unit, Ms. Dixon invited us inside. Roughly half the incubators were occupied, with a few open-air infant hospital cribs containing babies as well. Nurses in soothing pink scrubs flitted from patient to patient, checking vitals such as heart rate, blood pressure, and oxygen saturation, to name a few. Decorations had changed since the expansion, and I smiled, noting the cartoon jungle animals hand-painted on the walls. Several upholstered glider rocking chairs were scattered around the room, some containing parents as they kept a watchful eye over the other half of their hearts behind glass.

I was still noting the changes since my last visit when I heard a familiar voice call out in hushed tones, "Well, look who the cat dragged in. If it isn't Lucky Lucy!"

My eyes landed on the portly woman with her gray hair pulled back into a tight bun. She'd aged in the past ten years, but the kindness in her brown eyes remained the same. Rushing forward, I threw my arms around the older woman who had been our lifeline during Jameson's time here.

Pulling back, a smile stretched my face. "Nurse Cindy, it's so good to see you!"

Squeezing my hands tightly in hers, she asked, "How's our boy?"

"Growing like a weed!" Pulling my phone from my clutch, I brought up a picture taken during Thanksgiving, showing it to Nurse Cindy.

She threw a hand to her chest. "My, he *has* grown! I can remember when he was barely bigger than my hand. How old is he now?"

"He'll be eleven before spring." I beamed.

"Will miracles never cease?"

"Natalie sends her best. She will never forget all you did for her."

Waving me off, she couldn't help but smile. "Just doing my job." Looking over my head, she noticed Preston, asking, "And who is the gentleman you've brought with you today."

I was so caught up in the nostalgia that I'd almost forgotten I wasn't visiting alone. Stepping back so that I was again by his side, I introduced him. "This is Preston Scott."

Nurse Cindy looked between the two of us. She'd been around long enough to put two and two together so didn't press for more of an explanation. Addressing Preston, she asked, "Do you know why we call her Lucky Lucy?"

Oh, boy. I could feel the heat creeping onto my cheeks, but Preston simply replied, "No, ma'am. I don't."

Nearly bursting with pride, she began to tell the story. "Well, this one here would come to visit her nephew every day after school while he was in our care. No matter what kind of day he was having, when Lucy held him in her arms, it calmed him. She had a way of soothing him like no one else. We thought it was a lucky coincidence the first time, but by the time we realized it wasn't, the nickname had already stuck. So now, she is forever Lucky Lucy."

Almost embarrassed, I glanced at Preston, who was watching me intently. Under my breath, I uttered, "It really wasn't a big deal."

"Shall we test to see if you're still lucky, then?" Nurse Cindy offered.

"If that means I get to hold one of these precious babies, count me in."

"Right this way." She led me to an open glider, encouraging me to sit. I knew the drill by heart and watched as she opened the side of a nearby incubator, pulling out a baby that wasn't the tiniest I'd seen within the unit but was still smaller than a full-term baby. Carefully managing the cords attached to his monitors, she placed the featherlight infant in my arms before grabbing a blanket to keep him warm.

"This is Silas," Nurse Cindy introduced the tiny little boy.

"Hello, sweet Silas," I cooed, rocking the glider, enjoying his slight weight tucked safely against my chest.

"Looks like she's still got it," Nurse Cindy announced to those gathered.

I blinked, realizing a crowd had gathered to watch my interaction. I'd almost forgotten the public relations teams present—not only for the hospital but our in-house royal team. As much as I wanted this visit to be more personal and low-key, that wasn't how the world worked when you were a member of the royal family. Maybe someday, if I could figure out the current mess of my life, but not today.

The photographers were smart enough not to use flashes near such a tiny baby, but that didn't stop their cameras from clicking away. Then came the questions . . .

"Princess Lucy, you're quite the natural. Are there perhaps children of your own on the horizon?" a voice called from the crowd.

I kept my eyes on baby Silas in my arms, not wanting to give anything away with my facial expressions. "Perhaps one day." I kept my tone light, my answer vague.

"How many do you imagine having?"

My body tensed, and I was moments away from a verbal strike at whatever reporter dared to ask such a personal question when my brain caught up enough to realize the question came directly from my right, by a voice I knew almost as well as my own.

Turning my head, I locked eyes with Preston, who was now on one knee beside me. For just a moment, I thought I saw compassion in those hazel depths as he dropped his gaze to Silas. His question had been uttered so softly, and if the circumstances were different, I might have thought he genuinely wanted to know. But reality crashed down on me hard. We weren't a real couple; he didn't want to have children with me. This was just a trick to throw me off, having figured out I brought him here to make him uncomfortable.

Clearing my mind, I plastered a fake smile on my face, answering flippantly, "At least half a dozen. I'm not getting any younger, so we'll really have to bang them out."

I was taking a page out of his book, trying to spook him by suggesting I wanted a gaggle of kids born in rapid succession, but to my bewilderment, he simply nodded his head thoughtfully. "Seems like a tall task, but I could be convinced. I always thought more along the lines of three or four, but I find myself leaning toward four. Three, and there's always someone left out, but with four, everyone has a buddy. Growing up, it was only me and Max, and while I love my brother, it would have been nice to have a buffer sometimes. A larger family always held an appeal to me."

Was he fucking with me? He was supposed to be running out that door like his hair was on fire at the prospect of a house full of children. There were too many reasons not to believe he meant what he said.

One, he was Preston—he was never genuine with me.

Two, his job was his life—how would he carve out time to raise one child, let alone four or more?

And three, I saw him surrounded by Natalie's kids, and he never once chose to interact with them, electing to watch from the sidelines while the rest of us loved on them the way they deserved.

He had to be fucking with me. There was no other explanation.

Shaking my head slightly as if to clear it, my eyes searched for Nurse Cindy. When I located her, I asked, "Where are Silas's parents?"

Nurse Cindy gave a rueful smile. "His family resides in one of the more rural communities outside the city. They have older children and a farm to run. When he was transferred here shortly after birth, they could not come with him. His mother visits when she can, usually once a week if she's lucky. We send them regular updates and pictures via text."

My heart broke in two, not just for the little boy I held but for his family, whose circumstances did not allow them to be by his side. No one should have to choose between their livelihood and their devotion to their child requiring medical care. That's when my brain began working overtime, thinking of new ways to direct funding to benefit families like Silas's. If anyone could help me come up with ideas and how to implement them, it would be Amy. I'd have to sit down with her when she and Liam returned home from America.

"How many other babies are here without family nearby, unable to visit frequently?" Preston asked. It was like he could see what was on my mind.

That's not unsettling at all.

"Five at present," Nurse Cindy replied.

"All from rural communities?" he questioned.

"Not all. Some just live too far and have nowhere to stay for as long as their child needs care."

"Hmm," he mused. "Can you take me to one of them?"

"Certainly." She led him to the incubator across from where I sat. "This is Eliana."

Nodding, Preston asked, "May I hold her?"

Beaming up at him, Nurse Cindy enthusiastically replied, "Of course!"

The shock of Preston asking to hold a premature baby had barely worn off when I noticed him shedding his suit jacket before loosening his tie and undoing the top buttons of his dress shirt. Eyes wide, I asked in alarm, "What are you doing?"

Taking a seat in the chair opposite mine, his shirt half undone, Preston didn't falter. "My brother, Maxwell, is soon-to-be a father, and I've been helping him prepare for the arrival of my niece or nephew. I read that skin-to-skin contact has many benefits for premature babies. As Eliana's family is absent, I am happy to step in and provide that for her."

Thank God I was sitting down because you could have knocked me over with a feather.

Who was this man? Were we being invaded by aliens, and they'd already taken his body as a host? That was the only explanation I could think of because this wasn't the Preston I knew.

What if—what if he had meant what he said about wanting children? Four, to be exact. I could barely breathe as I watched Nurse Cindy place the diaper-clad baby girl against his bare chest before covering them with a blanket. Any other man, and this would have been endearing, heartwarm-ing even, but as I stared at him, my world was turned upside down.

Time seemingly stood still as we rocked our respective babies, and I was unable to tear my eyes away from the scene before me, even when Nurse Cindy whispered in my ear, "You picked a good one, Lucky."

Preston was seemingly lost in the little girl held carefully in his large hands. Was I hearing things, or was he actually humming a tune softly to her? Before I could stop it, a rogue thought crossed my mind.

He'd make a good father.

Maybe I was the one whose body had been taken over by aliens.

Where had that come from? And since when did being able to hold a baby equate to being a good father?

Parenthood was hard. It was stressful, putting a strain on even the best of marriages at times. You didn't get to go home at the end of the day and relax. You were always responsible for another human life—to guide them, teach them, and keep them safe. It wasn't always sweet baby cuddles.

Reluctantly, I handed the baby I held back over to Nurse Cindy as our visit drew to a close. Before we left, Preston and I made the rounds to each bed occupied in the NICU. Not all the babies were premature. Some were full-term, requiring a little assistance with various breathing issues, battling an infection, suffering from low blood sugar, or being born with a birth defect. I noted each one of their names so that I could keep them in my prayers at night.

Leaving the unit the way we came, I was more confused than ever about the direction my life was headed. Preston was in perfect step beside me, and my failure to scare him off today had sealed my fate.

Over the past couple of weeks, I began to accept that I might fall short in my quest, making mental plans on how to survive as Preston's wife. I would throw myself into my work, and hopefully, he'd leave me to my own devices. Thoughts of being intimate as man and wife made me physically ill.

I couldn't stop replaying his words regarding a future family in my head. They seemed sincere, but I learned long ago that he couldn't be trusted. Words were cheap; I had no choice but to take them at face value. I pretended to be someone I wasn't in the public eye every day, so who was to say he wasn't doing the same thing—especially after I outed our relationship? He had to make himself look good. I could only imagine the vultures watching were craning their necks to hear his words, and they were carefully crafted to be overheard.

But then, there was that image of him holding that baby with a knowledge of skin-to-skin. I, of course, knew that, having sat with Natalie as she'd done the same for Jameson what felt like a million years ago now, but he was a bachelor.

Preston had no warning of our visit here today, or I would have believed he did research to rattle me. As it stood, I was shaken to the core that he may have been telling the truth about helping to prepare his brother for impending fatherhood. That went beyond the normal expectations of brotherhood. Women stuck together in such matters, but not men.

Taking a deep breath as we exited the hospital's back entrance, I pushed all those thoughts aside. I had to focus on my future now—a future that promised a lifetime with Preston.

'Til death do us part.

CHAPTER 18

Preston

LUCY AND I SPENT nearly three months playing the world's highest-stakes game of chicken, and neither of us saw fit to swerve before we crashed in a blaze of glory. We were both losers and would now burn together.

Christmas brought our engagement, but you could clear your head of any notion right now that it had been a romantic affair. There wasn't any grand gesture where I got down on one knee and slid a ring onto her trembling hand as tears of joy leaked from her eyes.

A more accurate depiction would be that I handed her a velvet box in the privacy of our master suite sitting room while she eyed it like a snake about to strike, not bothering to even open it before she disappeared into her bedroom. I was pretty sure I heard her crying herself to sleep that night.

It was the stuff fairy tales were made of.

Seeing her now, you'd never know she was upset about our impending nuptials. Standing like puppets on a stage, we were placed before the royal press pack in the throne room to address our engagement before we adjourned for official photos. Lucy's smile was so wide, it nearly split her face as she beamed at the flashing lights that threatened to blind us both.

I'd heard stories of the press being a bunch of vultures, but I hadn't realized how bad it was until this moment. Their voices called over each other as photographers practically elbowed each other out of the way to get a closer shot.

This is my life now.

We stood smiling silently, with Lucy's left hand tucked strategically into the crook of my right elbow to showcase the rock on her finger until the royal press secretary took charge, identifying which reporters could ask questions and in what order.

First question: "Tell us about the proposal."

Oh, boy. Such a simple question, but at the same time, it was a doozy. Lucy's right hand joined her left on my arm as she gushed, "Oh, it was lovely. We celebrated Christmas Eve quietly at home, and as we were cuddled up under a blanket watching the fire roar, he surprised me by proposing. It was so unexpected."

What a crock of shit, but the lies fell so easily off Lucy's tongue. I wasn't sure I had it in me to lie flat-out, even to a bunch of strangers. I got that she was saving face, but this was too much.

Second question: "The ring is gorgeous. Any special story behind it?"

This was one I could answer—truthfully—so I took the lead. "It belonged to my grandmother, the late Duchess of Ashbridge. She was very special to me, and a creative mind very much like Lucette, so it seemed only fitting to present her with this particular family heirloom."

Oh, yeah, I'd been briefed on how to address Lucy in front of this audience. It was formal to the teeth, apparently.

Lucy's gasp at my response was so quiet, I barely heard it myself. Glancing at her with my own falsely painted-on smile, I saw hers falter slightly. The way her thumb worried the back of the ring in question, I knew she was trying to determine if my words were lies like hers or the truth.

I may not have wanted this marriage, but I was all in now that we were past the point of no return. For better or worse, Lucy would be my wife, and it was in my best interests to try and make it work.

We lived to push each other's buttons but had at least one thing in common when all was said and done. Only time would tell if that dynamic ever made its way into our marital life—there was no denying the chemistry we shared. But if I were a betting man, I'd put those odds at a million to one.

Lucy would likely shut me out if she learned of my true self, not wanting me to taint the world she held dear.

Lost in my thoughts, I allowed Lucy to answer the following few questions, not paying much attention to her answers. She was polished and perfect, falling into her role with ease. She knew how to play the game, having been a participant since birth.

Suddenly, one question piqued my interest: "When's the big day?"

Lucy fidgeted, for once not having an answer, whether true or false.

Without thought, I blurted out, "October 7th."

Yeah, I knew I was playing with fire, but I'd be lying if I said there wasn't some tiny part of me that wished Lucy knew I was the man she called Tony at Desire.

The cameras continued to flash, and I saw Lucy's head turn in my peripheral vision, so I looked down to meet her stare. To the casual observer, with our smiles never slipping, it would appear like a tender gaze between lovers, but that was the furthest thing from the truth.

Bracing for the backlash of showing my hand, Lucy's brilliant blue eyes were wide, but there wasn't any hint of recognition in their depths. Another emotion clouded those eyes—guilt. Was it possible she felt remorseful about sneaking out to meet another man, not once but twice since our arrangement began? What she didn't know was that I didn't have a leg to stand on in that regard because that first time, I hadn't expected to run into her. I was just as bad, seeking comfort in the arms of a stranger, knowing there was a woman I was expected to marry. The semantics of a formal engagement didn't matter—we both knew what we'd done was wrong.

The royal press secretary thanked those in attendance before effectively ending this portion of the day. The press filed out, and I envied them for being allowed to leave. Answering questions and pretending to look the picture of the blissfully in love couple from a distance was child's play compared to getting close and personal with Lucy and creating that same image for a private photographer.

The moment the door latched behind the final straggler, Lucy dropped her hold on my arm, and the smile vanished from her face. My cheeks and jaw ached from holding my own smile for so long, and I rubbed a hand over the sore muscles, opening my mouth repeatedly in an attempt to ease the tightness, to no avail.

How did Lucy do this almost daily? Granted, her normally muted public smile was on steroids today, but still. I could see why she wanted to leave this part of her life behind—today unintentionally revealed another piece of what made Lucy tick. I suppose that was something, right?

We were ushered out of the throne room toward the gold drawing room. After seeing our announcement outfits, the photographer deemed the room a perfectly complementary color scheme.

Lucy, a fashion designer to the core, coordinated our look. She had plucked a navy suit from my closet that paired perfectly with her burgundy dress.

I had to give her credit. Not only did she have an eye for colors, but her personal fashion sense was spot on. The burgundy color looked amazing against her winter-pale skin, and long black locks—currently tamed into loose waves—hung down her back, offering a perfect contrast. It was fitted without being too tight to be immodest, with a scoop neck, a hem that stopped just below the knee, long sleeves that flared past her elbow, and an enticing, exposed gold zipper that went all the way from the nape of her neck to the hem.

It also hadn't escaped my notice that she was wearing a pair of those come-fuck-me heels, with the red soles flashing from the bottom of the black pumps.

She had no idea how much she was tempting me.

Clenching my fists to stop myself from doing something I'd regret later, I followed her into the room where our engagement portraits would be taken.

The gold drawing room was aptly named; the walls featured an intricate gold design laid over ivory, with rich navy upholstered furniture strategically placed throughout the room. The photographer was right—this was the perfect room to complement the colors we wore today.

A young woman dressed in all black, with a state-of-the-art camera hung around her neck, greeted us enthusiastically as we entered the room. "Hello, lovebirds! I'm Carolyn, and I'll be your photographer today. I have a few planned poses requested from the palace, but beyond that, we can have some fun, allowing the shoot to showcase your unique couple style."

Oh, I do not have the energy for this today.

Lucy was much more practiced at keeping the polite mask on her face and took the lead in discussing the intricacies of the photo shoot. Funny, she could fake it for strangers and even members of her own family, but there were no holds barred when it came to her interactions with me over the past two decades. Perhaps I would be honored that she dropped the act for me, that I alone was afforded a rare glimpse of her fiery personality—if she didn't hold me in such contempt.

"Preston, if you could join Lucy over here, we can begin with the traditional shots," Carolyn's voice called near the ornate golden fireplace that perfectly fit the theme of the room.

God, give me the strength.

Following orders like the good soldier I was, I reached Lucy's side, awaiting my next instruction. Carolyn fussed over us, maneuvering our bodies into position—a hand here, a chin angled just so—before finally stepping back and getting behind her camera.

"Relax your faces and give me a nice natural smile," Carolyn called out, ready to get to work.

Closing my eyes, I took a deep breath. Opening them, I threw on my most charming smile and prepared for what promised to be at least another hour of torture. A few rapid-fire flashes from the light umbrellas pointed at us, then we were moved into another position.

The first had been just as we were in the throne room, side by side, the ring showcased as Lucy's left hand held my elbow. The next was slightly more intimate, forcing Lucy and me to face each other, her left hand on my chest as my arms circled her back, keeping her close.

Lucy was stiff as a board in my arms, but with how I held her curves pressed against the hard planes of my own body, I was reminded of those stolen moments I enjoyed with her at Desire.

A genuine smile graced my lips as I looked down at her, and Carolyn's tone was near orgasmic as she enthusiastically praised, "Yes! Just like that!"

Her excited tone didn't help the situation one bit. It was all I could do not to imagine those words in Lucy's voice as I cradled her body close to mine.

Don't get hard. Don't get hard.

Forcing myself to think of anything and everything that I found unappealing, I managed to keep my composure and not embarrass myself in front of these women.

After a few more traditional poses, Carolyn encouraged us to act natural and forget she was in the room. If I was forced to do this, I would comply to get us out of here as quickly as humanly possible.

Catching Lucy off guard, I wrapped my arms around her waist from behind, pulling her backside flush with the front of my body, forcing her to grip my forearms to steady herself. Dipping my head, I placed it beside her ear before seductively whispering, "Tell me a secret, Princess."

Gasping, she turned her head to meet my eye. There was a fire in their blue depths, but the simple act of her turning her head as we stared at each other intensely would create the look of lovers lost in each other. Carolyn's gushing as she snapped away was evidence that it had worked.

On and on it went, as I continued to shock and surprise Lucy into genuine reactions that the photographer ate up before she finally declared that we were done, much to our mutual relief.

It didn't go unnoticed that our forced body contact had Lucy on edge. I'd dedicated my entire adult life to reading the signs of arousal in women, developing eyes like a hawk, not missing a single signal their bodies gave off. Most times, they didn't even know they were sending them.

Lucy's brain might not know I was the mystery man who sent her soaring into the realms of mind-numbing orgasmic bliss, but her body had some idea.

As we made our way back to our apartment and she disappeared into her bedroom, I smiled to myself, knowing she was likely grappling with the agonizing decision to be a good girl for me and deny herself relief, or to take matters into her own hands. I had a feeling I knew which option she would choose as I relieved the same aching need she was suffering from.

———⊰⊱———

We were mere days away from the annual New Year's Eve Ball turned engagement party. My anxiety was through the roof—my only outlet now off-limits—at the prospect of Lucy and me being the focal point for the country's most prominent members of society.

Last year, Liam and Amy's elopement had been the talk of the party, and I'd watched Amy struggle to find her place in our world, going through the motions, her personality hidden behind hollow eyes. Sure, she had come out of her shell since then, but I could vividly recall that evening, when everyone felt entitled to a moment of her time and she was powerless to deny them.

That's what I was up against, and it didn't matter that I knew a majority of the attendees most of my life. It felt like an invasion of my privacy for them to feel as though they could now demand a window into my private life because of who I was asked to marry—who I *would* marry.

I began spiraling, going down the rabbit hole, with thoughts of my potential children being offered up as public domain. The images of those happy children at Thanksgiving flashed through my mind. Would my children ever be granted the opportunity to be that carefree? Or would they be treated like animals in the zoo, behind glass for spectators to watch their every move?

What kind of life was that for a child? I wasn't sure I could handle it as an adult.

Thankfully, Liam texted, announcing that he and Amy had returned home just as I was on the verge of hyperventilation with the weight of it all. It was nearing midnight, but I needed to vent. Praying he wasn't too jet-lagged, I replied, asking if we could talk. I held my breath as those three dots indicating he was typing flashed across my phone screen. Finally, his response came through that I should meet him in his office.

This late at night, it was unlikely that anyone else was up and roaming the hallways, so I left the apartment clad in only my flannel pajama bottoms and a long-sleeved T-shirt. While it was slightly eerie traversing the dimmed palace corridors, it reminded me of the night I snuck out to meet Lucy at the club.

Damn, I couldn't stop thinking about it. Images of Lucy uninhibited and free were popping into my brain with alarming frequency.

Reaching Liam's office, I found him inside waiting for me, a glass of brown liquor in his hand.

Relieved at seeing a friendly face at last, I breathed out as I entered the room, "Please, tell me you have one of those for me."

Fixing me with a knowing look, Liam silently poured me a glass, and I took a sip, allowing the high-quality bourbon to burn as it traveled down my throat.

Not quite ready to talk about my troubles, I asked him, "How was the flight?"

Liam raised an eyebrow. "That's why you begged to meet in the middle of the night?"

I shrugged. "Humor me."

"Smooth skies, no complaints."

"That's good." I nodded.

"You're obviously dragging your feet, so I'll cut to the chase. Would you like to tell me why I had to find out about my sister's engagement from an online news article?"

I took another sip of bourbon. "Maybe I didn't want to hear you gloat about how you were right from day one."

Liam sighed. "You know I'd never do that. What happened?"

"Since I last saw you? Let's see. I acted like a damn fool, staking out Lucy's nightly activities only to find out she's designing and sewing—all by herself, I might add—not only Amy's wedding dress but those of all three bridesmaids. Then, she dragged me to the women's hospital and took me to the NICU to try and scare me off. As you can probably tell, we both refused to blink, and I provided her with the most unromantic proposal you've ever heard."

"Try me."

"What?" I didn't understand what he was asking.

"I meant what I said. Try me. I bet I've heard a worse proposal story."

Rolling my eyes, I wanted to drown in my glass of bourbon. "I get what you're doing. You're trying to make me feel better, but it won't work."

"I won't ask again. I'd rather hear it from you instead of whatever twisted version finds me after Lucy tells Amy."

"Fine," I huffed. "I just handed her the ring still enclosed in its velvet box before she locked herself in her room and cried herself to sleep."

"That's bad, but I think I can do you one better with mine."

I scoffed. "Very funny. You love your wife."

"I do." He nodded. "That doesn't mean my proposal was worth a damn."

"Look, Liam. I don't need to hear some story about how you were so nervous you dropped the ring or some shit. I'm not in the mood."

"Maybe it's time that you to shut up and listen for once. You don't own the market on crappy proposals. Mine ended with me crushing a wine glass with my bare hand."

I blinked at Liam. "I'm sorry. I think the bourbon hit me faster than I thought. I thought I heard you say you crushed a wine glass with your bare hand at the end of your proposal to Amy. That can't be right."

Shrugging, he replied, "That's exactly what I said. Amy and I weren't always the lovebirds we are now."

"I find that hard to believe." I couldn't keep the sarcasm from my tone.

"Well, believe it. I asked Amy to marry me because she needed a husband, and I needed a wife. Hell, we even signed a contract."

"You're fucking with me."

"No, it's true. Remember how Jaxon said something about me holding out on Amy? We agreed on no sex, and yet, somehow, lines were crossed, and she fucking lured me into her trap. I tried to stay away from her, which was easier said than done while living in the same house, but it was no use. She kept coming for me until I gave in, and before I knew it, I was falling for my own wife." He chuckled for a moment, musing, "Damn, she was wily."

That was the last thing I needed to hear right now. I was already confused as hell, trying to figure out which parts of Lucy were genuine and which were fake. I didn't need to learn of Amy and Liam's unlikely love story, believing that maybe Lucy and I could work past our issues and develop a partnership. I wasn't foolish enough to believe that we might ever find love, but I held out hope that we could eventually find our way to a place where we didn't despise each other.

Trying to shake the idea of declaring a truce with Lucy, I mocked, "Boo-hoo. Poor Liam had the hot redhead begging him for sex. Some of us have real problems here, man."

Liam's blue eyes grew hard, and his jaw clenched, voice deadly as he warned, "Careful what you say about my wife."

Admitting I overstepped in my frustration, I apologized. "Sorry, you're right. So, tell me. Where does the broken wine glass come into play?"

Liam's voice was edged with steel. "She told me something about her past that was deeply upsetting."

Now, *that* did sound like the Liam I knew. "You always were a caveman." I chuckled.

"You don't fuck with the people I love and live to tell the tale," Liam uttered darkly.

Putting my hands up in mock surrender, I was sincere. "Noted. We might not get along, but I have no intention of hurting Lucy. I can promise you that."

Softening, he grabbed my crystal tumbler for a refill, and I let him. "You're really going to go through with this?"

Sighing, I declared, "I don't really have a choice anymore. The engagement is official. If something happens between now and the wedding day, it won't be because *I* called it off."

"If you want my opinion?" He paused, handing me the refilled tumbler, and I nodded for him to continue. "Put aside your pride and everything you think you know about my baby sister, and get to know the funny, caring person she is underneath your perception of her."

Liam's advice struck a chord with me. The past few months had shown me I didn't know Lucy as well as I once thought. The dressmaking alone would be enough proof that she cared deeply about those closest to her. But throw in hearing stories from the nurse in the NICU about how she used to come to visit her nephew daily while he was a patient of the unit, and the evidence was mounting that she was not as she appeared. Even this past week, I had a front-row seat to her turning it on and off, portraying different versions of herself to different audiences.

Then, there was the Lucy I saw underground at Desire. You couldn't fake the perfect submission she exhibited down there. Maybe I was just as wrong about her as she had been about me all these years. We saw what we wanted to see instead of what was actually there.

The bourbon warmed me from the inside out. I grew confident that after a good night's rest, I could try to start fresh with Lucy in the morning. She might not be ready to pivot on a dime when it came to our relationship, but we had all the time in the world. Eventually, I'd make her see that I was ready to turn over a new leaf.

Bidding Liam goodnight, I walked back to our apartment. Locking the door behind me upon entry, I trudged up the stairs, my body feeling weighed down after the two glasses of liquor. Reaching the top, a sliver of light fell across the hallway, and I noticed the door to Lucy's home workspace cracked open.

Sighing, I knew the endless engagement press was stealing precious time away from her design work. Deciding in a split second that I didn't need to wait until morning to show her I supported her, I padded silently to the door, pushing it open slowly, not wanting to startle her.

Expecting to find her in the midst of one of the many tasks I'd watched in the creative process during our time in her Milan studio, I stopped dead when I saw what she was working on.

Gone were the mannequins donning bridal attire, and in their place were new ones, dressed in various types of lingerie. Lucy knelt before one with her back to me, dressed only in another silk shorts set—the kind featured in every adolescent boy's fantasy of pillow fights—making minor adjustments. There hadn't been a single hint in Milan that intimate apparel was a part of the Lucy Remington brand, so I was caught completely off guard.

Then, the irony hit me that she was designing lingerie when I told her to destroy all her panties. In my loosened state, I couldn't stop the chuckle slipping past my lips at the thought.

Lucy's gasp reached my ears—a clear sign that my presence had been discovered—and I watched her black hair whip around, nearly smacking her in the face as she turned to face me. Those blue eyes were bigger than I'd ever seen as she stared at me with a mix of fear and anger.

What was she scared of?

I almost couldn't breathe past the thought of her being frightened of me. That was the last thing I'd ever want.

The silence stretched on for what seemed like hours, and when it became evident Lucy wouldn't be the first to speak, I took the lead. She might not realize it, but there were subtle hints of her submission even in this moment, and I intended to use that to my advantage.

Commanding, I asked, "What's going on here?" Lucy's eyes darted around the room, and I knew, right then and there, she was trying to think up a lie, so I added firmly, "I want the truth."

Dropping her eyes, her voice was barely above a whisper. "Working."

"These are your designs?" I gestured to the five mannequins scantily clad around the room.

Biting her lip, she nodded, saying nothing more. Venturing further into the space, I walked from mannequin to mannequin, surveying her work. Each piece was beautifully made and designed. I would expect nothing less from Lucy at this point.

Color rushed to her cheeks, but her eyes stayed fixed on the floor as she fidgeted with her hands. "Yes."

Maybe it was the liquor heating my blood and making me bold, or perhaps my secret carnal knowledge of the woman before me, but I couldn't stop myself from tilting her chin up with my fingers.

"Beautiful," I declared.

One single word, but it held so much meaning at this moment.

Thinking my declaration was aimed at her designs, not realizing I meant it for her, she whispered in explanation, "No one knows."

It was borderline terrifying how well this woman I was set to marry kept secrets. Lucy was leading a double life in multiple arenas. What else didn't I know about her?

Daring to push my luck, my thumb moved from her chin to tug at the plush lower lip she held between her teeth, pulling it free. "Naughty, naughty girl."

The reaction to those words was a shiver so visible that I had to hold back a groan from the memory of the last time I had my hands on her. Playing with fire, I lowered my hands to her hips and gently turned her body to face the scantily clad mannequins, standing behind her. Pulling her long black hair over one shoulder, I exposed the column of her neck before placing my mouth next to her ear, whispering, "You are so talented."

With that simple praise, I felt the tension leave her body. I began moving my thumbs where they still rested on her hips, drawing light circles over the silk of her shorts, further propelled in my actions by how her breathing changed, now coming in short staccato bursts.

Boldly, I tugged her earlobe between my teeth, and the resulting gasp was music to my ears. Releasing my new chew toy, I decided to paint her a little picture, the words rolling off my tongue as thick as honey a breath away from her ear. "I can picture you in the black teddy, the lace caressing your soft alabaster skin. The deep V-neck accenting your perky little breasts as they heave, ready and waiting for my attention." I allowed myself to groan at the mental image I created. "Hmm. I can see you shifting your thighs, using the friction of the thin scrap of lace between them to ease the ache—an ache you know only I can ease. Can you picture it, baby?"

Lucy's head dropped against my chest, and she moaned out, "Yes."

Damn, I was rock-hard, and primal instinct had me pulling her hips back so she could feel how badly I wanted her. That's when I knew Lucy was fully in a trance from my words because she engaged in our little dance, grinding her ass against my erection.

I decided to continue. "As stunning as you look draped in black lace, I wouldn't be able to take another second of it concealing your perfect body from my gaze. Slowly—fuck, it would be *so* slowly—I'd unwrap your body like it was a gift on Christmas morning. A gift for my eyes only." A shuddered breath worked its way up her chest as I placed a feather-light kiss to the side of her exposed neck. "Once fully revealed, I would take my time, worshiping each incredible inch until you were writhing beneath me, desperately begging me to put you out of your misery."

"Please," Lucy whispered.

"Not so fast, sweetheart," I chided softly. "You'd be begging for my cock to fill you, stretch you, and take you to the stars as you know only I can, but first, I would need to slake my thirst between your creamy white thighs. God, you taste fucking incredible, just the perfect hint of sweetness. I could live there, feasting on your pussy for the rest of my life."

Lucy was full-on panting now, her hips shifting restlessly, and I bet if I dipped a hand beneath the tiny scrap of silk between her legs, she'd be soaking wet. Emboldened by the buzz in my veins, I let one of my hands drop to the hem of her shorts, teasing the heated skin with my fingertips. Slowly, I began to venture beneath the hem, wondering if she was a good girl, and obeyed my order not to wear panties, when she placed one of her tiny hands atop mine.

"I can't," she forced out breathlessly.

There was always some part of my brain that knew Lucy would come to her senses eventually, but that didn't stop the disappointment and frustration from coursing through me at her words.

Sighing, I dropped my forehead to her shoulder, asking, "Can't or won't?" Each answer held a different meaning.

Lucy paused, thinking over how to answer. Finally, with regret in her voice, she replied, "Both?"

Holding true to my firm belief in consent, I took a step backward, creating space between us. I could pinpoint the exact moment Lucy's brain cleared enough for reality to crash down on her, revealing how intimate we'd been. Her body language gave her away as she tensed, and she threw a hand over her mouth before turning and fleeing the room.

She might have regrets about what we shared and how turned on my words made her, but it was a moment of clarity for me. If it weren't for my persona at Desire still having a hold on her, she might have been open to working on our relationship, beyond the show we put on for the public. I was the one standing in our way when it came to moving forward.

I couldn't live with this secret any longer. I needed to come clean to Lucy.

CHAPTER 19

Lucy

I WAS LIVING IN a constant state of denial.

Denial that Preston discovered the secret of Arabella Reign.

Denial that I allowed him to put his hands on me as he whispered dirty words in my ear, explaining in vivid detail everything he wanted to do to my body.

Denial that those words turned me on beyond belief, and I was a breath away from sleeping with him.

Denial that I was still thinking about it two days later.

Panicked and confused out of my mind, I ran from him that night. I still couldn't understand how I ended up putty in his hands, or even why he would think about me the way his words described.

We hated each other and always had. Right?

The more cynical part of my brain tried to convince me that it was just another trick, to see how far he could push me and then use it against me later. But there was no denying he was just as turned on as I was—I had shamelessly ground my ass against the proof.

Then, there was the fact that my body still felt like Tony owned it. It's why I stopped Preston when I had. His fingers were dangerously close to discovering I was bare beneath my pajama shorts, which, combined with the fact that I was teetering on the edge of an orgasm with his words alone, was enough to remind me that there was another man in my life. Even though I wasn't sure our two encounters constituted much of a relationship, I was suddenly very aware of how inappropriate our liaisons had been given my current circumstances.

I was an engaged woman now, as evidenced by the large emerald-cut solitaire diamond gracing my finger. I couldn't run to Desire whenever I needed an escape from my everyday life. I knew that. And that was why tonight, after our engagement party, I was headed there to break things off with Tony—if there was anything really there to break off.

At least to me, it felt like there was.

It was the right thing to do, and if anything, I'd gain the closure I needed to move on with my life—a life that apparently would be spent with Preston. If the other night was any indication, maybe it wouldn't be all bad. There was some chemistry there, even if we couldn't stand each other most of the time.

We were the guests of honor tonight, and I absolutely loathed knowing we would be the center of attention. It's why I agreed to this ludicrous proposal in the first place, to get far away from events such as this, where I was trussed up like a show pony and paraded around. I deserved the opportunity to live freely, something so many others took for granted.

From the outside looking in, my life appeared charmed. It was anything but.

Preston was waiting for me in the living room of our apartment—yes, I could finally admit it belonged to us both—with his back to me, looking out the window into the night sky. Wanting nothing more than to get this night over with, I cleared my throat, announcing my presence. Preston turned, the picture of a perfect gentleman in his White Tie evening apparel. Undoubtedly, I'd seen him dressed this way dozens of times over the years, but this was the first time I saw him for what he truly was—a handsome man.

His golden-green eyes raked over my body leisurely, scanning from the top of my head to the tips of my toes. Usually, I was confident in my appearance but found myself suddenly self-conscious, wondering what he saw when he looked at me.

Stalking toward where I stood, he reached for my white-gloved hand, bringing it to his lips before placing a kiss across my knuckles. Meeting my eyes, he quirked a small smile. "You look stunning, Lucy."

My chest tightened, and I blushed, unable to hold his gaze. "Thank you."

Releasing my hand, he tipped my chin up like he had that night in my workspace, and I felt my body reacting similarly. "I mean it. You're a vision in that dress. A goddess."

How had I never noticed his way with words? Granted, usually, his words were aimed at riling me up to the point of blinding rage, but I was quickly learning that there was more to Preston than my skewed perception allowed me to see.

My mother insisted I look "bridal" for the party this evening, so I scrambled to find a gown in white for the event. On such short notice, my options were limited, and I was forced to settle for a one-shoulder, floor-length gown with a silver trimmed band across the waist. It wasn't what I would have designed for myself, and I would have loved to alter it by adding some personal touches, but there simply wasn't time.

No matter my own feelings on what I was wearing, the look on Preston's face made me feel like a million bucks. I was reminded of my personal mission when creating gowns—and lingerie—for others. The clothing didn't make the woman; the woman made the clothing. I'd never experienced it myself until this moment.

Preston offered me his arm, and I took it, offering him a small smile. My palm tingled, even though several layers of clothing separated us. We would need to lean on each other tonight, and then it was time for me to take the necessary steps to commit to him fully.

It seemed only fitting to go into the new year with a clean slate.

***

I stayed at the party long enough to watch the fireworks from the balcony, celebrating the start of a new year, before I claimed to be tired and retreated to the apartment.

Preston was a perfect gentleman all evening, barely leaving my side as we accepted the well-wishes of what felt like the entire population of Belleston. He offered to escort me to our rooms, but I declined, imploring him to stay and socialize. There was a moment's hesitation, where he looked like he would force the issue, but eventually, he let me go.

Thank goodness, because I needed to sneak out before he retired for the night.

Tonight, I was ending things with Tony and planned on canceling my membership at Desire before I left. It was time to close that chapter of my life as I embarked on a new one.

I dressed slightly more conservatively than I normally would when headed to the club, opting for a long-sleeved black dress that hit mid-thigh, but

I couldn't bring myself to don underwear, even though I had no plans to engage in any kind of sexual activity. Maybe after I made a clean break, it would release this hold he had on me even when he wasn't around.

Pulling every pin from my elaborate updo, I let the remaining curls cascade down my back. Grabbing a faux fur shawl, I wrapped it around my upper body to ward off the winter chill I would encounter in the tunnels, before slipping on a pair of black flats.

Carefully, I opened my bedroom door just a crack, straining my ears for any sounds that might signal Preston's return to the suite while my eyes scanned the area. The coast appeared to be clear, but there was still a chance I could run into him at any point in my journey to the tunnel entrance. He would demand an explanation I was unable to give.

Crossing my fingers, I ventured forth. Clearing the apartment, I hurried down the hallway, further into the residence wing, stopping at the tapestry hung on the wall concealing one of the many entrances to the tunnels. Looking left and right to ensure there weren't any witnesses to my escape, I slid behind the tapestry and unlatched the door.

The further I traveled toward the city, the colder the air in the tunnels became. Winter in the Alps was no joke, and halfway to my destination, the temperature became so frigid that the exposed skin of my calves stung before they descended into numbness.

Great, I was so focused on the task at hand that I was risking frostbite. I could read the headlines now: *Princess Lucy Loses her Legs Sneaking Out in the Middle of the Night Headed to Unknown Destination.*

Doubling my pace to reach the exit faster, I was still mindful of where I placed my feet on the worn stone steps. A broken leg would be even worse than potential frostbite. Cell service this far below ground was non-existent, and no one would think to look for me in the tunnels when they discovered I was missing. Losing the ability to walk and being unable to call for help was a veritable death sentence.

Was this chance at closure worth it? I wasn't so sure anymore.

I heaved a sigh of relief when I finally reached the exit into that familiar alleyway in Remhorn, taking a moment to slip on my mask before venturing through the door. Stomping my feet, trying to bring some feeling back into my legs, I hustled to the bolted door of Desire, the password rushing desperately past my lips, just so that I could feel warm again.

Handing over my cell phone at the hostess stand, I elected to keep my shawl when they offered to check it for me. I fully intended to wrap it around my bare legs once I reached Room 203. Thankfully, there was a pins-and-needles feeling to them now as they came back to life, but I didn't relish the thought of my return trip through the tunnels.

Since I wasn't the member paying for the private room we used, a club employee escorted me, punching in the code and granting me entry. I was silently grateful when I found it empty; I needed a moment to gather my thoughts. This wasn't the first time I ended a relationship with a Dom, and it was always amicable, but something about this time felt different. Tony felt different.

Taking a seat on the plush bench situated at the foot of the bed, I covered my legs, rubbing over the faux fur to bring circulation back to my weather-abused extremities.

I can do this.

My plan was to be honest, telling him about my change in circumstances. I knew communication and trust were the cornerstones of this world, and he would accept that we couldn't see each other anymore.

Maybe I was being presumptuous in thinking that he even wanted to continue what we had. Hadn't he questioned the last time I asked for a meeting? It was entirely possible I was blowing this way out of proportion, but I couldn't deny how I felt when we were together. Didn't he feel that too?

Finally, regaining full feeling back in my legs, I removed my shawl, placing it carefully on the bed behind me, just as I heard the digital unlocking of the door before me. Taking a deep breath, I steeled my nerves watching the door open, revealing the man whose mere presence had tingles running across my skin with the memory of how well he commanded my body.

There was no hiding the surprise in his eyes when he found me seated. I couldn't blame him after how he'd found me the last time. He was expecting the submissive he knew as Ari, ready and willing. My heart broke knowing that girl would be packed up and shoved into a box in the back of my mind, never to see the light of day—or night—again.

"Ari?" Tony asked, uncertain.

I patted the quilted fabric of the bench beside me and gave him a small smile. "We need to talk."

Nodding, he strode to where I sat, dropping onto the bench beside me. There wasn't much room, and I couldn't prevent our thighs from touching. The brush of his suit pants against my bare thigh muddied my thoughts momentarily, but I regained my composure, determined to follow through with my plan.

Tony's clasped hands rested in his lap as he waited for me to open the conversation.

Taking a deep breath, I began, "I'm getting married."

Expecting some kind of reaction, I was disappointed when Tony gave none, stating without emotion, "I see."

Guilt gnawed at my conscience, and I felt the need to explain myself, even though he hadn't asked me to. "The engagement only happened this past week. I wasn't sure it was ever going to happen." Sighing, I huffed out, "It's complicated."

Nodding, his demeanor gave me no sign of how he felt about my news. "Relationships usually are."

Frustrated, I rushed out, "I don't even know if I can call it that."

"Care to explain?"

"Without getting into too many details, he's not the person I would have chosen for myself."

"Do you have feelings for him?"

Did I have feelings for Preston? I wasn't sure. I was learning there was more to him than I previously thought, and maybe if I could get past my own ego, we could fall into some form of comfortable companionship.

Holding to my vow of honesty, I replied, "Maybe? I don't know. He's different than I thought he was, and I haven't exactly made it easy on him. If he can put up with me at my worst, I feel like I owe it to him to give what we have a try."

"That's fair. Not all great love stories burn hot and bright right from the start."

Love? That was a stretch.

Protesting slightly, I countered, "I don't know that I'd go quite that far."

Taking my hand in his, he looked me right in the eye. "Promise me you won't close yourself off to the possibility. You deserve to find happiness."

Who was this guy? I was sitting here telling him our purely sexual relationship was over, and he was telling me to open my heart to love.

Squeezing his hand, I replied, "I promise."

A corner of his lips turned up, and he squeezed my hand back. "You were honest with me, so I think it's only fair that I do you that same courtesy."

"What do you mean?" I was confused.

Was he about to tell me that he, too, was in a committed relationship? My stomach turned, thinking perhaps he had a family, and I was the other woman. Before I could conjure up more possibilities, he released my hand, reached up to his face, and began to remove his mask.

Panic gripped me, and I blurted out, "No! Don't!"

Ignoring my protests, the mask left his face, and my panic turned to shock. It was like I was having an out-of-body experience; I could see myself jumping off the bench and staring at the man before me—a man who had a striking resemblance to Preston.

But that didn't make any sense. Maybe my mind was playing tricks on me; any tall man with a dark beard and hazel eyes would look like him.

"Lucy," he pleaded.

The use of my real name snapped me out of my stupor, and my shock switched to a rage so deep that I couldn't see straight. "Are you fucking kidding me?" I screamed at him.

"Let me explain. Please."

"Explain," I scoffed. My heart was beating so fast that I feared I might pass out. "How long have you known it was me?" His eyes lowered to the ground, and I had my answer. "Did you follow me here? Was this your plan all along? To blackmail me with exposure?"

Standing, he reached for me but dropped his hand when I visibly flinched. "No. It was a coincidence, I swear. I didn't even know you were a member until that first night."

I thought back to the night of our first encounter. "You initiated contact, sending me a drink that night. You knew it was me even then? How?"

Sighing, he ran a hand through his dark, messy hair. "I can't explain it. I've always been able to sense when you are near. I thought my mind was playing tricks on me, but then I saw you across the room, those blue eyes shining like a beacon, and I knew beyond a shadow of a doubt that you were the one behind that silver mask in the nearly see-through dress."

"I'm such an idiot," I breathed out. "You knew this whole time. Was it a joke to you? Were you laughing behind my back as we fucking lived together these past two months, knowing what we'd done down here?"

"Of course not. The first time, I didn't even know you'd accepted your grandfather's proposal. I found out the next morning."

Laughing bitterly, it finally made sense. "You saw me down here, and you couldn't resist the temptation to have me under your command, obeying your every order. Is that it?"

"It wasn't like that, please Lu—"

I cut him off, not done with my tirade. "How long were you going to let this continue?"

Preston's body sagged, and he dropped back onto the padded bench. "I was going to tell you tonight."

"Before or after you fucked me?" I shot back.

Those hazel eyes snapped to mine so fast, and it was satisfying to see I'd finally struck a nerve. I could handle a pissed-off Preston better than the version fumbling over a half-assed apology.

Clenching his fists next to his thighs where he sat, he finally engaged in the argument. "Are we going to sit here and pretend that you weren't the one to initiate contact beyond our initial meeting?"

I saw red, charging at him, stopping just short of where he sat, putting my finger in his face. "Oh, no. You're not going to turn this around on me. Don't. You. Dare."

Preston unclenched his fists and took a deep breath. "You're right."

"Say that again." I wanted to savor watching him eat crow.

"You got it once, Lucy. Don't push it. I know what I did was wrong. I came down here tonight with the intention of coming clean. Why would I have voluntarily removed my mask if that wasn't the case? And for clarification, I had no plans to have sex with you tonight, but are you really going to say that what we've shared in this room wasn't special? I know you felt it too."

Fuck him. Fuck him for playing these games and messing with my head. "It doesn't matter what I felt. It was built on a lie. Your lie."

"I'm sorry."

"Sorry isn't going to cut it. You broke my trust in the worst possible way. The second you realized who I was down here, you should have walked the other way, not engaged in play with me. You crossed a major line."

"I know." At least he had the good sense to look ashamed for what he'd done. "And I promise I will spend the rest of my life making it up to you."

Those words hit me like a slap to the face. "I'm sorry. Are you on crack right now? In what universe do you think I'm going to marry you after what you just pulled? No fucking way."

Standing, he wrapped his arms around me, and I fought against him like my life was on the line, but they held me like twin steel bands, unyielding. I used every ounce of energy I possessed to try and free myself, but it was no use, and eventually, the dam broke, allowing tears to stream down my face as my body went limp.

Preston's voice was soft in my ear. "Lucy, I've seen how much your career means to you. Breaking off our engagement would only see all your hard work go down the drain. As much as you'd love to see me walk away, there's something here between us, and I'm willing to find out exactly what that is."

"I hate you," I whimpered into his chest, defeated, giving up the fight.

"I hate me, too," he replied. Realizing I was no longer a flight risk, he lifted a hand to smooth the hair away from my damp cheeks. "Let me take you home. It's been a long day, and we can talk more in the morning."

Twisting my lips in thought, I debated declining out of spite, but damn if the offer to avoid a second trek through the freezing cold tunnels didn't sound good.

Tilting my chin up, he asked, "How did you get here anyway? I have a hell of a time making it past security myself." My body tensed, and he felt my reluctance to give up more of my private life. "Lucy, I already hold two of your secrets locked firmly within the vault. What's one more?" There wasn't a hint of mockery in his tone. He was being sincere, but he'd already effectively destroyed any scrap of trust we ever had.

Shaking my head, I declined to divulge my secret path to the club. It wasn't my secret to tell. Until he was an official member of our family, sharing that information would be deemed a security risk.

"Take me home," I whispered, too tired to talk any more.

My mind was numb as he led me from the club and into a car he had parked down the street. I was non-responsive as he tried to speak to me on the drive up the mountainside, and I refused to answer the questions the security team had for us at the gate about where we had been and why I was without Myles. I knew I would catch hell from my parents, but I didn't care.

The fact that I was about to marry a man I hated with every fiber of my being—who was also the man who pushed my body to the highest peaks of pleasure I had ever known—took up every available brain cell I possessed. I didn't have the capacity to think beyond that crushing reality.

The news that Tony was Preston changed everything.

The talk Preston wanted to have the morning following his shocking revelation hadn't happened. Six days later, I was still holed up in my room. I didn't want to talk to him. I didn't want to even look at him.

Beyond my blinding rage at his deception, I was mad at myself. He was able to see right through the protection aimed at creating anonymity at the club, so why hadn't I? Instead, I was utterly ignorant, allowing a man I hated—a man I would never trust with that kind of power in a million years—to work his way into my brain. So much so, that I hadn't gotten off once since that fateful night in October unless it was by his hand, and I no longer owned a single pair of panties.

His revelation added another layer to the confusion swirling around me before learning he was my mystery man at the club. Now, every interaction we had, every word he said, could be brought into question. He had cast a permanent shadow of doubt over the future of our relationship.

Relationship. That was rich.

I went to Desire because I felt I owed Preston a chance—a chance to see if we could work out our differences and find our way to a peaceful coexistence.

I was such an idiot.

Preston knew the whole fucking time.

He knew when he came out wearing nothing but a towel. Mulling that over now, he probably would have called my bluff and shown me the goods.

He knew when he told the press pack that our wedding date would be October 7th, the same night as our first encounter. God, how had I missed that clue?

He knew when we had that moment in my workspace, where I turned to putty in his hands as his words painted a picture so vivid that I found myself craving every intimate act he described.

Worst of all, he knew that I ran to him for comfort unknowingly, when he was the one pushing me past my limits. That pissed me off the most. He must have gotten a real kick out of that.

I hated him. I hated myself for letting him fool me. And yet, Preston still expected us to be able to work this out and get married. He was out of his damn mind. There was no coming back from this. If it meant giving up my dream, so be it. He'd already stolen what little dignity I had left. He might as well strip me all the way down until I had nothing.

I'd lost an entire week of work on the dresses for the bridal party in Amy and Liam's wedding, but the rest of my fashion empire couldn't be put off. My self-imposed solitary confinement was spent orchestrating both my fashion labels from my bed. I could still sketch and scan designs with my tablet, sending them to my respective teams, keeping momentum heading into the spring fashion shows. It was bittersweet knowing that after I ended this sham of an engagement, I could lose it all in an instant.

Tears sprang to my eyes at the thought, and that's when I heard a soft knock at my door. Amy tried several times to get me to open up this past week, not knowing why I locked myself in. I had turned off my phone as well. I was so ashamed, and even though I trusted Amy with my life—including my Arabella Reign secret—I would take what happened underground this New Year's Eve to my grave.

Wiping the tears from my cheeks, I sighed. "Amy, I don't want to talk about it. I just need some space. Please." I was practically begging, my voice weary.

The knock sounded again, but the voice on the other side wasn't Amy's. Preston's rich timbre filtered through the oak of my bedroom door. "Lucy, we need to talk about this."

Narrowing my eyes, willing myself the superpower of shooting laser beams through them so I could burn a hole right through the heavy wood and into his brain, I forced out through gritted teeth, "There's nothing to talk about."

There was a heavy thump on the door once, then twice. Was that his head beating against it? "You can't hide in there forever. Adults talk through their problems. Please."

Wanting nothing more than to push him over the edge as he had done to me, I looked around the room, searching for something, anything I could use to my advantage. My eyes landed on my bedside table, and inspiration struck. I had an idea to show Preston he no longer held control over me, and then he could stew on that.

The table's top drawer held many tools and implements I used to pleasure myself when the need arose. Scanning the contents, I decided to go with a classic. There was nothing more reliable in the realm of female self-care than the standard wand with a vibrating head. I lovingly called mine Wanda—do you get it? Wanda never let me down, and tonight, she'd help me get a little payback on the man who blew up my life.

Snuggling under the covers of my bed, I was conveniently already dressed for bed in a silk nightgown—one benefit of becoming a hermit for a week was that I was always in my pajamas. And thanks to dear old Preston on the other side of the door, I was completely bare underneath. Perfect for what I had planned.

Hitting the power button, I brought the bulbous vibrating head between my thighs, a soft moan escaping my lips as the vibrations teased my clit, reminding me just how much I missed this. But keeping quiet wasn't going to accomplish my goal. I needed to put on a vocal performance worthy of an award to push Preston past the breaking point.

My hips began to rock as the sensations teased my sensitive flesh. The next moan I let out was lewd and loud.

That seemingly did the trick as I heard Preston's voice through the door in response. "Lucy . . ." There was an edge of warning in his tone that I decided to ignore.

Committing fully, I turned the vibrations up a notch and started making sounds like a porn star. There would be no doubt about what I was doing in here.

"Oh God." I moaned. "Yes!" I screamed as my orgasm crested, proving more to myself than to him that he no longer held power over me.

Panting, starting to come down from the intensity of my manufactured release, I had barely opened my eyes when what sounded like an explosion startled me enough to sit up and search frantically for the source.

Light flooded the room, and as blood rushed back to my brain, I was able to focus enough to recognize Preston's form, his chest heaving, standing in my now open doorway.

He'd broken down the damn door!

CHAPTER 20

Preston

I LET LUCY STEW for a few days. I knew what I did was wrong, and she needed time to sort it out and calm down. That was fine. What wasn't fine was that after almost an entire week, she still hadn't left her room once. This had crossed the line into juvenile behavior. Lucy was hiding from her problems instead of facing them head-on.

She was pissed, that much I understood, but how long did she really expect to camp out in her bedroom? I knew for a fact she canceled all her public engagements indefinitely. Amy came to me asking what was wrong, and when she told me that Lucy had shut her out as well, I didn't know what to say to her. It wasn't my place to tell her the truth, not that I wanted to—it was too personal. Liam would have my ass if he knew what I'd done.

Lucy was right. I should have looked the other way when I saw her that first night at Desire. That was the mature thing to do, but I couldn't stay away. And I wasn't sorry in the least for discovering how incredible she was when she was fully submissive. But I was sorry that I hurt her. I couldn't erase the image from my brain of how she broke before my eyes, then went nearly catatonic on our drive home. I did that to her, and I wasn't sure I could ever forgive myself.

I gave Lucy her space until it became apparent she intended to act like a child, and I finally allowed myself to knock on her door. When she assumed it was Amy, I should have left her alone. The sound of her voice, so small and defeated, was enough to indicate she wasn't ready, but I pushed anyway. Beating my head against the door was less painful than the silence engulfing us for the past six days.

Now, here I stood, after breaking down her bedroom door, angry as hell and more than a little turned on.

When I first heard the whisper-soft moan through the wood separating us, I convinced myself I was hearing things. It hadn't made any sense. Then she turned it up a notch, and I knew exactly what she was doing. Lucy was trying to show that she was in charge.

I held myself in check for as long as humanly possible, rationalizing that she was faking it. Truth be told, she could have herself a promising career narrating dirty books. The straw that broke the camel's back was when I heard her climax. I'd witnessed that breathtaking sight in person, and the screams coming from the other side of the door were real. If I strained my ears just enough, I could hear the unmistakable buzzing of a vibrator.

The next thing I knew, I was rearing back my leg and kicking right above the doorknob, splintering the wood as the door burst open. Lucy sat up in shock, taking a moment to register what she was looking at. There was no mistaking the moment when awareness dawned as she pulled the covers up to her chest—not before I caught sight of another silky creation barely concealing her erect nipples—and anger clouded her features.

"What the hell, Preston?" she screamed. "Good luck explaining your rage issues to the palace staff before they report you to my family for shattering my door and have you escorted out for good."

Oh, so that's how she wants to play it? Fine.

Striding forward, I reached the foot of her bed as she clung tighter to her covers. It didn't help that I could still hear the muffled vibrations coming from beneath them as well.

I leaned over menacingly, placing my hands on the bed. "Don't worry, baby. I'll just be forced to explain how dear, sweet Princess Lucy likes it rough. And I wouldn't be lying, would I, sweetheart?"

Her gasp reached my ears as I held eye contact, but she didn't back down. "It would be your word against mine."

"You're right, but your family is no stranger to your feisty personality. Who do you think they're going to believe?"

Lucy knew I had her, but she still had that fire in her eyes as she spat, "Fuck you."

Careful what you wish for, Princess.

She purposely pushed past the limits I set for her, and now she would have to deal with the consequences.

Standing up straight, I walked around the side of her bed, stalking slowly toward where she sat. I kept my tone calm and level, but there was no mistaking that I'd transitioned from Preston to her Dom—that happened the moment I broke down the door. She had no one to blame for that but herself. "Admit it. You're just pissed that I know how to play your body better than any other man who has come before me. Or maybe you're pissed that it was me all along, and you want to hate me. Well, hear me now, Princess. You can hate me all you want, but you and I both know your body fucking belongs to me. If I want to eat nothing but your pussy every day for breakfast, lunch, and dinner, I will. Do you understand me?"

Those big blue eyes stared up at me unblinking, digesting my words, but there was no mistaking the lust shining through them as her pupils dilated. That, combined with how her breathing changed, I knew she wanted—no, she *needed*—our dynamic to continue, even if she was pissed about how it had developed.

Only the sounds of our breathing filled the room, so I prompted, "I won't ask again."

Lucy's face was expressive as she ran over each of my words carefully, trying to determine the question before she answered. Finally, she breathed out, "Yes, Sir."

Fuck me sideways. That was all I needed to hear. She was ready to play, but unfortunately for her, she'd been a brat, and that needed to be addressed.

Pulling the heavy down comforter off the bed, I revealed the rest of Lucy's body, clad in a navy-blue one-piece nightie instead of a shorts set as I had initially suspected, and the still buzzing proof of her act of defiance.

Grasping the handle of the vibrating wand, I held it up for inspection before asking, "Well, what have we here?"

Lucy didn't cower under my harsh gaze, answering, "Wanda."

"Wanda." I chuckled. "Clever. And what were you and Wanda up to in here?"

Her dark eyelashes fanned her cheeks as she lowered her eyes, knowing she was in trouble. "Getting off, Sir."

I tsked. "Naughty girl. You were given very few rules, yet you saw fit to break one. What do you have to say for yourself?"

Flashing those brilliant baby blues at me, I could see it in her eyes—she knew a punishment was imminent. She wasn't wrong. "I'm sorry, Sir."

Shaking my head, I gripped the vibrating wand tighter, allowing the shockwaves to move up my forearm. Glancing at it, I noted that the setting was only at the second highest of four. Damn, this thing could really pack a punch. Perfect for what I had in mind.

If Lucy wanted to be a little brat and come without permission, fine. The punishment would fit the crime. I smiled to myself. Forced orgasm was hands down my favorite form of punishment for a submissive. By the end of the evening, Lucy would be begging me to stop the overwhelming pleasure I pulled from her body over and over again. If she could still form coherent thoughts by that point, that was.

"How many days have you been in this room, Princess?" I questioned, already knowing the answer.

"Six, Sir."

"Six," I mused. "Then that's how many times I will bring your body to orgasm before you are allowed to rest. I expect you to count out each one, is that understood?"

Lucy's throat bobbed, the muscles working as she swallowed, accepting her fate. Her voice rang clear in her response. "Yes, Sir."

"Very good." I climbed atop the bed, using my knee to force her legs apart. "Don't be shy," I chided, causing her to open her legs fully so I could sit between them. "Now, I expect you to be a good girl while I take my turn playing with your toy."

Lucy's whimper reached my ears as I ran the vibrator up the inside of one thigh before skipping over to the other and running it down without making a pit stop between them. I wondered if she had ever been punished this way before because if she had, she wouldn't be quite so eager for my ministrations to focus on her core so quickly.

Using my free hand, I pushed the hem of her nightgown up and over her hips, baring her to me, revealing a lack of underwear. She may have blatantly broken one rule in a show of strength, but there was no denying who was really in charge here. That pretty pink pussy was staring me right in the face, glistening from her earlier release.

I smirked, knowing the orgasm she pulled from her body while alone wouldn't count in the six I had planned, and would also make the first stages of her punishment much more intense. That was too bad for her. I wasn't going out of my way to make this harder for her, but I wasn't about to pull back and make it easier, either. This time, Lucy had flown a little too close to the Sun and was about to learn a valuable lesson.

Bringing the bulbous vibrating head to her distended clit, I was satisfied when her hips bucked, and she hissed out, "Fuck."

"Such a dirty little mouth on you, Princess," I chastised, doubling my efforts, cranking the setting on the wand up to the third level of vibration and adding more pressure.

Lucy's back bowed, and I watched her mouth open in a wordless scream, indicating the first of many orgasms she'd suffer at my hands tonight.

"Count," I demanded.

Panting, Lucy forced out, "One."

Without warning, I turned the vibrator up to full blast, causing her to squeal as her hips tried to escape the intense vibrations so soon after her climax. Using my free arm, I draped it over her lower abdomen, holding her in place.

"Please, I can't," she begged as her head thrashed side to side.

Twisting the wand to and fro to hit every sensitive spot she possessed, I denied her any form of mercy. "Buckle up, Princess. You're in for a wild ride."

A cry of despair left her lips, the truth of what would transpire tonight finally sinking in. Those perfectly white, straight teeth sunk into her lower lip as she tried to stifle the moans slipping from her mouth beyond her control.

Lucy was fighting it, trying to hold back, and that wouldn't do. I needed her to give in to me—only then could we regain what we'd lost. I knew it was asking a lot, and I didn't care. I was very used to getting my way.

"Give in. Let me make you feel good." My words sent her flying over the precipice, this time much more forcefully than the last, as her body jerked violently against the soft bedding, her screams ripping through the air. Satisfied I'd wrung every ounce of pleasure out of her, I pulled the wand away, switching it off and discarding it on the bed.

"Two," Lucy breathed out.

Shoving the scrap of silk she wore higher, I exposed her pink-tipped breasts, running my hands over their stiff peaks as she arched into my touch before I lowered my mouth to nip them gently.

"You're absolutely breathtaking when you give yourself over completely," I growled against the skin of her breast before sucking the nipple into my mouth, eliciting a groan from above. Giving her a temporary reprieve, I teased with featherlight flicks and bites across her creamy smooth skin.

Lucy sighed and melted into the bed, lulled by the sensual way my hands roved her body as I moved above her, stealing her mouth in a kiss. This was something we hadn't done enough in our earlier interactions, and I sank into her mouth, tasting her as our tongues tangled. I drank her in, nibbling her lower lip before diving right back in. She met me stroke for stroke, a full participant in the lazy way we consumed each other.

Convinced I gave her enough rest before continuing with the rest of her punishment, I ripped my lips away from hers, asking while she was still lucid enough to understand, "Do you remember your safe word?"

"Red." Lucy showed no signs of hesitation, anything that would tell me she didn't understand that tonight she was mine to command.

"Good girl." The words were barely out of my mouth before it descended on hers again. This time, it wasn't slow and easy; it was a clash of lips and tongue and teeth. It was a battle for dominance—one I knew I had already won.

My cock was throbbing behind the fly of my slacks, aching to join the fray, but it would have to wait. That was until I gave Lucy's nipple a tweak, and her hips rose just enough that she was able to grind against my aching length. My lips broke contact as I hissed, feeling her heat through the layers of clothing separating us.

"Needy little thing, aren't you?" I teased Lucy, resulting in her taking two handfuls of my ass and pulling me closer between her legs to increase the friction. I nearly growled as I moved my mouth along her jaw, stopping when I was next to her ear. "Careful what you wish for, Princess."

Her resulting moan was all I needed to hear, and I gave in, thrusting my hips against hers, allowing her hands to guide them as the roughness of my fly rubbed against her needy little clit. I knew it wouldn't take much of this with how sensitive she was from her earlier orgasms, but I had better plans. Plus, if I let Lucy dictate how she got off, there would always be the idea in the back of her mind that I wasn't in total control. Nothing could be further from the truth—the sooner she learned that, the better.

Pulling back, I kneeled between her thighs, and her hands fell away, no longer able to reach me. Rolling my shirt sleeves past my forearms, I eyed her silk nightie pushed above her perky little breasts. "Take it off," I demanded.

Crossing her arms, Lucy grasped two handfuls of the blue material and lifted it over her head before dropping it over the side of the bed. It hadn't hidden much in the end, but now her flawless alabaster skin was completely unadorned, and I was nearly dumbstruck by how stunning she looked sprawled out before me. My mind raced with all the wicked things I wanted to do to her perfect body, and I felt myself smile as I remembered that we had all the time in the world. I would have a lifetime with this woman in my bed, to do with whatever I so pleased. She might be a handful outside of the bedroom, but in here, she was all mine.

It wasn't lost on me that I was still fully dressed while Lucy lay before me naked. Leaving my clothes on was the only thing keeping me in check right now—that was how badly I wanted her. This was turning out to be exquisite torture for us both.

Using my knees, I nudged her thighs further apart as the tiniest hint of her arousal reached my nostrils. My eyes closed, trying to regain any semblance of control—apparently, Lucy drove me insane in every arena. Unable to wait a moment longer, I lowered my face to the heaven between her thighs, taking my time breathing in her scent.

My hands came up to force her legs open even wider for my perusal. Fuck, if this wasn't the most mouthwatering pussy I'd ever laid eyes on. My tongue darted out to lick my lips in anticipation of what I was about to do, but I heard the tiniest whimper from above as Lucy's hips shifted beneath my hands.

Peering over her mound, Lucy's lust-filled gaze met mine. Lowering my mouth a breath away from her slick core, my eyes never left hers as I asked, "Does my dirty girl like to watch?"

She tried to buck her hips, but my hands gripped tighter in response, not allowing an inch of movement. "Please," she begged.

Shaking my head, my nose came close to grazing her clit, as I countered, "As much as I love hearing you beg, Princess, that wasn't the answer to my question."

Those blue eyes flared, and she nodded slightly as a single word rushed past her lips, "Yes."

"See? That wasn't so hard." Mentally, I cursed myself for uttering that word as it brought my attention back to the painful erection I had pressed into the bed, hoping to provide even a modicum of relief. Gritting my teeth against the sensations that threatened to overwhelm me and cloud my judgment, my voice was firm as I commanded, "Keep those eyes on me then, Princess. Watch as I devour this sweet pussy of yours."

I groaned against her slick flesh as her teeth sank into that kiss-swollen lower lip of hers in anticipation. My eyes remained locked on hers as I stuck my tongue out for a lazy first lick, swiping through her pussy from entrance to clit, drinking in her essence. Goddamn, she tasted incredible. I would never get enough.

Fuck me. From the way she licked her lips, it almost looked as if she craved a taste as well. That was a request I was more than happy to oblige, but not until I had my fill first. As much as I wanted to savor this moment, taking my time devouring every inch of this delectable pussy, that wasn't the mission this evening.

Committing to the task at hand, I abandoned my slow, tasting strokes, moving my focus to that tight little pearl that would make her come apart. Circling her clit once, teasing it out from beneath its hood fully, I went to work with quick flicks of my tongue. Lucy gasped at the change of pace and focus as her thighs tried desperately to close around my head, but I held her open. There was nowhere to hide as I ravaged her tender flesh.

Sucking that swollen nub between my teeth, I tugged gently, sending her careening over the edge into the abyss as her eyes slid closed.

My reaction to her disobedience was visceral as I pulled back enough to bark out, "Eyes!"

A whine left Lucy's lips, but she obeyed, forcing her eyes open just enough that I could view a hint of glassy blue as the pleasure racked her body in waves. I waited just long enough for her to come down before I thrust two fingers inside her tight passage. The shock of their entry caused her eyes to open wide as her lips formed a little "O" of surprise.

"More," I demanded as I curled my fingers, massaging that rough spot on her front wall I knew held the power to force her past the breaking point.

I felt her pussy flutter around me with the aftershocks of her last climax and the beginnings of the next. Groaning, I could almost imagine how incredible it would feel when I compelled it to squeeze tightly around my cock.

Moving my thumb, I grazed her clit as my fingers started to pump inside her. Lucy's back arched as her moans grew in pitch. Allowing her some movement, her hips jerked against my hand, half squirming to escape the relentless pleasure and half begging for more. I could appreciate the war raging between her body and mind, but I already knew who would win—this was my game, and I was always victorious.

"Give yourself over, Princess." My voice was husky, shadowed by my own lust as I pumped harder, adding a third finger and bracing myself for the show Lucy was about to put on.

She didn't disappoint; her scream rent the air as her entire body tensed before she shattered around my hand. Her pussy gripped my fingers so tightly, I was half convinced it was trying to suck them in further as she became a whimpering, trembling mess in my arms, coming down from the intense high of back-to-back orgasms.

Pulling my fingers from her silken sheath, I brought them to her open mouth as shaky breaths slipped past her lips in warm puffs. Rubbing a tiny taste of her arousal on her plump lips, I watched her pink tongue dart out to lick it off eagerly, searching for more.

God, she couldn't be any more perfect if she tried.

Giving her what her greedy little mouth demanded, I pushed my fingers inside. Lucy's tongue swirled around them, cleaning off every last drop of her desire. When her lips closed around my digits and her hot, wet mouth sucked them deep inside, I couldn't wait a moment longer to be inside her.

Four orgasms down, two to go.

Speaking of which, that reminded me she hadn't bothered to count the last two. I couldn't blame her, they were intense, but it would undermine my authority to let it slide.

Slipping my fingers from her mouth, I relished the sound of her whining in protest. It almost had me dragging my fingers back through her slickness so she could have another taste, but I had to deal with her disobedience.

"Oh, Princess," I chided. "You've been a bad girl." Those dazzling blue eyes looked at mine in confusion, so I explained, "Someone forgot to count."

Awareness broke through her haze, and panic filled those blue depths as she stumbled over her words. "I-I'm sorry, S-Sir."

Standing from the bed, I slowly undid the buttons of my dress shirt—I'd just returned home from the office when I knocked on her door wanting to talk. Lucy's eyes drank in the sight of my chest as it was revealed to her, but the hunger shining through them was erased when I mused, "I should tack on another two to make up for it."

"No, please, Sir. I can't," she begged on a whimper.

She could, I was sure of it, but I wasn't a monster. Seven total on the evening would be enough to teach her the lesson I intended. Scanning the room as I undid my buckle, I caught sight of the open drawer on her nightstand. Unbuttoning my slacks as I walked around the bed, I was welcomed by the view of a veritable treasure trove containing Lucy's secret stash of sex toys.

Lucy's form laid limp, sprawled across the bed where I'd left her, but her head followed my movements. The drawer was deep and surprisingly organized into categories, containing all manner of implements used for her solo sexual delight. Surveying the bounty, I raised an eyebrow in Lucy's direction. She was as knowledgeable as she claimed that first night we were together. Wanda was the tip of the iceberg. Nestled within the confines of her nightstand were several other types of vibrators, butt plugs of both the silicone and jewel-tipped crystal variety, and one more very intriguing item.

Plucking that last item from the drawer, I held it up for Lucy's inspection. Her resulting moan as she caught sight of the set of nipple clamps connected by a thin silver chain told me I'd chosen correctly.

I was never into some of Desire's more seemingly sinister pursuits, but that didn't mean I would deny Lucy a little bite of pain with her pleasure. She claimed to have no limits, and if these clamps were a part of her personal play collection, she enjoyed using them even when alone.

This woman was an enigma, and I would enjoy taking the time to figure out what made her tick, especially when we played together in the bedroom.

Reaching inside my pants, I gripped my cock, squeezing hard against the ache that threatened to consume me. Soon, I promised myself. Soon, I would sink between her thighs and take what was mine.

Climbing atop the bed once more, I laid next to Lucy's overly relaxed form. Taking one nipple between my teeth, I tugged on it, savoring the gasps that reached my ears as I plucked its twin with my fingers. Switching between them, I gave each equal treatment before grasping them one at a time, pulling them away from her body before gently attaching the clamps. A sharp hiss escaped Lucy's lips once each clamp was firmly in place. Giving a gentle tug on the chain connecting them, I enjoyed watching her body squirm in response. If she was like most women, that tug sent shockwaves straight to her clit.

I couldn't have planned this better if I tried.

Leaving her there to soak in the sensations the clamps provided, I stood, removing my pants and boxer briefs, kicking my socks off, and leaving my clothing in a heap on the ground.

Lucy was a sight to behold as I rejoined her on the bed. She was flushed head to toe, a light sheen of sweat coating her body, even as goosebumps raised along her skin with the barely-there brushes of my fingertips. Her long black hair was a tangled mess, creating a halo around her head. And fuck if she wasn't thrusting her hips gently, ready for more.

She was perfection personified.

Finding my place perched between her wide-open thighs, I ran my hands up and down her soft, smooth skin before bending her knees and pushing them up so high they rested near her armpits. She was a tiny little thing, and now I had her bent nearly in half, open and waiting for my next move.

Every fiber of my being was screaming to sink deep inside her, and it was finally time. With my hands holding her knees down, keeping her in position, I rolled my hips, allowing the head of my cock to slide through the wetness it encountered between her creamy thighs, effectively coating it in preparation for what came next.

Lucy's hips rocked the best they could, pinned the way she was, and the moan that reached my ears when my cock nudged against her engorged clit was so raw, so primal, I couldn't hold back a second longer. Lining myself up against her waiting entrance, I penetrated her slowly, stretching her inch by inch, gritting my teeth against the sensation of how tightly we fit together.

When I finally bottomed out, I could barely breathe—the depth of our connection literally stole my breath away. I was acutely aware that there were no barriers between our joined bodies. Never in my life had I skipped the added layer of protection I wore, regardless of a woman's precautions, but it seemed only fitting that tonight be the first. Everything about Lucy was different—perhaps something deep within me always knew that.

Forcing those thoughts to the side, my body demanded I move to create friction, if not for her continued pleasure, but for my own. There was nowhere for her to run, nowhere to hide, as I set a steady but strong pace, battering into her pussy with intention as she writhed beneath me.

Fucking hell, I wasn't going to last very long like this, and I needed to wring another two orgasms from her body. The combination of how stunning she looked, the near-shrill moans falling past her lips, the way my lower abdomen was being coated in her juices with each thrust, and the sensation overload of being bare inside her, was almost too much to withstand.

Releasing my grasp on Lucy's knees, she almost wept with relief before I hooked my elbows beneath them, pressing her open with my entire body, creating an even deeper angle I hadn't thought possible. Capturing her lips with mine, I drank her in greedily, caught up in the total-body experience I created. I felt her pussy tighten around me, nearly causing me to blow my load. If I let her come around my cock, I would be a goner.

I needed to think of something quickly to get her off one more time before I succumbed to the pleasure we created together. My chest pressed against her clamped nipples, and when her guttural groan in response reached my ears, I knew I'd found my life raft in a sea that threatened to drag me under.

Pushing back to kneel before her, I freed my hands, allowing her legs to drop. Before she could think of bringing them around my hips and locking her ankles, trapping our bodies together, I thrust quickly three times, bringing her right to the edge before pulling out and yanking on the chain connecting the nipple clamps so hard that they pulled right off with a snap.

Lucy's eyes rolled back into her head as a tremor consumed her entire body, and I watched as her pussy clamped desperately around nothing as her release hit her with such force that the scream torn from her throat was so animalistic and loud, I feared it could be heard beyond the walls of our apartment. It might sound like I was killing her, but it was the most breathtakingly beautiful sight I'd ever seen.

Not giving her a moment to come down from the sudden rush of her release, I pulled her by the ankles to the edge of the bed before flipping her onto her stomach. Her body was so loose it was like maneuvering a rag doll, but I wasn't done with her just yet. Gripping her hips, I pulled her further toward me so that only her torso remained on the mattress, allowing her legs to hang over the side until her feet grazed the ground.

"Five," she managed to whisper out.

It pleased me that even blissed out of her mind, her obedience through submission shined. She learned from her mistakes quickly through punishment—a nugget of knowledge I stored away for the future.

My moldable little Princess.

Holding her steady, I kicked her feet apart with my own, baring her battered and abused pussy before I slammed into it once more, pulling her hips to meet my own as our bodies slapped together.

Instantly, I realized that not giving her any time to recover threatened to become my downfall. The white-hot pleasure that engulfed me with my cock buried deep within her still-spasming pussy threatened to throw me over the edge of ecstasy before I completed my mission.

"Oh God," Lucy groaned into the bedding.

Honestly, I was surprised she could form a coherent thought at this point. I'd have to remedy that.

Thankful to have a focal point to distract me from the blinding pleasure radiating through my body, I bent over her back, bringing my mouth to the shell of her ear, replying darkly, "That's right, Princess. You better pray to whatever god you believe in that your birth control doesn't fail you because I'm about to fill you up and claim you once and for all."

Her resulting moan was all the motivation I needed as I rocked my hips into her, still curled over her back, trying to prolong this grand finale for my sake. I never wanted this to end.

Lucy's hair tickled my chest, nearly getting into my open mouth as I panted, trying to hold back my impending release, and I had a wicked thought.

Grasping a handful of her black tresses, I growled, "This would be much easier if your hair was pulled back into a braid."

Her gasp was unmistakable. Neither of us forgot how I'd teased her in our youth, and I remembered that one day, she'd stopped wearing braids after I told her braided pigtails were for babies. Even all these years later, I never saw a braid adorn one of her elaborate hairdos. She might not want to admit it, but I was always there, commanding her, even when I wasn't physically present.

Gritting my teeth, I slowed my strokes into the heaven between her thighs, trying to stave off the orgasm looming in the shadows that had the power to sneak up on me if I wasn't careful. That's when I saw the full-length standing mirror across the room, positioned perfectly to capture the fireworks of Lucy's final climax.

Tugging on the fistful of hair I held tightly within my grasp, I raised my torso, allowing me to stand upright, pulling her head up off the bed. Lucy didn't fight it, and I caught sight of her face in the mirror. Her eyes were glazed over in lust, tears streaking down her face. Her mouth hung open as moans flew out endlessly.

She was stunning, and she was mine. All that remained was to hear her say it.

"Look at yourself, Princess," I growled.

Lucy's eyes focused just enough that she was able to see the sight of me thrusting into her from behind. That wasn't what I asked for.

"Not me. You." I commanded. Sliding her gaze further down to catch her own reflection, she groaned. "Look at yourself and tell me who you belong to?"

Lucy was so deep within her submission that there was no hesitation. Without pause, she nearly wept her response. "You, Sir."

Fuck me. It was one thing to know what the response should be, quite another to hear this vixen—the one who was so contrary she'd insist the sky wasn't blue if I claimed it was—say those words, accepting my claim on her body.

"You're goddamn right. You belong to me. You're mine. *Mine*," I forced out through clenched teeth.

Releasing her hair, allowing her head to drop back to the mattress, I hooked my arms under her armpits, pulling her to a near-standing position against my chest. Lucy was so much shorter than me that her feet couldn't reach the ground the way we were joined, but I kept her hips pinned against the side of the bed, anchoring one of my arms across her chest, the other around her hips.

In this room, with our reflections staring back at us, there were no masks to hide behind, and there was no denying that *I* was the one she willingly surrendered her control to tonight.

Pistoning into her, I watched our coupling in the mirror. The sight alone was almost enough to rip the release from the depths of my soul. Each thrust tested the limits of my restraint, and I had to get her off one more time before I succumbed to my own orgasm.

Lucy was close, each stroke of my cock inside her bumping against her G-spot, and she clenched around me, trying to draw me deeper.

My voice was low next to her ear as I whispered, "Six."

Moving both my hands to cup her breasts as I held her against my chest, I pinched the tender flesh of her nipples, sending her blasting into the stratosphere, her pussy gripping me like a silken glove as her body vibrated beneath my touch. Carefully dropping her torso to the bed, I let her ride out the waves as I pounded into her like my life depended on it. I was right there with her. One, two, three more pumps and my balls tightened almost painfully in anticipation, mere seconds before I finally let go.

"Motherfucker!" I swore as the impact hit me with the weight of a freight train, as I rammed into her repeatedly, emptying myself deep within her body. Lucy may have been the one who had multiple mind-numbing orgasms tonight, but they all led to this single moment for me, and the magnitude of what we'd done hit me square in the chest.

Lucy's body was splayed across the bed as I rocked into her a few more times, savoring every last bit of pleasure I could steal before we separated, her moans still echoing through the room. Leaning down, I dropped kisses along the curve of her spine, cherishing these moments of calm after the storm.

Reluctantly, I broke the contact between our bodies, taking a step back to assess the damage. She was stunning bent over like this, but what really got me was watching our combined release leaking out and onto her inner thighs. For a fleeting moment, there was an impulse to push it back inside.

As much as I wanted to believe her willingness to accept her punishment was the reset we needed, I knew tomorrow she'd go right back to being furious with me. A night of passion and seemingly endless orgasms wouldn't solve our problems, but I was willing to put in the hard work. I could only hope she was willing to do the same.

The future could wait. Right now, Lucy deserved care after what I put her body through. Rolling her over onto her back, I scooped her into my

arms, carrying her into the ensuite bathroom. Placing her on the edge
of the sink, I turned on the faucet of the giant clawfoot bathtub, testing
the water until it was hot enough to soothe her muscles but not hot
enough to burn her soft skin.

Returning to Lucy, I carried her to the tub, gently easing her into
the steaming water and slipping in behind her. Reaching forward, I
turned off the water before it overflowed. I relished the feel of my body
curling around her tiny frame. Soothingly, I ran my hands over every
inch of skin I could reach, the water letting my fingers glide easily over
her slippery skin. My touches were meant to provide comfort as she
came back to reality.

She was so quiet, I was afraid I pushed her too far, but eventually, she
sighed, relaxing into my body and moving her hands along with mine.
Kissing the top of her head resting under my chin, I knew deep within
my bones that I could easily spend the rest of my life doing just this.

Lucy and I were fire and ice, but damn if that wasn't explosive in all
areas of our relationship.

When the water eventually cooled enough to chill, I helped Lucy
from the tub, carefully toweling every drop of water from her perfect
skin before wrapping a towel around my waist. Guiding her to the vanity stool, I sat her down before brushing her long black hair. Smiling
to myself, I plaited it—a symbol of our past but also a hope for our
future. Even if her mind was hazy now, when she awoke, there would
be a reminder of our night together.

Leading her to bed, I tucked her in gently, pulling the covers under
her chin. Lucy's heavy eyes fluttered closed once before reopening
slowly. She was fighting to keep them open.

Kissing her forehead gently, I whispered, "Rest now, Lucy. You were
such a good girl tonight. You deserve it."

Those beautiful blue eyes slid closed once more, and a tiny smile graced her lips a moment before her breathing leveled out, and I knew she'd fallen fast asleep. Tiptoeing out of her bedroom through the broken-down door, I chuckled to myself.

This was not at all what I had in mind when I knocked on her door tonight, but I think it might have been just what we needed.

CHAPTER 21

Preston

As EXPECTED, LUCY CONTINUED to give me the silent treatment after our first night together as ourselves, but at least she stopped hiding. Granted, it would have been difficult without a bedroom door, but I would accept that small victory.

Speaking of which, that broken door led to a lot questions.

We were able to sell a story to the palace staff about how Lucy was inside when the lock became stuck, and she panicked, unable to get out. I simply broke it down in desperation to get to my hyperventilating fiancée.

Liam wasn't so easily convinced. He and Amy knew that Lucy had locked herself inside for a week, and the shattered door was no accident. Liam pressed hard for the truth, but he wouldn't get it from me. Amy listened to the story and Liam's wary inquisition with a knowing smile on her face. I had a feeling she would be a valuable ally and made a mental note to foster the relationship with my soon-to-be sister-in-law.

Their wedding was now less than three months away, and they were in the throes of planning, drowning in press engagements as the country eagerly anticipated the first royal wedding in over a decade.

The citizens of Belleston had waited thirteen years between the Remington brothers' marriages, but luckily for them, they would be treated to a second wedding before the year was out.

There would be no intrigue surrounding a chosen royal bride, but Lucy was the princess they watched grow up. Ours was bound to be a veritable circus compared to those of her brothers, and I was already being hounded by the press anytime I left the palace as they begged for exclusive details.

Thankfully, Lucy dragged me back to Milan, and this time, I was grateful to put some distance between us and the prying eyes back home. Before we left, I tendered my resignation at work, accepting that my life would revolve around Lucy's from this point forward. I was hoping it would be a show of good faith and Lucy might open up to talking to me again, but no such luck. Regardless, caring for her and supporting her career was now my job, and I was never one to give anything less than my all in my work, so she'd have to deal with it.

I wasn't going anywhere.

Arriving late evening at her apartment in the city, all I could think about was how tired I was.

Tired of her shutting me out.

Tired of the decades we'd spent hating each other.

Tired of everything if I was being honest.

Dropping onto the couch I slept on during our last stay as she headed for the only bedroom without a word, I sighed before calling out wearily, "Lucy."

She'd spent the past few weeks ignoring me, so I half-expected her to keep walking and slam her bedroom door to punctuate that she had no interest in speaking to me. But she had always been unpredictable, and tonight was no exception.

Pausing, Lucy turned to face me. The exhaustion I felt was mirrored on her face. "What do you want from me?"

I hated seeing her this defeated, knowing I was the cause. Rubbing a hand down my face, I knew I needed to be honest with her from this point forward. No matter what.

"I know it's too much to ask your forgiveness, but maybe I can ask that we get to know each other better?"

Lucy huffed out, "We've known each other almost our entire lives."

"Maybe we get to know the people we are when we aren't deliberately trying to piss the other one off," I countered.

She chewed on her lower lip, thinking it over. Finally, she asked, "Like the guy who reads the baby books with his brother?"

That brought a smile to my lips. This was the opening I needed.

Nodding my head, I patted the seat beside me on the couch. "Exactly. That guy wants to get to know the girl who handcrafts wedding dresses for the people she loves and is moonlighting as a lingerie designer."

The way a blush crept up her cheeks and her eyes lowered did things to my insides. How had I never noticed how naturally beautiful she was in all these years? Maybe I didn't want to see past my perception of her to realize there was so much more to her than I ever realized.

"Please?" I practically begged.

"Okay," she whispered, joining me on the couch but keeping some distance between us. That was just fine, this process would take time, and I was a patient man.

"Would you like to start, or shall I?" I was quickly learning that the key to breaking past Lucy's walls was by not being pushy. Well, at least outside of the bedroom, anyway.

Watching her closely, I searched for any clues that might tell me what she was thinking when I noticed she twisted the engagement ring around her finger as a nervous habit.

Gently, I took charge. "Do you like the ring?"

Startled from her thoughts, Lucy's head snapped up for a split second before she focused her attention on the ring gracing her finger. Quietly she asked, "Is this really your grandmother's ring?"

Reaching out slowly to grasp her hand, I was surprised when she didn't pull away. Turning the hand containing the sparkling diamond so it was on full display, I gave her a shy smile. "Yes. She was very special to me."

"Will you tell me about her?"

"Of course. Like you, she loved her family very much, her grandsons especially. She would have loved you. Your passion, your loyalty, your compassion."

"You said she was creative-minded?"

My smile grew. "Oh, yes. She loved to paint. Our ancestral home, Foxway Manor, is full of her work. In another life, I know she would have loved the opportunity to showcase her pieces in a gallery. I think she'd have very much approved of how you can balance a career and still fulfill your royal duties."

"Why didn't your brother give this ring to his wife?"

"It wasn't his to give. Grandmother—Marisol was her name—left it to me when she passed. She told me it would take a strong woman to tame me and that she would be well-deserving of the ring that symbolized her many years of love with my grandfather." Lucy blushed again, so I squeezed her hand, emphasizing, "She wasn't wrong about that part. You are stronger than you know. I truly don't know how you handle it all."

Those blue eyes flashed to mine, and her shaky voice replied, "I tread water every day. Some days, I fear it will all pull me under, and I'll drown."

I would have given anything to pull her into my arms and tell her she could lean on me, but I knew it was too soon. Instead, I offered, "Soon, you won't have to. Will you tell me why you're secretly designing intimate apparel?"

Pulling her hand from mine, she hugged her knees to her chest. "I meant what I said. No one knows. Well, beyond my sisters-in-law, but I can trust them with my life."

"Why? Every piece I saw was stunning. Why wouldn't you want to attach your name to such incredible work?"

Her eyes never left mine, but I saw a shadow of doubt cross them. "My *name* is exactly why I keep it a secret."

My brows drew down. "I don't follow."

"With Addy June, I'll never know if my success was because of my designs or because of who I am. My family name carried enough weight that I could get investors right out of design school, but I wanted to prove to myself that I could stand on my own two feet."

Was she truly insecure about her talent? There was so much more to Lucy, and I knew this was just scratching the surface of the woman buried deep—the one hidden by her polished outer shell.

Carefully, I asked, "And have you found success with your lingerie line?"

Biting her lip, she looked down and nodded. "It does well enough that I could have afforded to walk away the day my grandfather asked me to marry an unknown man. I was halfway out the door at his suggestion, ready to leave that part of my life behind if he made me choose."

Impressed, I countered, "Then why didn't you?"

"Because I love my family, even if I don't want to live the same life they do. Walking out that day would have fractured relationships; I would never have been truly happy living the life I always dreamed of, knowing someone else had to lose for me to win. It was impossible to refuse when he offered me the chance to have the best of both worlds." She shrugged. "So, here we are."

"Here we are," I repeated.

She covered her mouth as a yawn threatened to split her face. While I'd learned more about the woman beneath the mask in the past hour than I had in the past twenty years, I could appreciate how draining it was to be vulnerable, and we had plenty of time to continue getting to know each other later.

"You should get some sleep," I offered.

Taking the out, she nodded, standing. "I think you're right."

I smirked, every fiber of my being wanting to point out this was the first time she ever admitted that to me, but I didn't want to push my luck. Instead, I simply said, "Goodnight, Lucy."

"Goodnight, Preston." Those were the last words we said to each other as she disappeared into her bedroom.

Tonight was a fresh start for us, and tomorrow, I would begin my quest to regain Lucy's trust.

⟡

"What made you get into fashion?" I asked out of the blue.

Tonight, Lucy was working late at her studio, offering me the perfect opportunity to continue the discussion we started the other night in my crusade to get to know each other better. The rest of the team was sent home over an hour ago, and all who remained were Sophie—who I learned during our last trip was her right hand—and Myles keeping a watchful eye. Lucy brought Amy's wedding dress with us to Milan and was working overtime to get it done in time.

Lucy paused her meticulous work on the dress, pulling out the pin she held between her teeth. "I guess I started to fall in love with it when I was five or six."

That surprised me, but I took a vested interest in the origin of her ultimate passion. "Really? That young?"

A corner of her lips quirked up. "I used to sit with my mom for hours as she got ready for fancy state events and balls. She wore a new gown to each one, and I found myself entranced with the many different styles and fabrics. To a casual observer, they might assume that meant I fantasized about wearing them myself, but it was never about that for me. I viewed each dress as a piece of art. Most were made custom for her—they were always the perfect complement to her body shape and coloring."

"I've noticed your eye for color and design in every piece you wear."

"That's a part of what I do, but I love the idea of a woman wearing one of my pieces and it making her feel as beautiful as she is within."

I may have done my research on her debut fashion week this fall, so I was able to ask the question that found its way into every article about her line. "Is that why you cater to a wide range of body types and sizes?"

That caught her slightly off guard. "What do you know about that?"

Smirking, I retorted, "Other than the fact that you said you had a model my size and proceeded to build a dress around my body?"

Blushing, Lucy bit her lip. "Yeah. Sorry about that."

I waved her off. "No need. We both did a lot of things we aren't proud of."

She tilted her head. "I didn't say I wasn't proud. Just that I was sorry."

There she was. My spitfire. Slowly, she was coming back to me.

Reinvigorated by her flash of fire, I prodded, "You didn't answer the question."

"There are so many reasons why I cater to a wide range of sizes and shapes. Mainly, I think the pressure society puts on women to be perfect is ridiculous. Women shouldn't be pushed past the boundaries of what their mental health can handle because they don't fit inside a box created by a man."

"Mental health?" I wanted to truly understand. As a man, it was simple—you put on clothes that fit and went about your day.

Sighing, she explained, "I'm sure you noticed Natalie's transformation when you last saw her. She was so sickly, starving herself for so many years, we worried we might lose her. All because the press claimed she wasn't thin enough."

"Nothing was wrong with how Natalie looked when she married Leo."

Lucy scoffed. "You think I don't know that? But it didn't matter. She literally couldn't see what was in front of her in the mirror. Her brain was so altered from years of verbal attacks on her size that her vision of herself was distorted. You wouldn't believe how shocked she was when we showed her pictures of her at her thinnest. I can still hear her crying, claiming it was photoshopped. She couldn't see what we saw until it was almost too late."

My heart broke for Natalie. I couldn't put myself in her shoes, but Lucy's account of her struggles made me re-evaluate every fashion ad I'd ever seen. She was right. They were all unnaturally thin women.

"So, Natalie is your inspiration?"

"Amy is too. She's curvy and confident, and I want that for all women, no matter their dimensions." Lucy hesitated momentarily before adding, "What I really want is to normalize that women's bodies change through-out their lives. It's natural, sometimes unavoidable, and they shouldn't have their clothing choices restricted because of it."

I was floored. Impressed wasn't a strong enough word to describe how highly I thought of Lucy's mission to improve the fashion world. She was a thin woman but could think beyond herself, advocating for all women.

Before I could vocalize how incredible I thought she was, Lucy asked a question of her own. "What is it that you do, Preston?"

Wryly, I answered, "Nothing now."

Rolling her pretty blue eyes, she huffed, "I meant before."

"Well," I began. "As you know, I'm a second son. It's why Liam and I got on so well. We were more than happy not to have to step into our fathers' shoes one day." Lucy coughed slightly and avoided my gaze, focusing again on the dress before her. Her reaction piqued my curiosity, but I continued, "While he re-enlisted, choosing to serve our country physically, I chose to do the same, but in an intellectual capacity."

"I remember Grandfather mentioning you were an attorney for the Crown," she mused. "But that is the extent of my knowledge of your profession."

"Yes. While Liam continued with the Bellestonian Army, I attended university and law school. Until recently, I was working to support the royal family's charitable pursuits and foundations, but that was only a stepping stone for me."

"Will you tell me what you were working toward?"

I sighed. "What I really wanted to do was move into treaty law. I wanted to help our country by constructing and amending the documents that built bridges between us and our allies."

Lucy was pensive, remarking, "That's admirable, Preston."

I didn't want to think about a life that now could never be, so I stood from my chair, needing some air. When she looked at me in question, I explained, "I think I'll go grab us some food since you're working late."

Lucy opened her mouth to say something more, but I left before she could. I didn't need her pity or apologies. I'd made my choice, and now I had to live with it. Nothing she said would ease the gnawing feeling in my gut that I would always know something was missing from my life. Not everyone had the luxury of fulfilling their dreams.

CHAPTER 22

Lucy

"WOULD YOU LIKE TO see a picture of my new nephew?" Preston called from the couch after we returned home from the studio.

This had become our thing for three weeks—him asking questions randomly and me answering honestly. Not every topic was easy to talk about, but I dug deep within myself, knowing that our life together would be easier if we figured out a way to get along.

I was still angry with him, and I wasn't sure I'd ever be able to trust him fully, but with each passing day—each question—the anger I felt ebbed a tiny bit.

Today's question wasn't exactly about me, but I was happy to focus on someone else. Preston held his phone out silently, inviting me to take it. Stepping forward, I grasped the offered phone, glancing at the picture of a pink-faced bundled-up baby in a hospital bassinet.

A smile crept across my face as I quietly gushed, "Oh, Preston. He's precious."

He chuckled in response. "He is quite the handsome little fella. Must take after his uncle."

Ever so slowly, we were crawling out of our protective shells and becoming more comfortable with each other. As my perception of him changed, I saw his comment as less arrogant and more playful. The urge to roll my eyes at him lessened daily.

"What's his name?" I asked.

Patting the seat next to him on the couch, beckoning me to join him, he replied, "Henry. The future Duke of Ashbridge."

Sitting down, I sighed as I handed him back his phone. "Poor thing." Here was this brand-new baby boy, and his future was already decided for him. I hated that for him.

Preston shrugged. "He'll be all right, I'm sure. Well, that is if he doesn't end up betrothed to one of Belleston's future princesses."

He was joking about our predicament, so I shoved his shoulder, retorting, "Yes, that would be a fate worse than death."

Reclining against the back of the couch, he put his hands behind his head. "It's not all bad. He could do worse than a pretty Remington."

Did Preston Scott just call me pretty?

I blushed like a teenager whose first crush said hi in passing in the school hallways. I told myself not to read too much into it. Redirecting the conversation, I asked, "When was Henry born?"

"Earlier this morning. Perhaps a visit from his Aunt Lucy would be in order when we return home?"

Slightly uncomfortable, I protested, "Oh, I don't know. I'm not really his aunt. I wouldn't want to intrude."

Sitting up, he slid closer to me on the couch, taking my hand, and I let him—only God knows why. "Are you saying he's not worthy of the famous Aunt Lucy treatment?"

His voice had a teasing tone, and I found myself loosening up. "Famous, huh?"

Nodding, he kept his face serious. "It's well known throughout Belleston that Lucy Remington is hands down the best aunt around."

"Is that so?" I arched a brow.

Placing his free hand over his chest, he swore, "On my honor." Those three words had the power to open a can of worms regarding my feelings of trust toward him, and I dropped my eyes from his gaze. Realizing his mistake, he changed course quickly, asking, "Tell me about your nieces and nephews?"

I had to hand it to him—he was good. Mention of the children I loved was enough to steer my thoughts away from dangerous territory.

Teasing, I asked in return, "How much time do you have?"

Squeezing my hand, his answer was sincere. "All the time in the world."

Well, if that isn't the truth.

Shyly, I mused, "Where would I even begin?"

Logical to a fault, he offered, "Perhaps oldest to youngest?"

"Good plan," I praised. "The oldest is Amelia, and she fits the role so well. She's protective of her mom and younger siblings, probably something she learned from Liam. There must be a gene in there somewhere they share. She's also very thoughtful. She can assess and analyze a situation before taking action or finding the words she wants to say. I can say with certainty she does *not* get that from me."

Preston laughed at my attempt at self-deprecation. "She seemed so mature. It's incredible how much she's grown up."

"She'll be a teenager before we know it," I lamented. "Then, there's Jameson."

"His striking resemblance to Leo is uncanny."

A chill ran down my spine at the mention of my oldest brother. He had done unspeakable things to Natalie and those children, and I was beyond grateful to my parents for ensuring he couldn't ruin their newfound happiness. Shaking off the sense of foreboding I felt, my tone was sharper than intended in my response, "That's where the similarities end." Preston's eyes widened, but he kept quiet, allowing me to continue. "As you know, he was born prematurely, so it's nothing short of a miracle that he's a healthy, strong little boy with no lingering health issues. He's the sensitive one. The divorce was more difficult for him than the others, and he had to work through some of his anger. He has blossomed now that there's a permanent father figure in his life."

"I couldn't help but notice little Beau is his stepfather's shadow," I mused.

"Jaxon is the only father Beau's ever known. He was a baby when they left, so he doesn't have any of the baggage the other two carry from their life here. He's this incredible, carefree boy, and he loves so freely."

"And the baby?"

"Who, Charlie?" Preston nodded, so I touched on Natalie's youngest. "Charlie came along, and she healed that family. She might not be my niece by blood, but damn if Liam and I don't love her with our whole hearts. She might be young, but her personality shines through, and I can't wait until she gets older. She doesn't take crap from anybody, and I'm willing to bet she will give her older brothers a run for their money."

"Are you sure you two aren't related?" Preston needled.

"Charlie might be a classic case of nature versus nurture. She's fortunate to have a plethora of strong female role models. The world better watch out."

"Consider me warned."

"Smart man." Preston usually opened our line of questioning, but sometimes, I kept it going by turning it around on him. This conversation lent itself to asking about something I had been curious about for a while now. "That day in the NICU," I started, and just like that, the air in the room changed from joking to more serious. "Did you mean what you said? That you wanted three or four kids?"

He searched my eyes, likely for cues as to which way to answer. I schooled my features like I'd been conditioned to do my whole life, not giving him any inclination of my feelings on the matter.

Eventually, he answered, "Yeah. I mean, I never really gave much thought to settling down, but in the back of my mind, I could picture having kids someday." Chuckling to himself, he added, "I know I'm not getting any younger, but I figured I was a guy, and our clocks don't tick quite the same way as the girls'."

Teasing him as he'd done to me, I quipped, "Oh, shoot. Did I ruin your dreams of geriatric fatherhood?"

Swinging an arm before his chest, he snapped his fingers. "Darn you, Lucy Remington. But seriously, though, I'm open to whatever you might want." Pausing, he thought it over. "Is that something you want? Do you want to have kids at all?"

Whoa, this got deep really fast, but I started the conversation, so I had to hold up my end. Pushing him off only slightly, I countered, "Why would you ask that?"

"Come on, Luce." Well, damn, if him giving me a nickname didn't give me butterflies. "I've seen how you reacted whenever someone brought up the idea of babies. You flipped out. Hell, I used it to my advantage. It's not something I'm particularly proud of."

He was right—I had gone off the deep end more than once at the mention of having a baby, and I was ashamed to say that the idea of having said babies with Preston in particular fueled those overreactions.

Diving into that part of it wouldn't do us any good, so I focused on the other reasons. "Is it too much to ask that I get to decide when I put my body through the trauma of a pregnancy and birth?"

Preston tilted his head. "Trauma?"

I scoffed. "That is such a man thing to say. You may have read the baby books, but theoretical knowledge can't compare with experiencing the reality. Why don't you call up your sister-in-law and ask her to describe every horrifying thing that happens to a woman's body during the nine months of pregnancy in vivid detail? That's before you have your body split in two forcing a human being the size of a watermelon out the hole the size of a lemon, leaving a wound on the inside the size of a luncheon plate that takes six weeks to fully heal. It's practically barbaric that some countries don't provide paid leave for new mothers."

Eyes wide, Preston was sufficiently chastised and mildly horrified, uttering, "Point taken."

"That's only the beginning. Parenthood is for life. It's not something to jump into without careful thought and consideration. You are responsible for another person's emotional and physical well-being, education, and safety."

"Is that a no, then?" Preston hedged.

Sighing, I pulled my hand from his to rub both of mine over my face. "It's not a no. It's just a 'not right now.' My life has belonged to others since the moment I was born. For the first time in my life, I'm faced with the opportunity to spread my wings and do what I want. I would like to enjoy that newfound freedom before committing the rest of my life to being a mother."

"So, what you're saying is . . . I still have a chance at being an older dad."

His joking lightened the mood of this serious conversation, and I laughed. "I live to serve." Preston's laughter joined mine, and when we calmed down, I couldn't help but ask, "So, you're not mad?"

I watched his hand twitch, wondering if he wanted to grab mine again. I wouldn't stop him if that's what he wanted, but I could tell he was debating in his mind on how best to proceed with physical contact. I couldn't blame him.

Softly, he said, "I'm not mad, Luce." There was that nickname again. "We are just starting to get to know each other; jumping right into having kids would be madness. You're building this incredible business, and I can't wait to see how it grows when you can finally give it the attention it deserves."

Okay, he was being a little too nice to me, and I didn't know what to do with it. If I didn't get into my room quickly, he might see me cry, and I wasn't ready to be that vulnerable with him yet.

Pretending to yawn, I lamely excused myself. "I'm tired, so I think I'll head to bed. I'll see you tomorrow, Preston."

"Until tomorrow, Lucy."

<hr>

"Will you tell me about how you ended up at Desire?" We were eating dinner alone in my Milan apartment, and his question shocked me so much that I almost choked on a mouthful of food.

"Excuse me?" I sputtered after hastily swallowing.

"Would it make you feel more comfortable if I answered the same question first?" he offered.

Was this actually happening? We'd been in Milan a month now, and somehow, we managed to ignore the elephant in the room. Was I fooling myself to think we would never discuss our shared private interests? We were going to be married; we couldn't sweep our secret desires—our secret selves—beneath the rug forever.

Steeling myself for probably our most uncomfortable conversation yet, I nodded. "Yes, please."

Setting his fork down, he paused for a moment. "There was always something deep within me that craved control. I couldn't explain it. When I got older, I met a girl who liked role-play. It was innocent enough, but I got into it. Like, really into it, to the point where I craved that dynamic every time we hooked up. She just wanted to have fun now and again to spice things up, so we parted ways, but she suggested I take a further look into the BDSM community. I brushed her off because I wasn't into the idea of beating women. She explained it was much more than that, and if I did my research, I might find the sexual gratification I was searching for. So, I did. And I discovered this whole world that allowed me the control that I craved with willing partners in a fulfilling way for all involved. I joined as a member at Desire and never looked back."

He'd shared his personal journey, but I knew it would be difficult for me, so I teased, "So you're not into impact play, but the hair-pulling is right up your alley?"

Preston laughed heartily. "What can I say? I thoroughly enjoy a good hair-pulling. Always have." He emphasized that last part with a wink, and I felt heat rising to my cheeks.

Oh, boy. We were in dangerous territory now, discussing the club and our preferences regarding sex.

"How about you?" he prodded. Preston had been gracious in offering his journey first, but now it was my turn.

Chewing on my lower lip, I gathered the courage to tell the tale of my self-discovery. Taking a deep breath, I began, "I'm sure you've noticed by now that there's always someone watching me. And I don't mean Myles."

Bowing his head slightly, he acknowledged the reality of my fishbowl existence. "I've had a taste of that myself these past few months, and it's overwhelming, to say the least."

Preston validating my feelings gave me the strength to continue. "Beyond the press, we live in a world where everyone has a camera in their back pocket. Having sex with anyone had the potential to leave me vulnerable. I wasn't sure who I could trust not to secretly film me in a compromising position or even to sell a story about their sordid affair with the princess."

"Trust is a gift, but it's hard-won and easily broken." Preston's words were quiet, and they hit home. We both knew he'd broken mine.

Swallowing, I forced myself to push on with my story. "So, one day, I thought, there has to be a way to lose my virginity discreetly. That was the day I found out the internet had a wealth of information on the topic if you knew how to look for it."

Processing my words, he asked in disbelief, "You lost your virginity at Desire?"

"Yes," I confirmed.

"Jesus. How old were you?"

From his reaction so far, I knew my answer would shock him, but I was done hiding. "Nineteen."

"Fucking hell." He dragged a hand across the dark shadow of a beard along his jaw.

"I wasn't kidding when I said I'd been a member for a long time."

Preston's eyes widened in shock. "Wait. Are you saying you've never had a sexual encounter outside the club?"

He was figuring it out, but I felt myself blushing, remembering our one night together in my bedroom. "Well, until recently, I hadn't. I couldn't risk it. But now, I find myself doubting if the protection of my mask was enough, and some of my partners knew of my identity."

"Lucy, I'm sure none of them knew," he tried to reassure me. "You and I have a history. It might not be the best history, but I'd know you anywhere."

"Anywhere?" I challenged.

"Anywhere," he confirmed. "I will say, I was surprised to learn you were a submissive. You didn't strike me as the type."

"Yeah, well, I guess years of conditioning to obey couldn't be undone and leaked into my sex life. But honestly? Down there, my submission is a choice, not an expectation. There was something so liberating about handing over that power to another human being and trusting them explicitly to take care of you. The feeling was out of this world, and the club became my safe space—a place where I could be myself and not fear the repercussions from the outside world. You know what it's like. The stigma attached to the things we enjoy. My reputation would be torn to shreds if anyone ever found out."

"I canceled my membership," Preston blurted out.

The weight of his admission settled in my gut, and it was heavy. He was committed to what we were required to build together, and the past month had shown he was willing to wait for me to be ready. I wasn't there yet.

Softly, I stated, "I don't know how to move forward."

"I'm still the same guy from the club." The look in his hazel eyes stole my breath. He was practically pleading with me to give him a second chance.

"Yeah, but you're also the guy I've hated most of my life. I don't know how to reconcile the two."

"We just keep doing this. We take our time. There's no rush."

"Our wedding is in less than eight months, Preston." I couldn't keep the sharp bite of cynicism from my voice.

"So what? Who says we have to be madly in love by the time we walk down the aisle? I'm content to continue taking baby steps. We make the rules when it comes to our relationship. No one else. Just us."

I wanted to believe him, but I was jaded. He'd lied to me before. And if the night he broke down my door was any indication, he wouldn't tolerate my attitude. If he pushed me too fast, I might pull away completely. My entire life was on the line, and I could lose everything if I let him get too close.

My sense of self-preservation won out, and I thanked him for dinner before retreating to my room once more. Most of our conversations ended this way, with me running when it got tough and him letting me go without question.

Would this ever get any easier?

CHAPTER 23

Lucy

"It's so good to be home." I sighed.

Preston raised an eyebrow at me. "You are a walking contradiction, do you know that? You're chomping at the bit to escape these walls, claiming you can finally breathe in Milan, yet you're glad to be home?"

He was right. We landed in Remhorn barely an hour ago, and it wasn't so much that I missed the life I led here but the people I cared about within the palace walls. No matter where my life took me, this place would always be home.

Brushing him off as he brought our carry-ons inside the apartment before closing the door, I moved toward the stairs, asking over my shoulder, "You want me to have dinner brought up?"

"Sure, sounds good." I heard his voice behind me as I climbed the stairs, ready to decompress for the evening before diving headfirst back into public engagements and the pre-wedding madness with only a month to go before Amy and Liam tied the knot—this time, for the world to see.

Reaching the landing, I turned into our open master suite, dropping my purse on the coffee table. I was about to plop onto the couch when I felt

Preston so close behind me that the hairs stood up on the back of my neck with awareness.

"Looks like someone fixed the door." The hot kiss of his breath caressed the shell of my ear.

A shiver ran down my spine at his closeness, and I started to lean into him when I remembered why my door needed to be replaced. Jolting to my senses, I spun to face him, taking two giant steps backward, pointing a finger at Preston. "Don't even think about it."

Feigning innocence, he stuck his hands into the pockets of his jeans, rocking back on his heels. "I have no idea what you're talking about."

Narrowing my eyes at him, I could feel my body vibrating with the memory of what he could do to my body. Mentally berating my traitorous body, I tried to calm my racing heart. "I'm not kidding, Preston."

Stepping forward in a silent dare to see if I would retreat again, he smirked when he realized I was rooted to the spot. My brain screamed at my body to move, but I couldn't make it obey. Leaning down, he dropped a kiss on my forehead, and I closed my eyes against the overwhelming rush of feelings such a deeply intimate act caused.

Reminding myself I still wasn't ready, I opened my mouth to verbally push him away when I heard him behind me, declaring, "I'm going to take a shower."

Great, that's all I needed. The knowledge of him naked, soapy, and wet, with only a few doors separating us.

His bedroom door clicked shut, and I finally came to my senses. Sitting on the couch, I grabbed my purse off the coffee table, digging inside to find my cell phone so I could call the kitchen and order dinner to be brought up. That's when a manilla envelope caught my eye. My purse must have been covering it, and I hadn't noticed it when I entered the room.

It was addressed to both Preston and me, and the return address was Alpine Slope Women's Hospital. Curious, I put my purse aside and reached forward to pluck the envelope off the coffee table, opening it carefully. There were several pieces of paper enclosed, as well as a smaller envelope. The first page read:

Dear Lucky Lucy and Preston,

There aren't words to express how grateful we are at the NICU for your kindness. Your compassion and generosity truly know no bounds. The families you've helped wanted to express their gratitude, but since you wished to remain anonymous, I offered to forward any words of their appreciation personally. Contained are letters and pictures of the lives you've changed. They may not know who you are, but I do, and I am proud of the young people who will someday help guide our great country.

Appreciatively,
Nurse Cindy

Forget curious. Now, I was flat-out confused.

What was Nurse Cindy talking about? I could understand a thank-you letter after our visit—I received dozens of those monthly—but she mentioned us wishing to remain anonymous. That didn't make any sense. Our visit had been well documented. It was no secret who we were.

Then there was mention of helping families, and beyond holding a couple of preemies, I wasn't sure what she meant. Life had gotten crazy, and I had every intention of discussing a fundraising event with Amy, but I never got around to it. Did my press office send something? But that still didn't explain the anonymous part.

Placing Nurse Cindy's letter on the coffee table, I read through the rest of the letters. Each one was from a different family, some thanking us for providing hotel accommodations so they could be near their baby, some overly grateful for funding childcare for their older children, and another even mentioned the sending of extra hands to help on their farm, so they didn't have to choose between their livelihood and their sick baby.

The smaller envelope enclosed contained photographs.

Photographs of parents with their babies in the NICU.

Photographs of babies getting ready to go home.

Photographs of babies thriving in the outside world.

It was the final picture that struck me. The baby boy was smiling, his face filled out with a healthy glow. He was older and bigger, but I'd know that face anywhere. I'd held his tiny body against mine not so long ago. That baby was Silas.

"Lucy?" Preston called my name through the whirling storm of emotions threatening to pull me under, but I barely heard him. All I could do was stare at the picture in my hand.

"Lucy!" He tried again. The couch dipped next to me, and he cupped my face in his hands, turning me to look him in the eyes. "Lucy, what's wrong?"

"What?" I didn't understand him. I didn't understand anything right now.

"You're crying. What happened?"

Was I? Reaching a hand up, I felt the warm wetness seeping through where Preston held me so gently. "I . . . I don't understand."

Using his thumbs, he wiped the tears from my cheeks, but they were quickly replaced with more. I couldn't stop them. Preston's eyes searched mine. "Understand what? Let me help you."

"Help," I repeated, and the pieces began to fall into place. The letter was addressed to both of us. Holding the picture in my shaking hand out to him, I asked, "Did you do this?"

Preston's brows drew down, and he reluctantly dropped his hands to take the photograph of baby Silas. Glancing down, he questioned, "What am I looking at?"

"Silas," I whispered.

Understanding dawned on his face. Good, that made one of us, then. "Oh, that."

"So, you did this?"

Placing the picture on the coffee table, he took my hands in his. "Yes, I went back to the NICU about a week after our joint visit and had Nurse Cindy compile a list of families who couldn't be with their baby for various reasons and what it would take to get them there."

"But why?" None of this made any sense.

He shrugged. "I saw a need, and I filled it. Nothing more."

"Nothing more?" I exclaimed. "How can you say that? It was *every-thing* to these families!" Quietly, I added, "It is everything to me."

Had I really been that blind? Had I let a few years of teasing color my perception of this selfless man?

Reality hit me that maybe I hadn't wanted to see who he truly was, but there was no denying it now. I was set to put a plan in motion to help families like Silas's, but he went out of his way to personally help Silas's family. I could only imagine he used his own funds, but what stood out was that he wanted no recognition. Preston simply wanted to help them.

It was incredible. *He* was incredible. My stubborn ass just needed someone else to show me.

"Luce . . ." I could tell he was trying to find the words, but I didn't want to talk anymore. We'd spent the last six weeks talking. I knew everything I needed to know.

This time, I placed my hands on the sides of his face. My thumbs toyed with the rough texture of his beard, loving the contrast against the softness of my hands. Closing the distance between us, I placed my lips against his softly. This was the first time I chose him, and it was terrifying. What if he didn't choose me back?

That uncertainty was squelched when he pulled me into his arms, opening his mouth and kissing me deeply. He poured everything he was feeling into our kiss, and I did the same. I didn't have the words to express how I felt at that moment, but I hoped I could show him.

Running my hands from his face into his hair, I took two fistfuls, pulling on the short strands gently. He moaned into my mouth, and I climbed onto his lap. Preston's hands held me gently, caressing up and down my back, allowing me to take the lead. I could only imagine it was killing him, but his restraint spoke volumes. He was here for me, allowing me to take what I needed from him.

Breaking our kiss, I dropped my forehead to his, breathless. His ragged breathing was the perfect complement to mine, and I smiled. Was this what it was like for other people? For the ones who didn't participate in kink? I had no regrets about my sex life, but it was nice getting a taste of what it meant to have a more conventional relationship.

Pulling back, I lost myself in the hazel depths of his eyes. Preparing myself to say the words, I took a deep breath. "I want you."

Preston's hands moved into my hair, and he tried to pull my mouth back to his, but I resisted just slightly. Confusion spread over his face. "Are you sure?"

He wanted consent. I couldn't blame him. It was such an integral part of what we had shared to this point.

"Yes, I'm sure." Then I clarified, "I want it to be just us—Preston and Lucy."

His eyes flared, and he nodded, confirming, "Just us."

Scooping me into his arms, he stood. I clung to him, needing an anchor against the emotions swirling through my brain, threatening to overwhelm me.

After a few steps, he paused, and I looked up at him in question. Smiling down at me, he teased, "I need a little help with the door. That is, if you don't want me to break it down again."

That moment of levity was needed more than he would ever know. Reaching my right hand down, I turned the doorknob, allowing him to carry me over the threshold and into my bedroom. This was such a departure from our previous sexual encounters, but that was exactly what I needed. *He* was exactly what I needed.

Preston placed me gently onto the bed. Sitting up, I grasped the hem of my sweater, pulling it from my body. I bit my lip as I watched him devour me with his eyes, not daring to make a move. Reaching behind my back, I squeezed the clasp of my black lace bra, allowing it to fall away, baring my breasts to his already hungry gaze.

Getting onto my knees, I crawled to where he stood, still by the bedside. His chest rose rapidly as I took my hands and skimmed them underneath the t-shirt he now wore. Until now, I had barely been able to register that he dressed for bed after his shower.

Feeling his abs tense under my touch wasn't enough. I wanted to see him. Grabbing two fistfuls of the white cotton, I raised it up and over his head. Tall, dark, and handsome wasn't strong enough of a descriptor for the man standing before me. His body was sin incarnate. And he was all mine.

Capturing his lips with mine, I melted into him. Sensing my needs, he slipped his arms around my back, holding me as our tongues took their time tasting and teasing, sharing dominance.

I smiled against his lips, and he murmured against mine, "What's so funny?"

"Nothing," I replied truthfully. "I'm just happy. Is that okay?"

"More than okay." This time, he took over the kiss, and I sank into it, allowing him to ravage my mouth as if it were his last meal on Earth.

I felt him pushing me backward as he joined me on the bed. Falling back against the covers, I watched as he undid the button of my trousers before moving to the zipper. I lifted my hips as he slid the fabric down, exposing my heated flesh to the cool air of the room.

The pants barely cleared my ass before he paused, raising an eyebrow at my lack of underwear. "Still?"

My face flamed, and I brought my hands up to cover it, embarrassed.

"Look at me," he softly commanded, but I shook my head. "Lucy, please," he begged, and I couldn't deny him, dropping my hands and finding his hazel eyes shining with a need to hear me say the words.

Afraid that if I said them, I'd lose Preston, instead releasing the Dominant I knew lurked right beneath the surface. I tensed but forced them out anyway. "I belong to you."

His pupils dilated, leaving the tiniest hazel ring visible, before he closed them and took a shaky breath, dropping his forehead to my belly. I almost didn't hear him when he said, "We belong to each other."

Oh, wow.

My chest tightened, and I couldn't breathe. What was he doing to me?

Resuming his earlier actions, he pulled the pants down my legs, leaving me completely bare before him. Sitting back on his heels, he scanned my body from head to toe.

"You're so beautiful it hurts, Lucy." He must have seen the doubt on my face because he asked, "How can I prove it to you?"

Nudging a knee between my open thighs, I couldn't resist the urge to grind against him, needing friction almost as much as I needed air. Lowering his body over mine, he dropped hot, open-mouthed kisses down my neck, over my collarbone, around the outside curves of my breasts, and across my belly, before peppering kisses down my thighs until he reached my feet. It didn't escape my notice that the two places he skipped were my nipples and pussy—the two places most desperate for his attention.

"Baby, I will worship every inch of this body and take nothing for myself if it means you can understand that you're the most stunning creature to ever walk this planet, and for some reason, I'm the lucky bastard you've chosen to gift yourself to."

"Please," I whispered desperately, his words stealing the breath from my lungs. "I need you too badly."

"Then say it."

Closing my eyes, I whispered, "I'm beautiful." Like any woman, I played the comparison game and knew I had flaws. I wasn't perfect by any means.

"No. Eyes on me." When I forced my eyes open, he commanded, "Say it again."

That's when it dawned on me. I could list every imperfection I had, but in his eyes, I was beautiful. It reaffirmed everything I worked for—men loved the woman within, making her even more attractive to them. It didn't matter if their size and shape changed over time, they still found the woman they loved stunning.

But Preston didn't love me. He couldn't. It was too soon. Or maybe it was too soon for me to put how I felt about him into words. Either way, it just didn't seem possible.

"I'm waiting." Preston squeezed my foot, his eyes seemingly staring into my soul with their intensity.

This time, there was no hesitation. "I am beautiful."

He didn't falter as he reaffirmed, "So beautiful, Lucy."

A wave of something warm washed over me, but I couldn't name it. Instead, I begged, "Take off your pants."

"Is that a direct order?" he teased.

"It's whatever gets you naked faster," I huffed out, frustrated and needy for him.

"Well, when you put that way, how can I say no?" Without further delay, he stood, hooking both thumbs into his flannel pajama pants, drawing them down his legs, and taking his boxer briefs with them. His erection bobbed as it was released, and I groaned, desperate to feel him inside me. Hearing the sound, his eyes flashed to mine, and he smirked. "Like what you see?"

I moaned at his words. "Not interested in seeing. Make me feel. Please, Preston."

Gripping his length, he stroked it a few times, teasing me, but when I started to move toward him, he rejoined me on the bed, his dick pressing against my clit as our bodies aligned. Arching my back, I shifted my hips, trying to line him up enough to feel him slip inside.

"Careful, sweetheart. Let me take care of you first."

My head thrashed against the bed, and the thrusting of my hips became more insistent. "No. I need you now. Please don't make me wait."

He kissed me deeply, which only ratcheted up my need for him. I felt his hand graze over my hips and between my thighs, slipping easily through my folds.

Ripping his lips from mine, he growled, "Fuck, Luce. You're so damn wet already."

"If you don't get inside me right now," I panted, "I will flip you over and take what I need."

His thumb passed over my throbbing clit, and I gasped as he teased me with his fingers. "Well, that doesn't sound so bad either. Maybe next time, though." Those were the last words he said before he removed his hand and penetrated me with aching slowness.

"Yes," I hissed when he was fully seated to the hilt.

"Fuck yes," he groaned in response before rocking his hips gently, igniting a fire within my blood.

Our bodies moved together in a slow, sensual dance—the same dance humans have been participating in since the beginning of time. It was primal. It was intoxicating. And it was maddening, all at the same time.

I wanted him to move faster. I wanted him to move slower. I wanted this to never end.

My climax built slowly, the coiling sensation within my body increasing with each slow thrust of his hips. I clutched at his back, needing him closer, holding on for dear life as he held me teetering on the razor's edge of release. Preston reached down, hooking one of my thighs over his hip, changing the angle and throwing me past the brink of ecstasy.

I gasped, struggling to breathe as my release tore through me; every muscle in my body pulled taut before I shattered into a million tiny pieces. It was powerful, it was raw, and it was everything I never knew I needed. This closeness, this intimacy, only served to heighten the pleasure.

Moaning as the aftershocks faded and Preston continued to thrust with a steady rhythm, the beginnings of another orgasm stirred, my core clenching around his length buried deep inside me. He felt it too, and I could hear as he grunted, trying to hold off until I reached that peak for a second time.

Hooking my other thigh around his waist, I locked my ankles and gave myself over the sensations building between my legs. Shuddering violently, I came again, pulling Preston over the cliff with me as he roared next to my ear. He was always so expressive in his release, and I was satisfied to see that didn't change, regardless of our dynamic.

Preston rolled off me but didn't go far, allowing me to curl into his side as we both came down from arguably the most intense sex I'd ever had.

I began sliding into unconsciousness as he rubbed soothing hands over my bare skin, but not before I came to the realization that it didn't matter how we did it—the connection between me and Preston was explosive. What we did tonight was more than sex—it was meaningful. But that was something to dissect another day.

CHAPTER 24

Preston

DURING OUR TIME IN Milan, I kept myself busy focusing on Lucy. Most days were spent finding new ways to grow our budding relationship. I learned more about her in those six weeks than I had in the previous twenty-plus years combined.

I especially enjoyed when she let her guard down just enough that I was able to do the same, as she countered my questions with her own. It gave me hope for a future where we worked together instead of against each other at every step.

Then we came home, and she discovered how I'd helped the families in the NICU who could not remain with their children for various reasons. There was a reason I did so anonymously—I didn't need or want praise. I only did what I felt was right. Lucy was never supposed to know.

I'll never forget how I found her, with tears streaming from her eyes as she held photographs in her trembling hands. It didn't matter how long we spent talking—Lucy was still wary of me. But reading the words of others, hearing what I'd done to help them and expecting nothing in return, she could finally lower her defenses to see the person I was deep inside.

Our night together was incredible. I'd never felt so close to anyone in my entire life, and when she fell asleep in my arms, I held her close, praying it was the new start we so desperately needed.

Since then, we were taking our time, dipping our toes into the relationship pool. We got used to eating dinner together in Milan, so we continued to do so in our private suite. Some nights, Lucy worked in the other room. Other nights, we cuddled together on the couch, either reading independently or watching television. I continued not to rush her, and some nights she invited me into her bed. On nights she didn't, I retreated to my separate bedroom without question or complaint.

We were making progress, and I couldn't ask for anything more.

Being home made it glaringly obvious that I had nothing to do. Quitting my job right before we left didn't hit me until now. Lucy continued with her public engagement schedule and occasionally asked me to accompany her, but more often than not, she went alone.

Left to my own devices, I learned every inch of Stonecrest Palace that was accessible for my clearance level. It was a massive castle with hundreds of years of history held within its stone walls. Often, I found myself strolling leisurely through the portrait gallery, brushing up on my knowledge of Bellestonian monarchs long past. It was strange to think that if someday Lucy and I did have children, they would be part of this grand lineage. Any man would be proud to have their bloodline tied to the Remingtons, but none of that ever mattered to me. If there was anything I learned from my and Lucy's upbringing, it was that children should be allowed to have their own identities. Family was important, but finding yourself was paramount.

Bored out of my mind, having run out of places to explore, I ventured into Liam's office. Lucy and Amy had gone to a shelter housing women and children who were the victims of domestic abuse, so I knew he'd be home for the day. Lucy made it clear that this was not a trip where the men would be overly welcome, and I could appreciate that. It made my blood boil thinking about the weak men who needed to beat on their wives or girlfriends and kids to feel big.

Liam was only slightly surprised to see me, glancing up at the intrusion with a smile. "Hey there, stranger."

Dropping into the chair opposite his desk, I sighed. "I need something to do."

Laughing, he replied, "You'd think Lucy was handful enough to keep you busy."

"Not funny. I'm serious. I'm going crazy," I vented.

Crossing his arms, he leaned back in his desk chair. "You know I'd be happy to hand you one of my projects, but it wouldn't make much sense. You're not going to be living this life for long."

I hated that he was right. "I can do background stuff, clerical work. Anything, man. I'm desperate."

Eying me, he asked, "Things not going well with Lucy still?"

"We're fine." I sighed.

"The broken-down door begs to differ." Liam leveled me with a glare.

Returning his glare, I countered, "Are we really doing this?"

"I think I have a right to know if my sister is in a bad situation. Not that you'd tell me if something untoward was going on." He scoffed.

If he wanted to play, then fine. "How's your sex life, Liam?"

Liam's normally pale skin turned bright red as he sputtered, "That's none of your damn business!"

Smirking, I raised an eyebrow at him, making the implication clear about why I broke down Lucy's door. "Then I think the same should apply to mine, don't you think?"

Eyes wide, he muttered, "Jesus."

"What can I say? Your sister is a freak in the sheets."

"Enough! I get it!" Liam raised both hands to cover his ears.

Smugly, I leaned back in my chair. "I trust this will be the last time we discuss the damn door?"

Shuddering, Liam replied, "Yeah."

"Now, can we get back to the topic of me doing something to keep my mind occupied before I lose it completely?"

Sympathetic, he sighed. "I want to help you, I really do. But work is about to be set to the side anyway."

"What are you talking about?"

"The circus known as my wedding is about to begin. It'll require all hands on deck."

Frowning, I ran the date through my head. "Your wedding is two weeks away."

"Tell me something I don't know," he muttered. "It's going to be the giant spectacle I never wanted."

"You do know you're already married, right?" I stated the obvious.

Liam's blue eyes, an exact replica of Lucy's, rolled dramatically. "I'm well aware. It's . . . complicated."

The way he said it didn't invite clarifying questions, so I let it go. "What are we expected to do for two weeks? The wedding is a single day."

"The *extravaganza* is set to kick off on Friday night with the joint bachelor and bachelorette parties."

"Again, I'll point out you're already married, but who am I to say no to a night out? And why are we starting with that and not ending with that?"

"One, we aren't going out; we're staying in. Most of the younger wedding guests are set to arrive on Thursday, turning this palace into a hotel bursting with people. Two, the girls will be so busy with preparations—final dress fittings and all that—that this is a good way for them to unwind before reality sets in. And three, we want to do it before Amy's parents arrive."

The first two points I could understand, but the third gave me pause. "What's wrong with her parents?"

That question was enough to have Liam leaving his chair to pour two glasses of bourbon, offering me one before retaking his seat. "For starters, they haven't met my parents yet, so there's no telling which way *that* will go. Then, there's the fact that they hold Leo's sins against me."

I winced from more than the burn of the bourbon as it worked down my throat. "Yikes."

"Yeah. Beyond all that, Amy and her mom tend to butt heads. Her mother wanted her to be a society wife, and Amy was hell-bent on having a career, independent of reliance on a man."

Tipping my glass in his direction, I made a toast. "To strong women."

"Amen to that." We both sipped our drinks before he added, "In-laws, am I right?" Catching himself, he amended, "On second thought, maybe don't answer that."

"I have no complaints," I offered.

Satisfied with that answer, he took another sip. "I'm sorry I couldn't do more to help you today. Let's get through the next couple of weeks. Then, I can take my wife on a proper honeymoon while you and Lucy head back to Milan. Well, at least until planning for your own wedding ramps up."

"Right." I threw the remaining contents of my glass down my throat.

"Hey, Liam, do you think tonight we could—" Amy's sultry voice filtered into the room as she entered the office but stopped abruptly when she realized Liam wasn't alone. I turned my head just in time to catch the hint of a blush that crept up her neck and onto her cheeks. "Oh, Preston. What a pleasant surprise."

Not wanting to make my future sister-in-law any more uncomfortable, I stood, nodding to Liam as I placed my empty glass on his desk. Walking to where she stood, frozen to the spot and slightly embarrassed, I dropped a kiss on her cheek, not having to bend down much as she was almost my height in heels.

"Amy," I acknowledged her quietly before exiting the office, knowing that if Amy had returned, so had Lucy.

Entering our apartment, it didn't take much guesswork to determine where Lucy might be. As expected, I found her busy as a bee in her workspace, putting the finishing touches on the dresses for the wedding. Leaning against the doorframe, I paused for a moment, content to watch her work. Her passion was only matched by her attention to detail—she was meticulous in her quest for perfection.

I could have watched her all day, but she turned around to grab something off her desk and caught sight of me enjoying the view.

"Oh!" she exclaimed, startled by my presence.

I had to bite back a groan at how her mouth formed into a perfect "O" shape as she said the simple word, and I pictured her doing that on her knees before me.

"Have a nice afternoon?" I drawled.

"It was bittersweet at best." She sighed. "The shelter is doing its best for its residents, providing a physically safe place, but it will take years to heal the emotional wounds. If they can heal at all."

"What can I do?"

Lucy's smile was genuine. "Is this how it's going to work from now on? You trying to save the world?"

I shrugged. "Well, I do seem to have a lot of time on my hands. Why not channel it into righting the wrongs of this world?"

Chewing her lip, she asked, "What if I could do you one better?"

"What are you talking about?"

Lucy twisted the engagement ring around her finger. She was nervous. "How would you feel if I told you I managed to secure an offer for you to act as a consultant to the treaty law team?"

I could only stare at her, trying to make sense of those words. "I don't understand."

"You shared your dream with me, and I got to thinking that maybe there was still a way for you to achieve it."

It still didn't make sense. "How would that even work? I learned the hard way that trying to work remotely is challenging on the best of days. There was so much lost in translation."

Lucy's blue eyes sparkled as she stepped toward where I stood, skimming her hands up my chest and looping her arms around my neck once she was within reach. "I have been told that marriage is about compromise. Perhaps we could make it work like Amy and Liam do."

Sighing, I breathed out, "I can't ask you to do that. The whole reason you agreed to our marriage was so that you could commit full-time to your career."

Rising on her tiptoes, she brushed her lips against mine. "You didn't ask. I offered." Pulling away, leaving me speechless, she tossed over her shoulder as she returned to work on the dresses, "How else do you expect to support yourself?"

The teasing tone in Lucy's voice jarred me enough that I snapped out of my trance. Stalking toward her, I joked back, "Um, I'm sorry. The contract I signed said I would be provided with a sugar momma. Do I need to look over it again? Because if not, I will need to hire a new lawyer and find out how it can be broken."

I caught her from behind, pulling her into my arms as she squealed. Turning her head to peer up at me, the smile on her face took my breath away.

"Seems like you are out of luck. That contract is ironclad. The Crown only employs the best lawyers."

Stealing her mouth in a kiss before I left her to finish her work, I was floored by her selfless gesture. I was determined to spend every day for the rest of our lives showing her my gratitude.

―――⸘⸘⸘―――

The ballroom was transformed for Amy and Liam's joint bachelor/bachelorette party. I was used to being in this room for large-scale formal events, so the casual party atmosphere was a shocking contrast.

Instead of a string quartet playing classical music, a DJ pumped out the latest hits through massive speakers. The soft lighting signature of a ball was replaced with flashing neon lights. This giant room resembled a dance club more closely than one that regularly hosted some of the world's most influential people. Granted, influential people were still present, but they represented the younger generation—the world's future rulers and diplomats.

Natalie and Hannah had arrived last night, and Lucy and Amy were glued to them every waking moment. I could imagine how isolating her upbringing must have felt, so I was glad she had a group of ladies she could trust to be herself with.

Liam and I sat at a table with some of his distant European cousins, who were expected to stand up with him at the altar, when Lucy sauntered up to me, dropping onto my lap. She hadn't stopped dancing since we arrived, and I was enjoying the show. It didn't hurt that she wore skintight jeans topped with a shimmery halter top. She looked good enough to eat.

Maybe later.

Looping her arms around my neck, she swayed to the music, nearly toppling off my lap when she leaned a little too far.

Gripping her more firmly, I growled in her ear, "Are you drunk, Princess?"

Her resulting giggle gave me the answer, even as she protested, "No! Of course not!"

Squeezing her thigh, I countered, "So that wasn't you I saw doing gelatin shots?"

Blue eyes wide, she shook her head. "Must have been someone else. Wasn't me."

I knew she was lying but let it slide as she wiggled her ass, resulting in a rush of blood to my groin. Holding her steady, I warned, "Careful, Princess."

In a show of blatant disobedience, she struggled to grind her ass down further. "Are you going to punish me, Sir?"

Oh, fuck.

I couldn't stop myself from groaning. We hadn't slipped back into our dynamic since the night of her last punishment. God, how I missed dominating her, but I held back, giving her what she asked for when she begged for it to be just us. It looked like I wasn't the only one longing to regain our sexual roles.

Grabbing her by the back of the neck, I pulled her lips to mine in a punishing kiss, showing her exactly who was boss. Breaking away when we were both desperate for air, I put my mouth directly next to her ear. "You're walking a fine line, sweetheart. I have no problem throwing you over my shoulder and carrying you out of here while everyone watches."

Holding her so close, I felt the way her body trembled at my words, and satisfaction coursed through my veins.

Lucy breathed out, "Promise?"

"Don't tempt me," I growled.

She opened her mouth to retort, most likely to push me over the edge, when an old boy band song came over the speakers, and her eyes lit up. Jumping off my lap, she swayed on her feet, and I reached out a hand to steady her as she screamed, "I love this song! Where are my girls!?"

If she weren't so damn cute when tipsy as hell, I'd have rolled my eyes at her taste in music, but I couldn't tear my gaze away from her as she pushed through the mass of bodies on the dance floor to locate her friends. Just when I thought that was it, she pulled them toward the DJ's booth, and he handed them microphones.

The four of them danced, singing their hearts out and doing the iconic hand signals that went along with the song as the crowd watched. Lucy was so free in this moment, allowing her personality to shine through, and I wanted that for her every day. Not just when she was dangerously close to fall-down drunk. That was my job now, to see to her happiness and ease the burden she felt with the weight of the world—and her family—on her shoulders.

Smiling, I realized that seeing her happy made me happy, and I wanted to devote my life to making sure she could live as freely as she felt right now.

There was simply no denying it any longer. I was falling for the fashion princess.

CHAPTER 25

Lucy

I HAD BEEN IN rare form last night, as evidenced by the pounding in my head as I tried to force my eyes open. How much had I had to drink? Rolling over, not ready to face the day, I collided with a solid mass in my bed. My head was fuzzy, so I used my hands to explore what I'd bumped into as my eyes remained closed.

"Oof. Watch those hands, Princess."

Oh, shit.

Preston was in my bed. Inviting him to spend the night with me wasn't completely out of the ordinary, but I could only imagine how sloppy I'd been if I couldn't even remember it. That's when I realized what he meant by watching my hands as I felt his erection growing beneath my palm.

That was enough to wake me, and I sat up, my eyes opening suddenly, which I instantly regretted. Throwing both hands over them to shield them from the light, I groaned. "Sorry."

I felt him drop a kiss on my bare hipbone, uttering, "Nothing to be sorry about."

Glancing down, I noticed that I was indeed naked. Grimacing at the idea of begging him to fuck me while I was practically black-out drunk, I braced myself enough to ask, "Did we . . ."

Rolling over so his hand rested just below my navel, he chuckled. "No, I'm not in the habit of taking advantage of girls who can't walk to their own beds without assistance. Not that you didn't ask ever so nicely. However, you did get quite belligerent when I turned you down."

Of course I did.

"Sorry. I don't remember much of what happened after my stint at karaoke."

"Which stint? There were several." I could hear the smile in his voice.

"Oh God." I groaned. "I only remember the first one."

"If it helps, that was the most coherent one. They went downhill fast."

Rubbing my eyes against the pounding in my head, I asked, "If you turned me down, why are you in my bed?"

"Someone had to be here to roll you over so that you didn't aspirate on your own vomit. You're lucky you didn't wind up with alcohol poisoning. I got so caught up in watching you have a good time that I didn't bother to think about monitoring your liquor intake."

I groaned. "Thanks, I think?"

"You survived the night—that's all that matters." I felt the mattress shift under his weight and mourned the loss of his touch as his hand slipped from my body. "Let me get you a glass of water and some pain meds. Once those take effect, I'll bring you the greasiest items from our breakfast spread, and that hangover will be history."

Preston was clearly applying for sainthood, but I wouldn't complain. We were finding our groove and beginning to enjoy each other. I could finally see who he was beneath that false bravado, and I had to admit, he was genuinely charming. It wasn't a stretch to say he was quickly worming his way into my heart.

As I watched him walk away, his clothed form a stark contrast to my naked one, it hit me. Preston might have seemed like the worst possible choice my family could have made when picking out my future husband, but I couldn't imagine any of the self-centered pricks I grew up with taking care of me the way he had last night. Any one of them would have certainly taken advantage of my drunkenness and left me to fend for myself the morning after. Hell, they'd probably be in worse shape than I was—rich boys knew how to party.

It appeared that Preston was a diamond in the rough. Who would have thought?

The wedding festivities were in full swing, with more guests from around the world arriving daily. Guests most essential to the wedding and those with the highest international status were invited to stay at the palace.

Simply put, the place was a madhouse, and I was required to always be on.

Thank God Preston was there to keep me grounded. All it took was a gentle touch from him, and the tension dissipated, reminding me this was only temporary and that he had my back.

I wasn't just the groom's sister and a bridesmaid; I was the gown designer, and the second Natalie and Hannah arrived from America, I set to work altering their bridesmaid dresses to perfection. Sophie also flew in to help with any last-minute alterations to my dress.

As if I wasn't stretched thin enough, Grandfather declared that a family dinner with the new in-laws and the bridal party would take place this evening. All I wanted to do was take off my bra in the comfort of my apartment and hide from all the people crowding our space, but clearly, that wasn't an option until the bride and groom said, "I do."

I shuddered to think about my own wedding barely six months from now. If I couldn't escape the fanfare leading up to my brother's wedding, how would I handle being in the spotlight? Maybe I could persuade Preston into eloping. Liam and Amy ran to Vegas when they first got married, effectively paving the way for us to do the same.

Yes, technically, Liam was the new heir—even if almost no one knew it yet—so this grand spectacle after the fact was necessary, but I had hope that I could talk my way out of one for myself. My mother's heart might be broken at the thought of not attending her only daughter's wedding, but I was sure when Amy and Liam produced more grand-babies, it would smooth it all over.

It was a nice dream, but I knew it was just that—a dream. I wasn't willing to risk my chance to get out of this life for good. I would forever be a princess but no longer belong to the people. I would be my own person, living my own life, so a big fancy state wedding was a small price to pay.

You might think a family dinner in the middle of the chaos would be relaxing, but you couldn't be more wrong. We weren't your typical family; it was a formal affair when we were summoned to dinner. The men were practically wearing tuxedos, and the women were trussed up in evening gowns. The only difference from how we dressed for a ball was that we nixed the tiaras. There were drinks before dinner in the formal sitting room, then, at minimum, a seven-course meal that took hours—it was tedious in the extreme, and I was not in the mood.

The only thing making it slightly more bearable was the sight of Preston dressed to the nines in a perfectly tailored dinner suit. His reflection stared back at me in the mirror of my vanity as I affixed my earrings, and there was no mistaking the hunger in his hazel gaze as he raked it down my body.

Moving my long black hair off the side of my neck, he held my gaze and pressed a soft kiss to the spot where my neck and shoulder met.

"I know you're tired and wish we could stay in tonight, but I can't say I'm sorry about being forced to attend dinner when you look this incredible. God bless formal seating arrangements, where I get to stare at you from across the table all night."

His words caressed my skin as smoothly as the red silk draped across my body. I leaned into his strong body behind me, closing my eyes and wishing we could continue what he started with that simple kiss. Even now, I shifted in my seat against the growing ache between my thighs, and I needed to get a grip before the wetness of my arousal soaked through the thin fabric. While I could change before we went down for drinks, I would have some explaining to do if he continued to devour me with his eyes throughout dinner.

Pulling back with a lingering graze of his fingers over my shoulder, he smirked. "I have a gift for you."

Frowning in confusion, I asked, "What's the occasion?"

Preston shrugged. "Do I need to have a reason to spoil you, Princess?"

I bit my lip. Him calling me Princess had the power to push me over the edge. We hadn't played together in so long, and I missed it. Sure, the vanilla sex we were having was deep and emotional, but surely there was room for both in our relationship. Was he implying he wanted it just as much as I did?

Deciding to test the waters, I replied, "No, Sir."

Preston groaned in response. "Good girl."

It was official. I needed to change. The silk beneath me was slippery and wet. I just couldn't control myself with the promise of him dominating me later tonight. Standing, I turned to survey the damage in the mirror. Sure enough, there was a wet spot right below my ass.

Shaking my head, I playfully chastised him, "Look what you did. I can't go down there looking like this."

Stepping closer, Preston brought his hands down to cup my ass before pulling me flush against him. The obvious bulge pressing against my abdomen showed me he was similarly affected by our little exchange.

Dipping his head next to my ear, he whispered provocatively, "My gift might help with that."

Rearing back to look at him, my brows drew down. "How could whatever you have possibly keep me from soaking through every dress I have when you talk to me like that?"

Releasing me from his arms, he strode through the open door to my bedroom, returning with a gift bag and offering it to me. "You'll see."

Curious, I took the bag, removing the tissue paper, before pulling out a pair of black lace panties. Twirling them over my finger, I teased, "I thought I wasn't allowed to wear panties?"

His hazel eyes flared. "These are special panties. For tonight only, I'll make an exception."

I narrowed my eyes at him before focusing on the panties I held in my hand. I designed underwear for a living, and these didn't look any different than any I'd seen. "What makes them special?"

Crowding my space, he reached into the gift bag, pulling out a bullet vibrator, causing my eyes to widen. "There is a special pocket, allowing you to place this inside the gusset."

He was insane! "There's no way I'm wearing that to dinner with my whole family! You've lost your damn mind!"

In a flash, he transformed into the Dom who could bring me to my knees and command me like no other. His tone was firm as he countered, "I wasn't asking. You *will* wear these tonight. Is that understood?"

My mouth suddenly went dry, and I swallowed uncontrollably, but I managed to nod.

That wasn't good enough for him, and he demanded, "Words, Princess."

"Yes, Sir," I managed to croak out.

Softening slightly, he smirked. "Don't worry. I'll only have to use it if you're naughty."

My knees threatened to buckle. He knew exactly what he was doing, and God help me, I was so turned on that I feared that when I donned these panties, the brush of the lace against my throbbing clit would be enough to send me over the edge.

While I made my way into my massive walk-in closet to find a new dress, Preston took the scrap of lace from my hands, inserting the vibrator into its special pocket.

I was so fucked.

<hr>

Pre-dinner drinks went the way they usually did, with everyone breaking into groups for more intimate conversations, but all I could focus on was the ticking time bomb resting between my thighs. I wasn't naïve; I knew

Preston had some kind of remote control hidden, and we were playing a game where only he knew the rules. I was completely unaware of what transgression would cause him to turn on the vibrator in a room full of my entire family and closest friends.

"Lucy!" I heard Natalie call out beside me.

"Huh?" I murmured.

"Where are you? You look like you're a million miles away."

"Oh, um." I had to think of a believable lie and fast. "Just thinking about all the work still left to be done on the dresses." That would work.

Natalie flashed me a smile. "Don't worry about the dresses. They're gorgeous."

Before I could respond, Hannah huffed, "Not like it matters. I don't even have a date for this thing."

"Neither do I," Natalie stated with a roll of her eyes. Jaxon's hockey team was in their final playoff push, and she traveled to Belleston with only her three oldest children.

"That's different." Hannah pouted.

"You're right, it is. You should take advantage of not having a date and maybe open yourself up to meeting someone who isn't forbidden." Natalie was referencing Hannah's life mission to land a hockey player, even though her dad, Jaxon's team's coach, had banned any of them from touching his daughters.

Hannah thought it over. "Well, I wouldn't exactly say no if one of these rich royals wanted to whisk me off to the Maldives for some post-wedding fun, but eventually, I would get bored."

Enjoying the distraction, I joked, "If there are no fists flying or any blood spilling on the ice, it's not exciting. Am I right, Hannah?"

Natalie shot me a glare. "Not helping, Lucy."

Hannah sighed. "Lucy gets me."

We all shared a laugh as the dinner bell rang, and Preston appeared by my side to escort me.

As the grand procession from the sitting room to the dining room began, he leaned down to whisper, "How are you hanging in there?"

Scowling, I whined, trying to remove any trace of fear from my voice. "It's uncomfortable."

Chuckling, he replied, "Don't worry, Princess. Be a good girl tonight, and you have nothing to worry about."

That was easy for him to say. He wasn't the one dodging invisible land mines all night. Bringing me to my assigned seat, he pulled out my chair, allowing me to gracefully fall into it before pushing me in and rounding the table to sit directly opposite me. Amy was seated to my right, and Natalie was on my left.

Amy leaned over. "Are you okay? You were walking a little funny."

Leave it to Amy not to miss a single thing.

I shrugged it off, trying to remain casual. "It's nothing. I just tweaked my ankle a couple of days ago. Should be right as rain by the wedding."

She didn't look convinced but dropped it as the first course was served. The conversation was light, primarily consisting of excited chatter surrounding the upcoming wedding, less than a week away. I sat silently eating my dinner as the din of voices faded into the background. I'd already had my fill of wedding talk.

"Lucette!" Uh oh. I was caught not paying attention, and Grandfather's booming voice alerted me to that discovery.

Looking up demurely, hoping to portray an air of innocence, I asked, "Yes, sir?"

Immediately, I felt the buzzing between my thighs and clenched against the sensation, which only made it more intense.

What the hell did I do wrong?

Gripping the table against the rolling waves of pleasure, I felt my face heat.

Before Grandfather could repeat whatever part of the conversation I missed that required a response, my mother's concerned voice called out, "Gracious, Lucy! Are you all right? You look flushed all of a sudden!"

The sound of Preston clearing his throat across the table caused me to glare in his direction, pleading desperately with my eyes to make it stop before I gave the entire dinner party a show.

Gritting my teeth, I forced out, "I'm fine, Mother. It's warm in here, is it not?"

Everyone gathered shook their heads, uttering various words indicating they had no issue with the temperature of the room. I almost wept with relief when the vibrations stopped abruptly, but my heart still raced, trying to beat right out of my chest.

Smiling slightly, I fanned my flushed face. "Guess it's just me, then."

Conversation resumed around the table, whatever topic pertaining to me long forgotten as I returned to concentrating on my food. The main course was served, a rack of lamb with roasted potatoes and carrots, and my mouth filled with saliva at the intoxicating aroma wafting off my plate.

While waiting for everyone else's meals to be plated, Grandfather made a toast to the happy couple. Everyone said, "Cheers," and then we began to eat once more.

Barely two bites into the savory lamb, Grandfather commented, "It pleases me to think that all my grandchildren will be settled in a few short months. I'm proud of you, Lucette."

I wanted to retort that he was prouder of himself for strong-arming me into a marriage I never wanted, but held my tongue, graciously accepting his false praise. "Thank you, sir."

The words had barely left my mouth when the vibrations started again, this time more intense than the last. Fuck. I wasn't going to make it out of here alive. My brain raced, trying to find a commonality between the two incidents as I desperately tried to stave off a very public orgasm.

"We are very grateful for your support, *sir*." Preston's voice was strong and clear, emphasizing that last word, and that's when it finally clicked.

He set me up!

He knew that coming down here tonight, I would be required to address my grandfather—my King—formally and with respect, and he was punishing me for it.

There wasn't much time to plan the ways I was going to kill him because the vibrations increased in intensity again, and a moan slipped past my lips as I placed a hand on my lower abdomen, struggling to hold back.

Amy's voice cut through the haze. "Lucy, you don't look so good. Are you sure you're all right?"

Shaking my head, my voice was breathy. "Actually, I don't feel so well."

Preston, the bastard, feigned concern, addressing my grandfather. "Your Majesty, would it be all right for Lucy and me to be excused? I think she's feeling a bit under the weather."

I couldn't dare to meet anyone's eyes, hunched over, right on the edge, clenching my teeth against the overwhelming urge to let go and succumb to my impending release.

"Yes, yes, of course." I barely heard Grandfather's voice over the roar of blood in my ears.

Just as he granted us permission to leave, the vibrations ceased, and I placed a hand on my chest as I took in shaky breaths. Sweat had formed on my skin due to the exertion required to keep my climax at bay.

A hand came down on my shoulder, and I nearly jumped out of my skin.

"It's all right, darling. I'll have you upstairs and in bed before you know it." Preston's voice was smooth as silk as he played the doting fiancé. Helping me out of my chair onto shaky legs, he slipped an arm around my waist to keep me steady before addressing the rest of the room. "I'm sorry to have ruined what promised to be a lovely evening."

My dad gave me a sympathetic look, speaking for everyone, "Don't bother yourself too much about it. Just make sure Lucy gets the rest she needs."

We were barely out of earshot when I heard Grandfather remark, "I certainly hope it isn't contagious. It wouldn't do to have the entire wedding party sick for the big day."

Preston chuckled under his breath as we cleared the dining room, but I elbowed his side, gritting out, "You are so dead."

Walking me carefully back to our apartment, he teased, "Oh, come on. That was hands-down the most entertaining dinner I've been to here at the palace."

"I'm so glad you had fun." My words dripped with sarcasm.

Reaching the entrance to our apartment, he opened the door, not allowing me to enter before whispering in my ear, "Don't worry, there's plenty of fun to be had this evening, Princess."

Damn him. Damn him and the way he could melt my insides with a single word.

Prepared to give him the tongue-lashing he deserved for his behavior at dinner, I never got the chance as he pulled me through the door, kicking it closed and using his body to pin mine against the wall.

I opened my mouth to tell him to go to hell, but he took that opportunity to claim my mouth in a punishing kiss, and I cursed my body for reacting. I wished for the dominant side of Preston to come back out to play only earlier this evening, and here he was. I guess I should have been more careful about what I wished for.

Or maybe not. It felt so damn good to let him take control.

His strong body pressed into mine, restricting how far my chest could expand to draw in air, and I felt lightheaded, but my panties were drenched. Without warning, he stepped back enough that I was able to draw a huge gulp of air. Grabbing a fistful of my hair, he pulled it so I was forced to look up at him.

I felt him move his other hand and cried out as the vibrator in my panties turned on again.

Growling, he brought his face close to mine. "Any time you even think of calling another man 'sir,' I want you to remember this."

Whimpering in response, I tried to reason with him, "What else am I supposed to call my superiors?"

Not budging, he snarled, "I don't care. Figure it out."

Choking out a sob, I egged him on. "Yes, Sir."

"Fuck." He turned off the vibrator but crushed his mouth to mine again, using the leverage of the wall to pull me into his arms. Instinct demanded that I lock my ankles around his waist as he carried me up the stairs toward our master suite. My dress rode up my legs—thank God for the slit up one thigh—and I shifted my hips, grinding into his hard-on, satisfied to hear him groan as we crossed the threshold into my bedroom.

Dropping me onto the bed, he had a dangerous look in his eye, but I wasn't scared. He would never hurt me. I would bet my life on that.

Shaking his head as he shed his suit jacket, Preston's voice was so calm it sent a chill down my spine. "Oh, Princess, you are going to pay for that."

Yes, please.

CHAPTER 26

Preston

STARING DOWN AT LUCY breathless on the bed, I marveled at how stunning she looked with her flushed skin and kiss-swollen lips. I knew the little game we played downstairs at dinner wasn't fair. Hell, she didn't even know the rules, thus ensuring she had no chance of winning.

Well, that wasn't entirely true.

I didn't know how she could view a hands-free orgasm as losing. But then again, she didn't quite get there—a fact I was acutely aware of and planned to exploit. It didn't matter that I was rock hard—I intended to play with my food before I ate it.

Grasping the control in my pocket, I tapped the button again, reveling in the sight of Lucy as her blue eyes widened and her body arched on the bed. Her hips shifted, finally able to enjoy the pleasure the panties provided, but I watched for signs she was about to fall apart. The second her toes began to curl in her open-toe heels and her eyes drifted closed, I pressed the button to turn it off.

Lucy gripped the covers so tightly that her knuckles turned white as she whined, "Please, Sir."

"Did you really think it would be that easy?" I taunted.

The reality of my plan of attack this evening sunk in, and those twin blue flames flared. It would be exquisite torture bringing her to the edge of release repeatedly before backing off, but she knew as well as I did that it would result in an orgasm so intense it would rival all others.

Pulling at the knot of my bow tie, I slipped it through my collar before working down my shirt, undoing the buttons.

Needing to hear her say it, I commanded, "Tell me who you belong to, Princess."

Her greedy gaze drank in each inch of my chest as it was revealed. Licking her lips, she replied, "You, Sir. Only you."

Rewarding her for answering correctly, I allowed her another twenty seconds of feeling the buzzing between her thighs. "Good girl," I praised as I turned it off again, watching her pupils dilate even further at my words.

What could I say? I was a sucker for a submissive with a praise kink.

Shirtless, I crawled over her body on the bed before sucking a nipple through the black silk dress she wore, before biting it gently, eliciting a breathy moan from Lucy's lips. I'd watched her change after she ruined the red dress with her arousal and knew that while she wore panties, there was no bra underneath. Once the fabric was soaked through, I thumbed the sensitive peak, letting the friction of the silk gliding over it fan the fire undoubtedly simmering right beneath the surface.

When she was writhing beneath me, I turned her on her side, pulling the zipper down her back before easing the smooth silk from her body and discarding it on the floor. Now, all that was left were the special black lace panties I'd gifted her earlier this evening, but I couldn't hold back the primal desire to see her bare. Gripping the sides, I pulled, yanking the fabric away from her body until the sound of ripping threads filled the air.

Eyeing the shredded panties, I growled, "That's better."

My cock was throbbing, begging to be buried deep within her hot pussy, but it would have to wait. Pressing it into the mattress to relieve some of the ache, I kissed a path down her body from her breasts to her mound.

Inhaling deeply, I dropped my forehead to her belly. "Fuck, Princess. You smell incredible. Let's see if you taste as good as I remember."

Moving down further, I held her thighs open with my hands, baring her glistening pink pussy for my viewing. Her clit was swollen, no doubt from the earlier attention of the vibrator pressed flush against it all night. I wanted nothing more than to tug that little bud between my teeth and make her scream, but tonight was all about the tease.

Taking my time, I tantalized her with my tongue and my lips, circling but never quite focusing my attention on her clit, no matter how she shifted her thighs, silently begging for it. I watched as her pussy clenched, desperately needing to be filled.

Soon, Princess, but not yet.

Placing a soft kiss right over the hood of her clit, I heard Lucy gasp. I barely had grazed it with my lips, and she was dangerously close to exploding. Maybe it was time for a little detour until it calmed down.

Kissing the inside of her thigh, I rubbed the sensitive flesh with the sides of my jaw, relishing the knowledge that the scruff of my short beard would leave the skin red and raw. Tomorrow, she would feel me with every step she took, a reminder of who she belonged to. The moans I heard from above spurred me on, and I added a little love bite to the reddened skin, marking her.

Lucy grew restless, her body squirming against the sheets. Desperation looked good on her. If not for the pressing need to claim her, I could have toyed with her all night.

Easing two fingers inside her, I relished the sound of her breathy groan as her walls squeezed tightly around me. She tried to ride my hand, but

I placed an arm over her hips, keeping them immobile. Lucy would take what I offered, nothing more.

Pumping slowly into her silken depths, I watched for the subtle cues her body gave. Her thighs began to tremble, squeezing together to trap my hand, and I knew she was right on the brink. Cruelly, I pulled my hand away just as I felt the first tremors of her climax from within.

"You fucking asshole," Lucy growled.

Glancing up, she was near feral, baring her teeth in sexual frustration. The way her chest rose and fell as she huffed out breaths with her nostrils flared reminded me of a fire-breathing dragon. She was fired up, and I had her just where I wanted.

I was torn between amusement and the need to turn her over my knee and spank her ass for daring to speak to me that way. Never in my life had I laid a hand on a woman, but damn if I wasn't tempted beyond belief right now. Knowing her, she'd enjoy every second of it, and that would defeat the purpose.

Sitting up, she reached for me, desperate for anything more, but I left her on the bed, standing to the side to remove the rest of my clothes. When my cock bounced free, she licked her lips, and I had to stifle a groan. I knew what she wanted, and I wanted to give it to her, but maybe next round. I wasn't done with her yet, and I needed to feel her squeezing the life out of my cock as she came around it.

Resuming my place above her, I nestled into the cradle of her thighs, allowing her slickness to coat my cock. Reaching down, I hooked one of her legs around my hip before rolling over so that she was above me, straddling my lower abdomen as my dick nestled against the pillowy cushion of her ass.

Gripping her hips, I raised her just enough to place the tip of my cock at her entrance, holding her steady as she tried to impale herself onto me.

Lucy pushed against my chest, raising herself above me, anchoring her hands on my chest. She thought that by me putting her on top, I was about to relinquish some control, but she had no idea.

Letting my cock slide through her folds, bumping her clit, I hissed as fingernails dug into my chest. She was still full of fire, even in her submission, and I fucking loved it.

"Tell me what you want, Princess," I demanded.

Shifting her hips, she moaned. "You."

"You already have me. Tell me what you want," I pressed.

Biting her lip, she let out a shuddering breath. "Fuck me. Claim me. Make me yours."

Christ Almighty, that was more than I could have ever asked for. My grip on her hips grew punishing, knowing it would leave bruises on her perfectly creamy skin, a lingering reminder that she was mine. I might not be the first man—or Dom—to stake my claim on this woman, but I would be the last.

Slowly, I slid her down my shaft until she was seated to the hilt. I gritted my teeth against the blinding pleasure coursing through my veins at our joining. I wondered if this would ever get old? I sure as hell hoped not.

The way our bodies fit together, it was as if they were made for each other. And maybe they were. What if something deep inside my brain always knew she was my perfect match, the submissive to my Dominant, even when we were children? It had been a compulsion to intervene when she acted bratty even back then, like she was always mine to handle.

Before I could lose myself too deep in that thought, Lucy shifted above me. That little minx thought she was in control. It was time to show her who was in charge.

Instead of raising her hips and sliding into her, I rocked her back and forth. The motion put friction on both her clit externally and her G-spot internally, creating the perfect storm to send her plummeting over the precipice I'd held her on all evening.

I started gently, allowing her to feel the delicious double threat, but my patience was wearing thin, and the primal need to watch her come apart at my command became overwhelming. Holding on for dear life, she gripped my chest as I moved her back and forth, shaking her near violently above me until her body seized, her pussy clamping down on me with a vise grip as she came, screaming my name.

The tremors were still coursing through her body when I raised her a few inches and pounded into her from below. With each thrust, she screamed against the unrelenting pace I set. My blood was on fire, and I had one goal—claiming this woman.

Gritting my teeth, I felt my orgasm building, and I tried to hold it off, but it barreled through me, stealing my breath, as I spilled myself deep inside her, painting her walls with my seed. I knew Lucy wanted to concentrate on her career, and I supported her, but a part of me longed to see her pregnant with my child, her belly swollen with a life we created together. She might be the one person on Earth who could unlock a breeding kink I never knew I had.

Lucy collapsed atop my chest, our sweaty bodies slippery as I held her in my arms. This felt so right that it seemed ridiculous how we'd both resisted. I silently thanked those who thought they knew better than us when arranging this match. They saw something we couldn't see, but they were right—we were perfect together.

CHAPTER 27

Preston

THERE WAS NOTHING QUITE so hectic as a royal wedding. When Leo and Natalie wed, I was away serving my requisite time with the Bellestonian army. My parents and brother had attended, but being a guest was different from being on the inside, privy to the chaos behind the curtain of the picture-perfect final product the world saw.

The wedding ceremony itself would be held in the city at Remhorn Cathedral, the oldest church in the country. Most, if not all, the Remingtons had been married there, and the most prominent ones were entombed beneath its marble floors.

Lucy and I were no exception to the family tradition. Six months from now, our wedding would occur in the same cathedral as the world watched on.

The reception following the ceremony was set to take place inside the ballroom at Stonecrest Palace, so in addition to the numerous guests taking up residence within its walls, there was a bustle of activity as vendors set up for the big day. Security was on high alert with the number of people entering the palace daily. Not to mention a large-scale event such as this—

where most of the world's leaders would be in one place—was considered a potential target for an attack.

It was *so* romantic to think that what was supposed to be the happiest
day of your life could also become a tragedy. It was unimaginable but a
reality of the world I lived in now. Lucy was right to want to get away
from it all.

I saw less and less of Lucy as the wedding drew nearer. Most nights,
I went to bed before she returned for the evening, and she was gone
by the time I awoke. I could only imagine her level of exhaustion and
would have loved to take the edge off for her, but we were hardly in the
same room together. I reminded myself this was temporary, and once
the insanity died down, we could go back to Milan to reconnect—at
least until it was our turn to marry.

The night before, the girls—Amy, Lucy, Natalie, and Hannah—took
up residence in a guest suite. It didn't matter that Amy and Liam
were legally married for over a year—they were keeping with tradition,
dictating that the groom should not see his bride until the wedding.

Liam must have been lonely because he invited me to his apartment
for a drink. Sitting down in his living room, I was happy for the
company. There hadn't been much for me to do in the preparations.

Pouring us each a glass of bourbon, he sat in the chair opposite mine
as we savored the liquor.

Breaking the silence, I joked, "So, are you nervous about the big
day?"

Liam chuckled. "Can't be worse than the first time."

So much had happened in the past few months. I only vaguely recalled that during a late-night conversation over drinks, Liam confessed
their initial marriage had essentially been a sham.

"Was it really that bad?" I pressed.

He sighed. "It sure as hell wasn't romantic. Amy wore a suit. Granted, she looked stunning, but it's not exactly every little girl's dream to get married in Vegas with a bodyguard as a witness. We barely even kissed. Probably wouldn't have if I didn't need to send home proof that we were officially married. My parents have no idea it started off as fake. They'd probably have my head for fucking around with the future of our country."

That caught my attention. What would his marriage have to do with the future of our country? He was the second son, and his older brother had three heirs. Remaining silent, I didn't push for clarification. I might be marrying into this family, but I would likely never know about the inner workings—not that I needed to add more drama to my life.

The silence stretched until Liam said, "I actually wanted to ask you a favor."

"Oh?" I raised an eyebrow at him.

"One of my cousins got caught up and won't make it in time for the ceremony tomorrow. I was wondering if you might consider standing up with me in his place."

"I don't know," I protested. "We've been friends a long time, but that's a big deal."

"You're marrying my sister, which makes you my brother. Who better to stand by my side?"

I guess I hadn't really thought of it like that, but it set the wheels turning in my brain. Liam had a brother, but in all my time dealing with Lucy, I hadn't seen him once. Leo was—simply put—an attention whore, always needing to be front and center. Where was he, and why hadn't anyone mentioned him in months? Shouldn't he be here for the wedding? It seemed strange that his own family pretended like he didn't exist.

"Please, Preston?" Liam asked again before smirking. "It comes with perks. You get to escort my beautiful sister instead of seeing someone else put their hands on her."

Damn. He had me there. I hadn't thought about some other guy holding her arm, even if only for a few minutes leaving the church and in the car ride back to the palace. She was mine, and Liam knew how to play to my possessive side.

"If I say yes, what would you have me wear? A last-minute change could throw off the aesthetics, and we know our little fashion princess might have a stroke if I don't match."

"Luckily for you, that won't be an issue. I'll be in my dress uniform, but the groomsmen will wear morning suits. I trust you have one of those?"

He knew I did. "Fine. I was really hoping I didn't have to do this song and dance for another six months, but I'll do it on one condition."

"Name it." There was no hesitation in his reply, and I had a feeling I could have asked him anything, and he would have granted it.

"You will do the same for me when I marry Lucy."

Liam smiled, something he did much more often now that Amy was in his life. "I would be honored. Lucy seems happy, and I have to say, I'd much rather she be marrying someone I know and trust than one of the douchebags we knew growing up."

Hope filled my chest. "You think she's happy?"

Chuckling, he raised his glass to his lips before replying, "Let's just say far too much of the girl talk finds me, whether I want to hear it or not. She's happy. Are you?"

"I never thought I'd say this, but I am." There was no point in denying the truth any longer.

"I guess it's true what they say—opposites attract. It sure was with me and Amy."

"Maybe it's more about finding your complement in another," I mused.

"Maybe you're right. Just promise me you'll take care of her, okay?"

The conversation had taken a serious turn, but I nodded. "You have my word."

Satisfied, Liam returned to savoring his bourbon, and I left him to his last "single" night in peace.

Amy and Liam's big day arrived, and if I thought the lead-up was chaos, it was nothing compared to the morning of. As an official part of the wedding party, I was now in the thick of it, and the wedding coordinators—yes, more than one—were all over us, directing traffic and barking commands. I felt like I was back in the military.

Everything was perfectly timed, and before we knew it, Liam and his groomsmen were being ushered to the palace entrance, where two sleek black sedans awaited to take us down the side of the mountain to the cathedral. It was surreal going through the motions knowing my turn was coming soon.

Leaving the palace grounds, I couldn't conceal my shock at seeing the road lined with citizens, all screaming and waving, hoping to eventually catch a glimpse of the bride on her way to the church. They were gathered along the entire route, some holding signs expressing well-wishes, but the sentiment was the same—everyone was thrilled for the royal couple.

Reaching the cathedral, the crowds were even more dense, requiring barricades to keep them at a respectable distance. Armed guards stood at regular intervals in case one went rogue and posed a threat.

Liam exited the car, and the second the door opened, the roar from the masses was deafening. Taking it in stride, having been born to this life, Liam nodded to those gathered, giving a respectful wave. I had a moment's hesitation before venturing from the car myself—even the most charismatic man would have stage fright under these circumstances.

Taking a calming breath, I pulled the door handle, stepping out onto the cobblestone street. Joining the rest of the groomsmen from the other car, we walked up the steps into the church, leaving the adoring public to wait for the girls. This might be my first time, but all four of those women had done this before, even if it was over a decade ago—only this time, a different one of them was the bride.

We were ushered into a small room just to the side of the altar, where we were expected to wait. Liam smuggled in a flask of his beloved bourbon since the rest of us didn't have pockets in our morning coats. Passing around the metal container, we all took a sip, letting the liquor warm us in the chilly church.

Liam's calm demeanor was almost unsettling. But why wouldn't he be relaxed? He was already married. I knew I would be an absolute wreck waiting for Lucy's arrival on our wedding day. It didn't matter that we were already committed to each other—there was a weight, a finality, to saying marriage vows.

Most of the guests arrived before us, so we were only waiting for the girls. We didn't have to wonder when that moment arrived because the crowds roared so loudly that we could hear it through the thick stone walls.

The sound gave me chills.

It was so strange that these people were enthusiastically happy for two people they probably had never met yet felt a strong connection to them as the face of our country. Every moment of the Remingtons' lives was so well-documented that people felt like they knew them, allowing them to celebrate and mourn with them when the occasion presented itself.

One of the drill sergeants with a headset on burst into the room, declaring it was time for us to take our place at the altar. Liam led the charge, always in command, but I couldn't begrudge him that—it was in his blood. He exhibited his authority in public while I did the same in private, and no part of me wanted to trade.

Following Liam to our proper place, I just about jumped out of my skin when the organ blared to life suddenly behind me. For some reason, this whole event seemed bigger than all of us. We lived in a world that no longer believed in divine right, understanding that bloodlines and mere accidents of birth brought forth our current and future monarchs, but the grandeur of this event was enough to make anyone believe in fairy tales.

This wedding symbolized a modern monarchy. Both Remington brothers brought home commoners from America to be their brides, showcasing that being royal was no longer an exclusive club accessible only to those with the bluest blood. Our future King was being raised on another continent, and I was sure that any offspring brought forth from this union would also spend significant time abroad. Lucy and I were the only ones whose marriage was stuck in the old ways, a last-ditch effort by an outdated and dying generation to hold onto what once was the standard.

My musings were forgotten the moment I caught a flash of blue out of the corner of my eye. Craning my neck from my perch to look down the long aisle, I saw her.

Lucy was a vision in a long dress of her own creation, the same color blue as her striking eyes. Her long black hair was pulled off her neck in an elegant updo, showcasing her bare shoulders—quite scandalous for church—as I moved my gaze down her lean body, noting how her nipples stood out against the bright blue silk draped over her petite frame. I knew she wasn't wearing panties, but the naughty girl had also gone without a bra.

Willing my body not to embarrass me in front of not only all those gathered here today but the millions watching around the world, I kept my eyes on her face, which wasn't a hardship. Lucy was stunning. I hadn't seen Amy yet, but in my mind, Lucy already stole the show.

When those blue eyes flashed to mine, widening in surprise as she saw me waiting at the front for her, it knocked the breath from my lungs. A shy smile graced her lips, and her eyes lowered, allowing her coal-black eyelashes to fan her cheeks momentarily before bringing them back up to meet mine. The impure thoughts rolling through my mind at that simple act were enough for God to strike me down in church, but I couldn't help myself. Lucy's body spoke in a language only we knew, and I itched to get her alone as soon as this ceremony concluded.

Reaching the altar, she took her spot across the aisle from mine, followed in turn by Hannah and Natalie. I had to hand it to Natalie—she had guts to come back here after all these years to stand up for her best friend on such a public stage. She'd done nothing wrong, leaving what I understood to be an abusive relationship. Still, the court of public opinion was strong, and the picture painted by Leo had been less than favorable.

Next came the children—Amelia and Jameson as a pair, preceded by their little brother, Beau. The people of this country hadn't seen the royal children in almost five years and were thrilled to have them home, even if just for a short visit. They were our future.

The organ boomed even louder now, signaling the arrival of the bride. The aisle to the cathedral stretched impossibly long, cast in the soft colors of the sun shining through the stained-glass windows on either side. Light streamed in as the floor-to-ceiling double doors opened at the front of the church, and the crowd's roar filtered in as Amy appeared.

There were two groomsmen standing between me and Liam, but I could hear his audible gasp when he saw her. The look on his face—full of love for the woman striding toward him on her father's arm—was enough to make a grown man cry. Honestly, I didn't know how he was still standing.

Amy portrayed the picture of beauty and grace in the flowing white gown Lucy lovingly made for her. The dress itself was a work of art, with its hand-stitched embroidered overlay and scalloped hem. The silhouette accented Amy's curves perfectly, giving life to Lucy's mission of creating fashion for real women.

Amy appeared to be floating on air, the dress only highlighting the natural beauty she exuded. Her signature auburn hair was curled and left loose, the top of her head adorned with a sparkling diamond tiara. Her makeup was barely there, allowing her green eyes to shine as brightly as the emerald drop earrings gracing her ears. A hint of pink on the apples of her cheeks accented her pale skin as a smile split her face. I had no doubts she loved my friend just as much as he loved her.

I was starting to understand that all-consuming feeling myself—courtesy of the raven-haired beauty standing fifteen feet away.

———— ❈ ————

My eyes never left Lucy's throughout the ceremony, and I could only pray the cameras positioned throughout the cathedral hadn't noticed.

While I didn't mind a headline portraying us as having only eyes for each other, today's story wasn't about us. It was Amy and Liam's day, and the focus should be on them.

The couple shared a kiss, and those gathered to witness their celebration of love clapped. The music blared from the organ once more as they walked back up the aisle. Each bridesmaid met up with a groomsman as they were escorted out behind them, with Lucy and me bringing up the rear.

Keeping the soft smile plastered on her face as she looped her arm through my offered elbow, Lucy whispered, "Well, this is a surprise."

"A pleasant one, I hope," I teased.

"Very pleasant," she cooed.

Together we followed the procession, eventually reaching the open cathedral doors. Amy and Liam were already secured in a car featuring a glass dome so they could be seen by the people lining the road back to the palace, but when the crowd saw us, they erupted in cheers again—this time, yelling our names.

Lucy grumbled, her smile never slipping. "The wedding is barely over, and they're on to the next."

Even when she played the polished princess I'd tortured her for being, she hated every second of it. I had so much regret for not understanding what she was dealing with or seeing the need to live her life in peace. She was never being selfish; she was simply trying to survive the hand she was dealt.

Soon, we would get away from it all, and I couldn't wait to see how she blossomed in the wild.

A door to a black sedan opened for us, and I allowed Lucy to slide in before following, pulling the door closed behind me. Two members of the palace security team sat in the front, and we rolled forward to join the rest of the bridal party for pictures before the reception.

Snaking an arm around Lucy's waist, I pulled her body flush with mine, growling low in her ear, "Do you know how much it was killing me knowing you weren't wearing a bra? All I could think about was how I wanted to take those perky little nipples between my teeth, but God and the whole country were watching."

Gasping, Lucy pulled back enough to search my face. "You could tell?"

She was so fucking adorable. "First time in a drafty old church, Princess?" I teased.

Her face turned the most beautiful shade of pink, and she groaned in embarrassment. "Do you think everyone could tell?"

I could lie to her, but the stills and video of the ceremony would reveal the truth. It wasn't worth it putting a dent in the trust we were trying to rebuild, even if it would offer temporary comfort. "Only if they had eyes."

Blowing out a breath, Lucy grumbled, "Guess that's what I get for ditching the uncomfortable strapless bra."

"You know, they have these adhesive lifting bras these days."

Lucy's jaw dropped. "And what would you know of that?"

I shrugged. "I've done my research. My future wife is in fashion, in case you haven't heard."

"Very funny." She rolled her pretty blue eyes.

Sliding my hand from her waist to her ass, I gave it a squeeze. "What's not funny is that you gave everyone in that church—correction, everyone around the world watching—a peek at what belongs to me. That's a very serious offense, Princess."

Lucy's pupils dilated, and I watched that pulse point at the base of her throat flutter rapidly as she shifted her hips against the leather seat. "I'm very sorry, Sir."

"You will be," I growled in her ear. "The impure thoughts running through my head in a house of God were bad enough. But knowing that other men are going to use that image of you—with your nipples visible through the fabric of your dress—in their personal spank banks for years to come is enough to throw me into a jealous rage."

She bit her lip, knowing she was in trouble, and that I would punish her later. I pressed my thumb against her mouth, providing enough pressure to pull her lip from her teeth. Dipping my head, I was about to claim it for myself when I felt the car stop.

Damn, this would have to wait.

Disappointed, I looked up, ready to exit the car at the palace, when I noticed we were stopped by the side of the road just outside the city, nowhere near the steep switchback road that led up the mountain to Stonecrest Palace. My confusion was mirrored on Lucy's face. We were so lost in each other that we hadn't noticed we were going in the wrong direction.

Before I could ask why we'd taken a detour, the security agent in the front passenger seat opened his door, stepping out and opening mine.

"Time to go, lover boy," he snarled before yanking me out through the open door.

"What the hell is going on here?" I yelled, twisting my body, trying to escape his grip.

"Preston!" I heard Lucy scream from inside the car, and I stopped struggling long enough to see the second agent putting his hands on her.

I saw red.

"Lucy!" I fought back with every bit of strength I possessed, desperate to get to her, but I couldn't break free. "Get the fuck off her!" I shouted right before a blinding pain tore through my head, and my world went black.

CHAPTER 28

Lucy

I BEGAN TO REGAIN consciousness but kept my eyes closed against the persistent pounding in my head. My mouth felt dry, like it was stuffed with cotton balls, and every muscle in my body ached.

What the hell happened?

Thinking back, the last thing I remember was driving away from the cathedral after the wedding in a car with Preston. We were cuddled together in the backseat, and he made it clear he planned to punish me later when we stopped suddenly. By the time we noticed we were nowhere near the route back to the palace, he was being pulled from the car by one of the two security guards escorting us. The other grabbed me when I tried to reach for Preston, and I felt a sting in my neck before the edges of my vision closed around me.

I hadn't recognized either of the guards in our car, but that wasn't unusual during such a large-scale event. Additional agents being brought in was standard procedure.

Reality sank in that someone used the chaos of the wedding to kidnap me.

Panic clawed up my chest to the point where I almost couldn't breathe, but I willed myself to remain calm. I'd been trained for this my whole life. Granted, I never thought I would need to use the survival tactics drilled into my brain as a child, but I was suddenly very thankful for my parents' insistence on their importance.

The first thing I needed to do was gather information—figure out where I was, who I was with, and what they wanted to gain by abducting me.

Keeping my eyes closed, I didn't want to give away that I was awake while I cataloged what I could before adding the visual aspect. The first thing I noticed was that it was cold, much colder than the church earlier, and I would go so far as to say it was colder than the early spring air.

Taking inventory of my body, I gathered that I was sitting upright, but when I tried to move, I couldn't. My shoulders were burning, and I felt the sharp bite of something rough around my wrists when I wiggled my hands—they were tied behind my back, likely with rope, as it felt too prickly to be a zip tie. I couldn't move or close my legs, so my powers of deduction told me I was tied to a chair.

Go figure, my knowledge of bondage implements and techniques came in handy when my life was on the line.

I tried to take a deep breath but couldn't draw air through my mouth—something was stuffed inside it. Great, so I was bound and gagged.

This is bad.

My heart raced with the knowledge that whoever dared to take me was not afraid of the consequences. I was the King's granddaughter, and they clearly knew that with how my kidnapping was planned. They were either insane or stupid—neither scenario would bode well for me.

Trying to breathe through my nose was more difficult, but I managed. Craning my ears, I listened for any sounds that might give me more clues as to where I was and who I was with. The longer I pretended to be knocked out, the better my chances of overhearing something I wasn't meant to hear.

"You're not that good of an actress. I know you're awake."

There wasn't time to dwell on the fact that I'd been caught because that was a voice I recognized. It was a voice I'd known all my life but hadn't heard in almost a year.

Opening my eyes, the person standing before me didn't match up with the memory of the man I knew. His blonde hair was long now—reaching his shoulders—looking greasy and stringy from lack of washing. His brown eyes appeared sunken in his too-thin face, sporting a scraggly, unkempt dark blond beard. Tattered clothing hung off his body, but it didn't matter. I'd know that voice anywhere.

He might not look the same, but there was no doubt that the man behind my kidnapping was my very own brother.

"Hey, baby sis," Leo sneered.

Unable to respond with the gag stuffed in my mouth, it was probably a good thing because I would have given him a piece of my mind. Instead, I scanned my surroundings. We were in a ten-by-ten-foot room with stone walls. I knew exactly where we were—one of the many underground chambers accessed through the tunnels beneath the palace.

My heart sank, knowing that even if I did manage to escape this room, I wouldn't get far. There weren't many places to hide in the tunnels, and I had no way of knowing where we were located in the massive labyrinth created as a security measure.

I guess it only worked to keep you safe if one of your own didn't turn against you.

Pulling on my restraints, testing to see if they had any give, Leo's sinister laugh echoed off the stone walls. "Don't bother. You're not going anywhere." Then he added, "It's not my fault you've been spoiled by fancy silk ties."

That got my attention, and my eyes widened in shock as they snapped to his.

Casually, he stalked toward me. "What? Did you really think there was anything that goes on in this country that I don't know about? I have eyes everywhere. You'd do well to remember that." Thoughtfully, he added, "I suppose I should be thanking you. If it weren't for your *extracurricular* activities on New Year's Eve, I wouldn't have been able to access the tunnels without notice."

New Year's Eve. That was the night Preston revealed himself to be the man behind the mask and then drove me home. I'd been so distraught that it never crossed my mind that I would have left the tunnel access open by not going home the same way I arrived.

Had Leo been living down here since that night? With the dirty way he looked, it was hard to believe otherwise.

God, I was such an idiot. My recklessness put my entire family at risk as I allowed the monster to sneak in the back door. All because I needed my freedom.

Maybe I *was* the selfish brat Preston thought me to be. I hadn't cared about anyone else when I used the tunnels—only myself.

While my mind raced, Leo had gotten close enough to bend low next to my ear to taunt me. "If I knew the kind of sick shit you were into sooner, I would have had a taste for myself."

Bile rose up my throat, and I willed myself not to vomit—I was gagged and would choke on it. If Leo went so far as to take me, he likely wouldn't have any qualms about letting me die.

"Can you promise to stay calm if I remove your gag?" I nodded enthusiastically, desperate to take a deep breath so I didn't hyperventilate. Staying still, even as my skin crawled where he touched it, I heard him remark, "You always were too shrill."

The moment the cloth was removed from inside my mouth, I took in huge gulps of air. Now, it was time to get him talking so I could figure out his motives.

Putting all my effort into not letting him see how rattled I was, I kept my voice steady, asking, "What do you want, Leo?"

He walked away from me, and that's when I noticed the two security guards from the car sitting against the stone wall opposite me. Before Leo turned around, I glanced behind me to scan for additional accomplices, but thankfully, it was just the three men. Not that three adult men against a petite woman were great odds, but it could always be worse.

"I want my rightful place restored." Leo's voice was eerily calm.

"What are you talking about?" I knew the answer already, but my training told me I needed to keep him talking.

"Don't play dumb with me, you little slut!" I flinched at his harsh words.

Leo had never been a kind man, choosing to use his words as weapons in private, but it was still jarring to be on the receiving end. I skated under his radar for most of my life as he sparred with Liam—his natural rival—before eventually focusing on Natalie.

Keeping him talking was important, but aggravating him was borderline dangerous, so I conceded, "You must be referring to the fact that you are my half-brother."

"I am the first-born son!" Leo roared.

Calmly, I repeated my question. "What do you want?"

An evil smile curled on his lips. "It's quite simple, actually. I'm willing to trade an heir for an heir."

That didn't make any sense. I wasn't the one who would take his place—Liam was. Carefully, I pointed that out to Leo. "I think you took the wrong sibling if that's your goal."

"Don't patronize me, Lucy. Liam won't be able to resist playing the white knight to save his precious little sister."

"So, I'm bait, then?" Each question he answered gave me more pieces to the puzzle.

"Something like that."

Even if Leo took Liam out of the equation, that wouldn't be enough to restore him as my father's heir. I was still legitimate and posed a threat if he ever wanted to rule.

My blood ran cold as it hit me.

Leo was going to kill me—whether before or after he did the same to Liam was the only uncertainty.

My life was on the line, but only one thought crossed my mind.

I'd never get the chance to tell Preston that I loved him.

I didn't even know if he was still alive.

When I saw him today at the front of the cathedral waiting for me, the way his eyes never left mine throughout the ceremony, I knew beyond a shadow of a doubt that I was in love with him. The feeling had been growing for weeks, but at the same time, it snuck up on me.

He grounded me in a way I didn't know was possible, easing the burden of my heavy life. He was the first person I wanted to see when I woke up and the last one I saw before falling asleep. Our history might have been complicated, but it shaped our relationship in a unique way, and I couldn't imagine my life without him.

If Leo's goons eliminated him without a thought and I made it out of here alive, I wasn't sure I would survive. My heart would die with him.

Keeping my head held high, knowing I had nothing left to lose, I decided to press Leo further. Psychopaths tended to have big egos, so my goal was to stroke it and see what more I could get out of him.

"It's smart. Once Liam and I are out of the picture, they will be forced to let you resume your role as heir because they no longer have spares. It won't matter that you don't have a drop of royal blood—you will become their last resort."

What he hadn't considered was that my family would rather let a distant cousin take over in ruling our country before they let a depraved son of a bitch like Leo rule. But it wasn't my place to tell him that. I had to make him believe he was the smartest man in the room.

Leo laughed maniacally, sending a chill down my spine. He was seriously unwell.

"You think you've got me all figured out, don't you?" Gesturing to the two other men in the room, he challenged, "Since you know everything, did you know I plan on allowing those two to do whatever they want to your body before putting you out of your misery?"

I swallowed and shook my head. The two giant, hulking men leered at me, and a shudder involuntarily racked my body.

Terror gripped me, but I made a conscious decision to keep stalling for time, praying there was a rescue coming. Surely, someone had noticed I was missing and was actively searching for me.

"How will you continue your line? Will you remarry?" I regretted asking those questions the minute they left my mouth.

"The timing couldn't be more perfect. It just so happens that my children are somewhere above us as we speak. I can picture it now, Belleston rejoicing that I've brought the royal children they adore back home. But don't you worry—Natalie can keep her little bastard." That last line spoke to his conviction that he was not biologically Beau's father.

I couldn't contain my visceral reaction to him mentioning those kids, screaming, "You leave those kids alone! They're better off without you!"

Pain exploded beneath my eye as Leo brought the back of his hand across my face. "No one is better off without me! Not my children. Not my country. NO ONE!"

The crazed look in his eyes scared me into silence. He was coming unhinged, and I wasn't sure how long he needed to keep me alive. Maybe it was better for me to take some time to figure out a way to get out of this chair and plan a possible next move.

Silently, I prayed someone was on the way to rescue me.

CHAPTER 29

Preston

"MR. SCOTT!"

The words reached me through a haze, and I groaned. A searing pain sliced through my skull, and I screamed, opening my eyes to find Myles kneeling before me.

Myles.

Suddenly, it all came rushing back to me.

The church. The car. Being pulled out and Lucy screaming.

Lucy!

Sitting up suddenly, my vision swam, and I laid back down. "Where's Lucy?" I begged Myles.

The remorse on his face told me what I already knew as he sighed. "I was hoping you would be able to answer that for me."

Fuck. "Someone took her."

Myles remained professional, asking, "Did you recognize who it was?"

My memory was hazy, but I remembered one thing. "It was the security detail in our car. They pulled me out—knocking me out, I'm assuming—and took her."

Ruefully, Myles remarked, "You do have a nasty gash on your head."

"Where am I?"

"The side of the road leading out of the city. I tracked your phone the minute I lost eyes on Lucy."

"Is this the part where I'm supposed to be grateful for the invasion of privacy?" I grumbled.

"Would you like me to leave you here?" Myles countered.

Narrowing my eyes, I allowed him to help me up. Gripping my throbbing head, I pulled my hand away and discovered it covered in blood. There were only so many things that would split your head open like that. Lucy was in real danger.

Helping me into the passenger side of the car he'd driven to the edge of town, Myles hopped into the driver's seat and sped toward the palace. Try as I might, I couldn't stop myself from slipping in and out of consciousness as he drove, but I could hear him barking at someone on the phone, sounding the alarm that Lucy had been taken and ordering that the rest of the royal family be placed on lockdown.

Reaching the palace gates, we were stopped by armed guards and given clearance for entry. Judging from the long line of cars we passed on the way up the mountainside, they were refusing to let anyone in who was non-essential. Wedding guests would only make it past the gates once the security team determined the threat level to the royal family.

Racing the rest of the way up the drive, Myles pulled the SUV to a screeching halt at the open palace doors and jumped out, yelling to the rest of the security team within earshot.

Between the jarring motions of the car and the constant loud noises making me feel like an icepick was being driven into my brain, I wanted to throw up.

No, scratch that.

As soon as I got my door open, I heaved the contents of my stomach onto the gravel drive. The two security agents approaching to assist me out of the car paused, covering their noses.

Myles saw their hesitation and barked out, "Oh, for fuck's sake. There isn't time for you to be squeamish right now!"

Not wasting any more time, he hefted me up under one armpit, and one of the other two braced my weight on the other side. I swayed like I was drunk as they helped me inside the palace. I wanted to take a nap, but they dragged me through countless corridors until we reached a tapestry hung on the wall in a dimly lit dead-end.

Myles knocked on the wall beside it in a specific cadence. They must have hit me in the head hard because I could have sworn I saw a head pop out from beneath the tapestry. Startled by the hallucination, I jumped back, exclaiming, "Fuck!"

The head eyed me, asking, "What's his deal?"

Myles explained, "He's definitely got a concussion. Probably needs stitches too. Is the royal physician inside with them?"

"Yeah."

"Well, are you going to just stand there all day, or are you going to let us in?"

"Only you and the princess's fiancé. It's essential personnel only."

The body holding up my right side stepped away, and I nearly crumpled to the ground as he uttered, "Fine by me."

Myles grunted with the extra weight of supporting me solo. "Christ, Ryker, at least give me a warning."

The floating head disappeared, and a side of the tapestry was pulled back, enough to reveal an open steel door. Maybe I wasn't seeing things after all, as the head appeared to be connected to a body standing on the threshold of the concealed room.

Pulling me inside, Myles dropped me into a chair as I heard the unmistakable thud of the steel door closing and being bolted shut. I only had a moment to process where I was before the shouting started.

"Where the hell is my sister?!"

"What happened to him?!"

"Do we know who is behind this?!"

"How long are we expected to remain in here?!"

Grabbing both sides of my head, I screamed, "STOP!"

Well, shit. That seemed to do the trick.

Silence descended upon the room, and I jumped out of my skin when a hand touched my shoulder.

"Hey, it's okay." It was Amy.

Forcing myself to look up at the woman whose wedding was in the process of being ruined, there was nothing but compassion in her eyes.

"What happened?" she asked softly.

"Does everyone promise not to yell?"

Amy gave a pointed look to those gathered in this small room—clearly the designated panic room for the family. "We promise. Don't we?"

There were various murmurs throughout the room, so I chose to proceed. "Lucy and I were in the car between the church and the palace, and we weren't paying close attention to where we were headed. The car stopped, and by the time we realized we weren't going in the right direction, I was being pulled out, and one of them grabbed Lucy."

"One of who?" Amy prompted.

"The two security guards who were in the front seat of our assigned car."

Liam's voice was full of rage as he barked at Myles. "And where the hell were you?"

Myles kept his head held high, but he knew he'd fucked up taking his eyes off Lucy even for a moment in the midst of arguably the biggest security nightmare in over a decade. "Miss Sophie twisted her ankle. I stopped to help her up."

"Sophie?!" Liam roared, causing a stabbing feeling like a hot poker to my brain. "You're not paid to lay down your life to protect Sophie!"

"Yes, sir."

"Get him out of here!" Myles headed for the door voluntarily, but when he got close enough, Liam added, "You are hereby relieved of your duties."

Myles dipped his head in acknowledgment, and before I could blink, he was gone from the room. Liam ordered the royal physician to tend to my wound, and thankfully, the room grew quiet.

While I sat still and allowed the doctor to stitch my head, I took inventory of those gathered within the panic room. Natalie huddled with her three children, trying to soothe them. Princess Adelaide cried softly in a corner as Amy attempted to comfort her. King Victor, Prince Adrian, and Liam spoke in hushed tones, but given the way their hands gestured wildly, their conversation was anything but calm.

This was a side of the family I never wanted to see.

A heavy blanket of despair fell over the room, and it was unsettling, especially when Lucy was the only one not safely held within these secure walls.

What could I have done differently this morning that would have kept her safe? Should I have asked for identification from the guards before placing Lucy inside the car when I didn't recognize them? Why didn't Myles's absence raise a red flag?

I could play the what-if game all day long, but it didn't change the fact that someone took Lucy, and I wasn't enough to protect her.

I'd failed her.

The doctor finished with the stitches, placing a bandage on my head, instructing, "Try to keep this area dry for a few days." I mumbled my acknowledgment as he assessed me carefully. "Did you lose consciousness?"

Here we go. I had better things to worry about right now than myself, but I placated him. "Yes."

"How long were you unconscious?"

I couldn't keep the snark from my voice. "I don't know. I didn't exactly ask my assailant to mark the time before he knocked me out."

The doctor frowned but continued his line of questioning. "Any nausea, dizziness, memory loss?"

My patience was already stretched thin, and I snapped at the balding man. "Are you blind? Did you not see me being propped up on the way in here? Yes, I'm fucking dizzy. As for nausea, I'm sure the palace staff is hosing down the mess in the drive as we speak."

"Preston . . ." Liam warned.

"What?" I snapped at him next. "Am I supposed to sit here and act like this is okay? That my needs come before Lucy's safety? We need to do something to help her!"

Liam took the seat opposite where I sat. "I get it. You feel helpless right now. I do, too."

"Easy to say when your wife is within arm's reach, and you know she's safe," I shot back.

"I'm not going to let anything happen to Lucy," he countered.

"You can't promise that!" I shouted, despite how it shot lightning bolts of pain through my skull.

Liam was gearing up to respond when his phone dinged. Frantically, he dug into his pocket to retrieve it, but my heart sank when I saw him clutch it so tightly that his knuckles turned white.

"What is it? Is it Lucy?" I begged.

Standing, Liam walked toward his grandfather and father, but I could hear him even from a distance, the terror in his voice sending a trickle of fear down my spine. "It's Leo."

"Leo?" I asked, confused. What about Leo?

Liam's eyes shot to mine. "He has Lucy."

Pandemonium erupted inside the room, everyone talking over each other at this shocking development. The panic was palpable, but I didn't understand. Why would Leo take Lucy? It seemed everyone, excluding me, knew the answer but wasn't willing to clue me in.

"What does it say?" I asked, needing to raise my voice loud enough to be heard above the others.

Liam still held his phone in a vise grip. "There's a picture of her gagged and bound to a chair. He wants me and is using Lucy as collateral—that's the gist of it, anyway. I'm expected to meet him alone in an hour, and if I don't . . ." Liam's face contorted in way that made it look like he was about to be sick.

"If you don't, then what?" I needed to hear the words.

"Then he'll kill her."

Princess Adelaide's wails increased in volume as she said on repeat, "This is all my fault."

Liam was methodical. I could see his mind racing, trying to find hidden clues in Leo's message. Finally, he remarked, "I recognize where she is."

A flicker of hope sparked inside my chest. "Where?"

"It's hard to say which one exactly, but it's one of the chambers in the underground tunnels. Nowhere else would have the exposed stone walls like that."

"Tunnels? What tunnels?"

Liam glanced at his father, who nodded slightly, indicating that he could continue. "There are tunnels beneath the palace. They were built as an escape route in case an attack ever occurred and the family needed to reach safety undetected. They lead down into the city."

Oh, Lucy. So that's how she got to Desire undetected. It all made sense.

"The pin he dropped as the place he wants me to meet him is on the edge of the city limits," Liam remarked.

"Did he say anything about whether he would bring Lucy to the meeting?" Prince Adrian asked.

"No. He just says to come alone."

"We can send men down to the tunnels and set up a sniper team at the meet-up location in case he shows up."

Sniper team? Was he suggesting they take out Leo? I mean, I was ready to kill him with my bare hands, but that was his son.

Liam shook his head once. "No. I'm going into the tunnels. Now that we know he has her, moving her is too risky. He's not stupid—he'll know we will have men everywhere looking for signs of her. She's still in her bridesmaid dress, and that flash of blue will stand out."

"You're not going anywhere," King Victor declared.

"I will take Jasper as backup," Liam countered, not backing down.

"I'm going too!" I shouted.

Liam shook his head. "Out of the question."

Standing, I yelled, "The hell I'm not! That's the woman I love!" The effort caused me to feel woozy, and I dropped back into my chair, cradling my head.

Liam scoffed. "You just proved you're not in any shape to accompany me. If you love her, you'll let those who are capable handle the situation. You'd only be a liability down there in your condition."

I knew he was right, but I needed to do something to ease this helpless feeling churning in my gut. More vulnerable than I ever felt in my life, I said softly, "If anything happens to her . . ."

Glancing at his wife, he nodded in understanding. "I know. We'll get her back."

Princess Adelaide jumped up from her perch in the corner. "No! Liam, please, we can't lose both of you. Let someone else go."

Liam walked over to his mother, pulling her into a tight hug before releasing her. "I have to do this. If it goes sideways, you have the children."

All eyes turned to the three Remington children gathered around their mother. Natalie's brown eyes widened when she realized he meant that her kids would be what was left of the family if the unthinkable happened today.

"No," Natalie sobbed. "Liam, please."

For a moment, I thought Liam might reconsider—Natalie had always been his Achilles' heel—but he held firm. "I'm the best chance Lucy's got. I know you'll do what needs to be done if I don't make it back."

Natalie covered her face as she wept, but Liam didn't waste another second consoling her. Grabbing a gun from one of the extra security guards in the room, he tucked it into the waistband of his pants.

Turning to his wife, his long strides ate up the space between them and he grabbed her face for a hard kiss that lasted barely a second before breaking away. "I love you, Ames."

I don't know how Amy held it together, but her voice never wavered, staring up at her husband. "I love you, too. Bring her home safe."

The steel door opened, and Liam walked through it, followed closely by his security agent, Jasper, who was also armed. The sound of the door closing and bolting behind them was deafening, giving off an air of finality and foreboding as we all wondered if we would ever see Lucy or Liam again.

Soft sniffles were the only noise in the room until Beau asked his mother, "Is the bad man going to hurt Aunt Lucy?"

Jameson jumped in to clarify, "That bad man is our dad, Beau."

Natalie sprang into action, kneeling before her three children and gathering their attention. "You listen to me. That man might be your father on paper, but your *dad* is the man back home waiting for us in Connecticut. He's the one who is there for you every day and loves you more than anything in this world. Do you understand?"

"Yes, Mom," a chorus of three voices responded.

Those poor kids were dealt a crappy hand. Not only were they born into royalty, where their every move was of general interest to the public, but the man who fathered them was a piece of shit human being and mentally unstable. No one as young as them should have to deal with this situation, knowing that even someone who shares the same blood could be a threat. I wished they could be normal kids who never had to question whether their family loved them and put their safety above all else.

Being alone with my thoughts in the silence was dangerous. All I could think about was all the awful things Leo might do to Lucy. If he was crazy enough to take her, there was no telling what he would do.

I bargained with God, promising him anything if he could just let Liam bring Lucy home safely.

CHAPTER 30

Lucy

THE COLD SEEPED INTO my bones as the time passed, and the throbbing under my eye was relentless. There was no way of knowing how long I'd been in this room, being underground with no windows. All I knew was that one of Leo's henchmen left a little while ago and hadn't returned.

I kept quiet after Leo struck me, but I couldn't stand the silence a moment longer. My voice was scratchy with lack of use, but I dared to ask, "When are we expecting Liam?"

Leo picked at the dirt under his fingernail with the tip of a knife. "We aren't."

"How do you expect to eliminate him, then?"

If Leo was smart, he would learn to keep his mouth shut, but his ego won out. "Your heroic big brother is headed to a meeting point far from here—lured by a picture of you tied up here before you woke up—where Colt will be waiting to put a bullet in his brain. Once he returns with confirmation that the job is done, then it's your turn."

The last thing I wanted to give Leo was the satisfaction of seeing how terrified I was at the prospect of being physically assaulted and then murdered, so I used my years of practice and schooled my features to give an outwardly calm appearance.

Leo mentioned a picture—if taken in this room, then he underestimated Liam. He'd know this room was inside the tunnels. We used to play down here when we were kids. We couldn't resist a game of hide and seek, given the massive maze the tunnels created.

Liam had tactical training from his service in the military. He wouldn't bite on a promise of me if he had proof of my location. And he also wouldn't allow someone else to come for me. Liam would take charge, insisting that he be the one to rescue me instead of remaining in the panic room, sitting on his hands.

That meant he was coming for me. It was just a matter of when he found the right room, and if that came before Colt returned with news that he'd been a no-show at their meeting.

I needed to find a way to get out of this chair. Years of self-defense training would only be useful if I could get my hands and feet free. Sure, I was no match for a gun if either of them had one—Leo, for sure, had a knife—but I would rather go down fighting than remain a sitting duck.

My ass went numb from its immobile position on the wooden chair for God knows how long, and it gave me an idea. Squirming to make it look believable, I declared, "I need to use the bathroom."

Leo didn't even look up. "Tough luck, sis. There's not exactly indoor plumbing down here."

Trying again, I asked, "If you've been living down here, how have you managed?"

Tilting his head toward the corner, my gaze landed on a bucket there. "Figure it out."

"I'm not too good for a bucket."

"You might as well just piss yourself. You don't have much time left anyway."

Thinking quickly on my feet—or my ass, in this case—I yelled, "I have my period!" Leo finally glanced up, a disgusted expression on his face, and I watched as the remaining guard squirmed, looking uncomfortable, so I leaned into it. "I don't know how long we've been down here, but much longer, and things could get real messy."

Leo narrowed his eyes. "What do you want me to do? It's not like I'm stocked up on a bunch of feminine products down here."

"That rag you stuffed in my mouth earlier. That would work for a little while."

Snapping his fingers, he directed his accomplice to grab the rag from where he'd tossed it on the floor. "Carson, help the princess out, would you?"

Carson wrinkled his nose but grabbed the filthy rag and stalked toward where I sat. When he began to lift the hem of my dress, I protested, "I need to remove my tampon first."

"For fuck's sake," Carson mumbled. Turning to Leo, he held his hands up. "I'm not doing that."

Leo glared at me. "Fine. Untie her and let her have a moment." Pointing his knife in my direction, he added, "Don't try anything stupid. Just remember . . . I don't exactly need you alive."

Nodding, I agreed. "I promise." He couldn't see my fingers crossed where they were tied behind my back.

Carson started with my ankles, and I reminded myself not to be hasty—I needed all four of my appendages freed before I made a move. I rolled them once the ropes were untied and winced against the lingering rope burn I felt. Moving behind me, Carson deftly undid the tie holding my hands together.

Not letting me get far with my newfound freedom, Carson clamped a hand down on my upper arm so tightly that I cried out in pain. Half dragging me on cramped legs to the corner of the room, he let go suddenly, causing me to stumble as he tossed the disgusting scrap of cloth in my direction.

I allowed it to float to the floor as I squatted over the bucket, reaching under my skirt, pretending to remove a tampon. Keeping one hand up my dress, I leaned with the other toward the rag, which was just out of reach, huffing out an exaggerated breath of frustration. "Can't seem to reach it."

"What now?" Leo's annoyance was evident in his tone.

"The rag is too far. I'd grab it myself, but my flow is really heavy today, and I'm afraid I'll get blood on the floor."

Sighing heavily, he barked, "Carson, hand her the rag. Fucking disgusting."

Carson eyed Leo but obeyed his command, stepping closer and bending down to grab the rag before reaching out to hand it to me. Using all the leverage I had in my bent legs, I lunged at his face with my elbow. The force of the impact with his nose vibrated down my arm, as I heard a satisfying crunching sound as a result.

"You little bitch!" He screamed in pain as he clutched at the blood running down his face.

Bolting for the door while he was distracted, I didn't make it far. A hand grabbed a fistful of my hair, yanking me back violently enough that I feared my neck might snap. I had to fight the urge to gag as he gripped my breast painfully, his breath hot in my ear, as he spoke roughly, "You might think that a little blood will stop me from violating this body, but you have two other perfectly good holes I can use. There won't be anything left for Colt by the time I'm done with you."

Using his grip on my hair, he turned me forcefully to face him, and I saw the truth of his words in his cold, dead eyes. Terrified out of my mind, the only thing left to do was fight until I couldn't anymore. Gritting my teeth, I raised my foot and stomped on his with the sharp point of my heel, causing him to shove me away from him.

Unfortunately, the force knocked me right onto my ass, and before I could scramble to my feet, his large body was on top of mine. Rearing back a hand, he landed a punch right to my jaw, and I swore I saw stars.

Fuck, that shit hurt.

How did men get in fistfights and not call it quits after the first punch?

Carson took advantage of my stunned state, and I heard the ripping of fabric over the rising psychotic laughter from Leo's mouth as he watched on in amusement. Coming to my senses, I realized my hands were free because he couldn't restrain me while his hands were occupied tearing my dress, so I clawed at his face, trying to gouge out his eyes.

His screams filled the small space, and he shoved a knee between my thighs to hold them open as he gripped my wrists in one of his large, beefy hands. The other went to his belt, and I heard it jangling as he unbuckled it, along with the sound of his zipper lowering. As soon as I was confident his dick was out, I brought my knee up as hard as I could, and I must have hit the mark because he yelped in pain, grabbing himself with both hands, thus freeing mine.

I tried to turn onto my stomach and crawl out from beneath him, but his weight held me down—I was trapped.

Snarling, Carson attempted to mount me again, and I opened my mouth as I extended my neck, hoping I could get my mouth close enough to bite something off, but it was useless.

Grunting, he tossed over his shoulder, "You didn't warn me she was a fucking feral cat."

"Does it matter? Finish up, so you can hold her down and I can take a turn," Leo called back.

My stomach lurched. He was still my half-brother, and the idea of him violating me was sickening.

Deciding to use that, I pictured the vile act, willing myself to puke on Carson to get him off me, when there was an ear-splitting bang, and wetness splashed on my face. I couldn't stop the scream that left my mouth as the weight of Carson's heavy body crashed atop mine.

Another loud bang rang out, and I realized it was a gunshot.

Who was shooting? Was it Leo? Was Colt back?

"You son of a bitch!" Leo screamed in agony, and I could turn my head just enough to see him crumpled on the cold stone floor, gripping his knee as a blossom of red spread beneath his palms.

That's when Liam came into view, and I nearly wept with relief as he stood over Leo and landed a perfect hit to his temple, knocking him out.

Carson's weight pressed on my chest, and I couldn't expand my lungs enough to draw air. Struggling, I pushed my hands against him, but he was immovable, and my vision began to close in.

This can't be how this ends. Crushed to death after I've been rescued.

Gasping, my lungs burned with the need to draw air. Just when I was about to give up hope, the weight was removed, and I gulped in huge breaths of air as my vision swam.

"Lucy! Oh my God. Lucy!" I felt rather than saw Liam pull me into his arms. I wasn't sure if it was the adrenaline crash or the lack of oxygen, but that was the last thing I heard before I passed out.

CHAPTER 31

Preston

THERE WAS A BANG on the door to the panic room, causing everyone's heads to swivel toward it. I'd been here for less than an hour, but it felt like an eternity while we sat silently, knowing Lucy's life hung in the balance.

More knocking, this time more rhythmically, and whoever was out there must have known the secret code because one security agent cocked his gun, training it on the steel door, as another opened it carefully.

Liam burst through the doorway, carrying Lucy's limp body. I vaguely heard Liam tell his father to remove the women and children from the room as I stumbled to where he placed her down on a couch.

Kneeling next to her unconscious body, I cupped her face with both hands. "Lucy, baby. Please wake up."

I had been so relieved to see her that I didn't notice the blood splattered across her face and upper chest.

Looking to Liam in question, he quickly explained, "It's not hers."

Caressing the soft skin of her cheeks, I winced at the ugly-looking bruise forming at the edge of her jawline, noting another under her eye. Scanning the rest of her body for injuries, I saw the jacket of Liam's dress uniform draped across her legs. Thinking he was trying to keep her warm, I removed it, revealing the tattered remains of the lower half of her dress.

The breath froze in my lungs at the sight. Liam replaced the jacket over her bare thighs as I stared at her in shock, praying with all my might that I could erase whatever happened to her in those tunnels.

Liam had to physically pull me away long enough for the royal physician to examine her. Not straying far, I pulled a chair to the edge of the couch, keeping her hand held in mine.

"How was she when you found her?" the doctor asked Liam.

Liam spared me a glance, hesitating, and I could see the regret written all over his face.

"Tell him," I demanded.

Running a hand through his dark hair, he sighed. "There was a man on top of her." Fuck. Hearing him confirm it drove a dagger into my heart. "I took him out with a bullet to the head; that's the blood splatter you see. She was struggling to breathe by the time I got his weight off her chest. She passed out not long after."

Using a stethoscope, he listened to her lungs. "Her breath sounds are good. We're not looking at a collapsed lung, so it's possible she fainted due to shock." Pausing, he looked between me and Liam. "Shall I examine for signs of a sexual assault?"

"No!" I roared, gripping my head against the pain yelling caused. "Don't you fucking touch her!"

Liam put a hand on my shoulder. "I know it's hard, man. But we need to know for sure."

I wanted to rip him limb from limb. It was my job to protect this woman, and the idea of some other man putting his hands on her, forcing himself on her . . . It made me physically ill.

Just as I was about to grant permission, her tiny hand squeezed mine, and my heart leapt. "Lucy?"

She squeezed again, harder this time.

"Luce, can you hear me?"

Those blue eyes fluttered open and locked on mine. Relief washed over me like a tidal wave as her voice croaked out, "Preston?"

Knocking the doctor out of the way, I sat on the couch, pulling her into my arms. I was never going to let her go ever again. "I've got you, Princess."

Her body began to shake at the use of her special nickname, and I felt wetness soaking through my shirt. Before I knew it, tears fell from my eyes and into her dark hair. The feeling was bittersweet as I wept with her in relief that she was safe but also in heartbreak at the horrors she was forced to endure at the hands of her own brother.

Lucy pulled her face off my chest, her sad blue eyes glassy with tears. Placing both her hands on my cheeks, she whispered, "I thought I'd never see you again."

I knew how she felt, but I needed to push my fear to the side. What she went through was far worse, and I was determined to support her in any way I could.

Wiping the tears from her cheeks with my thumbs, I whispered, "I'm right here."

Lip trembling, she nodded. "Don't leave me."

"Never." I shook my head.

There was a touch on my shoulder, and I glanced back to find Liam with a sympathetic expression on his face, the question clear in his blue eyes. Taking a steadying breath, I forced myself to pull back from her clinging form, making room for the doctor.

Confusion clouded her eyes as she gripped me tighter. "Where are you going?"

This was killing me. "Baby, the doctor needs to examine you. If you want Liam and me to leave the room, we can."

Understanding dawned, and Lucy shook her head furiously. "No."

"I know it's difficult, but—"

"No," she stated again. "He didn't touch me."

"Baby, it's okay. We just need to make sure you get the proper care."

"You're not listening!" Lucy's cries rendered us silent. "He tried, but he wasn't successful."

"Are you sure?" Liam asked from above. Clearing his throat, we both turned to him, and his discomfort was evident. "He was . . . exposed."

Lucy never faltered. "Like I said, he tried. I got a good knee in right before he collapsed on top of me."

That's my girl.

A mix of relief and pride welled in my chest. My girl was a fighter. I shouldn't have expected anything less.

The physician asked Lucy, "Are there any other injuries that need to be addressed?"

Lucy shook her head. "No. My face hurts, but I don't think you can do much for that."

My entire body tensed when he reached out to cup her jaw, probing the skin gently with his thick fingers.

Frowning, he pulled his hand away. "There don't appear to be any broken bones that I can tell. Let me know if the pain becomes sharp instead of a dull throb, and we can arrange for X-rays. Other than that, if eating bothers you, opt for softer foods or chew on the other side. I'm sorry I can't offer more treatment than that."

Liam escorted him from the room, and Lucy burrowed into my chest. The words were on the tip of my tongue to tell her how much I loved her, but I couldn't do it like this. Not today. I didn't want my declaration of love for the woman I intended to spend the rest of my life with to be tainted by the events of the day, to be forever intertwined with arguably the worst day of our lives.

So, I would wait. Instead, I would pour my love into my actions and care for her until the time was right to say the words out loud.

Liam returned, settling into the wingback chair opposite where we sat. His jaw was set so tight, I wondered how he didn't crack a tooth. I knew my friend, and even though he had killed one of the men involved, he held himself personally responsible for his family's safety—especially that of his younger sisters.

"Lucy," he began, causing her to turn her head to face him, still plastered to my body so closely that there wasn't an inch of space separating us. "I need some information from you to determine if there's still a threat to our family out there."

Trembling in my arms, she nodded. "What do you need to know?"

"I don't know how much you remember, but I took out the man trying to assault you. Leo's been disabled, and all tunnel access has been sealed, with security teams clearing them now. Was there anyone else?"

"Yes. There were two men besides Leo. One left before you came in. He was—he was—" Her voice broke, and I could feel her start to cry again, but she forced out, "He was going to kill you."

Liam nodded. "We apprehended a man at the location I was sent via text. Can you identify him as the second man if I show you a picture?" He pulled his phone out and handed it to her.

Peering down at the picture on the glossy screen, she replied, "That's him."

"Good. We have him in custody. He'll never see the light of day again."

"And Leo?"

Just the mention of that son of a bitch's name had my body vibrating with rage. What kind of person kidnapped his little sister and watched while one of his accomplices tried to violate her body? If what she said was true and he wanted Liam dead, who was to say he wouldn't eliminate her as well? The man had no soul.

"A padded cell for the rest of his life is too good for him, but that's what Mother and Father have decided."

"So, it's really over?" Lucy asked, cautiously optimistic.

Liam sighed, running a hand over his jaw. "I'm sorry you got mixed up in this, Lucy."

Sensing he needed comfort, she pulled herself from my arms and hugged her brother. I watched as his arms tightened around her like a lifeline. "I'm sorry you did, too. But if it helps, Belleston will have the most badass king they've ever seen someday."

While that comment elicited a chuckle from his chest, it stopped me dead in my tracks.

Today changed everything for our country. Lucy was implying that Liam would become King after his father. Obviously, Leo was psychotic and couldn't be allowed to rule, but he had three children. How could they bypass them so easily? And if they did, that left Liam and Lucy as the remaining Remingtons in their family line.

That raised so many questions.

What would happen if neither of them had children? Who would rule Belleston?

Was our match more than what it seemed? Bloodlines were brought up more than once. Did they already know our children might one day be required to rule?

Why was Natalie so terrified at the prospect of her children being all that was left if something happened to Liam and Lucy? She always knew they were in the direct line of succession.

I had a feeling I was the only one in the room today who didn't have the whole picture. They all knew something I didn't. It was understandable because I was an outsider; I couldn't be trusted with deep family secrets until I was officially a member of the family. But at minimum, I should have been alerted if there was a threat out there. I could have been more vigilant, more aware—especially today.

Liam kissed Lucy tenderly on the forehead before picking her up like she weighed nothing and placing her back in my arms. "I'll have Amy get you something to wear, and then we can get you out of here."

At the mention of Amy, Lucy groaned. "Oh, Liam. I'm sorry I ruined your wedding."

Staring fondly at his baby sister, he shook his head. "At the risk of losing my tongue, nothing matters more than you do, LuLu."

I could hear her swallow as tears threatened to overtake her again. "I love you, Liam. Thank you for saving me."

Winking at her, he joked, "I know you'd do the same for me." Then he exited the room, leaving us completely alone.

I owed Liam my life for stopping at nothing to see Lucy brought safely back to me. He risked his own life for hers. His loyalty and love knew no bounds, and if what Lucy said was true—that he would someday be our King—we would be lucky as hell to have him.

Holding Lucy close, I knew that while the imminent threat was gone, the aftereffects of her ordeal would plague her beyond today. It was my job to remain steadfast, to provide her with the support she needed and however she needed it. It wouldn't be easy, but I loved her enough to weather the storm.

———⟨≫⟩———

"*Breaking news out of the small European country of Belleston today. Prince Leopold Remington has been admitted to the psychiatric ward at the Remhorn Mental Health Facility and is expected to remain there indefinitely, according to palace sources.*

King Victor has petitioned Parliament that Prince Leopold is mentally unstable and unfit to rule. In response, they have removed him from the line of succession. Leopold has three children—two sons and a daughter—who reside in the United States with their mother. Former Princess Natalie has petitioned Parliament that they be removed from the line of succession, in addition to their father.

This leaves Crown Prince Adrian's second son, Prince William, as heir behind his father and grandfather. Prince William recently married American oil heiress, Amy Michaels, and the pair have created many programs benefiting Bellestonians in need.

However, the future of the country's longest-reigning royal family hangs in the balance as they wait to see if their youngest generation provides heirs to continue their line."

Sighing, I turned off the news report on the television. It wasn't every day that a country eliminated not one but four people from their line of succession, so it was bound to make international news, but it dredged up so many bad memories for the family to have it constantly brought up.

It had been two weeks since Amy and Liam's ruined state wedding and Lucy's kidnapping, and I knew so much more about the underlying issues that led to Leo's psychotic break. Lucy told me that Leo wasn't her father's son, and only after her abduction did her mother share the details of her own assault that led to his conception. Liam knew before marrying Amy, but Lucy only discovered she was the spare when her grandfather asked her to marry me.

Leo hadn't handled it well when he learned the news and disappeared shortly after. He felt entitled after thirty-five years of being groomed to take over for his father, but the signs that he was deranged became too strong to ignore, and they made the decision to bypass him. He was only raised as the heir to save Princess Adelaide from the trauma of having her assault broadcast to the world. She'd been through enough already.

Having Leo declared insane was the best-case scenario for the family. It allowed them to have him formally removed from the line of succession without bringing up the circumstances surrounding his birth.

No one knew about Lucy's kidnapping either. The palace explained away the lockdown after the wedding as standard procedure, citing that they received an anonymous threat to the royal family.

The monster was in a padded cell, where he could never hurt anyone again, and the women would never have to worry about the public having private details about their trauma.

Adelaide, Natalie, and Lucy could finally heal without looking over their shoulders.

A soft shuffling sounded from behind where I sat on the couch in the private sitting room of our master suite. Turning my head, I saw Lucy, still in her pajamas, hair a tangled mess, as she moved through the room to sit beside me. Pulling her into my arms, I kissed the top of her head to comfort her.

Thank God Prince Adrian and Liam handled most of the press conferences due to Leo's commitment to the mental hospital. Lucy wasn't brought into focus much, which was a blessing.

Two weeks, and we hadn't left the apartment once. We had the occasional visitor, but she wasn't strong enough yet to venture outside the safety of our home within the palace. The bruises on her face had faded, but the emotional damage would take longer to heal—if it ever did.

She was a mess when she discovered Liam had dismissed Myles as her personal protection officer. He was her shadow for five years; she trusted him, and the thought of going out with someone new only caused her to draw further into her shell and the protection this apartment offered.

I begged her to let me whisk her away to Milan, away from all of this, but she'd refused. Lucy might have been hurting, but she was adamant that I begin my post as a consultant to the treaty law team. The shake-up to our line of succession had the potential to alter relationships with other nations as Leo was the prominent face in international relations for over a decade.

The only problem was that I didn't know how I could leave her alone in the apartment in this state. As it was, we slept with the lights on every night. She was struggling, even if she wouldn't verbally admit it. The signs were all there.

"The world is watching, waiting for Liam and me to fail to produce an heir." It was a statement of fact from Lucy—her voice had no emotion.

"I shouldn't have been watching," I apologized. "Don't worry about what anyone else thinks or has to say. Your only focus should be on getting better."

Pulling back, her blue eyes met mine. "I'm okay." Then, she stood up and went back to bed. It was 10 AM, and that's where she would remain for the rest of the day.

She wasn't fooling anyone. She was not okay.

———— ✦ ————

The shrill screams woke me from a dead sleep, and I bolted into action. Lucy was thrashing in bed beside me, her body covered in sweat as the nightmare played behind her closed eyes.

This was the third time she'd woken me like this in the past week.

The lights were on already, so I didn't waste any time pulling her into my arms, hoping to wake her up so she knew she was safe.

"No! Get off me!" Lucy screamed, her eyes moving rapidly beneath their closed lids.

It broke my heart when she called out in her sleep like this. I learned more about what happened to her in that cold room beneath the castle when she was asleep than she ever told me when she was awake.

"Luce, baby, wake up. I've got you. You're safe," I begged her gently and calmly so as not to scare her further.

Slowly, her body relaxed, and her eyelids fluttered open to reveal bright blue unfocused eyes. Patiently, I held her until she realized where she was and who she was with. Then those beautiful eyes filled with tears, and she began to cry.

"Preston," she sobbed, clutching me like I had the power to take away all the bad things that happened to her.

God, if only it were that simple. I would do it in a heartbeat. I felt so helpless while she battled these invisible demons.

"I'm right here, Princess."

"I can't do this."

"Can't do what, baby?" Whatever it was, I would move heaven and Earth to help her.

"I can't stay here. Every time I close my eyes, I see him, hear him, knowing he was right beneath us for months, just waiting for an opportunity. An opportunity *I* gave him."

Lucy was referring to the night I took her home from Desire, leaving the tunnels accessible from the doorway in Remhorn. She explained to me that's how he got in and that he'd been living down there since that night.

My response was instant. "Then we leave tomorrow. We can go to your place in Milan, Liam offered up his house in Connecticut, or we can go somewhere warm where we are alone and forget the rest of the world exists. I will take you anywhere—throw a dart at a map, and we're gone."

Tears streamed down her face as she searched my eyes. "But your job . . ."

"Fuck the job, Lucy. It's not worth it to see you in pain."

"But it's your dream. I can't ask you to give it up for me."

I knew what she was doing, trying to give me an out. We'd spent months trying to push each other away, and now she was telling me she would walk away if that's what I wanted. She couldn't stay here, but she was willing to leave and let me remain, giving me a chance to have everything I wanted before I fell in love with her.

Five months ago, I would have skipped out of this palace with a giant smile on my face if she decided to call it quits, but so much had changed since then. I needed her just as much as she needed me. My world would crumble without her.

I almost lost her once. I couldn't bear to lose her again.

Cupping her cheeks with my hands, I shook my head. "I have a new dream now. One that sees you safe, happy, and whole. You matter more than anything, Lucy. A life without you is a life I don't want to live. Jobs come and go. *You* are what I want for the rest of my life."

She choked back a sob. "You really mean that?"

"Of course, I mean that. I love you, Lucy. I realized it weeks ago, but I wasn't sure you felt the same, and I didn't want to pressure you. Maybe I thought you would think it was lip service because we were set to be married anyway, and I was trying to make it easier by saying I cared. Maybe I was scared that you wouldn't feel the same way. But then, you were taken from me, and I realized I should have told you every single day. You deserved to know how you make my life worth living, how you light up my world, and how the thought of spending one day apart from you makes my stomach hurt. You are everything I never knew I always needed. You, Lucy Remington, are my whole world. I love you now, and I will love you until I take my last breath. If you'll have me, that's where I'll be, by your side. For now, and always."

There.

I did it.

I poured out my soul to the woman I loved, and now it was up to her whether she was willing to accept my love. Even if she didn't, I knew I couldn't stop my heart from loving her.

"Oh, Preston." Lucy's voice trembled. "I love you so much." Those words had my heart soaring, but I allowed her to continue. "All I could think in that room was that if something had already happened to you, or if I didn't make it out, I'd never have the chance to tell you. That would have been the greatest regret of my life, not telling you how I felt. Our love story almost became a tragedy before we even got a chance to write it. We get a second chance, and I don't want to waste it here, surrounded by these bad memories."

Dropping my forehead to hers, I kissed her softly. Pulling my lips away, I said against hers, "It's you and me. From here on out."

I felt the smile creep onto her lips. "Just us?"

Laughing for the first time in weeks, I confirmed, "Just us."

Just us was all I would ever need.

Epilogue

Lucy

Five Months Later

"WHERE ARE WE GOING?" I asked Preston as we sped through the streets of Manhattan in a sporty silver coupe.

Grabbing my hand from across the center console, his eyes never left the busy roads before us. "It's a surprise."

Laughing, happier than I'd ever been in my life, I teased, "That doesn't always promise to be a good thing."

"Don't worry, Princess, you're going to love it."

I could hardly believe there was a time in my life when Preston calling me Princess had grated on my nerves like hearing nails on a chalkboard. I'd hated it more than anything in this world.

Now, I loved it. It made me feel safe and loved.

He made me feel safe and loved.

His unwavering support during some of my darkest days was the only reason I was still standing.

After the disaster of Amy and Liam's wedding, my family was forced to abandon the idea of a state wedding for me and Preston. The morning following our declarations of love in the dead of night, we packed up, left Belleston, and hadn't returned since. Maybe someday, I could walk the halls of my childhood home and not be haunted by the memories of what happened there, but it wouldn't be anytime soon.

My mom was the first to step in, supporting my wishes, and immediately began searching for alternatives. With the new studio I decided to launch in New York, we settled on having the ceremony at Trinity Church on Wall Street. It was intimate, with immediate family only, and the best part was that the press had no clue.

Being away from Belleston turned out to be the best thing for me, and Preston was the one to suggest settling part-time in America. It was comforting to know my brother and sisters-in-law—along with my nieces and nephews—were only a short drive away. It was like having a little piece of home away from home, and they provided the support system I desperately needed while I mentally recovered from my trauma.

I was living the fashion designer life I always dreamt of, and as of thirty minutes ago, I was now Mrs. Preston Scott. We would, of course, be bestowed with new titles as a married couple by my grandfather, but my title as Preston's wife would be the one I cherish most.

I asked my mom this morning why she suggested Preston to Grandfather as the perfect match for me—bloodlines and birth order aside—and she told me that it always made her smile when Preston would ruffle my feathers when we were children. She knew I would grow up to be a strong, independent woman and would need an equally strong man to challenge me and know exactly when to put me in my place.

If only she really knew.

No matter how it happened, I could only thank her for knowing what was best for me, even when I couldn't see it for myself.

Preston pulled the car up to a valet in front of a building in the Upper East Side, exiting the driver's side before rounding and opening my door, giving me his hand, and helping me out. Even in the busy New York street, I couldn't resist pressing my lips to his. These lips belonged to me, and I craved them constantly.

Escorting me to the double doors held open by a doorman, I looked at Preston, confused, as we entered what looked like an apartment building's lobby. "Where are we?"

Smirking, he walked me toward the elevator, hitting the button and calling it to the ground floor. "You'll see."

Trying to goad him into giving up a clue, I teased, "It's not like you to be so mysterious."

Those hazel eyes flared as his pupils dilated and his voice dropped an octave. "Oh, I can be very mysterious, Mrs. Scott."

Oh, yes, he could.

The elevator doors opened, and Preston pressed the button to the 20th floor. Up we went as I tried to figure out just what the surprise was. My mind was still spinning as the gold-plated doors slid open, and he pulled me down the hallway, stopping at the door with a placard that read Apt. 2003.

Hmm. After our few nights in Room 203 at Desire, I could have read more into it, but it was probably a coincidence. Right?

Pulling a key from his tuxedo pocket, he unlocked the door and opened it but stopped me when I tried to walk inside. There wasn't time to ask why because he pulled me into his arms, carrying me across the threshold, whispering in my ear, "Welcome home, Princess."

"Home?" I looked around in disbelief. We were standing in a wide-long entryway, but even from here, I could see gorgeous crown molding and stunning hardwood floors.

Placing me on my feet, he encouraged, "Look around. Let me know what you think."

I'd already cried once today when we said our vows, and it was almost a sure bet I was about to gear up for round two. My heels clacked on the wood floors as the hallway opened into a massive living space furnished beautifully with a comfortable-looking leather couch and antique wooden accent tables. Floor-to-ceiling windows showcased double doors leading out to a balcony overlooking Central Park. There was a decent-sized kitchen with a large island and stainless-steel appliances, a dining room set with a table that could seat up to ten people, and a powder room. Beyond the living spaces, I discovered a laundry room and two additional doors. The first opened to a master bedroom done in gold and cream, featuring a four-poster bed, two walk-in closets, and an ensuite bathroom.

"I can't believe you did this," I gushed at Preston.

Circling his arms around my waist from behind, he rested his chin on the top of my head. "The one-bedroom in SoHo wasn't going to work long-term."

"This is too much!" I protested.

Turning me in his arms so that I faced him, he countered, "Nothing is too much for you. You deserve the world, and I'm just the lucky bastard trying to give it to you."

Looping my arms around his neck, I pulled him down for a long slow kiss, showing gratitude for his thoughtfulness. Pulling back slightly, I whispered, "Thank you."

Breaking out of his embrace, I walked out of the master suite to the last remaining door, expecting to find a second bedroom. Turning the knob, I found it locked.

Frowning, I turned to Preston. "Why is this door locked?"

Reaching into his jacket, he pulled out a key on a long strand of black ribbon. Handing it to me, he said, "This is only for when you're ready."

"Ready for what?" I asked in confusion as I unlocked the door.

Turning the knob successfully this time, I pushed the door open and gasped. Inside was a mini replica of our room at Desire. Black silk sheets on a bed with a slatted headboard, a quilted bench seat at the foot of the bed, and an armchair to the side. But in addition to those, there were large pieces of equipment—most notably, a Saint Andrews Cross.

Preston had put together a playroom for us.

From behind me, I heard him softly say, "Like I said, only when you're ready. *If* you are ever ready. I don't need this more than I need you."

Turning, I looked at my husband. I learned in these past few months how truly selfless he was. He took care of me when I couldn't take care of myself. He put his life on hold, ready and willing to move anywhere in the world so that I could feel safe. He supported my career goals with enthusiasm, pushing me to be a better version of myself both in my personal and professional life.

The only drawback was that even now, many months later, he treated me as if I were made of glass. I was strong enough to admit that there was a short time after the incident when my own shadow was enough to spook me, but I was better now. I'd spent a lot of time in therapy, and I could recognize that I would probably never be able to forget what happened to me entirely, but I could move on and not have it impact every facet of my life.

I could sleep with the lights off now, and I wasn't looking around corners everywhere I went, but Preston still handled me with kid gloves. He hadn't tied me up once, and I knew why—he didn't want to trigger me. While I could appreciate that, I was a big girl. I knew my limits and safewords.

Maybe he needed a reminder of who he married. I refused to let the events of one day shape the rest of my life. Today was the first day of the rest of our lives, and I intended to start it off right.

Raising my right arm, I grasped the zipper to my wedding dress under my armpit and pulled it down. The dress pooled around my feet, leaving me in a white lace corset with attached garters.

Preston sucked in a breath as he scanned my scantily clad form before I gleefully watched the transformation—his eyes hardening when he noticed the white lace panties that matched the set.

His tone was firm and commanding, sending a shiver down my spine as he demanded, "What are those?"

Well . . . Hello, Sir.

Shrugging, I countered, "What? I couldn't very well go without panties when my sisters-in-law helped get me dressed. We're close, but not that close."

Stalking toward me, the promise of punishment in his eyes gave me a delicious thrill. "You think I care?"

Popping my hip, I placed one hand on it, giving an air of an attitude as I taunted, "Then I guess you'll just have to punish me."

"Don't test me, Princess," he growled.

Instead of answering him, I pulled my hair over my shoulder to reach it with both hands. I'd recently cut a good chunk of it off, so now it only fell to the middle of my shoulder blades, but there was still plenty to work with. With practiced ease, I broke it into three sections and began to weave them together.

"What are you doing?" Preston's jaw was set tight. I knew he'd missed this just as much as I had but was holding himself back out of concern for me.

"Braiding my hair," I shot back casually.

That was all it took for him to activate, and his hand was around my throat before I could finish plaiting my hair. Tilting my jaw to look at him, I wasn't afraid, instead feeling safer in his grasp than I had in what felt like forever.

This was right. This was us. We couldn't let someone steal it away.

"Do you think it's funny to tease me, Princess?" His face was right in front of mine.

"No, Sir."

"That's better." He released his grip, forcing me backward until my body bumped against the large X-structure of the Saint Andrews Cross.

Fuck yes.

Affixing my arms and legs to the cross so that I faced him, he shed his tux jacket before unbuttoning his crisp white dress shirt. His lean, toned upper body had me licking my lips. I wanted to taste him so badly, but I knew I would have to wait. I was on his time. He made the rules. All I had to do was obey.

Wholly at his mercy, bound to the cross, he stared at me for what seemed like an eternity, and I began to squirm, pulling on my restraints with the intense need to be touched by his masterful hands. Chuckling at my discomfort, he propped open the bench seat, moving items around until he found what he required.

"Do you know what happens to bad girls, Princess?" Preston asked, his back still to me.

"They get punished, Sir."

"That's right." Turning, I saw what he held in his hands—Wanda. I nearly moaned, thinking of how he would punish me with her. Pressing the power button, that familiar buzzing filled the air. "You will take what I give you tonight and be grateful for what I allow. Do you understand?"

"Yes, Sir."

"Let's see if we can turn this bad girl into a good girl."

He knew I would do just about anything to be his good girl. And just like that, all was right in our world again.

———✦———

Don't you worry, Preston let me come plenty, but he made sure I begged for it. Sweaty and sated, we laid naked on the bed in the playroom together, coming down from our intense play session.

Stroking his chest, with my body curled into the crook of his arm, I mused, "This room is nice, but where will the baby sleep?"

Trailing his fingers up and down my spine, Preston replied, "Luce, I told you, don't let the pressure get to you. If that's not something you want, it's okay. If it is, we have plenty of time to convert this room or move if necessary."

I knew he couldn't see me twist my lips into a smile, but that was half the fun. "Well, not that much time . . ."

Without warning, my body fell face-first into the mattress as he sat up abruptly. "What?"

"Hmm? What's that?" I mumbled into the covers, playing dumb.

"Lucy . . . That's not funny."

Daring to look up at him, I knew the moment he saw the truth on my face. "Looks like Grandfather will get that summer baby he was hoping for."

"A baby. *Our* baby?"

"Is that okay?" I watched his expression closely, but it gave nothing away.

"Is that okay?" he repeated.

Honestly, at this point, I think I broke his brain.

Sitting up, I crawled onto his lap. I knew this news would come as a shock, but I didn't know if I could handle it if he was upset.

Cupping his face, I held his gaze. "Hey, I love you."

"Are you sure?"

When I nodded, his face morphed into one of pure joy. Pulling my face to his, he kissed me with so much love that I felt it all the way down to my toes. Breaking away, he asked, "What made you change your mind?"

Happy tears welled in my eyes. "It took a near-death experience to teach me that tomorrow isn't always guaranteed, and I realized that I didn't want to keep saying someday to a life I could have today. I'm ready to live my life to the fullest in the moment we have now. With you. With our family."

"A family. God, do you know how incredible it feels to say that?" Reaching between us, he placed his hand on my bare lower abdomen. "Our baby. Tell me I'm not dreaming."

Placing my hand on top of his, I reassured him. "You're not dreaming."

Suddenly, his eyes went wide in panic. "Oh my God!"

"What?"

"I probably scrambled its brains with Wanda!" I couldn't stop myself as I busted out laughing as he reprimanded, "It's not funny!"

Taking a moment to come down, I rolled my eyes. "Honey, it's smaller than a grain of rice right now. Wanda won't harm it. You would know that if you really read those baby books like you claimed."

Narrowing his eyes, he pinned me beneath him on the bed. "Oh, is that how it's going to be? Are you itching for another punishment so soon, Princess?"

"God, yes," I breathed.

"You're lucky I'm in the best mood of my life because what my Princess wants, my Princess gets."

As my brand-new husband promised all kinds of sexual delights, my only wish was that I could go back in time and let that little girl with the pigtails know that it would all turn out all right in the end. I needed that fire he created within me to push me to become the woman I was today, and now, the only place we drove each other crazy was in each other's arms. The future was looking very bright indeed.

For a bonus scene where Preston and Lucy embark on a new endeavor, you can find it under the Bonus Scenes tab at https://sienatrapbooks.com/

Sad to say goodbye to our favorite girl gang that never backs down from a fight and always comes out on top? Don't worry, Hannah's quest to hook up with a hockey player continues in the upcoming Connecticut Comets spin-off series with *Bagging the Blueliner*.

If you missed out on Natalie and Jaxon's story or Amy and Liam's, you can catch up with *Scoring the Princess* and *Playing Pretend with the Prince*.

Acknowledgements

To my husband, thank you for reading every word I write, even when you make silly noises and say words wrong on purpose to elicit an eye roll response.

To my family, both immediate and extended, for their continued support as I pursue my career in writing.

To Katie, my editor, for late nights spent pouring over my manuscripts line by line until they're perfect.

To Nina, my proofreader, combing through my edited work, making tweaks until it's polished for publication.

To my readers, a giant THANK YOU. Not just for reading my books, but for reaching out and sharing in your excitement for future works.

About the Author

SIENA IS ORIGINALLY FROM Pittsburgh, Pennsylvania, where a love of sports is bred into a girl's DNA. Her love of romance novels came early as well. She would often accompany her romance reviewer mom to book lovers' and romance writer's conventions, where she sat in on workshops and met numerous best-selling authors. It wasn't long before she was filling notebooks with her own stories, which often starred herself and a certain real-life prince.

As luck would have it, she met and married a handsome athlete instead. After several temporary residencies in multiple states and Germany, they finally settled in Michigan, the land where youth hockey reigns supreme.

Her stories no longer feature herself, but draw from her past experiences as an educator, businesswoman, fashion consultant, and world traveler when creating her strong heroines. "Oh yes," she says with a wink and a smile, "There are bits of me in all of them." Now, she spends her days writing happily ever afters for fictional characters and her evenings at the local hockey arenas cheering for her three children.

Siena loves to hear from her readers. You can email her at:
siena.trap.books@gmail.com
Or find her on social media (FB, IG, and TT): @siena.trap.books

More Books by Siena Trap

Remington Royals Series
Scoring the Princess
Playing Pretend with the Prince
Feuding with the Fashion Princess

Connecticut Comets (Hockey) Series
Bagging the Blueliner
Surprise for the Sniper
Second-Rate Superstar

Indy Speed (Hockey) Series
A Bunny for the Bench Boss
Frozen Heart Face-Off
Goalie Goal

Rust Canyon Series
Festive Faking
Coming Home Country
Crashing the Altar
Before You Can Blink

Bellini Mafia Series (coming fall 2025)
Bellini Born (Matteo's story)
Bellini Bound (Enzo's story)
Bellini Bred (Gio's story)

Made in the USA
Middletown, DE
13 May 2025